The Best of

Heroic Fantasy Quarterly

Volume 2

also available

The Best of Heroic Fantasy Quarterly, Volume 1

The Best of
Heroic Fantasy Quarterly

Volume 2, 2011-2013

compiled by the editors of
Heroic Fantasy Quarterly

Founding Editors: David Farney & Adrian Simmons
Editorial Team: James Leckey, William Ledbetter, James Rowe, Barbara Barrett
www.heroicfantasyquarterly.com

Cover art by Robert Zoltan
www.zoltanillustration.com

Chapter glyph from openclipart.org

Additional glyphs by Jennifer Easter
pages 8, 128, 146, 214, 244, 246

Internal Art:
page 122 by Katarina Deggans
pages 28, 92 by Raphael Ordoñez
pages 130, 194, 198, 222 by Simon Walpole
pages 12, 24, 46, 64, 68, 88, 108, 142, 166, 170, 234 by Miguel Santos

Design by Keanan Brand
www.keananbrand.com

Printed in U.S.A

DEDICATED IN MEMORY OF

Joe Simmons
Barry King
William John Rowe
Dorothy Beard

and to the examples of
Barbara Barrett and Stephen Sandifer,
who are still fighting the fight

Contents

Sword and Sorcery

Sword and Sorcery is dead. Long Live Sword and Sorcery!

It's with a heavy heart and a suitably sad countenance that I must announce the death of Sword and Sorcery as a genre. No, don't cry for me, Melniboné. It had a good run, from 1929 to 2012, if we're being honest with ourselves. And if you include those practice laps beforehand, well, that's a hell of a lifespan, wouldn't you say? Eighty-three years or more, depending on how you slice the pie. Certainly long enough that we can safely put it to rest.

After all, it's a new century, right? We're so much wiser, so much more knowledgeable, and so much more enlightened. We have no need for hoary old wizards, and crumbling ruins hiding tentacular horrors, or worst, clichéd dragons guarding piles of treasure. And oh! The cringing maidens in gossamer robes! The misogyny! The racism! Enough, already! Am I right, people?

And yet, here's the thing: the genre isn't going away. Oh, I'll grant you, many of the old trappings are going away. Joe Abercrombie broke quite a few idols with his *Books of the First Law* series. Scott Lynch re-invented the thieves' guild with *The Lies of Locke Lamora*. Charles Saunders is back behind the keyboard, and he and his protégé, Milton J, Davis, are re-introducing the world to sword and soul fiction. Howard Andrew Jones' 8th-century Arabian adventurers are informed by his love of Harold Lamb. Scott Oden's orc hero Grimmner spins the camera around to make the villain the hero. And, lest we forget, small press endeavors have cropped up recently, following the standard set out long ago by *Heroic Fantasy Quarterly*.

In addition to small press endeavors like *Skelos: the Journal of Weird Fiction and Dark Fantasy*, and the re-emergence of *Weirdbook*, role-playing games are again on the march. *Astonishing Swordsmen and Sorcerers of Hyperborea* just published an expanded second edition that's cut straight from the cloth of the original *Weird Tales* pulp magazine. And a new hybrid model, *Tales from the Magician's Skull*, will premiere soon, edited by Howard Andrew Jones and published by Goodman Games, the game company that publishes *Dungeon Crawl Classics*. They have a new setting for the game coming out next year as well: *Lankhmar*.

What keeps bringing life back into this seemingly played-out genre? Like the supernatural elements that make up the other half of the historical recipe called Sword and Sorcery (or Epic Fantasy, if you want to be all high-falootin' about it), what's old is new again, and the interest in heroic fantasy has never been greater. More people are fleeing New York Publishing to read and write about pragmatic, personal solutions in dark and troubled times. About heroes who keep their own council and personal compass on what is and isn't acceptable in a harsh and cruel setting. When the deck is stacked, they invariably know how to cut it — with the business end of a battle axe.

Sword and Sorcery isn't just Karl Edward Wagner, and Robert E. Howard, and Michael Moorcock anymore — and there's nothing wrong with that. There never was, to be honest. But times change. We're a different society than the one these luminaries railed against. And yet we're kinda sorta the same, too, aren't we? We still need someone to dismiss the prattlings of politicians, quiet the cries of the tormented, and smash the chains of oppression. I submit to you, we need it now more than ever. And that's always been what heroic fantasy does best.

But Sword and Sorcery is underground again. It's a sub-culture of the larger fantasy realm, though there are signifiers in the air, like the continuing popularity of George R. R. Martin's *Game of Thrones* series. It's lighter and heavier at the same time, and while it cleaves closer to a more Howardian world, its execution more and more resembles something from epic fantasy instead.

The real stuff is hard to find. You have to know what to look for. Who to ask for. There's a password, and usually you need someone to vouch for you. That's where *Heroic Fantasy Quarterly* comes in. It's a training ground for folks who are writing Sword and Sorcery, and a field guide for those who are reading Sword and Sorcery. Here's how to hone your skills, sharpen your senses, so that when you see it in the wild, you can pounce on it. You can read it, enjoy it, be inspired by it, and most importantly, you can pass it on. Tell others about what you have read, and why you like it. Keep the flame alive, as it were. You're one of us now. Here's your robe, and for Crom's sake, keep that blade covered, or they'll spot you coming a mile away.

Sword and Sorcery is dead. Long Live Sword and Sorcery!

— Mark Finn
Deep in North Texas

MARK FINN *is the editor of* Skelos Magazine. *He is also the author of the World Fantasy Award-nominated biography,* Blood and Thunder: The Life and Art of Robert E. Howard, *and of the novel,* Road Trip.

DEMON-FANG

BY R. MICHAEL BURNS

Having no means of crossing this life,
I make swordsmanship my hiding place.
Yagyū Muneyoshi
Heihō Kaden Sho, 17th Century

Somewhere in the deep of night, the Fang whispered, and Shadows stirred. The samurai Hokagé — Shadows-from-Firelight — opened his eyes on darkness, bitter voices crawling over him like insects. Such loss in those sounds, such mourning and misery — it struck him to the soul, as piercing as an act of seppuku. A man could lose his sanity in those murmurs, could drown in hopelessness.

Yet he dared not ignore them.

His eyes quickly adjusted to the subtle glow of moonlight on the paper shoji screens, and he gazed at the long arc of the sheathed katana in its sacred nook. In the cold blue gloom, the blade known as *Makiba* — Demon-Fang — called to him.

He knelt before it, placing a single hand on its hilt, its ghostly voices whimpering in his mind. At once his thoughts went stumbling back, wandering once more through the strange series of events that had first brought the cursed thing to him.

He saw again the towering phantom that had risen against the gray sky as he made his way home from the Mountain of Sorrows, a skeletal form as shifting and iridescent as the lights that danced in the skies far to the north. He had heard of such creatures — *O-dokuro*, wraiths born of unthinkable suffering, of deaths not attended by the proper rituals.

Somewhere nearby, a terrible slaughter had occurred.

Within his memory, he saw the skeletal giant wheel and flee, scudding across the sky like a storm cloud, its paces so long he imagined it could walk the length of the great *Sanjusan-gendo* temple in a single stride. Instinctively, he pursued, following it across the plains and through a maze of fallow rice paddies. Soon, at the foot of a low saw-blade of mountains, he came upon a nameless village.

Only traces of its inhabitants remained — abandoned huts, scattered belongings, furniture toppled and broken. Sliding doors wrenched from their tracks, *tatami* mats splashed with long-dried blood. Even the shades of the lost seemed to have forsaken that place, leaving only a profound emptiness.

The sky-striding wraith rose again and in two long steps came to the mountains, Hokagé sprinting along after it. At once his gaze snagged on a certain tangle of shadow behind a spray of bamboo. As he drew nearer, the gloom took shape — a low cavern, walls green with moss. From within came the thick odor of damp earth and stone, and something unnamable but far worse. *Naginata* blade probing the dark before him, Hokagé descended into the depths.

He found the Earth Spider crouching in a great net of webbing, its eight black eyes the size of rice bowls, dagger-like fangs jutting from a grotesquely feline head. Its emerald body bulged and throbbed, massive as a boulder.

For an instant, the two regarded one another, if such eyes could manage so casual an act. Then the demon lunged, maw agape, fangs snapping. Hokagé moved even as the creature sprang, stepping aside and thrusting with his long glaive. The *naginata* sank deep into the demon's bulk, came free with a gout of thick white blood. The Earth Spider mewled and spun with speed that seemed impossible for such an enormous thing, whipping its barbed backside toward him. Hokagé leapt, vaulting the demon's spiny thorax, narrowly avoiding the sticky tangle of spider-silks it expelled. He hit the ground and rolled to his feet, bringing the naginata up in a graceful waterwheel arc. With a muffled snick, the crescent blade struck the beast's head from its body.

The Earth Spider twitched and flailed for a long time before finally falling still.

Stifling a tremor of revulsion, Hokagé took up his naginata and split wide the creature's engorged belly. Ichor the color of rice wine dregs vomited forth, and with it a cascade of human bones — the remains, no doubt, of the lost inhabitants of that nameless village.

Then his glaive's blade snagged on something harder, something iron-solid in the viscera of the slain demon. Steeling himself, Hokagé reached into the monster's repulsive corpse and probed the warm, slick entrails until his gloved hand found what he sought. He wrenched it loose, drew it out, and stared at it.

It was a sword, half an arm's span longer than any he'd ever set eyes on, and deadly-beautiful. In the gloom of the Earth Spider's lair, the light ran over its tempered line like quicksilver, fluid and brilliant. On the naked tang, where usually the swordsmith etched his name, were two deep-cut characters. *Makiba*. Demon-Fang. He hefted the blade, feeling its weight — feeling it almost twitch, almost squirm in his grip, like an angry serpent.

He'd recognized it even then, of course, had known it for what it truly was — the monster's metal-hard, sharp-honed heart, the source of its malign life. Such blades were legend.

For a moment, he stood holding the gore-slathered thing, studying the deep arc of its edge, the sweep of its two narrow grooves. He knew he ought to just leave it, abandon it here and bring the cavern down on it by whatever means he might. Such an item would surely bring ill fortune, would draw misery like flies to carrion.

And then it began to whisper, to mutter to him in those terrible, strangled voices — the voices of all the dead whose bones were now interred in the Earth Spider's lair.

Then, as now, he had no desire to hear. Now, as then, he knew he could not ignore their words. The spirits of the Demon-Fang spoke only when they had something vital to tell.

Kneeling in the taut, unnatural silence of his moonlit chamber, Hokagé willed his hands steady, then took up the sword, grasped the hilt he'd fashioned for it and drew it from its lacquered scabbard.

At once the voices grew louder, harsh and dry as the crunch of dead leaves. And as they rasped their warning, the visions came as well:

— creatures with faces like half-melted tallow, moonlight shining on armor the color of dried blood;

— villagers, mad with terror, screaming through the streets of Yamagumo-machi, the village at the foot of the castle whose master Hokagé served;

— his fellow samurai rushing into the fray, meeting the battle-garbed ghosts and falling, one after the other, their weapons useless against this deathless foe;

— soil soaked with blood as if with summer rain, bodies crumpled, their heads plucked from their shoulders like overripe apricots;

— and, above it all, the white moon shining down, icily indifferent to the slaughter.

Without even seeing the clan *sashimono* the ghost warriors wore on their backs, Hokagé knew those men. They were Akkihito, the brigands who'd razed his birth town and killed the novice priest he had once been. The barbarians who had given him the straggling white scars that marred the left side of his face, cheek to jaw.

Hokagé's master had trampled their forces into the earth — Hokagé himself had claimed a dozen Akkihito. But some enemies, it seemed, could not be undone, even in death.

He pictured the full moon of his vision, and knew they would come the following night — *goryo*, wraiths reanimated by their lust for vengeance. They would attack by the dozens, by the hundreds, and no earthly weapon would touch them. Hokagé would call his men, would stand them between the phantom horde and the innocent souls inhabiting Yamagumo Town, but they could only delay the inevitable. In every meaningful way, he knew, the wielder of the Demon-Fang would stand alone.

* * *

Beyond the walls of Hokagé's compound, night crept slowly closer. Within, Hokagé dressed slowly, deliberately. He fastened his linen gaiters to his ankles and tied on his sandals, never rushing a single knot. Shin-guards, thigh-guards, tanned-hide gloves and padded silk sleeves, he gave every item its due attention, granted each equal importance. Adherence to procedure helped settle the mind, focusing him in the moment, denying any temptation to anticipate what might occur when night fell, to make dangerous assumptions. What *might* happen mattered not at all. Speculation too often proved wrong, led to error. One could but respond to events as they transpired, like a bamboo shoot bending with the swirling winds of a typhoon. He had cleansed himself with a long bath, and said prayers at the vermillion Hachiman Shrine perched on the hillside just beyond the village. The War God had saved him once before, but one couldn't expect too much from the notoriously capricious *kami*. The gods' wills were as the winds, ever-shifting, impossible to foresee.

Kneeling, Hokagé pulled his *dō* into place, lacquered flames blazing across the midnight-black breastplate like crimson serpents' tongues, afterimages of the conflagration that had consumed his home and burned away the boy he'd once been. He wrapped the linen *uwa obi* around his waist in three tight loops, bound it with a flower knot, then attached the *sodé*, the banded shoulder guards protruding like wings, emblems of his high rank. Rising, he slipped his dagger into place, tied the silk cord of its sheath to his linen belt, then fastened Makiba's scabbard to his side. Even now, the haunted *katana* murmured and whimpered, the chorus of the unquiet dead increasingly agitated as night drew nearer — and with it, the demonic host.

With great effort of will, Hokagé slipped the blade into its sheath and went on readying himself, never breaking the ritual. Throat guard secured, he donned his *hachimaki*, binding the cloth tight to his freshly-shaved dome.

In other rooms and barracks, he knew, other men now went through these same rites, readying themselves for the fight ahead. How many would not see the sun rise? Hokagé dismissed the question even as it rose to mind. Tomorrow might never come for any of them, but that didn't matter now. With hands as steady as stone, he lifted his *hoate* to his face, the mask smooth and black, hiding the ragged scars that straggled from cheek to jaw. Beneath the brim of his flame-horned helmet, his face became a shadow, darkness illuminated only by the foxfire-glow of his narrow eyes. Let the Akkihito demons come. He would face them as a phantom himself, the ghost of that novice priest they'd brought down so many years ago, the last lingering shade of the flames they had set upon his innocent village.

"You expect to die tonight, of course."

The voice, feminine dulcet and oh-so-sweet, came from behind him, but he did not turn to look at the intruder.

"That fish-boning knife of yours won't save you," the girl in the doorway went on, drifting into the room, sliding the screen shut behind her. "Those *goryo* will slaughter you and your brave samurai like so many wild boars — and then everyone else in this sorry little village." The voice, taunting as it was, had an air of resignation to it, perhaps even mourning.

Hokagé turned, gazing at the girl. She was beautiful, pale of cheek and clad in an elegantly layered kimono. But the illusion didn't fool him. He knew those eyes, that mocking tone. *Inari-no-gohachi-himago* had grown more adept at disguise, but the fox god's thirteenth great-grandchild couldn't hide his nature from this man whose fate karma had so thoroughly entangled with his own.

"Have you come to help, Sasa-kun," Hokagé said, emphasizing the old nickname, *Little One*, which rankled the trickster so, "or only to lap up my spilled blood?"

"Euch," the intruder muttered, wrinkling her nose, "sickening. My game is mischief, not carnage."

Hokagé said nothing, waiting.

"I came," the false maiden went on, "to be sure you understand just what you face tonight."

"The *Makiba* has shown me all too clearly."

"You see the angry ghosts of your old foes," Sasa said, sitting with knees folded in a very ladylike way, clearly enjoying this show of manners. "But still you do not comprehend what will fall on this village of yours when night comes."

"Enlighten me, then, please," Hokagé said, kneeling opposite him.

"Haven't you wondered why they come *now*? Why, so many years after your forces cut down the last of the Akkihito who didn't flee like rats into the hills, their spirits would stir so suddenly?"

"I do not claim to understand the workings of *anoyo*," Hokagé answered, using the cautious euphemism for the spirit-world — *the yonder-land*.

"No," Sasa agreed. "But I do. I visit it often, as a matter of fact. And I see things, Hokagé-san. I hear things, too." He paused. Hokagé waited. Sasa gave a frustrated sigh. "Wouldn't you like to know *what* I've heard, *what* I've seen?"

"I am sure you will tell me," Hokagé grumbled. Very little could try his well-worn patience, but this strange companion of his always seemed to manage.

"The Akkihito's warrior priest, the one called Kishin. He did not die on the field of battle. Well, not *entirely*."

Hokagé raised an eyebrow.

Sasa ran long fingers through illusory black hair. "His spirit fled his body, sank all the way into Yūkai, into the depths of the dead realm. But before the carrion birds could have his flesh, his spirit found its way home. He rose from where your warriors left him, with secrets he carried back from the underworld. For years he wandered and studied, discovering ancient arts and nasty little tricks from the necromancers of the Celestial Kingdom, learning how to use what he had learned in Yūkai. Readying his vengeance against Lord Kumamuné and all who serve him. He would be quite happy to take your head first, Hokagé-san."

"So — Kishin calls the ghosts of the Akkihito dead with this Chinese sorcery," Hokagé said, his voice registering no emotion.

"More than that!" Sasa said, abandoning the formal posture now and sprawling on the straw mats in a manner that was just short of obscene. "See — it's only his sorcery that sustains his army. He'll come with them as their general, leading their charge from behind the curtains of his commander's enclosure, poisoning the air with his incantations. Making the dead hop and dance and fight like so many ugly puppets."

"And if he is slain?"

Sasa shrugged, the gesture oddly unwieldy in his slight, feminine form. "Then perhaps the spell can be broken. But he's no man, Hokagé-san. He is neither of this world nor of the yonder-land. No blade of mere steel can kill him. I'm sure you understand what that means."

Hokagé touched the hilt of the sword at his hip, its whispers muted by the scabbard, but not silenced.

Yes, he understood.

Or so he believed.

* * *

He gazed into the dark beyond the town's northeast gate as twilight deepened to night and the stars bloomed overhead. The day's heat faded and crickets began to sing, but fitfully, as if uneasy about gracing this evening with their music. Behind the ghost in the flame-emblazoned armor, a vanguard of lesser samurai waited, while others lingered in the village, ready to give up their lives to prolong those of the villagers by even a few spare minutes. It was a paltry force, to be sure, for the bulk of Kumamuné's army had been dispatched to the south, to stake the lord's claim in the outcome of the war now brewing there. The rest — Lord Kumamuné's select guard — kept their posts inside the castle. If Hokagé failed, one among them would dispatch those members of Kumamuné's court too young or too old to fight or finish themselves, while another assisted Kumamuné's *seppuku*. None of his clan would die at the hands of the Akkihito — but they would die, and the vengeance of the damned would be complete.

Hokagé let his fingers rest on *Makiba's* hilt, feeling its murmurs as much as hearing them. Only the Demon-Fang could touch the coming enemy, only its unearthly blade could pierce the veil between worlds and bring down the *goryo*. But the knowledge brought no comfort, only another sort of misery — he knew the cost of striking down these foes. Each phantom the Fang sank its brutal tooth into would extinguish one of the innocent souls haunting the steel. Perhaps they escaped to the realm between to find their way to eventual rebirth, but even Sasa could not assure him of that. And as the human spirits guttered from the blade, the Earth Spider's cruel power grew stronger, its fiendish voice rising over the chorus, muttering bloodthirsty lies, terrible promises. For now, the others overwhelmed it...

But tonight he would face an army — scores of rage-driven specters, or hundreds. How many could he destroy before the demon's black heart reclaimed the sword — and took hold of its bearer?

It might be better to cast the weapon away and accept death, for death was surely preferable to surrendering his soul, such as it was.

Had his life alone hung in the balance, he might well have let them have it, or taken it himself before the enemy could. But hundreds of innocents, including Kumamune's sweet daughter-in-law, Kimiko, and her young son, Kumakichi, would also die, and many in ways far worse than the thrust of a blade into a soft abdomen.

He closed his hand on *Makiba's* hilt, gently, and waited. His men had their orders. If they fled when their enemy came, he would not blame them. He would only pity their inglorious deaths.

All around — in the space of a single breath — the cricket-song stopped.

Behind Hokagé, the men shifted in their armor.

Now the moon, full as a dewdrop in a spider's web, broke over the eastern hills, its silver light washing across the road, deepening the long tree-shadows there.

A sound rose, a drumming patter like a sudden, heavy fall of rain, though no clouds marred the star-strewn night.

Then the army of the dead surged from the darkness and came on in a storm, jaws agape in ravenous fury, eyes hideously wide.

Hokagé drew Demon-Fang and stepped into a ready stance. And as the ghostly horde cascaded toward him, he opened himself to the sword, let it reach into his thoughts, draw his mind into its terrible depths. Revulsion flooded through him at once, smothering. He felt like a man buried alive in a mass grave, crushed between writhing, deathless corpses. Submerged in *Makiba's* fathomless dark, he felt them — those *shōryō*, those imprisoned souls, straining and crying, their whispers turned to screams, their essences sizzling like lightning along the arc of the blade. Somewhere in their midst, the pitiless soul of the spider demon raged, mad with the hunger to keep those tortured spirits close — its prisoners, its playthings.

Every one of those voices, human and demon alike, cried out for carnage.

Hokagé lowered his head and rushed into the throng.

Makiba flicked and danced, hewing through malformed men as insubstantial as fog, obliterating them, one after another after the next. And as each *goryo* shattered and ceased to be, Hokagé felt a truly human soul within the sword vanish as well — an apprentice calligrapher, who did masterful work despite a malformed hand; an old farmer, whose skin had smelled of rice paddy mud; a girl child, who had dreamt only of learning the ways of a proper lady; a carpenter, who had thought the Earth Spider a mere figment of his drunken imagination, until its jaws split his flesh... Hokagé sensed the sudden extinction of each of them, as piercing-sharp as dagger wounds. Yet he fought on, slashing his way against the spectral current, cutting the Akkihito ghosts down just as he had when they lived, even as dozens more trampled past. From behind him came unthinkable sounds: wet, strangled shrieks of agony followed by dull crashes of armored bodies slouching to the earth. He paid no attention — he had none to spare.

Ahead, a vague rectangular outline hung oddly still amid the seethe and flow of the onslaught — linen curtains, tattered and ill-kept. He could see the eye-like *mon* of the Akkihito clan emblazoned upon them, gazing at him, daring him to approach.

Creatures with sagging, semi-human faces and too-familiar armor stepped before him, groping for him with hands twisted into massive claws, talons capable of wrenching a man's head from his shoulders. Hokagé dodged and thrust. Demon-Fang bobbed and pierced. Two *goryo* and two innocent souls ceased to be, and then three more. Hokagé's own spirit bled. From *Makiba*, he heard the mewling cry of the demon, ever louder, stronger.

But he could end it, now, if only he found the strength.

Hokagé slashed the *maku* curtains apart and stepped inside the battlefield commander's enclosure.

The sorcerer Kishin sat within, clad in a *daimyo's* wing-shouldered *hakama*, legs folded under him. His gaunt, gray-bearded face turned upward, lips twitching as he muttered unintelligible incantations. Hokagé raised his sword.

Kishin opened his eyes. Hokagé faltered. He gazed into those yellow eyes — and froze with hideous realization.

The deathless sorcerer's voice rose to a shout, a screech that pierced Hokagé's mind like daggers and he stumbled, staggered, fought to keep his feet. Tallow-faced wraiths in field generals' garb burst into the enclosure, their ghostly infantry following, rushing on like a tsunami. Hokagé cut them down in broad swaths like a farmer clearing young bamboo, swinging half-blind, mind ablaze with the agony of Kishin's hellish spell, and all the guttering whimpers of the innocent souls as they were torn from Demon-Fang's steel. He would not let himself hear them, would not let himself glimpse the lives he extinguished as he swept away the enemy. He could not allow himself such luxuries of compassion, even if the agony finally tore his sanity to shreds. Only the yellow-eyed sorcerer at the heart of the maelstrom mattered.

Whatever had reawakened Kishin's flesh, it was no human spirit, or human no longer — those fire-flicker eyes revealed the truth. They were the eyes of a demon, a denizen of the deepest Hells. Looking into them, Hogaké knew what had to be done — the only hope of ending this slaughter.

For the briefest of instants, he cast all other thoughts aside. He heard no screams, no deadly incantations, felt no injury, saw not a flutter of movement. He drew a deep breath, focused his consciousness to a fine, bright point.

Then he lunged, through the chaos of onrushing *goryo*, screaming out a battle cry that seemed to chill the dead themselves. *Makiba* plunged into the heart of the man seated behind the curtain, and as it did Hokagé poured himself into the haunted blade, filling the otherworldly steel with his *ki*, his life's vital force, feeling it join with hundreds of others. Together, the spirits fought, pressing, crushing, wringing the Earth Spider's essence from the metal, pouring it into the body of the jabbering sorcerer. The spirit leapt through Kishin like lightning through stormclouds.

Caught in the same flesh, the demons did as demons would — they fought one another for the territory. And tore it apart in their struggle.

Kishin's evil words turned into a thick gurgle. His eyes blazed wide and he doubled over, vomiting crimson gore. Blood bloomed like black flowers on his filthy coat as his skin split in a dozen, two dozen, ten dozen places. Bones snapped like kindling in a blazing fire. Kishin threw back his arms, made a twitching motion as if to rise...then sagged into a damp scarlet heap and moved no more.

The sounds of battle ceased at once. Only the murmurs of befuddled men and the moans of the still-dying stirred the night silence.

Hokagé withdrew Demon-Fang from the deflated remains of the sorcerer and held it aloft. For a moment, he thought the sword's voices had fallen silent, obliterated in that final act. But…there. A few remained — subdued, muted, yet present still. And yet…

As he listened, it seemed the sounds came not from the blade, but from within him, from the depths of his own mind.

"I wondered if you'd realize what was required of you," came a voice, close by. Hokagé glanced sideways, not surprised to see a small red fox sniffing at the tattered remnants of the *maku*. "Seems you're a scintilla more clever than I'd thought."

"And the Demon-Fang?" Hokagé asked. "I suppose it is mere metal now." As he said it, he found the idea rather comforting.

"Not *all* of the spirits are gone from it, Hokagé-san," Sasa said. "You gave a part of yourself to the Fang, and the *Makiba* returned the gift in kind. There is much of your soul in it now, and much of it in you. I'd keep it close, were I you. It is said that a samurai's sword is his soul, *ne*? Well, in your case, it's the literal truth. You are as tied to its destiny as…well, as I am to yours." Sasa snorted. "Rather sad, really."

Hokagé merely nodded. Then, silent, he slipped *Makiba* back into its scabbard, feeling its weight, its cool presence at his side.

"Let us hope, then," he said, "that fate shall be kind to us all."

R. MICHÆL BURNS *is an October child and the author of more than two dozen short stories and the novel* Windwalkers. *Born in Colorado, he lived for the better part of five years in the Kanto region of Japan, before settling in the deepest, darkest swamps of north central Florida. He is currently at work on a trilogy of novels featuring the samurai Hokogé and his companion, Sasa.*

CONFRONTING THE DEMON OF HIDDEN THINGS
BY DAVID SKLAR

On a winter day, at a mountain's feet,
from a dream more ancient than language,
three men went out to stand against
the darkness within the darkness:

the Oak Man with a bamboo staff,
the Reed Man with a staff of oak,
the Water Man with an ancient sword
so fearsome he dared not use it.

The three men found an empty house
and waited for the Darkness,
and when the winter wind blew in
and lanterns, stars, and moon went black,

the Oak Man struck with his bamboo staff,
the Water Man flung jade,
the Reed Man, waiting, listened and learned
the Terrible Name of the Darkness.

The Water Man spoke this name, and made
a light within the darnkess,
the Oak Man and the Darkness traded blows,
the Reed Man stood and waited for his time,

and when the Darkness had the Oak Man pinned,
the Reed Man struck a mighty blow
that shattered his wooden staff.
The Water Man still fought with light alone.

And as the Darkness turned
to strike the Reed Man down,
the Oak Man raised his bamboo staff
and struck the killing blow.

And so it was three heroes slew
the Demon of Hidden Things:
the Oak Man using strength and skill,
the Water Man with light and jade,
the Reed Man using patience and perfect timing.

DAVID SKLAR *grew up in Michigan, where the Michipeshu nibbled his toes on the days Lake Superior was feeling frisky. A Rhysling nominee and a past winner of the Julia Moore Award for Bad Verse, he has more than 100 published works, including fiction in* Nightmare *and* Strange Horizons, *poetry in* Ladybug *and* Stone Telling, *and humor in* Knights of The Dinner Table *and* McSweeney's Internet Tendency. *David lives with his wife, their two barbarians, and a secondhand familiar in a cliffside cottage in Northern New Jersey, where he almost supports his family as a freelance writer and editor.*

The Worship of the Lord of the Estuary and the Wages of Heroism

by James Frederick William Rowe

I t came from the sea, a thing of cold, slime, and teeth. Declaring its presence through murder, it took the lives of three men fishing on the open water before it claimed as its home the estuary at the orifice of the *Mor Oirthearach River* in Cacke. Ever since it has held this body of water, permitting none to pass but those who pay it in blood.

The people called him *Tiarna Inbhear*, the Lord of the Estuary, and their fear swelled to such a panic that it became necessary to convene a special assembly of the *tuath* so as to provide for what could be done. Petty-king Osgar thus sent out runners to the holdings of the families, alerting them to the assembly and urging them to haste, but such was the compulsion of the general panic that no such urging of haste was necessary. It hardly took but two weeks for all of the hundreds of families to muster on the plain where they congregated to hear his ruling.

Addressing the crowd, Osgar declared, "It has come to pass that a fierce creature has taken abode in the estuary. Of this we all are aware. But what we should do with this creature is unknown. The hardiest amongst you have called for a band of men to be dispatched so as to face it in combat."

Here, the petty-king paused to gesture to the band of men so mentioned. A small assembly of warriors nodded grimly at the king's recognition of their suggestion, but none strode forward to speak.

Osgar continued, "Whether we should accept this suggestion, however, is not suited to royal decree. My most trusted priest, Calbhach mac Breacan has told me that the proper way to choose what is to be done is to consult the soothsayers, whom in turn have told me that they must sacrifice a man by the threefold death in order to be certain on a matter as grave as this. Accordingly, they are now called to perform their divination in front of us all, so that the matter might be put to rest."

Upon the declaration of the petty-king, a trio of soothsayers emerged with their sacrifice bound at the wrist and elbow and drawn forward with much reluctance. He was a captive of war and even at this final hour he struggled mightily, but his bonds proved to render him impotent and he was soon forced to his knees. The brutal affair then commenced with the first soothsayer strangling him with a woven rope, the next bludgeoning him with a short staff, and finally the last slitting his throat with a ritual dagger. He died convulsing upon the scarlet stained grass until the open wound pumped only air and his heart gave way at last.

The crowd retained a stony, reverent silence throughout the affair of the sacrifice and the subsequent huddling of the soothsayers. This latter sequence took several minutes, throughout which the soothsayers hid themselves by way of their robes. Only after their consensus was met, which was signaled by a joining of hands followed by a series of three nods, did the soothsayers come to the petty-king to whisper their verdict.

Osgar declared then their decision, "The soothsayers have discerned by means of the sacrifice the path that ought to be taken. *Tiarna Inbhear*, as he has been so named, is not a mere beast, but like unto a god. As such, on the third night of every crescent moon a sacrifice of a man captured in war shall be made directly to the creature, in honour and fear of its might. So long as this is maintained it will largely be placated and attack infrequently, if at all."

He added, "If there are any amongst you who oppose this course of action, let them speak now and argue their case before all."

Amongst all of the throngs none raised an objection. Not even the warriors spoke out against the course, for though they may have contested against a brute, they were cowed by the declaration of its divinity. The matter thus decided the king turned to his priest who declared it law.

And it remained so for twenty years.

* * *

Garbhan mac Earnan was yet still in his mother's belly when the institution of sacrifice was announced, but it is widely thought that were he a man then, he would have challenged the ruling if only to boast that he alone had seen fit to do so. As it stood, it only took him till near his twentieth year to end up doing the same regardless.

He announced his attentions to face the Lord of the Estuary upon returning from a hunt, from whence he had killed an aurochs so large that it took a team of twenty men to hoist it back to the people. Garbhan insisted on this course of action so that none could deny that he had brought in a kill of such majestic proportions, for the people of Cacke were ever suspect of the claims of men, though they entirely swallowed the proclamations of the supernatural. But faced with such proof as the carcass of the slain beast, none could deny what their eyes had witnessed, and lavish praise was hoisted upon Garbhan till it came to pass that he boasted:

"There is nothing in land, sea, or sky, either man or beast, that can match Garbhan mac Earnan."

This was all it took for a rival, who was highly envious of his success in felling the aurochs, to chime up a challenge to this claim, "There is something which would contest that, braggart."

Garbhan looked venomously upon the interloper and his hand flew to his sword handle, "Scoithin, you speak as if you would challenge me."

Scoithin but laughed and held an open hand up as proof that he held no intention to draw arms against Garbhan. "You mistake my intentions: I do not challenge you. But it is evident that you have forgotten something."

"And what, pray tell, have I forgotten?" asked Garbhan, who though he drew his hand from his sword, yet retained the threat in his bearing.

The laughter was retained in Scoithin's voice as he defiantly retorted, "That the Lord of the Estuary would rip you to shreds ere you landed a single blow."

Garbhan minced no words, nor restrained his anger. He spat upon the ground at the feet of Scoithin and matched his defiance with his own, "I spit at you and your fears, coward, which alone can account for this foolish accusation."

Scoithin was unmoved. "If you disdain this claim so, then prove me wrong."

Without a thought, Garbhan declared, "I shall."

"Do you hear?" Scoithin appealed then to the crowd, his arm sweeping across the assembly as he turned to them. He pointed back at Garbhan as he continued, "Garbhan mac Earnan has proclaimed he shall face the Lord of the Estuary. Let he be known as a coward, a liar, a fool, and an empty braggart should he not match his boast with action."

"You do not need to bear the pressure of the people upon me, Scoithin," replied Garbhan who himself turned to the crowd. "For I would pursue this path were I alone the witness to my intentions. You have implied the Lord of the Estuary is mightier than I, and my honour and pride shall admit not of it. I shall, afore the next sacrifice to be made in three weeks, match the beast in mortal combat. Let this be known throughout the *tuath* — nay, let be known even by the whole of Cacke! — that Garbhan mac Earnan shall slay *Tiarna Inbhear*."

* * *

On the account that his summer service in the war-bands was not due for a whole month, and his winter hunting haul had been especially fruitful, it took merely a week and a half for Garbhan to ready himself for his departure. In point of fact, it would have even been sooner, were it not necessary for him to sell meat and skins to finance the furnishing of a fit set of travelling clothes, a spear equipped with a harpoon head, and half a dozen javelins. A shield, sword, and dagger he had all ready, but the latter two were also in need of sharpening, such that this added to the expense and the time necessary to procure things.

Still, a week and a half sufficed for the furnishing of these necessities and he did not tarry upon finding himself outfitted in full. Therefore, he set out alone and on foot the very morning after a celebratory feast that some had remarked sardonically was better to be conceived as a funerary one.

His departing words were themselves a boast, "When I come back you will bear witness to my triumph. I will prevail."

He left in high spirits while singing a jocund hunting song, such that few would have conjectured, based on sight alone, that he was pursuing a path many would reckoned would terminate in his death. Still, those who knew him would know that the very joy expressed by Garbhan was indication of the challenge he faced, for the prideful young man sought and faced such with eagerness. Indeed, Scoithin even remarked, "The damn fool is just happy to hunt the greatest quarry!"

However, in contrast with the goal of the jaunt to the sea, the journey itself should not prove challenging. All together, the trip from Garbhan's home to the point of sacrifice was reckoned as twenty one miles as the wolf runs. Walking from sun-up to after nightfall, Garbhan intended to cover this distance in a day of travel and take his rest by his foe so as to meet him bright and early the morning next. The way, he conceived, would be rather easy, consisting of a relatively gentle walk over land which only softly rolled with few points of difficulty and only light forest for obstruction.

He travelled at a steady pace until mid-day.

* * *

The mysterious standing stones, whose crafters and purpose even in those days were unknown, would be counted by others as a place entirely unfit for rest. Superstitions as to their nature and purpose, as well as the Strange Folk which frequented them, were enough to dissuade the common man of the *tuath* from doing little else but pass them in reverent silence accompanied to ritual repetitions of warding signs. Indeed, men would make a point to rush their steps when they came to these jutting masses of weather-beaten, stained rock, lest they fall victim to their native power, or else fall foul of a band of the strangers the common folk feared so.

But Garbhan was not so inclined toward such fears, but found his back soothed and his feet well calmed by the strong, smooth surface of the stone which supported him at rest. He could even prop his spear and sword against it and unburden himself of these heavy arms while he dined on coarse bread and dried meat, with but cool spring water, collected in his skin, for drink.

As he partook of his traveller's fare, the sky slowly darkened with the gathering of rain clouds. Thereafter, gentle rumblings preceded a quiet rain, which fell with a perfumed wind bringing with the refreshment of the storm. It was a mild shower and one which did little to disturb Garbhan, who in fact seemed to welcome the cooling droplets of water upon his face. Indeed, he even closed his eyes to feel the caress of the drops which stuck to his beard and played upon his hair.

But he would not retain this repose for long. The strange interruption of a heavy aroma of a floral perfume stirred his senses while a light, feminine grip upon his sword-arm arrested the violence of his startled awakening. Were it not for this gentle touch preventing such an act, Garbhan's first reaction would have been to grab his blade to the accompaniment of an outburst of shouting curses. As it stood, the curses were uttered even in the absence of the brandishing of the blade, which necessitated that the woman deal with this occurrence by whispering in a melodious, almost sing-song, voice, "Peace, peace. I mean you no harm."

But Garbhan, though he might not be superstitious, was yet not a fool and ill inclined to be awoken so peculiarly and suddenly. This was especially true on account of the strangeness of the woman, who aside from being bedecked with a floral crown which exuded the heavy perfume of the same, was finely attired in a gown of spotless white — which was of a cut and finery far beyond what was normal in these parts — and grew her raven-black hair down to her ankles. Furthermore, though he heard only that initial whispering, its singing delivery and strange accent made it apparent that she held no kin and converse with the locals.

All of this conspired for him to demand, "If you mean me no harm then you shall tell me who you are, and why it is that you have come upon me unawares."

The woman did not trifle with Garbhan by evading such a question, pregnant with the threat of harm, that he delivered her. She gave her identity without compunction, "I am known as Easnadh."

"Of what people and kind?" he further inquired.

She again held nothing back, "I am of those whom the people here call the Strange Folk."

Garbhan came near to laughing and the threat was lost to his voice, "I do not find this at all surprising, Easnadh of the Strange Folk. It seems somehow fitting that one of your kind should meet me here."

She did not share his humour. "My intention is not to surprise but rather to counsel."

Garbhan's eyebrow perked with intrigue and he gestured for her to continue, "To what end?"

"It is said that Garbhan mac Earnan seeks to vie with *Tiarna Inbhear*."

"It is as they say," he replied with a short nod of affirmation. "But I would be

33

interested as to how you learned this and came to know my name."

"What is to be known can be known," she remarked.

"Your candour has been lost for riddles."

It was her time to come near to laughter, "I speak no riddles: What is true can be determined and news travels fast. I would have to be deaf to not know of your intention. The clamour raised at your boasting was immense and you made no intention of hiding your purposes to the entire world."

Garbhan grinned like a child caught stealing sweets, "I suppose that is so."

"But it is not your prideful declarations that I counsel you against," Easnadh said with a return to sobriety, "but rather against this enterprise."

"So you are amongst the naysayers?" he asked with unhidden sourness.

"On the contrary, I think you shall prevail."

Confusion raised the eyebrow of Garbhan, "Then I do not follow you."

"You assume much, Garbhan mac Earnan, as to the nature of the response you shall receive from this feat of bravery,"

He was quick to question, "In what regard?"

"You rather think you shall be heralded as a hero, do you not?"

"I see no reason to think otherwise."

"Nor do I: But do you recognize what that entails?"

A single laugh, "Honours above honours, glory heaped upon glory, and the adulation of the entire tuath. Or rather I should say: At least this much, if not more! After all, is it not fitting? I shall render an inestimable service to the people in liberating them from the foul despotism of the Lord of the Estuary and the rites he demands."

"All of this might be conceded. But have you asked at what price?"

"The price is obvious: It is to risk my life and limb."

"But what if it is to forfeit it?"

"Are you suggesting I fear death?" and here the ire of Garbhan was slightly raised, such that more of the prior threat entered into his voice.

She did not shirk in the face of such, but persisted in her point, "Not at all, when it is from that which you know might kill you. But what if you're caught unaware?"

Garbhan retained his irritation, "Speak clearly, woman."

"There are more dangers than simply those of the Lord of the Estuary."

"And may I avoid said dangers and yet pursue this path?"

"I am afraid you cannot," she conceded.

"Then I care not. I am resolved to face the beast, kill him, and win fame."

"Even if they may be unworthy of this service?"

"Their worth is of no concern when it is my worth that is at stake, both in the public eye and in my heart."

"So it must be, Garbhan mac Earnan."

"So it must be indeed, Easnadh of the Strange Folk."

With those words having passed between them, Garbhan rose to take his departure. But he was stopped in so doing by Easnadh's grasp, which he saw was accompanied by a tacit pleading in her eyes. Still, he would refuse her, "Come now, Easnadh, I shall not stay."

"I ask not forever," she said, "but depart tomorrow at the least. The way to the estuary is long and you should not reach there until after nightfall. You cannot fight the creature in darkness and there is but a priest who lives there to provide you shelter. Tell me not that you would prefer to spend an evening with him over me?"

"I cannot, in truth, proclaim thus."

"Then come." Her grasp shifted to his hands. "I have meat, mead, and a warm bed."

With that, further protestations were silenced and Garbhan was lead by Easnadh to her cottage which was set away amidst a copse of trees a mile or so distant.

* * *

Garbhan rose to meet the day before dawn, but even then Easnadh had preceded him in awakening and was deep into her work. However, on the account that her form was obscured by a wrapped blanket and she worked in but the dim light of a single candle, he could not discern what she was doing.

"What are you working on, Easnadh of the Strange Folk?"

She did not reply but worked all the more quickly on what appeared to be the final part of her labours.

"All right, I shall bathe and ready myself for my departure, then," he said and walked outside to make good on this claim.

While tending to these matters, Easnadh finished her work and followed after him some minutes later. He was by then bathed and clothed and then affixing his sword to his belt and slinging his spear and quiver of javelins across his shoulders. However, he was interrupted in the latter task upon catching sight of Easnadh, and as the darts clattered to the ground he unleashed shout which awoke a flock of nearby birds into fluttering panic.

"Your hair!" he pointed in his shock.

Gone were the flowing locks of ink which streamed down to the soles of her feet. Replaced was a patchy mess of shorn tufts, boyish in appearance, through which the white skin of her scalp could be seen. A life's effort of growth was gone in an evening, but it was not in vain. In her outstretched arms she held proof of her labours: Woven from her own hair, a net had been crafted and strung with smooth stones for weights.

She explained, "Aye, my hair Garbhan mac Earnan, has been shorn, and from it I have sown a net that shall never break nor fail you, for I have woven my power and magic into every thread. With it, your victory is assured: You will trap the beast. Only cast it with care, for the Lord of the Estuary shall be fit to be contained by it but once, as he is crafty and a failed attempt shall not meet with success on the second trying."

For once the prideful young man was silenced. Indeed, he knew not what to say as she pressed her gift into his arms, such was the effect it had upon him.

At last, words did come to him, "It is rare indeed for me to be silenced by any act of man or woman, but this act of devotion has so tied my tongue and I will not profane the effect by speaking more to it. Instead, I shall do justice to the gift by using it well, as shall be proven when word reaches you of my victory."

"Fight valiantly, Garbhan mac Earnan," she said as she pressed his hands to her chest.

"I shall, Easnadh of the Strange Folk."

And with a passing caress of her cheek, Garbhan turned to pursue the estuary again.

* * *

Upon leaving Easnadh, Garbhan proceeded directly to the estuary — that place where sea and river intertwine and vie for dominance — which he reached by noon the same day. There he passed the sea-ruined remains of a fishing village vacated for fear of the beast but for the dwelling of the priest Calbhach mac Breacan — the very same who had declared the sacrifice law — who presided over the monthly sacrifice, and who hailed him.

"Garbhan mac Earnan," Calbhach called, "word of your intention has preceded your coming and I shall bear witness to your exploits."

"It is well and good this is so," replied Garbhan, "but it would have been better a poet than a priest by my reckoning, as I intend nothing less than the greatest display of heroism ever known amongst the sons of Cacke and I should want my exploits to be well recorded."

The priest grinned at the youth's bravado, "I assure you: I shall relate in depth the events of the day, whether you survive or no, such that no poet would want for lack of description. Now allow me to point you-"

"No need, holy one," interrupted Garbhan even as he began to strip bare. "It is well and apparent to me where the point of sacrifice is. All I require of you besides your eyes is that you should hold my clothes, that they might not be soiled."

"It shall be done," and with that the priest accepted the burden of the clothes given to him.

Upon attaining to full nudity and after having reaffixed his arms to his person, Garbhan spoke anew, "May you witness as I have boasted, or else a fine death. May I have a blessing, holy one?"

The priest raised his hand after tucking his burden of clothes beneath his other arm, "Proceed fearless, for shame endures where death is but the transition to another life."

With such said, Garbhan proceeded to the point of sacrifice which the people called Dearg Carraig. True to his declaration, it required no guide to point it out, for it quite unambiguously embodied the meaning of its name by being a large rock which jutted well into the estuary, stained a rusty red by the blood of nearly two-hundred and fifty victims. Though subject to the often violent waves and open entirely to the sea air, the deep set stain was too stubborn to be scoured clean by salt, water, and wind and no doubt it would long endure being so coloured.

But he would not direct his steps immediately to the rock, for he was in sore need of bait. Accordingly, he ducked into the woods to procure such, his javelin at the ready. As luck would have it, the detour proved extremely short, for he soon found a boar rooting for mushrooms. Coming upon it unawares was simple for Garbhan and the boar slumped dead upon the first cast of the javelin. Thereafter, it was a simple affair of hoisting the boar upon his bare shoulder and then walking swift enough to the rock that the animal would not lose all its blood from the sizable wound. He accomplished the latter task with ease and perched himself atop its uppermost prominence, which loomed some twenty feet above the water line.

From this height, the whole of the estuary could be surveyed, and though he did not spend long in looking, he noticed no sign of the creature amidst the choppy waters. Having expected this, Garbhan was not dissuaded and thus he slit the belly of the boar with his dagger and pitched the carcass off the rock with a sizable splash, which was itself followed by a spreading crimson froth from the blood and gore of the boar seeping into the water. Presently, he waited, and while he did so he readied the net of hair in hand after tying the casting line.

It took a full five minutes for the Lord of the Estuary to appear, and so subtle was he in his approach that Garbhan did not notice him till he was near fully upon the bloody bait. In fact, Garbhan did not even get a chance to cast the net before the terrible creature crested the waters with the tube of razors which consisted of his mouth opening to shred, tear, and suck the gory contents of the slaughtered pig into its bright pink innards.

However, this proved fortunate in as much as Garbhan recognized that the frenzying behaviour of the creature permitted a far easier casting than would have been able to if he had thrown prior to the creature claiming its feast. As such, he timed his casting until the boar was nearly wholly devoured, then threw the net out to cover the top most half of the creature, who was caught unawares by the man as he had not the cunning to draw his fishy eyes upwards throughout his gluttonous assault upon the bait.

The weights attached to the net drove down with surprising swiftness into the water, such that Garbhan had to pull the casting rope far quicker than he expected. Though this was critical in securing the creature, it also proved highly dangerous to the hunter. For in entwining the writhing beast, the great power of the monster nearly wrenched him clear off the rock and into the sea.

As it stood, it was only a stroke of luck which saw Garbhan react quick enough to release the line and to retain his balance by falling harshly on his rear end upon the blood-stained stone. This scratched well his posterior — adding more than a few more drops of human blood to the paint of the rock. He was fundamentally sound of body, and more importantly retained his weapons upon his person which would no doubt have flew even as he did, and more than likely have been flung entirely from his person into the splashing waters.

He was thus well supplied with javelins when he leapt to his feet and secured his strong advantage of height over the monster. But the horrible thrashing of the beast made aiming an uncertain affair, such that he had to pause lest he waste his missiles in vain throws. Likewise, Garbhan was arrested by the fact that only then, amidst its writhing and splashing, did the Lord of the Estuary appear to him in his awe-inducing totality.

A huge set of gills holes revealed the Lord of the Estuary as definitively ichthyic, a point which might otherwise be misjudged owing to the serpentine, thirty foot long, cylindrical body that was absent any lateral fins. Instead, the monster was fitted for propulsion by a length of fins that ran along both the dorsal and ventral sides of its body immediately after its gill slits, and which terminated at a caudal fin that wrapped around the tail and united the twin sides. As for the maw previously mentioned — which was, luckily for Garbhan, entirely encased by his net — it was a gargantuan thing which began immediately afore the gills holes, and which bulged wide in a cone that was ringed by a ridged, toothy surface. Inside this cavernous hole, concentric circles of jagged, razor-sharp teeth surrounded a bone-crusted tongue that seemed fit as much to impale as taste its gory meals. Lastly, the whole of the beast's skin was enclosed in a mail of scales covered in an unctuous slime, such that the monster appeared a shimmering, inky black.

Though impressed, and perhaps even indeed a bit scared, by *Tiarna Inbhear* in his revealed majesty, Garbhan was not transfixed, such that it took but a momentary calming of the beast for the hunter to shift from admiration to the pressing of the advantage. Tossing his dart with a lunge, the javelin lanced the sky and struck true with the metal tip breaking the scale and embedding shallowly in the flesh underneath. The beast bled a trickle into the waters, but such a prick as it sustained would not kill it were he to endure a hundred such barbs, and this fact caused Garbhan to curse loudly. The javelins would have to be abandoned and a new plan constructed.

Inspiration for his next move came by way of an errant gaze directed to the shore, where the hunter perceived the mix of sand and pebble as a fitting agent for blinding the large-eyed creature. He thus scrambled down the rock face and unstrung his shield from his back and used it as a scoop and filled it with the mixture. Thereafter, he waded into the churning water — which was so agitated by the thrashing of the monster — and flung the detritus against the eye. The material delivered its payload faithfully and it painfully closed, blinding the monster to Garbhan's approach, who proceeded forward then with spear drawn and shield pressed forward.

Blindness only doubled the ferocity of the Lord of the Estuary, whose convulsions began to churn not only the water, but the pebbles and shells of the shore floor up with it. Pelted with such debris, Garbhan protected himself by way of the shield, but found himself no less battered where the shield did not protect. He endured the sting of these missiles and the small cuts they drew upon his skin, until as such time that he closed the distance and was able to deliver a powerful lunge with the harpoon-tipped spear.

The blade sunk deep into the mouth of the monster and thick, bubbling blood flowed from the wound gouged into its maw. But an unforeseen consequence of such a fierce strike was that the blade became lodged underneath the roots of the teeth.

Garbhan proceeded closer to jerk the harpoon from where it was stuck, thinking it was key he should retrieve the spear for renewed strikes against the monster, but instead he found himself assaulted. For as soon as he draw near enough, the bony tongue jutted out like a lance of the monster's own through the holes in the netting, and were it not for the shield, Garbhan would be skewered. As it stood, the tongue penetrated the brazen shield as if it were straw, and stabbed the shoulder so holding it.

The wound was only shallow, but the pain and shock of the assault opened him to another blow. Following up the success of the stabbing, the monster rammed Garbhan with such force that he was lifted from the water and flung back to the shore. Laid flat and bleeding well from the wound in his shoulder, he did not stir for several moments, having been rendered unconscious. All the while, monster seemed almost to gloat over this fact by shredding the shield in its mouth to ribbons.

At long last, Garbhan recovered his senses and stumbled to his feet. Testing his shoulder, he found the wound had not severed the tendons nor broken the bone, and though it was painful to do so, it could be moved freely. He likewise found that his other injuries were mild enough, save for the ringing in his ears that betrayed the severity of the jostling of the brains sustained by the ram.

Being thus of sound body, if not of sound mind, Garbhan found himself fit to continue the fight against the Lord of the Estuary. All which was lacking was a plan, and lucky for the hunter, he was provided momentary respite in order to conceive of it. This was occasioned by the renewed thrashing of the monster, which saw the creature's attempts to not only liberate himself from the encumbering net, but also to free himself from the horrible pain of the dart in its mouth which remained lodged underneath its teeth.

Inspiration for the plan that finally formed in Garbhan's mind no doubt was rooted more in the injury of his head rather than sense, for Garbhan intentions resolved to a desperate act of brazen risk in order to subdue the creature. He thought this plan aloud: "The Lord of the Estuary shall prohibit my advance and has robbed me of my shield. Though he is netted, his tongue can yet stab me and his thrashing bulk will send me flying again. Nor can I wheel around and attack his tail, for it will do the same and I should lose my power should I have to swim. I thus have no other option: I must take his back. And if I am to take his back, I must pitch myself off the cliff and trust that I can grasp the net that grasps the Lord of the Estuary."

With that curious resolve that seeks hasty action, as if running ahead of the fear that would arrest one in one's pursuit, action immediately followed declaration. Garbhan quickly discarded his quiver of javelins, as he had no more use for the darts, and sped up the rock. Upon gaining the peak, he did not hesitate even for an instant, but ran to the edge with brandished sword, and while invoking the aid of higher powers as the sun played blazing upon his blade, he vaulted over the edge with hand outstretched.

Garbhan succeeded in not only landing upon the bucking, writhing monster, but in grasping in his hand a link of the hair net which secured him across the slickened surface of the beast. He spared no time in delivering great hacking strokes with his blade, which tore through the thick scales with such ferocity that the gore was flung from the blade with every clamourous strike. The beast wildly bucked in fury and pain from being so scaled, but Garbhan managed with the aid of the net to retain himself and make bare a wide expanse of the beast's flesh, which was then greeted with criss-crossing slashes that gouged the skin and fat until red cartilage shown naked underneath. Finally, with a great shout, Garbhan spiked the blood-coated blade down through the exposed skeleton, puncturing the thick cartilage of the skull, and penetrating deep into the brain.

The death throes of the monster were such that the blade was snapped even as it was spiked, and lost of this sure anchor, and the net itself cut to threads by the slashing of his sword, Garbhan could not retain his grip. In what might be construed as the last, desperate effort of the Lord of the Estuary, Garbhan was flung from the monster's back and was greeted with a fall broken only by the great rock itself. Thereafter, the beast gave up his ghost, and indeed Garbhan was hardly better, stretched as he was upon the rock senseless and battered.

* * *

Garbhan's recovery from the wounds sustained at the hands of the Lord of the Estuary owed much to the ministrations to the priest. Having seen the hero flung from the dying monster, he quickly rushed to Garbhan's aid. Finding him alive, though extremely concussed and variously injured, Calbhach brought Garbhan back to his house and there cared for him for him a few days. Thereafter, the pair set off together to bring news of Garbhan's victory over the monster to the people.

The triumphant return of Garbhan was reckoned a cause for celebration of a type seldom had. Though the Cackes were a jolly people they rarely were extravagant, but in heralding their returning hero they exceeded themselves. Not only was he greeted with celebrants in his home village, but immediately runners were sent out so as to alert the whole of the *tuath* on Calbhach's insistence that he would move the petty-king to call an assembly.

True to his word, the priest convinced Osgar — by then old, if not frail — and the people assembled within two weeks in the thousands. There they met two things: First, the massive skeleton stripped of flesh of the Lord of the Estuary, and secondly Garbhan bedecked in glory.

Indeed, Garbhan was allotted the honours of being carted upon a chariot to the assembly, crowned with a mistletoe wreath, arrayed in attire befitting the king himself, and permitted the king's seat, which Osgar conceded for the duration of the celebrations, which were to last for three nights. Garbhan also was given the right to judge over the games and feats of skill which consisted of the distractions of the days, while feasting filled the nights. In effect, he became temporary king over the *tuath*, and was assured of honours to last him the rest of his life of a lesser sort.

But on the feast held in last night of the celebrations, a team of three soothsayers drew the priest from the table and retained him elsewhere for some minutes. His absence was neither a cause of alarm nor of any notice, but his return drew the eyes of all present as it saw him holding aloft a large silver goblet — representing in its artistry and antiquity a rare sight to those accustomed primarily to woodcraft of recent make — while calling to the crowd, "Silence and reverence! It has been ordained that the hero should drink of this goblet in full. Delay not, oh champion, but hearken to divine honour!"

With the goblet pressed to his face, Garbhan did nothing to refuse it. He drank it down in several long gulps, and though the liquid was cloudy, held an extremely sharp and pungent aroma, and tasted a sickening sweet intermixed with undertones of dramatic bitterness, he endured until the last drop was quaffed from the basin of the goblet.

"Honour and blessings forever and anon be upon your head oh Garbhan mac Earnan," the priest proclaimed as he retrieved the goblet. "You will eternally be known as hero who has delivered us from the *Tiarna Inbhear*."

41

Garbhan moved his mouth in reply but found his tongue numb and the words choked in his throat. Confusion swept over and skewed his features at this effect, and as he looked up at the priest tacitly imploring an answer, his sight doubled and blurred. Pushing himself upon weakened arms, he went to stand from the table but was promptly forced back into his chair, where he then was lost to unconsciousness.

The stunning change in events set the crowd into confusion. Several men even jumped instinctively to Garbhan's aid, but the priest wheeled about to push them aside while thunderously proclaiming, "Stay your hands or suffer the wrath of the Gods themselves! He is our hero and it is his fate. Silence all of you! Back to your seats!"

Turning back to Garbhan, the priest quickly checked to see whether he was all right, and satisfied with his condition, only then did he address the crowd anew. He said, "Upon Garbhan's arrival to these celebrations, the soothsayers were sent by me to offer a sacrifice to determine how he should be honoured. They returned to inform me that he was no longer to be amongst us, and that the Gods have chosen him for exalted honours and that he might protect us from the monster's return. For be forewarned, though the monster is but bones, he shall return with a force far more terrible if the spirit of his slayer is not honoured!

He continued, "It has also been proclaimed that we, who are of his kin, must assure his seed passes to the generation next. As such, every family here present must render up a virgin daughter to lay with him, such that his line might not be extinguished with the ashes of his pyre which shall be lit upon the same day of his triumph on the next cycle of the moon."

What followed then was a week-long enterprise which saw the hunter kept in a constant daze, such that complete agency was robbed of him. Indeed, he was retained in utter insensibility, and kept up in his efforts with the small legions of maidens only by an invigorating drink forced down his throat. At no time was he permitted a return to sensibility, but dreamily he acted upon the urgings of the priest and attendant holy men who assisted him even to the point of moving his limbs. Thereafter, upon the month's anniversary of his triumph, Garbhan mac Earnan was lead to a pyre constructed atop the *Dearg Carraig*. Bedecked as majestically as at the victory assembly and while the people sang aloud a sacred hymn, Garbhan had first his throat slit by the priest and then was thrown into the flames.

Yearly, the sacrifice would be renewed.

* * *

Near to a year later, the famed poet Loman stood by the estuary for inspiration. To him fell the task of composing the song to commemorate the deeds of Garbhan, but he had found that life at the court of the petty-king was ill conducive to the task of composing a heroic poem. But here by the site of the monster's demise and near the blood-capped rock of sacrifice, he was beginning to feel the inklings of inspiration. Yet as he began to so compose his verses he was arrested by the appearance of a woman with swaddled child held in her arms. A heavy veil obscured her features.

"Hail to you," the poet called out, "young mother."

The woman nodded a greeting, "Hail to you. Tell me: are you Loman mac Marcan, the poet charged to relate the deeds of Garbhan mac Earnan?"

"Yes, I am doing such and I am he."

The woman drew her child nearer to her breast, "And you knew him in life?"

"In truth, I knew him but in passing," the poet conceded.

"Then listen well, poet," said the woman as she unveiled her face to the man, her chopped hair barely past her ears and her eyes alive with disdain, "to one who knew him better than his people. Garbhan mac Earnan did not die for you. He faced death, but he did not die for you, your priests, or your Gods. He fought that you might be free of the monster — an animal which you cravenly served with the sacred blood of man — and with the thought that you would honour him for rendering such a service. Instead, in your foolishness and superstition, your honours were to bring him to the pyre.

"Fools and savages! Those honours mean nothing to the one you betrayed so you might commemorate and live through him as any man amongst you ought to have lived, but only Garbhan dared! Your cowardice, your baseness, your meanness of soul is not assuaged by your supplications of the hero, but indeed becomes more monstrous, because you will never be as he by your ludicrous sacrifices. If truly you wish to be a hero as he, act as he did rather than celebrate your murder of him!"

She continued even as tears welled in those hateful eyes and the child at her breast wailed at the piercing shrillness of her tirade, "Would that I could have saved him from this fate, but he was naïve. Naïve that such evil lurked in your hearts, though he knew of your despicable practices. He could not fathom your wickedness, for though he might have known that a people may be moved to commit atrocious sins in the face of terror, and indeed be forgiven on account of this, no man of his spirit could countenance that cowardice could spur them on to retain these practices when they have been freed from terror. He died for your freedom from those rites and you dishonour him by their retention!"

"But I tell you this, poet Loman: His heir, his true heir, shall not be so naïve. This," she held the struggling, crying babe forward, "is Garbhan mac Earnan's true son and he will avenge his father."

"Aye, you savages may have given him your daughters that his line may forever persist amongst you, but I tell you that alone is this child his heir. Garbhan himself chose to lay with me, whereas your priests merely worked the senseless body to consummate the union of man and woman. And I will honour my son's father and so shall my people."

"Be forewarned: The sons of Cacke are the enemies now of what you call the Strange Folk. My father is king over my tribe and my mother his witch-bride and they have commanded it so. So tell your king, your Osgar the Fool, and his priest Calbhach the Idolater, to hearken to their superstitions. For the man, woman, or child to come to our dwellings or sacred stones shall be killed, until it comes to pass that the blood of Garbhan mac Earnan be redeemed by his son. So has Easnadh of the Strange Folk, wife of Garbhan, and all her people spoken."

All throughout Easnadh's lambasting, the poet held silent. Indeed, he did not answer her even as she left, only nodded once before she turned away and then watched in like silence until she was met by her people near the border of the woods and was embraced by both her father and mother. Only when they vanished into the tree line did he turn then gaze over his shoulder to the *Dearg Carraig* and declare:

"Evil is ever wrought when man does not aspire to ascend to the height of good, but beseeches the good to condescend to his level. Let the hero be mindful the wages of his heroism in the land of the coward."

JAMES FREDERICK WILLIAM ROWE *is a Rhysling-nominated poet and author out of Brooklyn, New York. His poetry and prose are known to bridge the gap between the philosophical and the fantastical, with work that can be characterized as "literary" and "speculative"—often at the same time. Since first published in 2010, he has seen three short stories and over sixty of his poems in print internationally, with many featuring in the speculative markets* Big Pulp, Tale of the Talisman, Heroic Fantasy Quarterly, Andromeda Spaceways, *and* Bete Noire. *His works have been described as having a "style that is bold, imaginative, crisp, and refreshingly simple, yet profound." He is especially proud to be a Frequent Contributor to* Songs of Eretz Poetry Review, *where his poetry is featured on a monthly basis, and which has done much to foster his growth into a contemporary, literary poet, drawing abundant inspiration from his thoughts and surroundings, while nevertheless retaining roots in the speculative field.*

He is often found writing his poems on the subway commute to his position as an adjunct professor of philosophy at Baruch College. His website can be found at http://jamesfwrowe.wordpress.com.

4

Death at the Pass

by Michael R. Fletcher

That this foul deed shall smell above the earth
With carrion men, groaning for burial.
Shakespeare, *Julius Caesar*

Somewhere there was a Necromancer. Of that there could be no doubt. Brushing a thousand years of dirt and rot from his robes, Khraen marvelled at how well preserved he was. Skin, sunken, cracked and grey, adhered to the bones of his long limbs. He'd never been muscular, but now he was downright skeletal. He chuckled at his little joke. A nearby dragon, still dragging its corpse from the earth and in a far more advanced state of decay, glanced toward him before shying from his gaze. Perhaps it recognised its ancient enemy. The creature was colossal — easily ten times the height of a man — but centuries of carrion insects had reduced it to a ragged and ratty skeleton. Its wings, once mighty and proud, hung like stained moth-eaten canvas.

Khraen examined the robes hanging from his bony shoulders. They were filthy but otherwise whole. Reaching back he felt for the cowl. It still hung behind him and was, as far as he could tell, intact.

"Remarkable," he muttered as he searched his memory. Though he had no doubt his brain had long since rotted to nothing, thought and memory still seemed to reside within his skull. A name came to him. "Fel, you still live and serve?"

The answer, heard only in what was left of his thoughts, was instant if somewhat faint. "Yes, Master."

Truly remarkable! That spirit-demon, bound to the very fabric of his robes of office, must have protected his body from insects and decay much as it had once protected him from the swords and arrows of countless assassins.

Khraen frowned in thought and dried earth crumbled from features that had not moved in millennia. Dirt dribbled unnoticed from empty eye-sockets. Fel had been one of the first demons the Emperor had bound to Khraen's service and yet still lived. If it lived, perhaps others had also survived, scattered and buried in the earth around him.

Khraen scanned his shattered surroundings. A few dozen leagues to the north the Deredi Mountains stabbed angrily at the sky, sharp, jagged, and black. Only at the peaks did they fade to an ashy grey. The ground around him was littered with rusted weapons and armour and fragments of broken stone, some larger than the dragon still trying to drag free a trapped leg. For the first time, he truly grasped the scope of the Necromancer's plans. As far as the eye could see the dead stood motionless or staggered about in dazed confusion. Dragons, many still mounted by their reptilian Dragon Lords whose once gleaming dragon-scale armour was now pitted and matte, towered above the undead horde. There were thousands of Deredi giants and hundreds of thousands of men. The Melechesh Pass, the only way through the impassible mountains that divided the two great continents, had been the site of countless battles. Khraen's Emperor had not been the first to attempt to conquer the Dragon Lords and wrest from them control of the pass and, judging from the strange garb many of the corpses wore, hadn't been the last. Some of the dead barely looked to have progressed beyond the first stages of decomposition. War had raged here recently.

Whoever this Necromancer was — Khraen couldn't see the man from where he stood — he had gathered for himself an impressive army. Even Palaq Taq's military, The Invincible Hand of Sorhd-Rach, paled before the host now gathered on the Deredi Steppes.

Apparently not so invincible, thought Khraen with some grim humour.

Palaq Taq, the small island kingdom had ruled much of the southern continent. Though he thought of it as home, he knew he had not been born there. Strange that some memories could be so diluted while others stood bright and sharp. Almost nothing of his day-to-day life remained to him and he missed none of it. What little he could remember consisted mostly of glowing success and crushing failure. Fear, he thought, had played an unhealthy role in his life.

And yet no twinge of longing or regret had survived his death.

"Time heals all wounds."

Dead or alive the days pass you by and time changes everything. When Khraen last walked the earth the Demonologists — under the leadership of Palaq Taq's Emperor — had subjugated the lesser magics. The Wizards with their filthy chaos-magic cowered in the far north where they'd fled after the Emperor's purging wars. Elementalists and Sorcerers, understanding the true balance of power, knew their place while Shamans were left to babble at their demented tribal spirits. Necromancers had been but unknown. This army of undead suggested that the balance had shifted, after long years, or centuries, in favour of the foul corpse-worshippers.

Khraen stepped around the struggling dragon to get a better look at the mountains. He couldn't remember the exact moment of his death, but his last memories were of being at the mouth of the Pass. If his army had brought his corpse out they would have carried his belongings as well, but retreat and failure were never options for the Invincible Hand. They would have stood and died, fought to the last. Most likely the spring floods had washed the corpses and garbage from the Pass as it did every year. The thought of being deposited here like so much effluent normally would have tweaked at Khraen's pride. Perhaps that had rotted away with his eyes and brain. He no longer felt like the Fist of Sorhd-Rach, First General of the Invincible Hand, loyal servant to the Emperor of eternal Palaq Taq. He wasn't sure how he felt but a weight had definitely been lifted from his shoulders.

If the palace at Palaq Taq still stood, who ruled there now? The Emperor had been thousands of years old when Khraen had served, could he still rule? It seemed unlikely. If the Invincible Hand had failed, Palaq Taq, bereft of it's army and First General, would have surely fallen shortly thereafter. That thought should have angered Khraen but instead left him feeling strangely — free. There were no demands being made of him. No Emperor gave commands he dared not question. No one begged his guidance and no god sought to dance him like a twisted marionette. The strings had been cut. His mind (and what little remained of his soul and sanity) were his.

Interesting. He hadn't given his god much thought.

"Sorhd-Rach?" Khraen asked quietly, neither dreading nor expecting a reply and yet still somehow pleased at the answering silence.

Again Khraen surveyed the vast Deredi Steppes, looking for The Sword of No Sorrows — his sword. If it was here it was hidden from sight. A thousand souls had been sacrificed in its making, fed to the ravenous evil the Emperor had summoned with the help of his deranged god. Khraen didn't miss the power that came with being First General and he certainly didn't miss the responsibility. He didn't miss spending lives and souls for the Emperor's territorial hunger and the amusement of Sorhd-Rach. He didn't miss the emptiness he had become. The sword, that he missed. It's name had been a joke, told once to one of his subordinates in a flash of rare whimsy. Kantlament was the demon bound to the blade. In a moment of introspective honesty he had to admit he was relieved to be free of the blade, too. Unable to feel the cold, Khraen still shivered. Some appetites can never be sated.

The Emperor had bound demons to Khraen's clothes, to his symbols of office, and to his very blood and bones. Dark deals were brokered with foul forces to extend Khraen's life and he had served the Emperor as First General for an unprecedented three-hundred years. Demons might have protected him from rot and decay, but here he was.

Dead.

And yet not.

Khraen shrugged. If there was a lesson here it escaped him.

With a final heave the dragon pulled itself free and shook millennium of filth from cavernous bones. Its mouth yawned wide, exposing row upon row of massive yellow teeth as dried lips pulled back in a fierce snarl. It turned its head in his direction and wheezed a gout of dust that covered him in grit. No smoke, no fire. Whatever had powered those bellows was long gone. The creature growled in consternation and ambled away, dragging limp and broken wings. Khraen was glad it hadn't decided to try and claw him apart. Fel might still protect him from such abuse, but the demon was beyond ancient. Best not to test its strength unnecessarily.

A wave of restlessness passed through the gathered dead and as one they turned to face north, Khraen included. He wondered at the strange compulsion that had suddenly overcome him. It had never crossed his mind that the Necromancer who could raise this field of dead might also be able to command it. Were he capable, he would have blinked in surprise. Whatever gods ruled now had a greater sense of humour than any he had known in his time.

The dead began their slow shambling march north. Khraen walked alongside a man who looked like he'd been dead no more than a few weeks. The crows had been at him. One of his eyes was missing, the soft tissue a carrion delicacy, and his face had been ravaged by something other than the normal wounds of war.

"You look fresh," Khraen said. "Do you know the Necromancer behind this magic?"

The man's mouth opened to spill damp earth and writhing maggots down the front of strange armour made of human rib-bones bound in strips of leather. His remaining eye rolled in pleading terror as he stumbled on the intestines hanging from a rent in his belly.

"Never mind." Some people just couldn't stomach death.

Khraen increased his pace and left the struggling corpse behind. He shouldered past men, ducked around giants and dragons, and steered well clear of the Dragon Lords. He didn't want to face one without the Sword of No Sorrows at his side. None of the dead seemed to pay particular attention to his passing, so lost in their own misery were they. He stumbled often on the uneven ground and several times found himself on hands and knees, crawling from craters blasted into the earth by ancient magics. He wondered how many of these his own demon-driven armies had caused or if the marks of his passing had been washed away by the ceaseless march of centuries. Emerging from a particularly deep crater, Khraen stood and brushed the dirt from his robes. More from force of habit than any desire to be clean. He marvelled at how little his pride chafed at having to muck about like a common man. When you weren't the First General, you did whatever needed doing with no worry of how it looked or whether some up-and-coming officer might see it as weakness.

He barked a dry laugh.

Struggling through mud and corpses.

Possibly enslaved by an unknown Necromancer.

He felt freer than he had in the last few hundred years of his life.

The ground fell away into a shallow valley or perhaps a very deep and old crater. The valley was empty of the dead and the corpses gave it wide berth as they marched north. Half a league away, where the ground evened out, he could see three tents and the makings of a simple camp. Two of the tents were shabby and old and bore the markings of some military cadre unknown to Khraen. The third tent was bright and colourful and looked out of place in this pale land of dust and the dead.

It was no great stretch for Khraen to decide the Necromancer would be found there. Once again longing for his lost sword, he stood staring down into the valley, hesitating.

"No gods-damned Necromancer's compulsion will stop me," Khraen muttered as he pushed himself forward. Once he was moving it became easier, though his feet kept trying to take him around the camp. Only by concentrating on his goal could he move in the right direction. As the only corpse not avoiding the camp Khraen felt strangely exposed.

They saw him coming. By the time he reached the camp there were five large men and women waiting for him with drawn blades. They looked discomfited at being confronted by the walking dead and, for a brief moment, he wondered what he looked like. One of the women, muscled arms stretching chain hauberk to its limits, waved a great-sword in his face. She wielded the ridiculous weapon single handed, like it was a fencing sword.

"Leave," she commanded in a brutal mangling of the Palaq Taqi tongue. "Dead belong on ridge. Not camp." She pointed the sword at the shuffling dead.

Khraen grunted. "What are you going to do, kill me?"

"Chop head."

Even dead that sounded unpleasant.

Khraen straightened to his full height but she still towered over him. He'd have happily killed to have his sword right now. "I am here to see the Necromancer," he said instead.

The woman's beady blue eyes darted toward the colourful tent. "She busy."

She? Khraen covered his surprise. "She expecting me." He grimaced at the slip.

The woman blinked in confusion and frowned thunder. No one expects the dead to lie. "You wait," she commanded as she spun away to march to the tent.

Khraen watched the warrior-woman stand at the tent's entrance trying to decide how to knock. Eventually she cleared her throat loudly enough that some of the distant dead looked in her direction. Moments later a slim woman exited the tent and looked about, shading dark eyes with a long-fingered hand. Her short black hair barely moved in the breeze. When she caught sight of Khraen she lifted a quizzical eyebrow. The Necromancer had no fear of the dead, no revulsion.

Khraen bowed low. He couldn't remember the last time he'd shown obeisance to anything less than god and Emperor. "I am Khraen, Fist of Sorhd-Rach, First General of the — "

"Sword-rock," she interrupted. "Is that a god?" Her Palaq Taqi was oddly accented but easily understood.

Khraen swallowed the impulse to anger. "First General of the Invincible Hand," he finished stubbornly. "And yes, Sorhd — "

"Never heard of him. Or you."

"Well — "

"When did you die?"

Khraen shrugged. "How would I — "

"You look remarkably well preserved."

"Does anyone ever get to finish a sentence around you?" Khraen caught the stifled smirks that passed between the Necromancer's minions.

"Turn and get down on your hands and knees," she said and, without hesitation, he was on the ground before her. She sat on him as if he were a bench. "You are dead," she told him from above. "A tool. An animated inanimate. An uncomfortable chair."

"I'm a bit more than that," said Khraen. "I'm — " He stopped. The man he was now facing stood with sword drawn but dangling casually in his right hand. The sword drew Khraen's attention, became his universe. Kantlament, there in the hands of some mortal. He must have found it lying in the dirt and, thinking it a pretty and well-made blade, thought to make it his own. Khraen hid his disgust, swallowed the hunger to once again possess that foul blade.

The Necromancer grunted and, her point made, rose gracefully from Khraen's back. "A General, you said?" She glanced toward the army of corpses. "Only one person in charge here. Are you anything more than a scrawny corpse?" She squinted at his gaunt frame as if imagining how he may have looked in life. "A Wizard? Kazsh, how many powerful Wizards do I have?"

"Dozens," the large woman answered instantly, as if awaiting the question.

Khraen stood and didn't bother dusting himself off. It would seem like wounded pride and there was no point anyway. "Wizards." He tried to spit but just sputtered dust. "We kept them as pets." It wasn't strictly true but sounded good. He'd hated Wizards and their easy power.

The Necromancer shrugged. "Elementalist? Sorceror? Gods, not *another* Necromancer!"

Her squad of hired muscle laughed dutifully and Khraen used the distraction to edge closer to the man holding Kantlament. "You missed a couple."

"I did?" The Necromancer frowned, searching her memory. "Shamanism hardly counts as a worthy branch of magic."

Khraen disagreed. He'd known a few dangerous Shamans. Anyone with the power to manipulate the countless tribal spirits (and a tribe's very spirituality) was worth some respect. He took another step toward his goal under the guise of a grand gesture to encompass the hordes of dead streaming past on the ridge.

"I am what you might call a — " Khraen spun and kicked the man square in the fruits. He snatched the sword from the man's hands and gave him a shove that sent him sprawling. He turned and found himself facing four drawn blades and an annoyed Necromancer.

"You're a gods-damned *swordsman*?" she asked, incredulous. "All of that for another swordsman?"

Khraen shrugged. "My sword," he said as if that explained everything.

The Necromancer turned back toward her tent and called over her shoulder, "Kill him. Again." She sounded bored.

Khraen flicked the cowl into place and hoped that enough of Fel still lived to get him through this. Kantlament, the Sword of No Sorrows, hung in his right hand like a dead weight. Lifeless. "Death and destruction," he promised the blade. "A thousand lives if you still live."

Nothing.

A sword crashed into him from behind, breaking ribs but not puncturing the robe. There was a time when Fel would have stopped everything and Khraen would have barely felt the attack, but the force of the blow sent him stumbling forward. He barely got Kantlament up in time to stop Kazsh from decapitating him. He didn't know if such a blow would kill him, but didn't want to spend the rest of his 'life' carrying his head tucked under an armpit. He stabbed at the big woman and she batted it aside contemptuously.

Four warriors now circled Khraen. They cracked jokes but knew that killing the undead was never a simple task. Feinting and probing, they tested his skill. The fifth, robbed of his blade, stood back and watched, calling out unwanted suggestions to his companions.

Khraen narrowly avoided another attack only to feel something slam into his back again. Another rib might have broken. He wasn't sure, he couldn't feel much of anything and certainly no pain.

At this rate they were going to pick him apart before long. *Why am I so desperately protecting this dead body?* No feeling. No pain. These were his advantages.

Can the dead be suicidal?

The next man that swung at Khraen met no defence. The once First General left himself exposed and, when his opponent's sword crashed against his body, stepped forward to run the man through. The demon-forged blade sheared banded mail, penetrated flesh and bone with ease. If there was resistance, Khraen couldn't feel it. Perhaps something of the old blade's strength remained.

Khraen spun away from the dying man and hurled himself at the closest target with little regard for his own welfare. The woman, a smaller, faster version of

Kazsh, stumbled backward in surprise. She was dead before she hit the ground, Kantlament neatly sliding free of her chest as she fell. The man Khraen had kicked in the groin leapt forward to snatch up a weapon from a fallen comrade. Khraen killed him next, stabbing through him into the earth. He could feel the grinding grit on the blade as he pulled it clear and backed away to face his two remaining opponents. Glancing past them he saw the Necromancer once again exit her tent.

"Perhaps we can talk," Khraen called out to her. "Or do I kill off the rest of your people?"

This was more feigned bravado than confidence. Even if he managed to kill them, he was far from sure what condition his body would be in by the end. Already his torso canted at an odd angle where ribs that had once supported him had been broken.

Kazsh and the remaining man circled Khraen warily, awaiting the command to finish him.

The Necromancer glanced about, taking in the fresh carnage. "Why don't I just raise them and have them finish you off?"

"I hadn't thought of that," Khraen admitted. "But I'm guessing talking would be easier."

"Maybe," she said, nodding at Kazsh. "Lower your weapons."

Kazsh, seemingly born to obedience, immediately sheathed her massive sword. Khraen killed her, driving Kantlament into her throat. Eyes wide with hurt surprise she stood motionless, trying to stem the torrent gushing from the wound with thick and blunt fingers before toppling like a felled tree.

"Unquestioning obedience is a weakness," Khraen told Kazsh's twitching body. Hollow words from a hollow soul. For three-hundred years he had been the very model of perfect obedience.

The man, having seen his companions slain by an undead creature of unknown power, chose flight instead.

Khraen watched the Necromancer as she watched her remaining warrior disappear into the marching dead.

"Was it always this hard to find good help?" she asked.

He shrugged, feeling the grinding of broken bones within his torso much as one hears a sound too low to be truly heard. "Do we talk now as equals, or must I kill you too?"

She lifted an eyebrow. "Equals? Have you forgotten already? Me Necromancer. You dead. I think you can figure out the rest."

Necromancy was a mystery. Could she simply negate whatever magic kept him alive? But then what is death to the dead? He shrugged again and began stalking toward her, lifting Kantlament in quiet promise of the violence to come. He had hoped that the sword would have shown some signs of life by now, but still it remained quiescent. Deader than he.

She frowned at his approach and waved a hand in his direction. "Drop your sword. Lie down in the dirt. Be a good corpse."

Khraen continued his approach. "The Emperor selected his Generals for their strength of personality. It takes a powerful will to command a demon, even one bound to eternal service. I was First General." He smiled. "And I have commanded an *army* of demons. Entire legions."

Showing no fear, she stood her ground. "The bench thing?"

"An act. It never hurts to be underestimated." A half truth. Her compulsion had caught him off-guard and pushed him to his knees. Once there he had regained control and made the decision to go along with it.

"You do realize that if you kill me, the spell I used to raise you ends and you fall back into the earth."

Khraen stopped. Death and dissolution should have been preferable to this pale shadow of life. Yet he clung to it as a drowning man clutches wood. He would not willingly slide back into darkness. Khraen might not be First General, but he was still the same man who had fought to achieve that position. Struggle was in his very blood. True dead was dead, devoid of options and choices. Undeath at least gave him the possibility of changing things. Perhaps he could find someone capable of bringing him back to life.

There was always the chance the Necromancer was bluffing, but Khraen couldn't see the advantage in testing that theory.

"So you can't command me, and I can't kill you," he said.

"Our relationship is a little more complex than that," she said. "If I die, you die. Where I am going, that is fairly likely. Perhaps even a certainty."

Khraen gestured at the unending army of the dead marching past. "Even with this? In my day I could have conquered the Melechesh Pass and enslaved the Dragon Lords with a force such as this."

"Times change. The Wizard's Guild hold the Pass. They control the only route north and tax everything that comes through. They've grown wealthy and powerful beyond sanity."

"In my day we'd crushed the Guilds and subjugated the Wizards."

"In my day," she mimicked scornfully. "There's only *one* Guild. It has always been that way. I've never heard of you or your silly sword god." She shook her head. "And there is no such thing as demons. I've raised a delusional fool."

"No. Just someone from another time." Khraen probed at broken ribs with skeletally thin fingers. "So, Necromancer, seeing as we are stuck with each other, what do the dead do about healing?"

"Leben, my name is Leben. Wait here," she commanded and ducked into her tent.

Khraen was glad that she'd turned away and not seen how her casually thrown command had momentarily rooted him to the ground. He'd have to keep his defences up at all times, ever ready to resist.

Leben returned with twine and strips of leather hide in varying widths. "Off with the robe," she commanded.

This time he was ready and barely twitched. "Why?" Though Fel hadn't sheltered him from all damage, the demon had still kept him from being hewn in half.

"The dead don't heal, they're *repaired*."

Khraen shrugged the robe aside. If Leben wanted him dead, she could turn a small fraction of her army against him at any time. Standing naked before her he could see the true severity of the damage he'd suffered. The lower ribs along one side had been crushed in and the parchment flesh torn. Bone shards projected through skin in a dozen places.

Leben prodded at his torso.

"I think your spine might be broken. I'm amazed you're still standing." She peeled a long strip of flesh away to expose the carnage below.

"Do you really need to peel me like that?" Khraen asked. "I'm not an orange."

She slapped his hand away as he tried to fend off her less than tender ministrations. "This isn't hurting you and I need to see what I'm doing." She drew forth a fragment of rib and tossed it over her shoulder. Reaching into his guts she felt around. "No, your spine is fine. The ribs supporting this side are broken. I'm going to tie them together and wrap some leather around your spine for additional support." She pulled out a long coil of desiccated intestine and dumped it at his feet.

"Might I not need that later?" Khraen asked.

Leben snorted. "Always the same with the dead. 'Don't toss my guts, I'll need them when I'm brought back to life.' Well it isn't going to happen. Dead is dead. This is as close to life as you will ever come. Don't waste your time on dreams of living."

It might be good advice, but Khraen was hesitant to accept it. There was always a way. He decided to change the subject. "So you plan to break the Guild's hold on the Melechesh Pass. And then what?"

Leben glanced up from where she knelt at his feet and Khraen could remember a time when that would have been an erotic sight. Now he didn't even want to think about what time had done to his manhood.

She talked as she worked, repairing ribs with twine and strips of leather, unaware of his distraction. Every now and then she'd grunt in disgust as she found something she couldn't fix and Khraen would feel a tug on his innards as she yanked something out and tossed it aside. "If I defeat the Wizards, I hold the Pass with my army of undead. I'll raise those Wizards that fall to help me with the reprisal they'll certainly launch from Paltaki when they learn what I've done. The more battles I survive, the stronger my army becomes as everyone who dies will fight on my side in the next."

"So, assuming you take the Pass and hold it, what then?"

"Same as the Wizards. Taxes and tolls. When I have my fortune, abandon my army in the Pass to act as a distraction as I flee to safety."

It seemed to Khraen a small plan, full of holes and wasteful. Something she had said caught his attention. "Paltaki. This is the Wizard's capital?"

"Yes, they — "

"An island kingdom, far to the south?"

She looked quizzical and seemed to find humour in being interrupted. "Yes. Why?"

After his death, had the Wizards taken Palaq Taq for their own? It couldn't be coincidence. He suddenly realized his fists were clenched and shaking. The thought of those filthy, godless mages walking the hallowed halls of the Eternal Palace rankled beyond all reason.

Khraen thought had death rendered him incapable of feeling and emotion. He had thought himself free of purpose.

He was wrong.

Life, even this anaemic imitation, required drive. One needed goals, something to live for. Well he had found his.

"I might suggest a change in plans. We should push south toward Palaq Taq, not north to the pass." Even as he said this he was envisioning the war to come.

"When you have something to offer we can talk about *your* goals. Until then, we do everything my way." She began wrapping his spine — where it had been exposed by her repair work — in thick leather thongs. "This might reduce your upper-body mobility a bit, but if your spine gets severed you'll spend the rest of eternity face down in the dirt. I've met undead who spent centuries as little more than severed heads. They're never sane. I wouldn't wish that on anyone." She looked up again, meeting his empty eye sockets unflinchingly. "Not even a delusional idiot."

There was a time when he would have killed anyone who talked to him in such a tone. That time was long gone. He found himself enjoying her blunt and fearless honesty. "Thanks."

Having completed her repair work, Leben stood and slapped him on the shoulder. "If you've been dead as long as you claim, you are remarkably well-preserved." She uttered a very unladylike grunt. "You must admit that it's more likely you haven't been dead all that long." She looked him up and down, appraising his state of decay. "Though I confess you look more mummified than this climate would account for. Was your body somehow preserved or stored in something?"

Khraen shrugged as he pulled on his robes. He didn't want to tell her that Fel had most likely preserved him. It never paid to give away secrets unnecessarily. Instead he pointed toward the Melechesh Pass. "So, how are we getting there? Walking?"

"I thought we'd find ourselves a few undead mounts. There must be a few thousand horses out amongst that crowd. They might not be the most comfortable ride — depending on the state of decay — but they never tire. That can be handy when you're fleeing angry Wizards."

Khraen decided not to mention the possibility of other mounts. Any dragon that recognized him would no doubt hold a grudge; his army had killed thousands. Another thought occurred to him. "So you resurrected horses as well as fallen warriors?"

Leben grinned, embarrassed. "I raised *everything*. Insects, rats, horses, men. If it was in the field of effect, it's out there wandering around and following my orders."

"Not a terribly specific spell, I take it. Seems wasteful," said Khraen, subtly probing for information.

She looked away, and watched the procession of dead for a moment. "Wasteful? Can you even begin to imagine how many dead animals and insects there are out there? I could probably take the Pass with them alone. To hells with your specificity."

Khraen examined her work on his torso. It was neat and effective. She'd obviously repaired corpses before. That lead to all manner of questions but instead he said, "Not everything you raised obeys your commands. You'd best hope there's nothing out there scarier than me."

"Everything out there is scarier than you," Leben scoffed.

Within minutes two skeletal horses presented themselves as mounts and Leben grumbled about the condition of their tattered leather saddles. Khraen asked why she didn't raise her fallen companions and she muttered something about the spell already being cast and not wanting to bother for a couple of half-wits who couldn't even kill a delusional and dead old man. He watched her as she talked and knew that she was hiding something. He might be dead and rotting, but his skills at reading people had not decayed to the point where this tactless Necromancer could hide something from him. For one thing she had called a horse for him. Had she really believed he was nothing more than a senile corpse, she wouldn't have bothered.

Despite her claims of the stamina of undead mounts, she set a sedate pace when they finally left for the Melechesh Pass. She rode like someone unaccustomed to the saddle, jolting awkwardly with each step, unable to find the horse's rhythm. Khraen, with centuries of unending war spent in the saddle, ever marching toward the Emperor's next conquest, rode with an unconscious grace. He watched Leben watching him from the corner of her eye, knowing what she saw; a man accustomed to command and at ease with violence. It was an act, the reproduction of someone he had once been. He felt none of the confidence he'd known as First General. He was dead and staring into an eternity of slow decay as he fell apart piece by piece. Some day he would suffer a wound that string and leather couldn't repair. What then?

Thinking back, Khraen saw that his entire life had been an act up until the moment he'd bartered soul and sanity for power, trading them to become the crushing Fist of Sorhd-Rach. After that the act had been replaced by the reality of being the puppet of an Emperor hungry for power and demanding a never ending river of blood.

River?

Khraen had shed *oceans* of blood in Sorhd-Rach's name. He may have led armies, but he now saw what he *truly* had been; a slave. He wished he could close his eyes and ride in blissful darkness, allowing the horse to find its way. Empty sockets cared not what paper-thin crusts of eyelid did. There was no escaping the future he could so clearly see splayed out before him like the grisly corpse he already was.

"Kantlament?" he whispered, hoping for both a reply and silence. "Are you still with me, or am I truly alone?"

There was no answer.

Khraen and Leben chatted as they rode. He spoke of the Emperor's wars to subjugate the five lesser magics. He told her of the wars to unite the southern continent under one rule and the later wars to take the Melechesh Pass from the Dragon Lords. Leben admitted she'd heard of Dragon Lords and demons but had always assumed them fanciful myths. She told him what little she knew of the rise of the Guild and how they had infiltrated virtually every kingdom. They talked of Paltaki, the Wizard's city and the centre of their power and when Khraen probed gently at her reasons for hating Wizards she snapped that they were at least as good as his and turned her back on him. All conversation died.

As they rode in silence amongst the marching dead Khraen wondered at how the world could have changed so much that the Wizards had taken Palaq Taq.

Kazsh rose to her feet, fierce eyes scouring the ground for her great-sword. That damned corpse would pay for what he'd — the sight of her companions also pushing themselves from the dirt stopped her.

She'd seen them die.

Kazsh glanced down at the red stain soaking the front of her hauberk and swore. That damnable Necromancer had been the death of her. After finding her sword she joined the ranks of marching dead. Her fallen friends walked alongside her.

"Idiots," she told them.

The staggering horde took days to reach the walled city the Wizards had built to defend the Melechesh Pass. Gone were the towering black citadels of the Dragon Lords. Gone was the colossal blood-red wall, fused with the stolen souls of those who had fallen trying to conquer it. The Wizard's city was small and mean in comparison, filthy with wretched humanity and reeking of their chaotic magic. Looking at this pitiful defence nestled between the peaks that framed the Pass, Khraen was surprised to feel scorn. His own forces would have conquered this city in minutes. The Wizards would be nothing before the gathered might of Leben's dead.

But the Wizards, unfettered by the iron rule of Palaq Taq, freed from the limits the Emperor had forced upon them, had been practising their magics. These were not the Wizards he had ruthlessly crushed under the heel of his demon-bound boots. One hundred generations of mages had gloried in their freedom, pushing the limits of their art far beyond what Khraen had ever seen.

All hells broke loose.

Foul clouds, boiling bruises of stained sky, erupted to rain thick oil upon the dead horde. Flaming meteorites shredded the clouds — exposing the burning red sky above — and crashed to the earth with devastating effect. In moments the oil was alight and Leben's army burned. Though they didn't feel the fires, the blast-furnace heat would eventually reduce them to ash. Even Leben, well back from the front lines, was soaked in sweat and stumbling as she screamed commands at her army.

Leben's orders, rendered inaudible by the cacophony of destruction, punched through Khraen's mind like a stiletto through soft belly flesh. It took every ounce of will to resist joining the other dead in their charge to oblivion. Perhaps part of him desired that escape, for he caught himself moving forward.

Those dead who commanded Wizardry of their own began hurling spells, blasting the Wizards defending the wall. Though Leben's Wizards were largely countered by the living mages, she also commanded Sorcerers, Elementalists, and Shamans.

Figures darted into the air, twisted into alien and terrible shapes, and disappeared over the wall to reek havoc upon the city's inhabitants.

The very earth turned against the Wizards. Massive sections of wall pulled itself free to rise up into towers of shuddering stone and fall upon them. Winds howled, spinning sharp dust and sending shards of stone hissing amongst the mages.

The sky over the city roiled.

Hurricanes.

Tornadoes.

The tribal spirits of a thousand long-dead cultures swarmed forward, answering the call of their undead High Priests. Godless, the Wizards had nothing to protect their souls from such an attack and quailed, sanity teetering on the brink as their thoughts and life-force were battered.

By the time the corpses of millions of insects and rodents flooded over the crumbling wall there was little to be seen of the city's defenders.

And still Leben screamed orders driving her army forward. Khraen's willpower shuddered under the assault and he found himself once again moving forward, Kantlament in hand, with the desire to kill Wizards. So closely did her commands mirror his own wants that he had trouble seeing where one ended and the other began. No matter how much he might desire vengeance on those who had desecrated his faded memories of all that was holy, this was not the way. If he followed her orders she would get him killed, or worse. Khraen had no desire to spend an eternity as a rotting skull, screaming in silent insanity. No longer was he First General of Palaq Taq. He might not be Fist to Sorhd-Rach, his ravenous and deranged god, but he was still Khraen, the man who had entered the Emperor's army as a lowly footsoldier and fought his way through the ranks.

Leben hurled orders into his mind and threatened to fray all thought and bend him to her will. He had thought himself free, able to brush aside her commands if he focused his considerable will. He saw now that he was wrong. Fear made her strong. In moments she would drive him away, sending him into the city, howling for blood and death.

Freedom is more than just an abstract concept. Even to a corpse.

Khraen ground ancient teeth, feeling them loose in his jaw, and turned to face the Necromancer. "Stop!" he yelled. Dried lungs lacked the air for volume and if she heard she didn't react. He grabbed her arm, pulling her close and wheezed into her face, "Stop!"

She yanked her arm from his grasp and unflinchingly met his empty gaze. "No." She spoke so softly he couldn't hear her voice, but still it echoed in his thoughts. "I command, you obey." She grinned and Khraen, for the first time, saw the insanity lurking behind her eyes. A memory clawed to the surface of his thoughts. He'd seen that look before. In the eyes of the Emperor as he sent Khraen and the Invincible Fist north. In the mirror on the morning he led his troops into the Melechesh Pass. He understood now that this war was not about money and taxes. Leben would not stop until she'd seen the death of the last Wizard and bent them to service. She would never free him.

"The dead are my tools," she said. "*Mine*. You are mine." She pointed at the fallen wall. "Go," she commanded, driving her orders into his thoughts. "Kill the Wizards. Kill them all."

Khraen had turned and taken a step toward the city before he managed to regain control. "No."

All his life he'd been a slave. To the Emperor. To his god. To his own unrelenting needs. Death, he realized, had truly freed him from the bonds of his old life.

He turned back and cut down the Necromancer, driving the Sword of No Sorrows into her heart.

Let this free you from whatever wounds your soul, he prayed to no particular god. *It worked for me.*

Eyes wide, she stared at the sword protruding from her chest. Her eyes spoke stunned disbelief.

"I thought — " she said, lifting a hand to caress the blade. She looked past Kantlmaent to Khraen. "Bastard."

Knees buckling she crumpled to the earth.

Khraen watched, waiting for dissolution. Waiting for that final end. He watched the light of life fade from her eyes. He watched the last small tremors as her dying body surrendered to the inevitable. He watched the dust of the Melechesh Pass gather in her staring eyes.

The din of battle faded.

The thunder of duelling magics echoed off the Deredi mountains and then fell silent.

Still Khraen stood. Motionless. Waiting.

Finally, after what seemed like an eternity, he looked up to find Leben's undead army watching him.

"The Necromancer lied," he muttered in surprise.

His second thought, born more of habit than desire, was 'can I command this army?' With such a force at his beck and call he could retake Palaq Taq, drive the filthy Wizards from the palace. If Sorhd-Rach still existed Khraen could rebuild his Empire. Khraen could rule instead of serve. For a moment he stood, lost in the dream. But with the memory of one recent thought that dream scattered like ash in the wind.

"Death has changed me," he told the gathered host, not caring if they heard. He drew the sword from Leben's chest and stood staring at the bloody blade.

So Many lives, so much death.

"Enough," he said.

Kantlament fell from numb fingers to lay at the Necromancer's side.

Khraen, once Fist of Sorhd-Rach, once First General of the Invincible Hand of Palaq Taq, turned his back on dead and living alike. Mounting his undead horse he rode out into the Deredi Steppes.

The future shouldn't be an attempt to rebuild the past.

Even for a corpse.

Khraen rode south, cutting a path through the army of corpses. The dead parted before him like a sea of grass. They watched with mute curiosity, not yet understanding. Could life (or unlife for that matter) be lived without direction, without goals? He would, he supposed, find out.

Leagues behind him, nearer the shattered city that once defended the Melechesh Pass, Leben rose from where she had fallen. Sobs shook her body, but no tears fell. The dead can't cry.

The spell went on as she had feared it might. Never again would the dead of the Deredi Steppes stay dead.

MICHAEL R. FLETCHER *lives in the endless suburban sprawl north of Toronto. He dreams of trees and seeing the stars at night and being a ninja.*

Beyond Redemption, *a work of dark fantasy and rampant delusion, was published by Harper Voyager. The sequel,* The Mirror's Truth, *was released in 2016.*

Other works include Ghosts of Tomorrow, *a Young/New Adult science-fiction novel, and the epic dark fantasy,* Swarm and Steel.

BEFORE THE VILLIAN

BY ALEXANDRA SEIDEL

Should I give up now because it's fate?
Should I bury the sword
handed to me through seven generations
of firstborn mages
in the watery soil of the moor?
in the coal-hot sand of the desert?
in the soft black earth behind the house?

The seer promised me a crown
and more riches than any man could spend
loyal sons and cunning daughters, everyone of them
a mage like me
should I melt the crown
before it's forged?
drown my children
before they are born?
abandon the wife
whose face I've not yet seen?

Should I cast off my fate
like a torn muddy shirt
leave it on the floor
like crone's spittle

just because the seer said that they would call me
evil?
Rich and wise and powerful
but also evil?

Should I end my life now before I take the name the seer
whispered in his trance, before
I get to kill six heroes
and wait for the seventh to finally free the world from me?
Should I?
And what am I
if I fight Fate
and win?

ALEXANDRA SEIDEL *dabbles in the alchemy of words. The results are less metallic, more inky: you can read them at places like* Lackington's, Mythic Delirium, Strange Horizons, *and others. If so inclined, you can follow Alexa on Twitter (@ Alexa_Seidel), or read her blog www.tigerinthematchstickbox.blogspot.com.*

THE PRINCESS TRAP
BY PETER DARBYSHIRE

Saleema was an orphaned sheepherder until her seventeenth year, when a talking dragon landed in the mountain meadow one summer day and ate all her sheep. Then Saleema was just an orphan.

Saleema, however, liked to imagine herself not as a mere orphan, or even an orphan sheepherder, but as the orphaned queen of her village. She imagined the grazing sheep as her army of servants, and the rock she sat on as her throne. She gazed down at the kingdom of her village below and imagined how she would run things differently.

For starters, she'd dig some irrigation canals from the river to the parched fields. And she'd dam up the channel that the men of the village had made to feed the artificial lake they'd dreamed up for their boat battles. And she'd put an end to the bull market — and the whole winter sacrifice of the bulls. The village needed cows for milk and meat, not bulls for symbolic offerings, but the men had traded away the last of the cows to neighboring villages for all their bulls.

Saleema had tried to bring up these ideas at the last village council meeting, but the men had all ignored her when she'd put up her hand, and even when she'd tried to speak. Most of them pretended she didn't exist since her father hadn't returned from the last war. Most of them.

But now the dragon had eaten her servants and Saleema was just a homeless orphan again, hiding in a cave in the mountainside, hoping to avoid becoming an after-dinner treat like the sweets the baker sometimes gave her when she ventured down into the village to trade a sheep or two for food.

But the dragon didn't seem interested in eating her and spitting out her bones afterward like it did with the sheep. Instead, it rolled around the mountainside, tearing up what remained of the good grass and sending a cloud of dust into her cave so thick it made her cough, thus ruining any chance of her remaining hidden from the fearsome creature. Then it lay on its side, twitching its tail like a contented cat, and stared down at the village. Or rather, it stared at the dirt road that led from the village to join the wider dirt road in the west, which led to the road paved with stones, which led to the river with its sailing ships, which led to the city in the west. All of these things had names, of course, but to Saleema they were just the dirt road and the big dirt road and the stone road and the river and the city.

Saleema had never gone farther than the first dirt road in her life, because this wasn't the sort of land where young women could travel alone. But she'd heard tales about the rest of the world from her father, who'd looked after the sheep himself until he'd signed up for military service and gone off to fight in the wars that had been going on her entire life. He didn't have the money to buy and raise a bull like the other men, which meant he would never truly be a man in the village. So when the military recruiter rode into the village, Saleema's father was the first in line to see him, and the first in line to sign the contract to serve the king. In those short times he came back to visit Saleema in the family hut, when they still had a hut, and he told tales about markets in the city that were bigger than the village. He told tales about men who worked their entire lives drawing pictures in books for a living, and were rewarded with gold for it. He told tales about women who sold themselves for that gold and sometimes less on the streets of the city. Like livestock, her father said, if your livestock were wolves that could pick pockets. Each time he returned he said he'd almost saved enough to come back to the village for good and buy his own bull. Maybe even two.

But then Saleema's father didn't come back after his latest stint in the king's army. Most of the men who'd gone off to fight in the last war hadn't returned. Travelers passing through the village said the king was dead and the city in ruins, but it was too far for anyone to go to find out the truth. And all people really cared about was that the tax collectors stopped coming. That meant more money for the bull competitions and boat battles.

When it was clear Saleema's father wasn't coming back, the village blacksmith strode into the hut one day and said it now belonged to him. He told Saleema her father owed him money for the sword and armor he'd taken to the wars with him. Saleema didn't know if the blacksmith was telling the truth or not, but she didn't argue. She knew it was the blacksmith's word against an orphan's, and the blacksmith was an important man in the village. He was one of the men who was the village. When the blacksmith said he'd look after her as well as the hut, and raise her like his own daughter, she went up the mountain with her sheep. But she didn't forget the blacksmith. She thought about the blacksmith a great deal.

Now, huddled in her cave, Saleema hoped her father was dead. She didn't know what he would do to her if he found the entire flock gone as well as the hut, but she suspected even a dragon wouldn't be a good enough excuse for her father. No excuses were good enough since the plague had taken her mother and half the village to keep her company.

"You can come out of your hiding hole," the dragon said without looking away from the road. "I'm not going to eat you. I don't eat princesses. Besides, there's not enough meat on your bones."

Saleema was surprised to hear the dragon speak, as she thought it was just a mindless beast. But she didn't really know much about dragons. She'd thought them legends until this one fell shrieking from the sky and herded the sheep into its jaws with those long wings. She decided to stay in her cave anyway. The dragon's tail kept flicking back and forth, and she'd watched enough cats with rats to know what that meant. And she wasn't about to be the rat.

Still, she thought if the dragon talked then maybe there was a chance she could reason with it.

"Um, I think you have the wrong person," she called to the dragon.

"Undoubtedly," the dragon said. "I have yet to find the right person."

Saleema didn't know what the monster meant by that, so she just cleared her throat and continued on.

"No, I mean I'm not a princess."

"Of course not," the dragon said, snorting. "What a ridiculous idea. Who's been putting such nonsense in your head?"

"You did," Saleema said, beginning to grow a little vexed now. "You said you wouldn't eat me because you don't eat princesses."

"Hmph. Right," the dragon said, swiveling one eye to glance at her before looking back at the road. "Well, I need a princess and you'll just have to do because all the real princesses are dead."

"Did you eat them?" Saleema asked.

Now the dragon turned its head to look at her, and she shrunk back in the cave.

"Are you not listening, child?" it asked. "I said I didn't eat princesses. What kind of dragon would I be if I did such a thing?"

Saleema had no idea what kind of dragon the dragon would be if it ate princesses. Saleema had no idea what kind of dragon it was now. Saleema had no idea what kind of dragons there were at all.

"What happened to the princesses then?" she asked, deciding she'd best change the subject before the dragon got angry.

The dragon gazed far into the distance now. "The plague," it sighed.

"Oh," Saleema said, then added, "I'm sorry." She remembered how she had felt after the plague had taken her mother. Sheep-eating dragon or not, nothing should feel like that.

She waited for what felt like a respectful amount of time, then said, "You owe me for those sheep. That's my family business."

The dragon snorted, but Saleema couldn't tell if it was amusement or contempt.

"I'm serious," Saleema said. She figured if the dragon wasn't going to eat her, then maybe she could bargain with it. Maybe it even had a conscience. Like the baker. "What am I supposed to do now?"

"Take it out of my treasure," the dragon said.

"What treasure?" Saleema asked. She peeked out of the cave entrance but couldn't see anything but the dragon and the piles of bloody fur and bone around it.

"It'll come," the dragon said, continuing to watch the road as its heavy eyelids slowly slid shut and its head drooped to the ground. "Once word gets out I've got a princess here, it'll come. It always does." The dragon's voice grew lower and lower, until it was muttering in its sleep. It muttered all night long, but Saleema couldn't make out what it was talking about because the cave was too far from the beast. Which suited Saleema just fine.

She couldn't sleep herself. It was too cold. And then, of course, there was the matter of the dragon. She didn't dare try to sneak past it, although she crept a few feet out of the cave, just far enough to look down on the village and see what the villagers were doing to come to her aid. But the village was dark, all the fires extinguished, even those in the bullpens to guard against thieves. They were hiding from the dragon. She was on her own.

The treasure turned out to be a knight who showed up two days later. Saleema spent the time in between trying to ignore her thirst and hunger, for she'd dropped her provisions bag when the dragon had swooped down out of the sky. She couldn't see the bag anywhere from the cave, so she assumed the dragon had eaten it along with the sheep. She tried to draw scenes of the dragon attack on the walls using a rock, in case she didn't get out of here alive, but her rendering of the dragon looked more like a deer with wings, so she gave up. She didn't want people to think she'd been killed by a deer with wings. At night, she dreamed of the baker's sweets.

The dragon spent the time arranging the piles of sheep bones and fur with its snout and claws. It built a large heap and then tore it apart with a snort. It built several smaller heaps and hopped down the hill to study them for a bit. Then it lashed its tail and knocked over the heaps and rearranged them in even smaller piles, so that each collection of bones looked like the skeleton of a man. Topped with a sheep's skull, of course.

"What are you doing?" Saleema asked, growing tired of this by noon on the first day.

"The view is perfect for a lair," the dragon said, pacing around the meadow and studying its work some more. "But it lacks that foreboding atmosphere, don't you think?"

Saleema thought the dragon was plenty foreboding on its own, but she figured it wise to keep that to herself.

The dragon sighed at its work. "It needs more than sheep," it said. "Are your people the kind of humans that bury their bones underground?"

"They're not my people," Saleema muttered, although more to herself than the dragon. She was still vexed by the fact no one had come from the village to help her.

"Perhaps I could dig up their bones and make a few more piles with them," the dragon went on. "Maybe even a nice bed." It looked down at the village and then cocked its head to the side, like one of the butcher's guard dogs whenever the butcher talked to it. "What are they doing?" it said.

Saleema crept a few feet out of the cave again and looked down at the village. Several of the men had dragged one of the larger brown bulls into the field nearest the foot of the mountain. As she watched, they tied it to a post and then ran away, back into the village. The bull looked around in obvious confusion. The bulls were usually only moved from their home fields for the bull competitions, but there were no other bulls in the field. The bull looked after the men, but they were hiding in the huts now.

"I think they're offering the bull to you," Saleema told the dragon. She could tell it was an expensive bull from its size and its impressive horns, but it wasn't the biggest bull in the village. That one belonged to the blacksmith and it was all black.

"Well, I suppose that's very generous of them," the dragon said. "But I'm saving my appetite for the knights now."

Saleema crept back into her cave, hoping the dragon wouldn't notice she'd exited it in the first place.

It turned its attention back to the bones and began to tell her about past lairs.

"I had a lovely one in the Frozen Spikes range," it said. "The icicles at the entrance looked like fangs, so it was like you were entering my mouth just walking inside. But it was too cold and remote for anyone to seek me out, so I had to leave it. After that I tried a lair in the Forgotten Swamp, but it was just too wet. My hole was always flooding, and I kept losing things in the muck. So then I took over this abandoned keep in the Borderlands, but keeps actually start falling apart if you don't properly maintain them, so one time when I landed on the tower, it actually just crumbled away underneath me. I could have been killed! Imagine dying because your lair collapses. So after that…"

Saleema began to believe the dragon mad, and she didn't hold out much hope for her chances of escape.

So when she saw the knight the next day, she almost screamed with joy. But she managed to keep quiet, because it was dawn and the dragon was still sleeping and muttering about its previous lairs. Each breath it expelled sent tufts of sheep fur up into the air, which drifted back down like snow.

The knight was riding a dirty white horse and carrying a lance pointed up in the air. Saleema had never seen a knight before, although her father had talked about them sometimes. Too stuck up to even whore, he'd said. Her mother, on the other hand, had told her knights were the kind of men who would give you everything they had, although Saleema wasn't sure how her mother could have known that. She watched the man and horse make their way up the rough slope, the morning sun gleaming on shining armor, and then she ran out of the cave and down the mountainside to him as quietly as she could, waving her arms to attract the knight's attention.

The knight drew up on his horse and watched her approach, but showed no sign of breaking out any bread or water. So be it. Saleema could wait a few moments. No doubt the knight had a few questions about the dragon he wanted to ask her.

But instead he bowed to her in the saddle, which looked to be difficult in a full set of armor, as he almost fell off. She looked over her shoulder at the dragon as the knight straightened himself with a great deal of clanking and swearing, and the horse staggered about under his shifting weight. But the dragon just sighed and murmured something about fiery heaths and mud goblins.

"My princess," the knight finally said when he'd managed to sit upright again. "I am here to rescue you."

"That's very kind of you," Saleema said. "Although I'm not a princess." She had trouble speaking the words because her mouth was so dry from lack of water.

The knight frowned at her and then up at the dragon.

"One of her handmaidens, are you? Where's the real princess then? In that cave yonder? Quick, run and tell her Sir Gladhand of the Fishmonger Clan has arrived to save her."

"There's no princess," Saleema said. "It's just me."

"Am I too late to save her then?" the knight said, his eyes widening. "Has the foul beast eaten her?"

"No, no, it's not like that," Saleema said.

"I came as quick as I could," the knight muttered. "But the roads are not what they used to be." He shrugged, which almost knocked him off the horse again. "Well, if I can't save her, I'll at least avenge her."

"I really think we should leave," Saleema said. "Quickly. And quietly."

Sir Gladhand smiled at her like the villagers sometimes smiled at the village simpleton, back before he'd burned down the village hall.

"Child, I am a knight," he said. "It would not do to scurry away from a dragon like some sheep."

"Sheep don't scurry, and even if they did — " Saleema began, but he kept on talking like he didn't hear her.

"I'll never become king that way," he said. He slammed his visor shut and the dragon snorted in its sleep.

"Fear not," Sir Gladhand told Saleema. "I can always find another princess after I slay the foul beast. I don't think the order really matters."

Saleema had no idea what he was talking about, but it didn't matter. She watched as he lowered his lance and spurred his horse forward and charged the dragon.

For a moment, Saleema thought perhaps he might be successful in slaying the creature. It was sleeping, after all. But then Sir Gladhand let out a war cry. "Wake to your death, O bane of the realm!" he shouted at the dragon. "Prepare to meet my glory!"

Saleema wasn't sure what he meant by that, and she doubted the wisdom of waking the dragon before attacking it, but she was impressed by the complete lack of fear on the parts of Sir Gladhand and his steed.

She was less impressed when the dragon opened its eyes at the sound of Sir Gladhand's shouting and then snapped its tail forward like a spear, skewering both Sir Gladhand and the horse. Sir Gladhand's armor made a sound similar to the sheep's bones in the dragon's mouth. Sir Gladhand himself made no sound other than a surprised whimper, which matched the horse's surprised snort.

"Umm," Saleema said, uncertain about what to do now that her salvation had turned out to be less than, well, a salvation. She looked around for another cave to hide in, but the only one in sight was the one back behind the dragon.

The dragon brought its tail closer to its head and looked at Sir Gladhand and his horse like a fisherman inspecting a catch. Then it gave a shake of its wings that Saleema thought may have been a shrug, and it set about eating its catch, ripping off limbs and swallowing them whole, armor and all. Saleema turned away. She wasn't sure if Gladhand was actually dead yet, and she didn't particularly want to watch this.

"You should have woken me so I could have talked to him and learned his name," the dragon said around a mouthful of something. "I do like to know what I'm eating."

"His name was Sir Gladhand of the Fishmonger Clan," Saleema said.

"A Fishmonger? Hmm." The dragon spat out bones and shards of metal: a piece of breastplate, the crushed and split-open helmet, the broken blade of the sword. "Not very auspicious. I far prefer the Warsouls and Ironbreakers. And the Deathseekers." The dragon got a far-away look in his eyes. "Ohh, how I miss the Deathseekers. They were so well seasoned."

Saleema nodded like she understood. She figured her only chance to survive was to humor whatever mental ailment the dragon had.

"Did he mention anything else about his lineage?" the dragon asked. "Any heroes among his ancestors? Kin to any magicians perhaps?" He spat out a jumble of bones. "He tastes awfully fresh."

Saleema shook her head. "He said something about becoming a king if he slew you," she said. "And he thought I was a princess."

"Oh good," the dragon said. "It's working then."

"What's working?" Saleema asked.

"My princess trap," the dragon said.

"Princess trap?" Saleema said.

The dragon let out a low, long groan that took Saleema a moment to realize was a belch.

"It's the best way to get the knights to come," the dragon said. "They can't resist a princess."

"But I'm not a princess," Saleema said.

The dragon sighed. "It's a sad state of affairs," it said, "but what can be done?"

"You could go look for knights yourself," Saleema suggested, "instead of eating all my sheep and holding me hostage in a cave."

The dragon snorted. "A fine dragon I would be if I went about challenging knights instead of doing things the proper way," it said. It pushed Sir Gladhand's bones into one of the piles of sheep bones.

"What difference does it make?" Saleema asked.

"It's custom," the dragon said. "It's the way things have worked since the first knight sought out the first dragon. Why would we want to change something that is working perfectly well?"

Saleema thought this particular custom wasn't working well at all for anyone but the dragon, but she kept that thought to herself.

"And I'm not forcing you to stay in that cave," the dragon added. "You can come out whenever you like."

"What I'd like is some food and water," she said. "But you seem to have eaten my provisions. And Sir Gladhand's."

"You humans always have something to complain about, don't you?" the dragon said. It coughed several times and then spat up a jumble of gear — more bits of armor, half a saddle, and the knight's saddlebags. Then it groaned and wiggled a bit on the spot.

"I shouldn't have eaten that lance," it said. "Or that armor." It spat out another shard of metal. Saleema wasn't sure but thought it could have been a mangled boot.

She took a few steps toward the saddlebag, but kept an eye on the dragon.

"Why don't you take off the armor first?" she said.

The dragon rolled an eye at her. "And how am I supposed to do that?" it asked. "I can't very well ask the knights to disrobe in the heat of battle."

"Just take it off after you've killed them," Saleema said. "Deshell them. You know, like turtles." She instantly regretted saying that, wondering if dragons and turtles were somehow related. She got ready to run for the cave, but the great beast didn't seem to take offense. Instead, it considered its massive talons.

"I don't think I could," it said. "I'm good at clawing and tearing but not so much at opening buckles and undoing latches." It looked back at Saleema. "But perhaps you could help?"

Saleema folded her arms across her chest. "You haven't even paid me for my sheep yet," she pointed out.

"You can keep whatever the knight had," the dragon said.

Saleema turned her attention back to the saddlebags. She couldn't resist anymore. She ran over to them and ripped them open. She was relieved to find the bread and sausage and water bag inside intact, if a little slimy. She drained half the water in one go, then devoured the food in seconds and finished the rest of the water. It was only after the provisions were gone that she searched the rest of the saddlebags and found several gold coins in a pouch. She rubbed the slime off them and held them up to the sky. Gold. She'd never seen a gold coin before, despite all her father's mutterings about them. They did look a little like the sun. She could see why people fought and died for them.

"All I have to do is take the armor off the knights after you've slain them?" she asked.

"And talk to them beforehand," the dragon said. "Find out their lineage."

"What difference does it make if you're going to eat them anyway?" she asked.

The dragon lashed its tail about, sending sheep bones into the air. Or maybe Gladhand bones. Saleema ducked as a couple of them flew over her head. "How would you like it if I just gave you some random pile of meat and told you to eat it without asking what it was?" the dragon asked.

Saleema thought that was more or less what the dragon had done with the saddlebags, but she was so happy to have finally eaten again that she didn't say anything. She looked down at the village instead. The bull was still tied to the post, still staring back at the huts where the men were hiding. Nobody was coming to save her. Nobody but the knights.

"What do the knights want with princesses anyway?" Saleema asked. "Whatever it is, it can't be worth the price they pay." She looked at the skull of Sir Gladhand, which the dragon had placed on top of one of the bone piles and was now adjusting with a talon.

"You need to marry a princess to be able to become king in this land," the dragon said. "And no princess is likely to refuse a marriage proposal if you've rescued her from me."

"How often do the knights rescue a princess from you?" Saleema asked.

"Never, of course," the dragon said. "I'm a dragon. They're just knights. They don't really stand much of a chance, do they?"

"So why don't they just find some other princess?" Saleema asked. She was trying very hard to understand all this, but it seemed a little like the bull sacrifice competition. That is, it was something that only made sense to men.

"There are no other princesses," the dragon said. "The plague wiped out the royal bloodline. Otherwise I would have made my princess trap with a real princess like in the old days." It let out a sigh. "Those were very good days."

"What are you going to do if they figure it out?" Saleema asked, polishing the gold coins some more. She wondered if she'd ever be able to spend them.

"I'm more concerned about running out of knights first," the dragon said. "It's not like in the past, when they were as plentiful as sheep." It shook its head.

Saleema couldn't help but ask the question on her mind. "So if you have to rescue a princess from a dragon to become king," she said, "then how did the king — "

The dragon sent bones flying everywhere across the meadow again.

"We need to clean up before the next knight arrives," it snapped. "Let's make this place look like a proper lair."

Saleema quickly discovered that dragons had very different ideas about "cleaning up" than humans did. She helped the creature gather the sheep bones again and arrange them in a large pile, topped by the bones of Sir Gladhand — she let the dragon handle those bits — and the shards of armor and weapons it had worked out of its system.

"It's not a lair without a good pile of bones," the dragon said, nodding to itself when they were finally done, near nightfall.

Saleema looked around the empty mountainside and thought it would always look more like a meadow than a lair but held her tongue. She was getting paid more than she'd ever been paid in her life, after all.

The dragon also insisted on making Saleema wear one of its teeth on a strap of leather it spat up.

"It'll mark you as mine," it said. "So no one thinks you're just a princess's servant or some smelly sheepherder," it said.

Saleema looked at the tooth before putting it on. She'd never worn a necklace in her life. None of the women in the village had. The men only gave necklaces to the bulls, and then only for the competitions. But she had seen them on the women that accompanied the traveling merchants.

"I don't give my teeth to just anyone, you know," the dragon said, eyeing her.

Saleema put the tooth around her neck but tucked it inside her shirt when the dragon wasn't looking.

That night she built a fire at the entrance to the cave with what sticks she could find. She stuffed sheep fur down her shirt and pants to add to the warmth. It was almost enough to make her stop shivering from the chill.

The dragon looked up at the stars overhead and let out a low croon. Saleema was afraid it was going to start talking about its past lairs again, so she asked it to tell her about the city to distract it.

"Oh, it's a lovely place," the dragon said. "Full of tall spires you can perch on at night so no one knows you're there. Sometimes you can even snatch soldiers off the battlements for a quick meal."

Saleema wondered if maybe the dragon had eaten her father. She wasn't sure how she felt about that. After all, her father wouldn't be mad at her for losing the flock if he'd been eaten.

"The smells are wonderful," the dragon went on. "A thousand cooking fires, a thousand different types of roasted meat, all mingling together. And the spices! So many even I can't recognize them all. And then of course, there are the people. There are the swordsmiths and the armorers, and the weapons trainers, of course. Did I mention the archers? And the soldiers on the walls? There are also the soldiers on the horses. And the soldiers on the ships, which aren't the same thing as the sailors on the ships, of course."

With each mention of a different profession, the dragon drew a line in the ground with one of its claws. Saleema took note that its tail also lashed a little more.

"Oh, and the royal guard," the dragon said. "The ones that protect the king and the princesses. Back when there were a king and princesses." It sighed again. It always seemed to be sighing.

Saleema remembered what she had wanted to ask the dragon earlier in the day. "If you have to rescue a princess and slay a dragon to become king," she said, "then how did the king become the king?"

The dragon didn't say anything for a moment. Then it closed its eyes. "Once, a knight did manage to slay a dragon," it muttered. "That's how the whole custom began. That knight went on to become the king."

"How did he manage that?" Saleema asked.

The dragon shifted about and dragged a talon through the lines it had drawn. "You may have noticed we are heavy sleepers. On account of our nocturnal habits."

"You mean talking in your sleep?" Saleema asked.

"Yes," the dragon said, looking away from her. "We talk in our sleep. The knight used the sound to cover its approach. It slew the dragon as it was remembering its travels in the cities of the cloud giants. A lance through the eye." It shook its head. "A nightmare."

"How do you know what happened?" Saleema asked. "How do you know what it was dreaming?"

"We remember," the dragon said, looking around the meadow like it saw another knight there now. "It is in our lineage."

"That must be a terrible thing," Saleema said, and she meant the words.

The dragon laid its head on the ground and stared down at the dark village and the dark roads beyond it.

"It is why we eat the knights," the dragon said. "It's like the saying goes, that which you consume cannot consume you."

Saleema had never heard that particular saying before. She decided it was time to change the subject again.

"What did the princesses look like?" she asked, closing her eyes. She tried to imagine a princess, but the dragon's words didn't help.

"Well, they were soft and pink, without too much meat on their bones," the dragon said. "Not at all like the queen. But they did wear nice spices. Maybe that would have made them tasty."

"Tell me about the queen instead," Saleema said.

"She was a very strong woman," the dragon said. "She was the one who made the kingdom great. She ran it like a dragon. But then she died in childbirth, and the king had to look after running the kingdom. That's when the wars started, and the wars brought the plagues."

"How did the queen run the kingdom?" Saleema asked. She wondered how a real queen worked, and if she'd been close in her imagination.

"She created taxes, but only on the merchant classes," the dragon said. "She used the money to help the farmers so there were more goods for sales. She had canals dug from the rivers to the farmers' fields, and started a ferry service for the shipment of produce..."

Saleema curled up by the fire and drifted off to sleep with a smile.

The second knight showed up the next morning, riding a white horse that was dirtier than the first knight's. The dragon pointed him out to Saleema, who lay dozing against the creature's great, warm side. She sat up and looked around with a start. She didn't remember coming out of the cave to the dragon. She also noticed the dragon's tooth was dangling on the outside of her shirt again.

"This one looks promising," the dragon muttered. It lifted a claw halfway, like it was thinking about waving. "Go down and find out his name and lineage," it said.

So Saleema went down the mountainside to the knight, who stopped a good distance away from the dragon and scowled at it. The horse snorted at Saleema, in a fashion that Saleema thought dismissive.

"Hello," Saleema said. "You should probably turn around and ride away now." She liked getting paid by the dragon, but she didn't really want to see it eat anyone else.

The knight eyed her and her tooth necklace, then looked back up the mountain. The dragon was moving the first knight's bones around on its pile, like it was making some finishing touches in preparation for the new knight's arrival.

"I appreciate your concern, princess," the knight said, "but I cannot leave you in such distress." He bowed on his horse with as much difficulty as the first knight.

"I'm fine," Saleema said. She didn't bother trying to correct him about the princess bit. She knew better now. "Don't worry about me."

He smiled at her. "How could I be any less brave than you, a simple princess?" he said. "I will slay the beast and then we will be wed."

Saleema stepped back from him. "Rein in your passion," she said. "We've only just met."

His smile turned into a grin. "You're feisty. I like that."

Saleema frowned at him. "It killed another knight and ate him just yesterday," she said, pointing at the dragon. "Impaled him on its tail like a hog on a stick."

The knight nodded. "Avoid the tail. Got it." He took several deep breaths and then slammed his visor shut. The horse shook its head at Saleema and pawed the ground.

Saleema shrugged. "Could I have your name at least?" she asked.

"Sir Farseer," the knight said, his voice echoing inside his helmet. "Of the Bookmonger clan. Riding the fierce steed Cyclops."

Saleema looked closer and saw one of the horse's eyes was clouded over with blindness. Then Sir Farseer spurred Cyclops forward and they charged the dragon, which let out a bellow of delight and flapped its wings excitedly. Saleema watched for the dragon's twitching tail to strike out and impale this new knight, so she was surprised when the dragon threw itself at the knight like a snake instead, knocking the lance aside and coiling around horse and rider. She looked away as the sounds of cracking metal and bone began.

"What did this one say his name was?" the dragon called to her.

"Sir Farseer of the Bookmonger clan," Saleema said, turning her gaze on the bull in field below rather than watch this scene. The bull had uprooted the post and was now dragging it behind itself as it grazed.

"A Bookmonger?" the dragon said. "Are those new?"

"Gggggggggggghhhhhh," Sir Farseer said.

It was difficult to extract Sir Farseer and his horse from their crushed armor after the dragon had finally squeezed the life out of them. Saleema had to use the knight's sword, the only intact thing remaining, to pry open parts of the armor.

"How much longer is this going to take?" the dragon asked, looking over Saleema's shoulder as she worked. "I like to eat my meals hot."

"How about you don't crush them next time then," Saleema said, finally managing to pop the breastplate off Sir Farseer. The dragon couldn't wait any longer and pushed Saleema aside with its great head to rip a chunk out of Sir Farseer's chest. It chewed slowly and thoughtfully, rolling the meat over in its mouth as Saleema hurriedly pried off the rest of the armor. She was worried the dragon would grow impatient and try a piece from her chest next.

"I don't much care for Bookmonger," the dragon sighed. "It's even younger than the Fishmonger."

"Why don't you try cooking them?" Saleema said.

"How would I do that?" the dragon asked.

"Roast them with your dragon breath," Saleema said.

"That's just a myth," the dragon said, snorting. The air turned foul and Saleema tried not to gag. "We can't actually breathe fire. Honestly, I don't know how these rumors get started." It wolfed down one of Sir Farseer's legs, then eyed Saleema. "Perhaps you could start another fire though," it said.

But Saleema shook her head and walked away for some fresh air. There were some things she wouldn't do, not even for gold.

She added the scraps of armor to the pile of bones, but the sword she placed in the cave. She had a plan for it.

That night, Saleema huddled against the dragon for warmth again. She hated herself a little for doing it, but the dragon was better than any fire she could make up here. If only the dragon would stop talking.

This night the dragon told her about other knights it had slain in the past.

"Now Hammerfist of the Trollkin Clan, there was a knight," the dragon said. "He hit harder with his fist than he did his mace. So strong. It took me days to eat him. But sometimes elegance is better than toughness. Take Hawkeye of the Free Archer Clan, for instance. He moved like water over stones, and he was very light, but with a sweet aftertaste. I think it came from all his traveling."

"They were all on quests to free princesses from you?" Saleema asked.

"A knight isn't a knight without a princess quest," the dragon said.

Saleema closed her eyes and started to drift off. "What happened to the other princesses you caught?" she asked.

"It's hard to keep track of them in the heat of battle," the dragon admitted. "Sometimes they get crushed when I roll around or get sent flying off a cliff by a stray wing. It's terribly embarrassing when that happens."

Saleema slept restlessly that evening, waking every few hours to make sure the dragon wasn't about to roll over on her.

The third knight arrived late the next afternoon, an hour or so after the sun had passed directly overhead. This one had a red sash tied to his lance, and the dragon crooned at the sight of it. "A pennant," it said. "Just what my lair needs."

"I'll go talk to him," Saleema sighed, and went down the mountain to greet the knight before he got too close.

"I don't suppose I could convince you to turn around now before you get eaten," she said to the knight.

"None of the Warehouser Clan have ever fled a dragon before, my lady," the knight said to her, "And Sir Tumble won't be the first."

Saleema suspected none of the Warehouser Clan had so much as seen a dragon before, but she kept that to himself. Instead, she decided to offer what advice she could.

"Watch for the tail," she said. "It uses it like a lance. And don't get close enough to let it constrict you. You won't be able to get out of that one."

"What about its fire breath?" Sir Tumble asked.

"That's a myth," Saleema said. "Who knows how these stories get started?"

"Are you coming or not?" the dragon called. "The day is wasting and it takes the princess ages to extract your kind from its shells."

Sir Tumble turned white. "It knows how to talk?" he said.

Saleema nodded. "Oh yes," she said. "But it doesn't know how to be silent."

"And it forces you to do its grisly work," Sir Tumble said, shaking his head. "What a vile beast."

"Actually, it isn't that bad," Saleema said. "Not unless you're a knight, I guess."

"Thank you for bringing the pennant," the dragon added. "That was very thoughtful."

The horse turned its head to look at Sir Tumble, who looked back at it.

"Look, you can still leave," Saleema said. "I'll tell it you're going back for more knights. It'll probably let you do that."

"Nonsense," Sir Tumble said, although his voice broke on the word. "I am a knight of the Shining Realm. I will rescue you and become king. And you will bear me many children."

Saleema shrugged and stepped aside as Sir Tumble spurred his horse forward — slower than the others, though, she noted.

The dragon couldn't wait. It charged down the hill at them, and the horse reared up at the sight of it, throwing Sir Tumble from its back. He fell to the ground with a mighty clang, and some swearing, and the horse galloped the way it had come.

Sir Tumble held up a hand as the dragon bore down on it. "One moment," he said. "Just let me fetch my steed again and — " The rest of his words were lost as the dragon lunged forward and bit off his head.

Saleema sighed and watched the horse ride off down the mountainside, back toward the road. The bull pawed at the ground and shook its head at the horse as it passed, then it went back to dragging the post around the empty field.

"There you go," the dragon said around Sir Tumble's head. "Now you can deshell — who did he say he was?"

"Sir Tumble of the Warehouser Clan," Saleema said, bending down and beginning the work of taking off the knight's armor.

The dragon spat out the helmet and chewed Sir Tumble's head thoughtfully. "Hmm, I think he may have been a bastard," he said. "I'm sure I can taste a little Regent in him. Or maybe Prophet."

Saleema dragged the armor back up the hill while the dragon ate Sir Tumble's deshelled body and debated the taste of it with itself. Instead of adding the armor to the bone piles, though, Saleema put it in the cave with the sword. She figured the dragon wouldn't notice because it was so preoccupied with its meal. She had a plan for the armor as well. Now she just needed one more thing.

The dragon continued to talk about past knights long after it had consumed the present one and Saleema had curled up against it again for warmth from the night's chill. "He could have been descended from the Noblelance Clan," it said. "He has that lingering taste. Not as strong as a Privateer, mind you — they're much saltier. Although that's fine if you wash them down with the blood of virgins." It reached out with a claw to stroke Sir Tumble's pennant, which it had tied to a leg bone sticking out of a pile.

"Why are none of those other knights seeking you out?" Saleema asked. "Why is it all Warehousers and Bookmongers instead of Hammerfists and Deathseekers?" She had to admit that she felt a little insulted about the quality of knights she was attracting.

The dragon was silent for a moment. Then, in a low grumble, it said, "I think I've eaten all the good knights. That's why we're seeing this sorry lot."

"You ate them all?" Saleema said.

"Well, some got killed in the wars," the dragon muttered.

"How many knights have you eaten?" Saleema demanded to know.

"You human females just need to have larger broods," the dragon said, ignoring her question. "It takes no time at all to work through your stock."

"Or maybe you could stop eating everything that moves," Saleema said.

"You think I like eating Bookmongers?" the dragon protested. "But it's all that's left! What choice do I have? It's a sad state of affairs for everyone, especially me."

Saleema shook her head and opened her bag to count her gold again. She had a hefty sum now, so much the bag was hard to move around. If she went back to the village with it, she'd be rich. Richer than even the blacksmith, probably. But she had other things than the village on her mind now.

"Tell me more about the city," she told the dragon. "The queen's city."

"Well, they have nicer lairs there than anywhere else," the dragon said. "Most of them are stone or mud and brick. And they have the most modern sewage system that she arranged, made of these clever pipes connected to the ditches. It all goes to this field outside the city, where…"

Saleema nodded as the dragon spoke. She could see it in her mind. Everything the dragon told her was the sort of thing she'd imagined when she was daydreaming up here instead of herding sheep.

When the next knight came the following afternoon, Saleema offered to hold his horse for him while he fought the dragon. The knight's armor looked as if each piece had come from a different armorer. The horse was so muddy she couldn't tell its original color.

"You'll never beat it on horseback," she told the knight, who declared himself to be Sir Boy of the Streetsweeper Clan. "But it has a weak spot on its belly you can reach by foot." She had no idea if that was true or not, but she felt she had to give the knight some small hope.

Sir Boy nodded and dismounted. "I will give you a share of the dragon's wealth as a reward when I am done slaying it," he told Saleema. "So you can buy yourself frilly things for when we are wed."

"No need," Saleema said and tied the horse to a tree as Sir Boy climbed the slope to his fate. It took Sir Boy several attempts to free his sword from its scabbard, for all the good that it did him.

After, when Saleema had taken off Sir Boy's battered armor and added it to the piles, the dragon looked down at the horse, which was trying to hide behind the tree.

"Excellent job stopping that one from running away," it said. "Bring it up here and we'll have a little dessert."

"I'm afraid not," Saleema told the dragon. "I'm keeping this one."

The dragon looked at her. "What are you talking about?" it asked.

"You can't eat the horse," Saleema said. "I'm claiming it."

The dragon snorted. "A princess can't claim anything."

"A princess can claim a kingdom," she said. "Especially if there are no other royals left."

The dragon paused. "You? You're not *really* a princess," it said. "Or did you forget?"

"Tell that to the knights," Saleema said. "They certainly think I'm a princess."

"What will you do then?" the dragon asked. "Wed one of this sorry lot?" It waved a wing at a pile of bones.

"Actually, I think I'm going to skip the knight part of things," Saleema said, "and go straight to being queen. It sounds to me like the city needs another queen more than it needs another king."

The dragon stretched out its neck until its head bumped against her. It sniffed her. "You still smell like sheep," it said. "How are you going to convince the people in the city to let you become their queen?"

Saleema brushed past the dragon and went into the cave. She put on the armor. By now she'd had enough practice taking it off the dead knights that she had a pretty good understanding of how it all worked, and it didn't take her long. She picked up the sword she'd taken from the second knight and went back outside.

"What if I'm a dragon slayer as well?" she said to the dragon. "I'm sure the people in the city will accept a dragon-slaying queen."

The dragon eyed her and lashed its tail back and forth.

"Are you going to challenge me then?" it said.

"After watching what you did to the other knights?" Saleema said. "Not a chance."

She slipped off her dragon fang necklace and tied it around her head instead, so the fang hung against her forehead. "I'll just tell them I slew you and show them my crown," she said.

The dragon snorted and shook its head. "They'll never believe you," it said.

"They will if they come here and find the bones of a dragon," Saleema said. "Or a collection of bones that at least look as if a dragon were slain here."

The dragon looked at its bone piles for a moment and then back at her. It tapped a talon against the ground. "I see," it said. "Very clever."

"I will reward you for your cooperation in this matter, of course," Saleema said.

The dragon nodded. "That was my next question. What's in this for me?"

"A most wonderful treasure that you can only dream of," Saleema said. "Once I am queen, I'll build up the knight bloodlines again. I'll identify the best men — the manliest men — and have them trained as knights. I'll make sure they have proper weapons and noble steeds. I will make them true knights worthy of my kingdom. The finest lineage imaginable. I will bestow upon them grand new names. Deathkillers and Ironhearts and Soulbreakers. Then, when there are enough of them, you can make a return appearance. And you will all have an enemy worth fighting."

The dragon was still and silent for a moment. Then it chuckled. "And so you'll be rid of any man who might want to seize the throne and become king," it said. "A fine way to get rid of the competition."

Saleema smiled and picked up her saddlebags of gold. "Come visit me some night at the castle," she said. "We'll work out the details."

"You think like a dragon," the dragon told her.

"Thank you," Saleema said. She thought it was a compliment anyway. She started down to the horse.

"Before you leave, you may want to pay a visit to the village," she called over her shoulder. "There are rumors the blacksmith once used to be a knight."

The dragon turned its gaze to the huts. "Of what clan?" it murmured.

"There's only one way to find out," Saleema said.

And then Queen Saleema untied the horse and rode down the mountain to her waiting kingdom.

PETER DARBYSHIRE *is the author of the Cross series of supernatural thrillers, about an undying angel hunter and the faerie, gorgons, dragons, ghosts, demons and other fantastic creatures that love/hate him (written under the name Peter Roman). He lives near Vancouver, B.C., where angels are scarce.*

Burying the Ploughshare

by Bethany Powell

Failure — wide open failure,
scent of hot dust and sunrays
on the green of weeds baking
where they're harvested all together,
walling this plot.

The dark king's warfare has salted the ground.
This is expected.
Nothing is coming up but the most perverse of weeds,
grasses hard enough to draw blood.
The cracked soil is a whisper of release:

"Go. Take that sword
you were supposed to bury with your father
but couldn't bear to,
not in this unhallowed and fruitless plain,
not with his old twisted bones.
Become the soldier he never was.
Become the rightful heir to it."

We've gone broke here,
telling ourselves we had a heritage to save,
ancestors to make proud
while the war-machine ground up bone of earth
and the crops along with it,
us running behind with more seed, more desperate hope.

I'm done with this.
The hair-tearing sting of it,
of nursing half-dead animals
that run off and join wild packs,
of digging up great heads of leaves
to find no roots beneath.

I'm selling the last cow standing,
one final milking in a skin
for the first day's walk.
My arms are strong
with tearing up masses of plants,
hoeing up rock-pregnant earth.
People won't laugh at me for long.

In two bites the last small fruit of my labor —
a hard, bitter radish — gone,
except for its taint in my mouth.
I'll stamp back over these sweat-sown fields.
There's nothing to crush,
only years of work to haunt each step.
No more crops will grow, anyway,
until I've changed the world.

BETHANY POWELL *read* The Silmarillion *in Japanese public school,* Harry Potter *on a night bus, and is now up to no good between piles of books in rural Oklahoma. She gardens there with mixed success but great relish. Her weird speculative poetry has been published in many magazines and is currently forthcoming in the* Sunvault *anthology,* Asimov's, *and* Liminality. *You can find more of her work at bethanypowell.com.*

CROWN OF SORROWS
BY SEAN PATRICK KELLEY

The mistress Paracevia is the only one who knows my real name at the brothel where they find me. Those who've come for me think they're clever — they wait deep into the night when they think I'll be sotted with drink and worn from the ministrations of the mistress's women.

They're mistaken, for I care not for the touch of slaves. I've come only to learn of the caravan schedules from the girls who service the masters of the camels.

I awake alone, sober and naked upon the horsehair mattress to voices beyond the door. I continue to snore as I pick up my sword. They argue what's the best way to take me. I help them make up their minds by shoving my long sword through the door's shuttering. A sense of pressure and a grunt are my reward.

There is a scream as the victim is pulled from my sword and the door bursts inward with guards dressed in black. I drop the first, slamming my dagger into his face until I feel the pommel break his jaw. I leave it and grab the cudgel from his flailing hand as I dodge a swing at my head.

Behind these first few I can hear men scrambling to get in, "Come forward you dogs," I shout, distracting another as I hit him hard enough with the cudgel to see brains scatter across the wall, "your two friends will be lonely in hell without you!"

Blows rain down on my back and shoulder as I twist and try to free my sword from the broken door while I kick another attacker to the ground and stomp his face.

The sword will not pull free so I retreat to the back of the room away from the swinging arms. My hands shake with pain from the beating I've taken.

"Who is next to die?" I ask the room as my vision narrows and grows dark. They pause to find their courage and charge. Blows fall all about me as I kick and punch. I spit a finger from my mouth as the world grows black and distant.

Somewhere far away I can hear a man screaming and drums beating.

* * *

In the highest room in the tower it stinks of herbs and shadows; it stinks of the ruler, the summoner-king Theisius. He, who has stolen lives beyond number to extend his meager flame, now seeks another taker-of-lives to further extend his frail reach. To him I'm brought, an iron collar around my neck with legs and hands bound in chains. I'm not surprised. I'm a mercenary and I've been caught.

"Your name is Ordwin. Yes?" asks the corpselike king, from under layers of silken robes. I'm surprised he knows my name, but I say nothing.

"Don't be thus, mercenary. I know of you. Do you know why I've spared you the gallows?" Theisius asks, lips greasy with hunger over long, grey teeth.

"To gloat," I say through swollen lips, not wishing to give this decrepit old spider his pleasure.

The troupe of followers around me laughs, and I imagine each face in the darkness split with an axe or sword. They who must balance their desire to place a dagger into their lord's back against the fear of one of their pack-mates plunging one into their own.

The old king coughs out humors, saying, "No, no mercenary. I've saved you from an uncomfortable death for a purpose: games. Perhaps you have heard of my love of games? Wagers?"

"Yes, I've heard of your arena. But I won't fight — better you cut off my thumbs and balls now and gut me."

"Bless us, this fellow has some spirit. You've chosen well, Kadir," Theisius says, nodding to his captain of the guard. "No, Ordwin of Silrafe. I need you not for gladiatorial games. You would be a terrible waste there, though entertaining. Megerae, show him."

A bald man with a face disfigured with pox scars limps forward and unwraps a parchment to reveal a human hand. It's small and delicate, with nails that have never been broken and skin that has never been callused from using a tool.

"The hand of one of my many daughters, Lothil, if memory serves. Kidnapped by your lord — "

"I've no lord you dried-up old pile of goat vomit."

Theisius gestures and a guard kicks me to the floor, filling my vision with motes of light.

"Watch your mouth, sell-sword, or I'll have Kadir shave your head and hang you by that precious Silrafian braid of yours. As I was saying, you've been in the employ of Archese — your lord — for whom you've raided my caravans. One of the things you have taken is a crown. The crown is a thing of power. Part of the game Archese and I play. I want it back."

"So take it back," I say, wondering what game this strange old creature is playing with me. "You've got soldiers, and creatures from beyond who serve you."

"Rules, mercenary. Rules to be followed. Games must have rules. A challenge must be overcome, and only by one of Archese's own followers."

"You want my help?"

"Yes, yes. I was beginning to think my men had beaten you senseless. Yes, mercenary. We must play a game together. Me a king, you a pawn."

"And if I say no?"

The captain of the guard laughs behind me. "Then I throw you off this tower tonight and into the river Reeth below. There's a chance you survive the fall, but the crocodiles prefer meat with a little fight left in it."

I frown and shift in my chains. I'm sure I could grab the king and make it out the window before the guards stop me. To see the horror in his eyes on the way down is tempting, but then again, perhaps I could survive this game and come out free to see Theisius' kingdom in flames. "Tell me more about this game."

The old king's face splits into a horrible smile. "You're young, Ordwin. Someone your age cannot understand the boredom of so long a life as mine. This game with Archese has been ongoing since he was a boy, when I sent him an envoy offering him the control of the Amarani littoral if he could beat me in game."

The old king pauses and gestures to a servant who brings a cup and sips it before passing it into the king's thin hands. Theisius watches the servant for a moment before drinking himself.

"Archese and I are playing a game for control over seven items of power. Each year at the autumnal equinox whoever holds the items gets a point for each. If ever one has twice as many points as the other, they win."

"Did you know King Archese is dying of the wasting disease?" I ask. "He will be lucky to live out the year."

Theisius chuckles in pleasure. "I know. I know. I sent the courtesan who gave it to him. I've arranged for Archese to have enough points this year to claim victory; he thinks he can spend his last breath gloating, then pass off the Amarani to his fat son Askelion. He also thinks the crown is safe with the beast people, who are his allies. Can you imagine the look on his face as he lies dying and finds out he has lost after a lifetime of trying to best me? That will be something. I've a spy in his court to observe the moment just so I can have a painting done to commemorate it for my trophy room."

"You seem sure of yourself. You're also mad."

"Yes, perhaps, but I'm also a king and you're a man with few choices."

"What would you have me do?"

"The crown is with my daughter. I ransomed her to Archese for the right to challenge for control of the crown. She's held by a monster, the king of the beast people, in a labyrinth to the west. There are challenges three, mercenary..."

* * *

I follow the cobbled streets of Sethiphera down the Reeth escarpment to the docks on the river of the same name, where a dozen nations mix into one shifting mass of trade. Everything is for sale; I'm offered wine, poison, women, girls, boys, weapons — anything for the right price. What I get is an escort by Kadir himself with a dozen of the Dragon guard in their blackened armor and horned helms.

Waiting for us at a dock conspicuously empty of porters, sailors, and traders is a galley, its oars shipped but ready to pull away and up current as fast as its taskmaster can wring the effort from the shoulders of his slaves.

"Where's this challenge to take place and when are you going to remove these chains and return my things, Kadir?"

"Patience mercenary. I'll remove the chains after we're on board the galley. Until then I can say nothing of our destination."

"Our destination?"

"Yes. My guard and I are to accompany you, to guarantee you keep your bargain."

"I keep my word, Sethipherian."

"As do I, and mine is to my king, who has been known to peel the flesh from those who fail him. Now quiet until we are aboard."

* * *

The warm cinnamon and grass smell of the plains keeps the reek of the galley slaves away from the forecastle where Kadir and I stand, our faces into the wind. The slow and steady heartbeat of the oars give the ship a feeling of life; through my bare feet on the deck I can feel the beat as the galley crawls through the muddy river water.

"We're on board, now remove my bonds," I tell Kadir.

"Yes, but first you must drink this." He hands me a clear vial filled with light blue liquid.

"What is it?"

"Courage of the boar, power of the tiger, vision of the cat and ears of the fox."

"What else?"

"A magical compulsion to do as you've promised."

"Why should I drink it? I could jump over the side and take my chance with the crocodiles."

"Because if the sun sets on the shackle about your neck it will begin to shrink until it cuts off your head."

"Horse shit — you play me for a fool."

"I do not. You know it's well within my king's power and you would do well not to question the depths of his cruelty. Even now I can see it start to grow more taut around your neck. Can you not feel it, mercenary?"

Curse his eyes to the six hells, but I could feel the tightness of the collar. I undo the wax sealed stopper and toss back the cool liquid in a swallow. It tastes of windblown snow, the sweat of a woman's thighs and the burn of twice-spelled brandy from the steppes.

"Damn you and damn your sorcerous king, Kadir. I've drunk the potion, now remove the collar and these chains!"

"As you wish. You've a fortnight to finish this task or the potion will give you the features of the beasts whose abilities you've stolen."

"How long will it take us to get there?"

"Not more than half a fortnight."

"Bastard. How will I make it back in time to avoid turning into a beast? You've doomed me."

Kadir laughs. "Your doom follows you like whores follow sailors, Ordwin. However, if you are successful there's a cure in a chest on this ship, which I'll have waiting on your return."

"What's to stop me," I ask, but Kadir cuts me off.

"From killing everyone and taking it now? You're too predictable by half. The chest the potion is stored in will only open in the presence of the crown. Bring back the crown and the potion is yours."

"What of Lothil, Theisius' daughter?"

"What of her?"

"Does he want her back too?"

"No. What good is a one-handed princess?"

* * *

The galley snakes upriver, leaving in its wake a trail of dying and dead slaves tossed over the side when they're unable to row any longer. Up the Reeth, we cling to the spine of Sethis, a rib of earth thrown up from the plains in ages past by one of the great wars. My grandfather's words speak to me of the ancient battles and our people's shame in failing the gods: "Thrice cursed are the men of the Silrafe," I think as I watch them throw another meekly protesting galley slave from the deck to a chorus of reptilian glee below.

The potion has wound its way into me like a barb and true to the king's promise my body has changed, as has my mind. I pace the deck filled with boundless energy, seeking only to begin my quest. I'm hungry for it now, like a man hungering for a woman's smell on his hands. I ache to be off this filthy slave-barge and on my way. Behind me Kadir lumbers up the deck like a pregnant cow.

"What do you want?" I ask him, without turning. In my mind's eye I can see him, hear him, and feel his presence like a blowfly on my skin.

"We will crest the great redoubt tonight. Are you familiar with the pass of the North?"

"Of course. I've ridden through it twice."

"There is a narrow canyon off the pass."

"There are many narrow canyons off the pass. Hundreds. It's also called the pass of the noose or the pass of thieves. What of it?"

"Patience mercenary. In one of those canyons is a cave. This cave is the entrance to the lair of the monster you must slay to capture the crown and save yourself from existence as a freak."

"How will I know the way?"

"That is easy enough — my men and I shall show you. But even alone you would find it. For someone of our — special senses, it has a certain smell you can't miss," Kadir says as he removes a small vial from his belt. Upon opening it a stench hits my nostrils like a mace.

"Gods of mountain fire and shit, stopper that back up and throw yourself in the river with it."

Kadir laughs softly. "Yes, it's quite strong isn't it?"

I look at him in the darkness and see his eyes have the same yellow glow as those of a predator, the same as mine.

"So you too share the senses of the beasts?" I ask.

"Yes, though perhaps not as strongly as you. The greater the gift, the greater the consequences. I pity what you'll become if you fail."

"Pity me not, Kadir. I plan to live to the end of this and see your king hung like a marionette by his own bowels." I growl.

"Easy words to say, but no one has succeeded at that task in three hundred years. Get some rest, Ordwin; you'll need your hate later."

* * *

Late spring storms swell the Reeth like the belly of a new wife. The waters turn to an angry dark froth and suck at the galley. I stand on the foredeck keeping my vigil watching the purple mountains climb the horizon to the west. I count the days.

In a carmine dusk on the ninth day out of Sethiphera, we raise the river port of Feric, sitting at the cross of the old imperial road and the bridge over the Reeth. The rains have caught them unprepared so their docks and low lying areas are a morass of flooded buildings, barges and rafts trying to rescue what they can of their goods. The captain chooses to put in at a ford a few miles upriver where he knows the currents and bank better, and away from prying eyes.

We are forced to remove our cargo from the galley standing in raging, hip-deep water in near dark. Kadir, six of the dragon guard, our horses, supplies and myself all make it onto land, safe but exhausted. We pack our gear onto the horses and strap on the unmarked armor we've been provided.

The imperial road runs past the ford which is a half day ride south-east of lake Fer, for which Feric takes its name. From here we're more than a day's ride from the cave, but we're wet and tired, so we make camp for the night in a copse of soldier's-thorn, perhaps a league up the road from the ford. We take time only to rub down the horses before dropping into fitful sleep.

The morning of the tenth day brings fog and the incessant chirp of frogs in the near dawn pallor. We waken sodden and eat salty cured meat with watered down wine before we saddle the horses and ride for the pass of thieves. I'm anxious to be there, for my imagination has begun to feed a paranoid awareness of my body. I feel my hair and wonder if it's getting coarser, or run my tongue over my canines; are they longer? Sharper?

I'm lost in this reverie like a foolish boy when the arrows begin to fall amongst us. The sharp crack of them striking the armor of one of the guards brings me to my senses and I goad my chestnut gelding forward in the direction I think best to meet our assailants. Through the thick fog I can hear others shouting out battle cries and following me while the gray-white air fills with projectiles.

I'm close enough to hear the whine of a breaking bowstring as I crest a small rise and see a group of four archers. I charge them, thrashing the side of my gelding to drive him screaming into the group of them so that I can dive off with a short axe in hand.

My leap carries me from the saddle and into a roll before a soldier trying to draw his blade. I use my momentum to spring forward and split him from shoulder to hip in a single swing. The shock on his face almost matches my own. I've no time to stare at the spectacle as I dodge the thrust of a short sword. One of the dragon guard stabs my assailant in the side while I take off his arm at the shoulder. Beside us the first archer attempts to maintain balance while his body hangs awkwardly to one side revealing layers of red meat, pink bone and yellow-white fat as blood sprays into the misty air. It smells sweet.

I hear a third coming before I see him and I lead into a turn with my axe in time to meet his incoming sword. A glancing blow grazes my shoulder and ear, but neither are more than annoyances. I square up to face him as he swings wildly, waiting my chance, but before I can act a sword bursts from his chest and he tries to howl through a mouthful of blood and bile. The blade slips out of his chest and he sinks onto the ground revealing a smiling Kadir.

"Where is the fourth?" I ask.

"He ran, but my men will chase him down. You should thank me, Ordwin. That was a poisoned blade — had he got a good poke at you, you might be frothing out your last words alongside him right now. Pity to see you die before your time."

Before I answer him I pull out my wineskin and wash the wounds on my ear and shoulder. "He caught me by surprise, though it would seem the poison is of poor quality. Either way I'd have dealt with him. But if you wish to hear the words, then you've earned my thanks."

One of the dragon guards hands something to Kadir and speaks into his ear.

Kadir holds out a patch. "Does this look familiar?"

The patch is from the mercenary company serving King Archese, of which I was a member. "My own gods damned company," I say and bark a laugh, "so was this one of the challenges?"

Kadir shakes his head. "No, those are formal and will be in the cave. I know that much about these things. This was more of an opportunistic attempt to put the odds in that dog Archese's favor."

"I thought there were rules."

"Wizards follow rules for shit, Ordwin. If you haven't figured that out by now, you can thank me for that bit of wisdom too."

"How well do they keep their word?" I ask.

"Better, but not much. That's the best I can offer you."

"So now what?"

"Now we ride hard and fast to get to the cave. I know you think I'm a bastard, and I am, but you'll not say I robbed you of a fair chance to win or lose."

Kadir smears black salve on my shoulder and ear which burn like demon piss while his guards get the horses together. Of the four that left with us, only two return with our mounts.

"Where are the other two?"

"Dead. We go forward, we four, now mount up," Kadir says pulling himself onto his saddle and urging his roan down the road at a reckless pace.

* * *

It's sunset of the eleventh day when Kadir and I reach the reeking entrance to the cave. What should have been a day's journey has stretched to two as we were ambushed three times more along the way. Behind us we left the guards and all the horses but Kadir's roan for dead. That and a trail of mercenary corpses. Once we find the path up the ravine it makes its way to an actual road not more than a league up the path. The twists and turns are carved into the cliff face, its smooth wall covered in hieroglyphics used by the lost empire.

"I can read some of this you know," I tell Kadir, who leans into his horse due to a deep cut in his thigh.

"Yeah? What does it say?"

"That this road leads to an imperial tomb; other glyphs describe the curses that will be put upon us if we desecrate the tomb."

"Do you believe in being cursed by the gods of the old empire?" Kadir asks.

"I do, but I'm a Silrafian. I'm thrice cursed already. What else can they do?"

"Best not to tempt the fates to show you," Kadir says.

An hour later, with the canyon already in evening shadows, Kadir points to the end of the path. "Look, there's the entrance ahead of us. We've made it."

"How will I make it back in time? Even if I take only a day it's unlikely I'll make it back to the ship in time with the crown."

"Perhaps the change will come slow like the abilities and take days? I cannot say. I've never seen it happen. If you make it back to the ship, beast or not you go back to Theisius — he can see you're made whole."

"I'll believe it when I see it, captain of the guard."

"So go get the crown and hurry back. I'll wait four days for you and no more. Then I shall leave you for the crows. Go."

"The devil take you, Kadir," I say with a nod and walk into the fetid tomb. The entrance is a simple arch carved into stone a dozen hands high. Once inside a vast gallery lined with pillars stretches into the darkness as far as my catlike eyes can see.

I'm soon so far down the gallery that the only light comes from the glow of ever-light rushes in sconces placed every fifth pillar. I pull one of the dusty bundles of reeds loose and swing it against the pillar, knocking loose ages of dust and cobwebs until the weak spell on it brightens to several candles worth of bluish light. It's enough to see, but offers no warmth or cheer.

The gallery continues unchanging and with a slight grade down into the living rock. I soon lose all sense of time and I begin to think this passage is somehow a magical challenge itself, until it comes to a wall with a door and before it an altar with a single chalice. Beside the chalice are two pitchers and a piece of parchment.

I silently thank my uncle's insistence that I learn how to read Old Imperial as a boy. I use my dagger to turn the parchment so that I can read it.

Luck:
What is a hero but one who has been luckier than the rest? So by luck or guile you must choose to go forward. Before you are two pitchers: one water, and one poison. You must choose and live, or choose and die.

"Damn, I hate wizard games."

I wish for a moment Kadir had come with me — it would've been amusing to make him drink first. I lean forward and look into the pitchers, both beaten copper. The contents are clear. I break a reed off the ever-light and stir the surface inside one of them; under its dim glow I can see a slight film. I sniff it, but it smells only of water, unlike everything else in this cave which smells of ancient death.

I examine the second pitcher and find it identical to the first, so I look into the copper chalice. I pick it up and look at my reflection in it. I don't like the distorted look of my face, so I put it down. I notice a sticky feeling on one thumb so I take my reed and draw it across the inside of the chalice and see the faintest trail left on its surface.

The bastards poisoned the damn chalice, I think, but also know there is only one way to know for sure. I take the pitcher on the right and turn it up, drinking it. It tastes like tepid water.

"Well," I ask aloud while waiting, but nothing happens so I step through the door into the passage beyond and hear the slap of bare feet on stone running ahead of me, and hyena-like laughter.

I consider making chase, but haste in an unknown environment is always a good way to end up in a pit full of spikes, so I grind my teeth and count the names of those who will pay for what has been done to me, one by one.

I can reach out and touch each wall, and there are no more ever-lights, only the one I carry with me. I walk for perhaps two hours, always forward and down, but I cannot say for sure because time has become obscured in these tombs. It must be nearing morning of my twelfth day out of Sethiphera when I decide I must rest. I lay my dagger and axe out next to me on the floor and wrap myself in a wool horse blanket before leaning against the wall and allowing myself to sleep.

I awake to the sound of rain and for a time I think I'm somewhere else, among my people still and my betrothed, the beautiful Vesgothe. I reach for her, but my hand only finds cold stone. I open my eyes to the dark passage. I can smell water.

Famished, I eat the rest of my provisions and leave behind everything I don't need for a fight wrapped in my blanket as a gift for the next fool who crosses a wizard. I resume my exploration into the depths and soon I step into ankle-deep ice-cold water. There is no way to go but forward, so I walk and the water rises with each step. Soon only my head is above the water and then I can go no further.

It's clear my path is forward, and I know I must choose soon for my body is on fire with pain from the freezing cold. I take a deep breath and plunge my head under water and open my eyes. The cold makes my eyes ache, but I can see down the passage in the dim, shimmering glow of my ever-light. Just ahead the passage opens into a chamber.

I raise my head up and take three deep breaths then push myself back under and swim forward into the room. It's circular, with a flat floor. In the center is a stone pillar. I swim up and find a curved roof and eventually reach air. Water pours in from above and I realize this chamber has begun filling recently. If I don't find a way to get past it soon there will only be failure.

I take several deep breaths and explore the room. There is no exit, only the pillar, so I examine it more closely. Words are written on it. I go back up once more into the shrinking air space to get a breath before I read it. My eyes fight me as I try to focus and I realize that I'm starting to go numb. I'm running out of time. I read what is written on the column.

Might:

What is a hero but one who is mightier than the rest? So by might alone you must move this pillar from your path to go forward. But be quick, for the cold robs you of your strength and wits, like old age. You must triumph and live or fail and die.

I surface once more, but now I can only get air if I face the ceiling. I gasp air until my chest feels like it will burst and I push off the roof with my feet and wrap my arms around the pillar. The water makes it hard to get a good grip and use leverage but I lock my body to it and lift with everything I have.

Pain erupts across my body as hot blood floods stiff, cold muscle and sinews stretch to the breaking point. I shift all of my strength into lifting the pillar and we are married in exertion.

Nothing.

Nothing, and my head is filled with the roar of the charge from the battle on the Ionien plain from when I was but a boy.

Nothing, and everything has become red and my all is screaming. The horses race down on our position, we hold the line with sharpened wooden stakes set in the earth and leather strips in our teeth so we do not crack them grimacing in fear.

Nothing, and my body is a thing of flame, burning upon burning. I'm a mote of effort; my young hands hold the stake as a black stallion plunges onto it throwing his rider, its blood bursting forth over me like a second birth.

Nothing, and I'm dying, my light fades and the plains are empty but for the screaming horse and myself. I will die.

Darkness, I'll die the victim of a wizard's grand game.

No. No!

My world becomes agony. I lift one last desperate time. It's unbearable, but the pillar rises. It rises and I can feel the sucking water below me escaping. I scream out my last breath and wrench the pillar free as the world goes black.

And the charge broke on the Ionien plain and we lived that day, and the water recedes and I lay on the floor of the chamber retching and coughing up water. My body shakes from the cold and I bellow like a wounded bear. I'll live this day.

I lay on the floor listening to the water rain down from the ceiling, wracked with cramps and my body burning from the cold, until I can get to my feet. I stand and everything is painful, but nothing seems permanent, so I stand in the room and look down the hole I've opened. Where the base of the pillar sat is a narrow spiral stair going down. For the second time I wish Kadir was with me now, but not because I crave human company. I wish for someone to share the view down into the wet, black depths, but I go forward alone.

I count five hundred steps, though I don't know why I'm counting when I stumble attempting to take a step and find an expanse of flat ground. In the flood my ever-light was lost so I'm near blind in the darkness. Only a slight glow in the walls shows the way. I feel about on my hands and knees to make sure it's not a landing, but indeed the end of the stairs. I bump into a wall with my hand and the room bursts into light.

I curse and cover my eyes, which sting in pain from the brightness. I get to my feet and look about, dazed by the pure white glow.

"Welcome, mercenary," says a voice.

"Who speaks?"

"I speak, but I've no name."

My eyes adjust and I can see a being wearing grey robes.

"Are you my next challenge?"

"No, mercenary. I'm only the arbiter of the challenge you seek. In this room is the final challenge before you reach the beast king. He has that which you seek, but first you must pass my test."

"What is your test?"

"Are you ready?"

"No, no. A moment," I say while I search myself for my weapons and then sit where I can see the stranger. When I feel somewhat rested I rise and stare at the figure in grey.

"Do you live here?"

"Are you ready?"

"Yes, I'm ready." I realize it won't answer my questions.

"Then know this, warrior. You've proven your luck and you're surely mighty, but a true hero must know sacrifice. To pass this room you must give of yourself into this golden dish before me, twelve-grain weight of your body. Not a grain more or a grain less will I take." From its robes it extends a gloved hand holding a golden dish.

"Will you answer my questions?" I ask.

"Not a grain more or a grain less will I take."

I stare long at the dish and sit once more on the steps in thought, then say aloud, "If I'm to survive to the next challenge how can I leave twelve grain of my body?"

"Not a grain more or a grain less will I take," it responds.

I sigh and run my hand over my face when I get an idea. The men of the Silrafe grow and braid their hair from the test of manhood until death. We never willingly cut it, for it's a source of our pride and a mark of our people. I consider the alternative and then begin to unplait my braid.

When my hair has been pulled from its braid I bunch it up and use my dagger cut off half an ell and pile it into the golden dish.

"Not a grain less will I take," it says, so I grab another handful and cut it free and lay it on the dish.

"Not a grain more will I take."

"Damn you," I curse and lift a small amount off the dish.

"A warrior who has learned sacrifice knows the measure of all things," it says and before I can step back bursts into flames, singeing what hair I have left.

The acrid smell of burnt hair fills the cavern and on its far side a rock wall rolls back to reveal a passage and the sound of laughter and cheering echo down it.

I pull my now shoulder length hair into a braid and tie it off with a leather thong while I listen to the tumult. I feel something sharp cut my wrist and when I pull back my hand I find my fingers have grown wicked talons.

"I'm running out of time," I speak aloud once more, but my voice feels foreign in my mouth and my tongue fits poorly around my enlarged canines.

"Damn."

I draw my weapons and walk into the den of the beast, standing upright like a man while I still can.

* * *

The court of the beast is a cavern stretching into darkness, carved into an amphitheater. It's lit with crystal and golden magical lanterns set upon stalagmites carved to look like fornicating men and animals.

As for the cavern's living inhabitants, the court is filled with every sort of combination of man and animal you could imagine. The grotesque, beautiful, crippled and graceful all dance and caper in the audience, talking and shouting. They cheer me on as I walk down the aisle, and they jeer and throw feces and pieces of food at which I try not to look too closely. Some thrust themselves lewdly at me in sexual poses, beckoning me to join them. All of the power, the glory, and the carnal lust of the feral kingdom are before me and I walk past it to my appointed time with its master.

At the center of the amphitheater is a central dais and upon it are two simple stone seats. Upon one is Lothil — this must be her, for I can see she is missing a hand — her head bowed. She is light haired and light skinned, but she is broad of shoulder and has the features of a lioness. Beside her is the beast; I cannot say what manner of thing he is or was, only that no animal of his kingdom was neglected in his making.

As I step onto the dais he rises from his seat on mismatched legs and stands upright, throwing his humped back up and raising his arms above his head, letting a golden cape fall to the floor behind him.

"Greetings warrior," he says through a many-toothed muzzle, his mismatched eyes meeting my own. "Have you come to test yourself against the beast?"

"I've come for the crown and nothing more. I've no contest with you, beast king. I only wish to avoid your fate. If you wish it I'll take the woman with me as well."

For the first time Lothil looks up. She has cat's eyes. She is beautiful — the most beautiful woman I've ever seen.

The court bursts into wild laughter and bleating.

"You'd take my new wife, oh generous warrior? You'd take my crown, my rightful crown given to me by king Archese? Shall you cut off my manhood and keep it for a trophy while you're at it? What would you leave me? My shame? My misshapen court? No, warrior. You can't have her, nor my crown. If you want them, you must come take them," he said with a grunting laugh.

I see the truth of it and waste no further words; I draw my axe and dagger and charge him screaming my own bestial cry.

He meets my axe with a club and catches my wrist with a hoof-like hand. He is fast, perhaps the fastest opponent I've ever seen.

His muzzle splits into a grin as we are locked together and he begins to twist my wrist holding the dagger. My shoulder grinds bone on sinew and lights into pain as I try to fight his awesome strength. It's a losing effort, his strength goes beyond even my own, so instead I kick him in his manhood twice in quick succession.

"Kill you!" he screams and shifts forward in pain, allowing me to break free from his hold. I shift back but his speed is better and swipes me with his steel-spiked club. A trail of cuts cross my chest and bleed freely down my torso.

"First blood to me," he calls, raising his club high.

I charge in and bury my dagger up to the hilt in his thigh before his elbow comes down like a fallen tree and knocks me to the ground.

I scramble to get up but a scaled hoof catches me in the face, tumbling me over onto my back. For a second I lay dazed while the court cheers madly and begins to chant for a kill. I roll to one side in time to dodge a swing from the club, which strikes the ground so hard I can feel it.

I get to my feet in time to block a second swing with my axe, but the blade sinks deep into the club and we are locked once more together.

We spin around each other, locked arm and arm on our weapons, kicking and punching at the other. My dagger leaves his left side a glistening lacework of ribbons and his fist forces me to spit out a dozen shattered teeth.

Finally his injured leg succumbs to one of my attempts to trip him and we go down to the ground, I on my back, and he over me. Blood and sweat run down his face onto mine as he breathes heavily and tries to force the spike of my axe into my face. My arms buckle under his weight and the spike touches my eye when a hot exhalation of breath and blood covers me. The beast rolls away clutching at his throat. I crawl to my feet to see blood spurting from the beast's neck. Over him stands Lothil, triumphant, a long dagger in her one, good hand.

I stagger to my knees. "Thank you." I offer, then pick up my axe and dispatch the gasping king of the beasts with three chops to the neck until his horned head rolls free.

I raise the head to the roaring cheer of the court and throw it into their midst. Lothil comes to my side.

"Am I a monster?" she asks me.

I stare into the slits of her pupils and see the start of whiskers growing from her cheeks. "I think you're fierce, and beautiful."

"But am I a monster?"

"Does it matter?"

"Yes."

"Can't your father cure you, like Kadir said he could cure me?"

"Cure? No, everyone who serves my father and takes the gifts of the beast will look like us sooner or later. There is no going back. Where do you think all of these creatures came from?" she asks, gesturing to the crowd. "We are all the discarded slaves of my father's sorcery."

My legs grow weak for a moment. "No going back."

"Never. So answer my question: am I a monster?"

I stare at my bestial hands and then her beautiful face. "I've killed the beast — what was his is mine, yes? His kingdom is my own?"

She nods.

I shout to a pig-faced man by the throne, "Bring me the crown."

It does as I say, bringing the prize to me with down-turned eyes.

I place the crown on my head, take Lothil's good hand in mine and smile though it hurts. "No, you're not a monster. You're a queen, my queen. I'm the monster. I'll be the monster and we shall make your father pay for what he has done to us."

And the court, my court, erupts in a hate-filled, joyous roar to offend the heavens.

SEAN PATRICK KELLEY *is a technology consigliere to a marketing agency by day and a fantasy writer by night. He co-found the Paradise Lost writing workshop, is a cook, gamer, marksman, gardener, foodie, husband and father of teenage twins. You can follow him on twitter @endiron.*

RHINDOR'S REMISSION

BY RUSSELL MILLER

He was pissing hot gravel.

Rhindor pulled his silver beard away and looked down, just to be sure. As always, there was no molten lava or bloodied bits of razor, it was just urine; just a maddeningly weak stream of plain yellow fluid.

His sunspotted hand slipped from the hem of his robe. Eyes widening, Rhindor clenched his teeth and scrambled to retract the errant length of cloth. The pain in his manhood mounted. He pulled his robe up unceremoniously, wadding the runes imbuing its hem. Taking approximate aim at the lacquered chamberpot, Rhindor clenched his brow and whispered an ancient prayer. It was the prayer of strength from the Bra'oic Kataa, or had it been the hymn of endurance from the Pogith Mardque?

The chamberpot resumed its simple melody. Rhindor let out a long breath. In times past, he'd have argued that the Elvin High Chorus or The Grand Symphony at Sar'lith produced Midlantia's finest music. But as the years piled, Rhindor had come to believe that the most melodious instrument in the world was lacquered white and played but one note.

Even the slow, steady discharge of his pent up fluids offered no real reprieve, however, it merely offered a different pain. Rhindor's shaggy brow furrowed as he tried to find just the right speed. Too fast and the urine became jagged yellow glass, too slow and his bladder filled with dragonfire. He curled his lips to a small O. His breath alternated between sucking gasps and stuttered grunts.

Oh, to be two-hundred again, Rhindor thought wistfully.

He looked about his tower-top room, if only to distract himself. The steps to the stone tower had become increasingly irksome, but his pride wouldn't allow him to move to the lower keep.

Besides, the view from his tower was lovely. It overlooked the garden which Mistress Polna tended. A bit farther on, the orchard, just coming into spring bloom, scented the air. Novice Gayln was staking a human-sized target near a flowering apple tree. *Too close*, Rhindor mused. *I'll have that moved before his practice begins.*

And then there was the idea of having to move all his stuff. There was too much by half, Rhindor knew. Sixty years ago, after he'd thrown away what he could, he was left with nearly three centuries of accumulated oddities and artifacts that couldn't bear further winnowing. Mistress Polna had complained that some of his treasures were morbid. Certainly, the human head was a tad...dark. But it had been well-preserved for all that; painstakingly dipped in the finest bronze and presented to him by a grateful queen. The casual observer might even think it a poor sculpture, rather than the last remains of the Dovnean king.

And the various bottles, scrolls, and books...some were too valuable, others too dangerous, to dispose of. The Book or Tor'rith hummed and smoldered during full moons—Rhindor had chained it shut, to avoid any accidents. The scrolls of N'dal, though sealed in wax, secured in lead, surrounded in steel, and ensorcelled with every relevant barrier Rhindor knew, still attracted butterflies. And the Fangiour rug, an eyesore of mottled brown and black hair, growled when stepped on. Polna complained that when she attempted to clean the pelt, it tried to bite her. How does one safely dispose of an undead icewolf rug?

And the crystal chest — Rhindor needn't turn to sense it; like a bonfire at his back. He'd spent countless hours admiring its sharp angles, geometric patterns, and illusory translucence. It was so beautiful a thing, so powerful a container, who'd guess it contained so dark a secret; so very, very dark. In spite of the spells painstakingly weaved into the crystal box, its contents still whispered, its muffled voice a harmony of round, seductive tones.

"Fatoriana!" came a shout from the orchard.

"Shite," Rhindor swore. The chamberpot ceased its wet symphony. He looked to the orchard and saw his novice waving his arms uselessly at the padded target. Rhindor closed his eyes, willing another release. *Please, just a little more. Almost done —*

"FaTOHrianA!" the novice bellowed, again waving his idiot hands.

Rhindor ground his teeth. A single drip fell to the bowl with an apologetic *plop*. Releasing the crinkled front of his thick robes, Rhindor nearly upended the chamberpot as he stormed to the window.

"Pha'Tor'ien-a!" the old man growled. Both the target and the flowering tree burst into flame with such percussion that the novice was thrown amongst Mistress Polna's cabbages. His hair was smoking.

Rhindor covered his mouth and bunched his shoulders as he peeked from his window. The boy was moving, struggling to regain his feet. *Good.* Rhindor's shoulders relaxed. Mistress Polna was hurrying across the garden, her pruning shears clenched absently in her hand. She was scolding the boy. She evidently thought the novice was to blame. *Even better.*

The novice was standing, he looked at the tree, and then to his hand. He scratched his haystacked hair, jerked his hand back, then began beating at his scalp. He must've found the source of the smoke. Rhindor grinned and stood straight. *Perfect.*

The mage retreated from the opening and swung the leaded glass window shut. Weak from disuse, a rusty laugh wheezed from Rhindor's lips. In his mind's eye, he replayed the boy looking at his own hand, as if *he'd* managed so powerful a casting. Another laugh took Rhindor, he gave the laughter a voice, a deep guffaw that rumbled from somewhere under his long beard. The boy would brag about it later, Rhindor knew. The notion fueled his mirth further; the old mage took hold of his bed post as his laughter sought to double him.

Something tickled in his throat.

Between chuckles, Rhindor tried clearing it to no avail. He balled his fist in front of his mouth and tried a cough, then another, then another. His mouth distended as the cough became a mirthless hack.

He rested his elbow on the bed as the dry barking spasmed through his thin body. His grey eyes watered and it became difficult to stand. Sinking to the floor, Rhindor sat on his knees near the edge of his canopied bed. He placed both knuckled hands on the cold floor and continued to cough. Veins stood from his forehead and his eyes blurred with tears, yet he continued to hack until he feared he might vomit.

An explosion from somewhere outside rattled his leaded window; a dull thud shook the tower stone, causing an empty beaker to roll from its shelf; it shattered with a sharp report. Rhindor hardly noticed the disturbance.

Am I dying? The thought toned through the old man as he struggled for air. *Is this how it ends?*

By degrees, however, the tremors subsided. He swallowed to wet his throat, gulping between shuddering breaths. He would live another day. Rhindor couldn't shake an unexpected disappointment. He blinked to clear the tears from his eyes and looked up from his knees at the debris cluttering his room. His treasure trove, a depository of endless quests and pyrrhic victories, looked very different from his place on the floor. He saw it at last as Mistress Polna saw it; as a bunch of useless trash.

He would be rid of it, he decided suddenly. All of it. Perhaps he could just bury it? Someone would dig it up someday, he knew. He found he didn't care.

New tears welled up in Rhindor's aged eyes and he began to shake with a new bout of tremors. How long had it been since he wept — or laughed, for that matter? He considered whether he would die before he laughed next. He was startled from this dark thought as something brushed along his hand. Rhindor snatched his arm back reflexively and wiped his eyes. The Fangiour pelt had drifted soundlessly nearer its master. Rhindor hesitated a moment, then scratched the mottled brown fur with his shaking hand. It was surprisingly soft.

Okay. He'd keep the rug.

A commotion rose beyond Rhindor's chamber door. He heard shouting of familiar voices, clattering steel, and a deep resonating hum — then silence. The door's bolt snapped open like a crossbow string, but the door swung inward slowly. Mist and smoke drifted into the bedchamber. The humming began anew; it charged the wisps of hair on Rhindor's spotted scalp, causing them to stand.

Rhindor sat up on his knees and hurriedly wiped the tears from his nose and beard. "Mortigar? Is that you?" Despite the danger, Rhindor's lips spread to an unexpected smile.

Mortigar drifted into the room like an angry ghost, his staff held before him. A red stone burned atop the black shaft, resonating malevolence.

"I'll have none of your tricks, old man," Mortigar sneered.

"No, no. No tricks." Rhindor held up his hands to evidence his good intent.

Mortigar jerked to the ready, leveling his staff.

"Really! There's no tricks," Rhindor insisted. "Anyway, I never used my hands — you know that."

Mortigar paused, "Yes, I suppose I do." He drifted sideways, glancing in all directions, placing his back near the wall. His dark eyes paused a moment at the sight of Rhindor kneeling. Mortigar's eyebrow arched. "I've discovered the Staff of Dar'Tith. Your powers are no match for me now."

"My *powers*?" Rhindor said. "Look at me!" His voice shook. "You needn't a staff. A shovel would have sufficed."

Mortigar hesitated. His staff's glow dimmed. "A shovel?"

Rhindor nodded. His chest began to shake, a single tear coursed its way to his ancient beard. "Besides, I've got the Wand of Glorin'twa. It's over there." Rhindor motioned weakly with his hand. "You're welcome to it. I don't want it anymore."

A smile spread Mortigar's lips. "You'll not distract me, wizard." He leveled his staff once more. Its tip began to resonate.

Snarling, the Fangiour pelt burst from where it lay near Rhindor. It lunged toward the darkly robed man. Electricity sizzled from the Staff of Dar'Tith. The hairy rug yelped and retreated back to its master's lap. A three-inch hole had been burned through its disheveled hair. Gods, Rhindor thought, now it's even more ugly. He patted the pelt as it continued to whine.

"What's this?" Mortigar laughed. "This is your last line of defense? A *rug*?"

"I told you, I — " Rhindor began.

"Enough!" Mortigar swept his hands.

Rhindor suddenly couldn't move, not even to breathe. It was a simple spell that Mortigar had used to paralyze him, he knew. But it was effective, for all that. Rhindor knew the counter-spell, of course, and since he'd no need to use his hands — as so many lesser wizards did — he would have no trouble breaking the spell. *Paralix'ish taha*, he let the words form in his mind. Nothing happened. *Pa'ralicish T'ha*, he tried again. Nothing.

His lungs began to burn for lack of air. *Pha'ralish Tahia! Paralyx Thi'a! PohRalich Te'Ah!* Nothing, nothing, and nothing. Mortigar was moving, but Rhindor couldn't turn his eyes to see what —

"It is the wand of Glorin Twa'!" Mortigar exclaimed. "Where did you find it?"

Rhindor, of course, couldn't respond. His vision was blurring, and his hearing became muffled. Tears, unaffected by the spell, formed in his eyes and ran chaotic paths down his weathered cheeks.

"Rhindor? Oh, for Hell's sake — Paralix'is Ta'he!"

Rhindor slapped his hands to the floor as his body went limp. He sucked in a shuddering breath. Great drops fell from his red-rimmed eyes onto the whimpering Fangiour pelt.

"Rhindor?" The menace left Mortigar's voice. "What's *happened* to you?"

Rhindor paused and pushed himself to his knees. "Three hundred and six years *happened* to me." He wiped his beak-like nose with the gaudy hem of his sleeve and looked to his old nemesis. He again felt a thrill of recognition; despite being sworn enemies, it was comforting to see someone from the old days. "I've spent the last eighty years living in this tower, surrounded by all this junk." He motioned weakly with his hand.

"Junk?" Mortigar cast his dark eyes about; he seemed to see a very different room. "Is that the hammer of Kaitlith?"

"Wha—? Oh, yes." Rhindor sniffed. "The dwarves don't have a kingdom anymore. They mixed in with the humans. They're just called 'short' now. You can have it."

Mortigar eyes narrowed, "It's very powerful."

"Yeah, but what good is it?" Rhindor's knobby knees were beginning to protest kneeling on the stone. "You can have it — all. I want none of it." He gripped a corner bedpost and struggled to rise. His legs had fallen asleep and were buzzing with horseflies.

Mortigar smiled, but his eyes looked uncertain. "You wish to appease me with gifts then?" He lowered his staff awkwardly; the wand remained clutched in his other hand.

"No, not really." Rhindor winced as his tingling feet protested. "I just don't need the clutter."

Mortigar's sneering gaze faltered. "Clutter?" He held the wand aloft as if showcasing his favorite bauble to a schoolchild. "You have the Wand of Glorin Twa'!"

"No," Rhindor answered. "You do. It's yours now."

"But" — Mortigar's lips moved soundlessly for a moment — "don't you realize how *powerful* this makes me?"

"Oh yes, sure." Rhindor barely nodded. "But you'll look silly running about with both a staff and a wand—don't say I didn't warn you." Rhindor sat on his bed. He knew it was rude, but his feet hurt and he was still shaking from the coughing fit.

"Are you mad?" Mortigar said. "I mean, you won't stand a chance."

"A chance?" Rhindor constructed a brace of pillows to rest his back against.

"I've come to kill you, Rhindor." The words left Mortigar's curt lips with a seasoned sting, as if he'd practiced them.

"Oh." Rhindor's mouth opened then shut. Mortigar's words pricked the old mage. While the prospect of death didn't appeal to him, there was something else — an unnamed sadness. Mortigar had been his enemy so long, surely that counted for something. "Wouldn't you rather — stay for tea?"

"Tea?" Mortigar said. His scripted baritone slipped to a frustrated falsetto. "Tea! You destroyed my minions and tore down my tower. You — " He pointed with the wand as he ranted. It began to hiss.

"Okay, okay," Rhindor placated. He held his frail hands up, palms forward. "I know we've got our differences — "

Mortigar's eyes goggled. "You melted my skin off!" His voice cracked as he said "skin." An awkward moment passed, broken only by a high pitched sizzle emanating from the Wand of Glorin Twa'.

"Yes, well, sorry about that," Rhindor said. "But it's not like you didn't have it coming — what with all you did to the elves — and Gods know what you were planning to do with the orb — "

"Hey!" Mortigar interrupted, "Those elves weren't exactly — "

"Fatoriana!" Gayln the apprentice crouched as he shouted from the doorway; he was gesturing with his fool hands again. Huntsman Kentos and Mistress Polna stood behind the boy. Kentos had brought a heavy ax.

Mortigar crossed the wand and staff before him in a defensive posture; the staff hummed and the wand crackled with ancient energy. "So it's a trap!" The dark mage's face twisted to a grim smile.

"A trap?" Rhindor snorted. "Use your eyes, Mortigar; it's a whelp, a woodsman, and a scullery maid."

"FaTOHrianA!" the boy shouted, waving his hands like a traveling show charlatan.

Mortigar's smile evaporated, he winced at the unpleasant sound of the novice's prepubescent voice. He turned from the struggling apprentice. "Is he yours?"

Rhindor scratched at his scalp. "Yeah, well, I haven't much time, you see, and — "

"FathoRhiannna!" the boy continued. Frothy spit collected at the corners of his mouth.

"But he's got no skill," Mortigar said. "None." The wand and staff abruptly ceased radiating energy. "No talent at all. Not a flicker." He sagged; his dark velvet robe suddenly seemed too large. "What happened to your last one?"

Rhindor knit his brow and looked toward the ceiling. He ticked on his fingers as if doing sums. "Petrina? She got sick after a — "

"She?" Mortigar arched his brow.

"Of course, you'd not have known her. It's a shame, really." Rhindor smiled weakly. "She wasn't much of a fighter, mind you, but she'd a clever touch." He began ticking on his fingers again. "You'd have known Hethan."

Mortigar's face quickened. "Yes." He pointed at Rhindor. "That's the one. Now, that one made me nervous."

"FatOOriaNNa!" the boy shouted doggedly. Both old wizards flinched at the interruption.

Rhindor recovered first. "You will stop that nonsense AT ONCE!" He slapped his small hand down on his bed; the sound it made on the thick coverlets was disappointingly powerless "poof." Rhindor turned his attention back to the dark wizard. "Now where — ? Ah, yes, Hethan — now *there* was an apprentice!"

"He seemed a bit whiny," Mortigar observed.

"Oh," Rhindor cast his eyes and hands up, "you've *no* idea. But then, at least he had a modicum of talent to work with." He gestured dismissively. "This one — " He snorted and rolled his eyes.

"It's not true!" the boy shouted, his voice was shrill and broken by the ravages of early puberty. Snot ran from his one of his nostrils. "I-I blew up the apple tree!" He pointed at the wall as if the ruined stump could be seen through the grey stone. He wiped his nose with his other sleeve.

Mortigar's face brightened. "It's true. I saw the tree explode."

"Oh, don't be ridiculous," Rhindor shushed both his hands through the air. "The boy couldn't blow up a wineskin. *I* did the tree."

After an awkward silence, the old mage wasn't sure what irritated him more: Mistress Polna's scolding look or the revelation's lack of hilarity. He'd hoped for another good laugh.

"Mistress Polna, would you be so good as to fetch a spot of tea? For two, please?" Polna stood rooted in place; she listened as if hearing a foreign language. Rhindor spoke more slowly. "I'll take mine with lemon, Mortigar?"

The dark wizard's eyes narrowed to slits and his lips curled. He bared his teeth and spat foreign words filled with hard consonants. Both the wand and staff erupted into full song; their long dormant power shook the tower. Priceless items that had been haphazardly stacked began to dance about on their shelves. The leaded window cracked, then shattered. Driven to an unnatural fury, wind penetrated the small opening; it caught up bits of colored glass and weathered pages of parchment, cyclonically scattering them about. Rhindor's bed danced away from the wall, he held up his hands to protect his face from swirling debris. Mistress Polna and the others huddled together under the huntsman's flapping cape. The bronzed head fell from its pedestal, its impact a distant *clunk*. Thunder erupted just outside the tower, pounding like a battle ram on mighty gates, scenting the angry air with the stink of charged sulfur.

Mortigar howled then. His eyes glowed black; his voice pierced the thunder and screaming wind. He held his clenched fists away from his body on straight arms as burning anger rose from his throat like an open forge. Shadow and light inverted chaotically as reality itself began to bend.

Silence.

Rhindor still hid behind his hands, fearing — hoping — that this sudden calm was death — that life could be escaped so painlessly. He was mildly disappointed to open his eyes and see his wrinkled palms. He peeked about the room. His bed stood near the room's center, and his collection of odds and ends, treasures and trivia, lay strewn about like hay in an untended stable. King Dovnean's head had rolled to where the woodsman still covered the others with his long cape; his face was bleeding. The crystal chest was the only item that hadn't moved; its gleaming implacability made it seem all the more beautiful.

Mortigar, too, remained rooted where he had stood before the fury, but he was hardly unmoved. His skin was ashen and his mouth drawn. His eyes were closed and the muscles around his eyes were slack. Sucking down a deep sigh, he exhaled into a slouch. His arms hung loose at his sides.

"Honey," he said. His voice was soft but clear. A single black tear coursed its way over his high cheekbone, trailing down to drip from his jaw. "I'll...take mine with honey."

Rhindor, atop his ruined bed covered with dust, dirt, and bits of glass, sat stupidly for a moment, then broke into a toothy smile. "Splendid!" He nearly laughed, his cheeks hurt from the unusual strain. "Mistress Polna. Two cups of tea please. Mr. Mortigar prefers honey. Chop chop, now. Don't dawdle."

"I want the orb," Mortigar said. It wasn't a threat, or even a demand, it was said as offhandedly as one might ask for honey. A bit of stubborn glass fell from the ruined window, it shattered crisply on the floor.

"But — " Rhindor hesitated, looked at the chest then back, "couldn't — "

"I want the orb." Mortigar's voice rose from a whisper.

It was Rhindor's turn to slump. ...so powerful, and so very, very dark. Rhindor had sworn oaths — to friends long dead and gone. A brief battle raged in Rhindor's mind; it made his head hurt. "Fine," he decided, "you'll have it." He heard Polna gasp and his novice mutter. Rhindor silenced them with a look. "But, please, let's have tea first, hmm?"

Mortigar's eye's narrowed and his lips hinted at their former curl. "Oh, we'll have tea — *after* I have the orb."

Rhindor paused a moment more before exhaling a frustrated sigh. "Fine," he said, "it's in the chest."

Mortigar's lips relaxed to an almost easy smile. He leaned on his staff and looked about the room, his eyes rested briefly on the crystalline chest before focusing on an upended chair. Stashing the wand in the folds of his velvet robe, the dark wizard righted the seat and sat down heavily. "Now," he said, sitting back, "about that tea..."

A titter ran up Rhindor's stomach. He swallowed a great apple that formed in his throat. "Yes, yes," he said, fighting an embarrassing mist that clouded his vision, "about that tea."

But, just as everything seemed perfect, it became — wrong.

Through his watery vision, Rhindor sensed movement from where his servants and student had lain. The movement was too quick to be casual. Rhindor blinked his eyes quickly and quailed at what he saw: His damned fool novice had taken the woodsman's axe. The weapon was a plain thing; heavy, crude, and effective for dull work. The boy was darting toward Mortigar's back now, the axe raised high. Time slowed. Rhindor formed words in his mind. The spell would kill the lad, the wizard knew —

But Mortigar was quicker.

The youth paused a moment before dropping the sharpened hunk of iron. It skittered harmlessly across the stone floor. Gayln's face set in a terrible frown and he began to emit a girlish squeal. He sought his master's eyes, seeking mercy. He found none. The lad burst into flame. He waved his arms about. Perhaps attempting a spell? He fell to his hands and knees, then finally to the floor. The tower filled with the stink of it.

"You!" Mortigar stood from his chair, pointing at his old enemy.

Rhindor showed his palms. "No," he pled, "I didn't — "

Mortigar's face twisted with anger and something new — something worse. He yanked the wand from the folds of his robe; it crackled to life like a whipped tigress. "You've failed, old man!" He hurried to the gleaming chest with long, fateful strides.

"Stop, Mortigar." Rhindor held his hands out, his fingers splayed. "Please."

Mortigar dropped his staff and jerked at the chest's lid. It opened with an innocuous click.

The dark mage stood straight, recognizing his folly. A pale mist whispered from somewhere under the lid; nearly translucent, the powder sparkled with the vibrancy of snow on a sunny day. Such a beautiful thing, really, to be so unrelentingly lethal.

Mortigar jerked back, his arms fell to his sides as he began to stiffen. With his last, he turned to his old nemesis. "I lose, it seems." He tried to speak more, but his lips and tongue hardened too quickly. A single tear froze in its track down his paling cheeks.

"Goodbye, old friend," Rhindor whispered.

Mortigar's frozen form fell backward. His impact against the tower stone sounded with a solid thud. Mistress Polna ran forward to where the dullard novice still lay in flames. She backed away; the heat was still too intense, as was the smell. Turning, she fell to her knees and emitted a heaving retch. She wept in a shrill voice between spasms.

But Rhindor hardly noticed Polna's travails; his red-rimmed eyes remained fixed on Mortigar's unyielding form.

Feeling every day of his 306 years, Rhindor stumbled from his bed to kneel near his dear enemy. Searing cold continued to emanate from Mortigar's body, leeching the heat from the very stone on which he rested.

"C-can you save him?" Mistress Polna seemed at the verge of retching further.

Rhindor didn't look up. "No." His voice caught for a moment. "The spell — too powerful. The elves wove it into the chest in the event of — "

"Not HIM, you idiot!" Polna's voice was seasoned with an unpleasant mix of sorrow, rage, and nausea. "The BOY! Can you save the boy!" She pointed to Galyn, as if his being on fire wasn't enough to draw Rhindor's eye.

"No. He's dead too — burned from the inside out, I'm afraid."

And no mean trick, to burn a single target from the inside out while one's back was turned, and with no foolish hand-waving either. Rhindor mused whether he could have managed such a feat.

"Then what good are you?" Polna shouted; her face had become mottled with unseemly patches of red. "Some 'all-powerful wizard' you are!" She waved her hands in mocking mystic motions. "Put him out!" She stabbed her finger at the boy's blazing form. "He's burning!"

Rhindor bristled at the hand motions. He *never* used his hands, and the last person who could appreciate that fact lay forever frozen —

"Now! Gods damn you! Put him out!" The normally stoic house mistress stood, her hands balled at her sides.

She was right, Rhindor thought sourly. She was always right. Knees aching, the old wizard stood and searched his foggy mind for the right spell.

"I can help," said a familiar voice.

"What's that?" Rhindor stood and shuffled as near he dare to the boy's burning corpse. Polna continued to motion at the boy; she'd heard nothing. The woodsman remained near the doorjamb clearing the blood that ran from a gash above his eye. Rhindor was sure he'd heard a voice, an old, comforting sound. The old mage's face went slack. *The orb.*

The voice came to him again; familiar, but different than it had been those many years ago. Gone were its promises of dominion and seductions of glory — those were the dreams of a younger man. Its voice was strangely bereft of its former arrogance. But it *was* familiar, so achingly familiar.

"No." Rhindor clenched his teeth and turned to close the chest that had stifled the orb's voice for so very, very long. The stone didn't burn as brazenly as he remembered; it glowed instead like a well-banked ember.

He could still shut the chest. The trap would reset —

"Put him OUT, you crazy old bastard!" Polna was shouting again, though she sounded far away.

Again, the voice toned through Rhindor's mind. It didn't beg or demand, it offered comfort, companionship.

Rhindor screwed his eyes shut. He'd been charged with the orb's protection — his life's work.

The orb's glow diminished till it appeared no more than a ball of dark glass; it was tired. It complained of its long stay in its crystal prison...of its loneliness. The world had changed. Even in the box, it'd felt the magic go out of the world; it'd felt the slow death of wonder. It doubted there remained a master capable of unlocking its secrets; it may as well be thrown on a well-pebbled beach. None understood its vast utility, both to destroy and to heal.

Rhindor turned his back to the orb and opened his eyes. The boy still burned before him and Polna was still shouting beyond. As always, he could feel the orb's warmth at his back — so comfortably warm.

The old wizard locked eyes with his house mistress. She stuttered a moment, then fell silent. He was tired of her voice, of her nagging, of her perpetual *rightness* — that most of all. He raised a single hand and held his palm backward over his shoulder.

The orb sprung from its prison, landing in Rhindor's palm with the eagerness of a long-awaited beau. Rhindor closed his fingers about the warm stone. His flesh tingled with forgotten vitality and his spine straightened as one removing a heavy pack. No longer numb, Rhindor's feet and ankles remembered the dexterity of his youth.

"Yes! Yes!" Mistress Polna said, clasping her hands before her. She seemed to sense her master's rebirth, his limitless power. "Save him! Please." Her eyes watered anew, not with sorrow's sagging flood, but with stinging tears of hope. The woodsman looked less pleased; he stood away from the doorjamb, his hands at his sides.

Grinning, Rhindor gripped the stone in the last three fingers of his right hand. With his left, he raised the hem of his robe. The stone was *so* warm...

Polna's mouth fell open, her eyebrows furrowed as if they sought to touch.

A graceful, steady yellow stream arced from beneath Rhindor's robe. "Yes, YES!" the mage exclaimed. He leaned his head back, his mouth opened. He didn't need to look to know his aim was true; his effort was met with steaming applause.

Rhindor's remission was interrupted by a sudden sound, like a sack of onions dropped from a counter. He looked and discovered that Mistress Polna had fallen —no, fainted. Worse, she'd landed in her own gory vomit. It coated the side of her untroubled face. It was soaking into her primly arranged hair.

They thought it very funny.

The orb laughed first, but Rhindor couldn't resist joining in. As the mage's hilarity shook him, his urine sprayed chaotically — and that was funnier still. Tears welled in the old man's eyes and his stomach ached. There was no tickle in his throat to fear — he would never fear mirth again.

They laughed until both voices rang together in two-part harmony. Its force shook dust from the eaves.

RUSSELL MILLER *used to want to be a novelist, but has since realized that his day job pays better and is less work. He still writes when he can't help himself. He lives in Utah and travels more than any decent person should.*

Advice on the Slaying of Wurms
by Michelle Muenzler

Sit, wurm slayer, and listen,
for I will speak these words but once.

There are three rules when it comes to slaying wurms, no matter what the city
farseers and pigeon-gutters might tell you.

Obey these, and your wurm will fall.
Fail them and...

Well,
I need not tell you the obvious consequences of that when you can see them so
easily before you, yes?

Rule, the first:
do not listen to the wurm's song.

You may think this a foolish rule.
What harm could the voice of one beast do?

But when a wurm sings, its voice cracks the very air.
Each note cuts the beast's throat,
slices the flesh ever wider to birth the next.

The more flesh cut, the higher the notes,
until not even the clouds pass overhead unscathed.
The sky breaks against that voice.

The shards of it litter the ground and are cupped by the wurm's silver-laced wings, the blood from its throat flecking every stained-glass sliver.

They tremble, those shards.

They tremble with the force of the song still playing in the reflections of light upon their surface.

You'll want to swallow them.

No, do not laugh. They are not glass;
they are liquid sky and voice,
hardened together for only a few moments
before they melt again like snow.

They sing with it, with the wurm.

You cannot help but want to swallow that song.

Resist. With all your strength, resist.

These fragments of song are the eggs that birth new wurms.
Only the foolish swallow the eggs of wurms.

Rule, the second:
once the wurm has completed its song,
do not look into its eyes.

You'll have eaten its song —
deny this as you please now, but I know the truth.

You'll have swallowed its song, as many shards as you could grasp before they melted between your fingers.

Yet you still have a chance to finish what you came for.
The wurm that sang now splays across the snow,
its once silver wings gray and limp, as though all the light has been sucked free of them by the treasures scattered before it.

Its voice hangs on the last remnants of sky,
soon to be lost as the winds rush into the void it has carved.

Without looking, remove its head.
That's why you brought the thrice-blessed knife,
isn't it?

An expensive knife for one such as yourself.

A wurm-slaying knife.

Slice the wurm's neck, working
from behind the pulsing curve of its jaw where the flesh is already tattered and spare
from the songs' birth.

Once torn free, the wurm breathing no longer,
drag its head down the mountainside,
a trail of blood behind you,
until you reach whatever village you came from.

There you'll be heralded a hero,
a wurm slayer in truth,
feasted until your belly is ready to split from too many roasted potatoes and lean
winter venison.
And in a week, when the local fervor dies somewhat,
you'll find a quiet night where none are likely to follow,
and you'll seek out a hedgewitch one village over
to extract the songs you swallowed.

At this point,
you can already feel their beats thrumming against your ribcage.

They grow fast, these songs.

You will do what must be done, though. Because,
when you are still standing atop that mountain
-- the wurm not yet slain,
its breathing labored from birthing pains,
and you wiping fresh trickles of blood from your song-stained lips --
you *will not* stare into the wurm's eyes.

Not if you have any intention of slaying it.

The nighttime sky dances in those eyes.

As they dim with the birthing's end,
each star flashes in turn,
one last cry against the oncoming emptiness.
A growing chain of fires joining their voices until all you can see is one bright white
flash,
infinitely hot against your own eyes,
then nothing but cold darkness.

The wurm is done now,
its songs emptied,
its eyes still as frozen ponds.

But your own eyes still burn,
deep behind the irises now speckled with the black of infinity.
Even stars need somewhere to be born.

You will no longer be able to stare into a mirror without seeing the glint of
constellations gleaming back.

You will do much staring into mirrors.

But this is how the wurm will make you love it,
and only the foolish fall in love with wurms.

Rule, the third --

Ah, never mind.
I see I have no need of a third rule.

Like I once did, you too will fail.
Don't waste yourself denying it.

You will fail,
and in a year's time it will be you sitting in this chair,
chaining words together as the silver scales harden along your legs,
as the fledgling wings press against your shoulder blades.
You thought because I still looked somewhat like the human I once was
that I could help you.
That I'd *want* to help you.

You were wrong.

You should have stabbed me as soon as you entered.

You know that now,
but it is too late.

I can see your face already hungering to hear my song,
to see the stars dying in my eyes and feel them born again in your own.

There is truly only one rule needed to slay a wurm. Any city farseer or pigeon-gutter could tell you that, and more the fool you for not listening to either.

Never listen to a wurm speak.

I look forward to seeing you atop the mountain, my child-bearer to be.

For you, my song will be glorious.

MICHELLE MUENZLER, *known at local science fiction and fantasy conventions as "The Cookie Lady", writes fiction both dark and strange to counterbalance the sweetness of her backing. Her short fiction and poetry can be read in numerous science fiction and fantasy magazines, and she takes immense joy in crinkling words like little foil puppets. If you wish to lure her out of hiding, you can friend her on Facebook or chase her down at a local SF/F convention where she will ply you with hundreds of home-baked cookies while gleefully describing the latest horror she's written. She supposes you could also contact her through her website, but she finds electronic cookies far less tasty than real ones.*

In the Meantime...

It's hard to believe it has been two years since the *Best-of Volume 1* hit the world. We hadn't planned for this long of a gap, but life is full of things not planned. We hadn't planned on doing a Kickstarter, but it seemed to be "the thing" in the late days of 2016 and early days of 2017, and we figured we'd better jump in before the wheat was eaten. We didn't plan on surpassing our goal by almost 400%. And although we said we'd do artwork, we had no real plan for how to pull it off.

But then, Gandalf the Grey had planned to just walk Frodo right on up to Mt. Doom, and we all know how that came out.

When you have a great crew, unplanned detours are not so hard to deal with. Artwork? Our writers hit the high points and our artists filled in the rest. Layout? Keanen Brand was, again, able to take our helter-skelter notes and files and create the book you hold in your hands. Cover art? Robert Zoltan dealt with our rabbit-assed decision-making progress, and our book has a cover that we can stack against any other. Difficulty lay in deciding what to include — 2011-2013 were a great two years for *Heroic Fantasy Quarterly*.

With our fine editorial staff and a firm base from the first two years of operation, we had a great wealth of fiction and poetry from which to choose. We're all four years older than when those stories first came out. In those four years, S&S fiction has undergone a bit of a renaissance — *Heroic Fantasy Quarterly* has been joined by other venues: *Sword and Sorcery*, *Skelos*, *Grimdark*, a recent Gardner Dozois *Book of Swords* anthology, and rumor has reached us that Rogue Blades Entertainment may be making a comeback. If that weren't enough, another heavy-hitter called *Tales from the Magician's Skull* appears to be taking form in the swirling mists.

Heroic Fantasy Quarterly has great company and great competition! Revisiting these works has been tremendous fun for us, and while four years is forever on the internet, it is our great pleasure to bring these tales of ages past to you. We hope you enjoy this edition as much as we do. With that, we send you on your way to adventure, and offer our hearty thanks to all Kickstarter contributors and fellow fans who have traded your hard-earned cutter for this hard-crafted book!

— *The Editors*

A Game of Chess

by David Pilling

O n the morning of one inauspicious day in early spring, with the sky as grey as the towers of Camelot and the incessant rain trickling into our chain mail, we rode out. One hundred and forty-nine brave young knights, eager to win glory and honour, and one miserable cynic lagging in the rear.

We rode to Canterbury, and there bent the knee before St Thomas the Martyr. Then we separated into small groups and scattered in all directions, though some of the bravest and stupidest decided to ride out on their own. Remarkably few of these survived. Those that did, such as Uwaine and Carados, were changed men when they came back to Camelot: savage killers, with all the youth and innocence beaten out of them.

Meanwhile, I, Sir Kay, was condemned to the company of Sir Gawaine.

* * *

Easily panicked, easily frustrated, easily enraged, with the blood of ancient Celts sizzling in his veins like cooking fat, Gawaine was the last man I would have chosen to accompany me to the privy, never mind a Quest. He was the son of the King of Orkney and the witch Morgause, which made him mad, brave and touched by the magic of the Old Ones.

We headed north from Canterbury, for Gawaine was eager to plunge into the unknown and opined that the best adventures were to be found in the North Country. I went along with it, swept along like a twig in the stream by his fierce charisma.

People forget that England was a different country then. Decades of Arthur's Peace, during which the land was steadily tamed and civilised, have stifled the memory of what a wild place it was in the old days. Much of the country was covered in forest, deep tangled labyrinthine forest, soaked in magic and half-submerged in the netherworlds of Faerie and the old pagan gods. Cities like Camelot were an oasis of law and sanity in a sea of chaos, but they were few and far between.

Into this strange, seething wilderness Arthur sent his knights, to bring peace and justice, by brute force if necessary, and to bring the light of Christ into dark places. That was the idea behind his Quests, and many brave young men died for it.

So Gawaine and I plunged into the unknown, leaving the rough roads far behind us in our — or rather, his — eagerness for encounters with black knights, malignant fairies, cockatrices, griffons and whatever else pricked his barbaric imagination.

Before long the forest ceased to be a simple collection of trees and undergrowth, and acquired an atmosphere of magic. The trees became strangely twisted and overgrown, their spindly branches overhanging like a witch's fingers, and strange horrors lurked in the shadows.

One morning, a strange portentous morning, the air heavy with magic and a fine golden mist, we stumbled upon adventure. A glade opened before us in the forest, and in the middle of it was a high tower surrounded by a moat.

From the branches of the trees that lined the glade hung dozens of shields, some ancient and half-rotted away or pitted with rust, as if they had been there for years.

A knight came out of the doorway of the tower, a big man armed from head to foot in black armour. His visor was down, and he carried a mace in one hand and a round sable shield with no device in the other. He crossed over the bridge and took up position at the far end, raising his mace in what I assumed to be a challenge.

"A black knight," I sighed, rolling my eyes, "how original. No doubt he means to fight anyone who wishes to pass this way. The shields hanging from the trees probably belonged to all the knights he has defeated. Perhaps he ate the bodies."

I spoke with heavy sarcasm, but Gawaine was too excited to notice. "Do you think so?" he roared, fumbling as he snatched up his helm, "look at him, the bonny warrior! Kay, man, help me lace my helmet, my fingers are shaking."

"Gawaine, life is not so simple," I warned. "There is bound to be some twist here. Knights don't just stand on bridges in the middle of the forest and kill people for no reason. Remember, we are in the heart of Faerie."

He was in no mood to listen. That was Sir Gawaine all over, a thick-headed fool and mad for fighting, but a hard man to dislike. I reluctantly helped him arm and then rode beside him into the glade.

I only half-listened to the formal challenges — it was the usual stuff, full of thees and thous and contrived outrage — but one thing the strange knight said did stand out. When asked by Gawaine to state his name, he spoke thus:

"I am the Guardian of the Dolorous Tower. I am fated to challenge any knight that passes this way, until one should arrive to supplant me."

He spoke in a mournful voice, more like a man attending a funeral than about to engage in deadly combat. I studied him further, and noticed an oddly listless air about him, as opposed to Gawaine's bristling aggression.

Despite my qualms I did nothing to interrupt, and within moments the two were hacking away at each other. As ever, Gawaine fought like a mad farmer attempting to get the harvest in before rain, mowing and slashing with his sword.

It was midmorning, which was significant, for Gawaine's blood was tainted by the magic of the Old Ones and his strength waxed as the sun rose in the sky. His opponent had a hard time of it, and could do little to counter the hammer blows that rained down on him.

Soon the grass on which they fought was speckled with the black knight's blood, and his breath could be heard wheezing inside his helm.

At last Gawaine's sword stabbed through the bars of his opponent's visor, and a torrent of blood and brain matter gushed over the blade. The black knight toppled onto his face with a dying groan and a clatter of ironmongery.

Feeling numb and weary, as though I had been the one fighting, I slowly climbed off my horse and walked over to inspect the body. I heaved him onto his back and lifted his visor, wincing at the carnage inside, while Gawaine got onto one knee and gave joyful thanks to God.

From what I could make out under the gore, the man had been youngish, with a matted red beard, aquiline nose and high cheekbones. It was a noble face, and I could not help but wonder what family he had belonged to.

"Oh, shut up, Gawaine," I snapped, irritated by his droning prayers, and at the hypocrisy that formed them. As if Christ would have anything to do with his wanton butchery.

I closed the dead man's visor, made the sign of the Cross over him, and stood up. As I did so I happened to glance up at the tower, and saw a woman staring at me from a window.

She had a wicked face, sly and deceitful, with a cynical twist to the mouth and black cat-like eyes that glittered with bad intentions. She was beautiful enough, in a pale underfed sort of way, but her charms were drowned by the awful malignancy of her expression.

I knew her at once for what she was, and that we had to get out of the glade. "Gawaine, come," I said urgently, for he had still not left off his prayers. "Quickly, get off your knees and on your horse! We are in deadly danger!"

He broke off, annoyance and confusion mingling on his simple freckled face. "Danger, what danger?" he demanded. "There's nothing to fear from yon knight. I slew him a moment ago, in case you hadn't noticed."

"Not him, you bloody fool!" I stabbed my finger at the lady in the window. "Look there!"

He twisted his head and stared up at her. Then, to my horror, he broke into a leering grin and ran an armoured hand through his sweat-soaked hair. "Well,

Kay, my luck is changing," he laughed, rising, "first I have a braw fight, and then a fine lady for dessert. Look at her smiling at us, the bonny lass. Call her down and we'll have a party."

"Are you mad?" I almost screamed. "Don't you know anything, you who has magic running in your veins? She's one of the Fair Folk, or the Lords and Ladies, call them what you will, and this whole wood is cursed. That poor devil you just slaughtered must have been under her spell. No wonder he didn't put up much of a fight. He must have longed for death!"

Gawaine wasn't much shaken by this. He was too damned stupid to be scared of anything. "Och, fairies," he said dismissively, "we have them in Orkney. Ugly wee things that live in barrows and steal milk. My auntie went off dancing in the woods with them, once, and we never saw her again. But by and large they are not to be feared."

"This is no common country sprite," I began, trying to keep my voice calm, but the fairy in the tower had heard enough. She waved her hand, pale as the moon and encrusted with jewels, and my tongue instantly stuck to the roof of my mouth.

"Enough of your chatter, ape," she said in a voice that was low, pleasant and melodious, "you bore me, and must go away immediately. Your companion, of course, will stay here with me."

Gawaine looked flummoxed at that, and turned to me for an explanation. I, unable to speak, gestured helplessly.

"What means this?" he growled, and the angry crimson flush started to creep back up his neck, "I'll go or stay as I see fit, madam."

The fairy laughed, a soft silvery noise, and leaned further out of the window. "Foolish man-thing," she sneered, "have you not guessed the riddle of my tower? It must be guarded by a champion, who challenges and slays any knight that passes by until he himself is slain. His killer then takes his place. That is the game I have devised, and it has kept me amused for three hundred years."

It took a moment for her words to sink in — Gawaine was never quick on the uptake — and then he exploded with rage.

"Trapped? Nay, never!" he roared between oaths, "no-one treats the Knight of Orkney so, man, woman or fairy!"

She merely rested her lovely head on the palm of her hand and smirked at him.

"Gawaine," I said, having been allowed to recover the power of speech, "you cannot leave the glade. This is old magic. I am so sorry, old fellow, but you must abide here for a while. I'll go fetch a priest and bring him back here to lift the curse."

He would have none of it, and advanced toward the tower, his face black with anger. Trying to restrain him would have meant my death, so I stood back, aghast, as he went to slay the fairy as he had slain her champion.

Realising his intention, she tried all sorts of tricks to defend herself. The bridge over the moat turned into a wild, hissing serpent, but Gawaine trod on its spine and chopped it in half. The door to the tower turned into a blank wall of stone, but he struck it down with one shuddering blow of his fist. His blood was up, and the sun was at its zenith, meaning his strength was at its highest ebb.

I waited, trembling, as Gawaine disappeared inside the tower. All was silence for a few moments, and then a terrible high-pitched scream erupted from inside the tower and echoed through the surrounding woods.

Gawaine reappeared. His sword was spattered with fresh blood, and in his left hand he carried the fairy's severed head by her long raven-black hair. Her dead face had a surprised expression, as well it might, and her eyelids still fluttered, a most horrible sight.

"Oh my God," I said, backing away and crossing myself, "what have you done? You have slain a woman!"

"Tut, man," Gawaine said cheerfully, all his high choler evaporated, "she was but a worthless fairy."

"She was still a woman, fairy or no, and you have compromised your knighthood. Arthur will be furious when he finds out. I know him, Gawaine. He will strip you of your spurs and have you flogged out of Camelot!"

"Nonsense! This was no noble lady I slew, but a wicked sprite. Arthur will not punish me."

As he spoke the earth began to tremble. Cracks appeared in the soil and green shoots shot up out of the ground at terrifying speed, twisting into thick ropes that coiled about Gawaine's body, pinning his arms to his side and wrapping tight around his neck and legs.

Green leaves burst through the surface of his skin, sprouting and multiplying to cover his eyes and fill his mouth even as he screamed.

I drew my sword and sprang to his aid, attempting to hack through the web of foliage. A thick tendril snaked out, wrapped several times about my blade and plucked it from my grasp. With a despairing cry I tried to snatch it back, but a couple of stout branches whipped against my chest and dumped me on my backside.

The swirling and rustling stopped, and it was done. Sir Gawaine was entombed inside a miniature forest that had suddenly appeared out of the ground. Barely a minute had passed since the first shoots appeared.

Once again, I had cause to thank my childhood acquaintance with Merlin. He had taught me many things about the Fair Folk, including their love of games.

"Everything is a game to them," he told me. "Life itself is a game to them. They cannot help themselves. Above all, they love challenges and riddles."

"All right," I said, clambering to my feet, "I accept. I will play the game."

There was a moment of dislocation, as though the world held its breath for a second. I looked to my left and saw that a path had opened in the forest.

The path was long and winding, made of spotless white flagstones, and led to a distant hill. High on the hill stood a fine stone house, though from another angle it looked like an ugly heap of rocks, like one of those ancient hilltop cairns the Old Ones buried their dead under.

I solved the problem by clapping a hand over my left eye, and the flickering images resolved into the house. Keeping my left eye covered, I left the clearing and stepped onto the path. My horse and Gawaine's, being sensible beasts, refused to go anywhere near, so I was obliged to walk.

In no time at all, though the house seemed at least a couple of miles away, I found myself standing at the foot of the hill. An elegant white marble staircase led up to the door, a handsome affair of yellow oak decorated with carvings of oak leaves and smirking cherubs. I mounted the stairs and knocked politely on the door, which opened silently.

Inside was a large airy round chamber with whitewashed walls and a domed ceiling. A small fire crackled in the grate and there was no furnishing, lending it a bare, cold atmosphere. In the middle of the chamber a man sat at a small table reading some ancient grimoire, carefully licking his fingers before turning the pages.

The man paid me no heed at all, so I had leisure to study him. He was of average height, slender and with hair the colour of spun gold falling to his shoulders. His eyes were remarkable, like a pair of green sapphires, and he was dressed all in black.

At last the man seemed to notice me and closed his book with a yawn. "Here you are, then," he said in a bored voice, "and I suppose you must be made welcome. Take a seat, Sir Kay."

He made a gesture, and a chair appeared on the opposite side of the table. Trying not to shiver, for I knew myself in the presence of a very powerful fairy indeed, I bowed and sat down.

"Now," he said, "there is this business of your comrade, Sir Gawaine, to be settled. I don't begrudge him killing the lady of the tower, for she was an enemy of mine and an irritating creature, but I can't allow humans to get into the habit of murdering my folk. After all, where would it end? I'm afraid he really must be punished."

I cleared my throat. "If it please you, sir," I said nervously, "may I ask your name?"

He looked at me in surprise. "I should have thought that was obvious. My name is Oberon."

Oberon, the King of the Fair Folk. I swallowed and tried to keep my voice calm. "I am happy to meet Your Majesty. On the matter of Sir Gawaine, I wonder if there might be some way I could persuade you to be merciful? I am happy to undergo any test or challenge on his behalf."

He studied me, and a slow smile crawled across his face. "Sir Kay, do not be rash," he said, chuckling, "you may be among the most loyal of your King's knights, but you are hardly the strongest. Even the great Lancelot would struggle against some of my champions."

"Nevertheless, I cannot abandon Gawaine."

"I only mean to keep him imprisoned for a couple of centuries, just long enough to teach him a lesson...no? Oh, very well."

He thought for a moment, tapping the side of his cheek with one long finger. Then he waved his hands over the table. A chessboard appeared, the like of which I had never seen, carved out of a single piece of ivory with the pieces wrought in precious stone.

"A game of chess to decide his fate," said Oberon, and now his thin face had adopted the sly look that all fairies wore when they thought they were being cunning.

Merlin's voice echoed down the years in my mind. "Remember, for such a powerful and clever race, the Fair Folk are strangely incapable of subtlety. They suffer from the sin of pride, and see no value in hiding their feelings."

I studied the board. Oberon had chosen black, and all his pieces were carved of shining ebony. The knights and pawns were sleek sinister shapes with horned helms and closed visors, and their king an intimidating figure in flowing robes and an oversized seven-pointed crown.

My pieces were made of opalescent pieces of crystal. I picked up one of the knights, and almost dropped it in surprise. The piece was bareheaded and its face was a perfect miniature replica of Sir Lancelot's. I picked up the other knight, and this time the face resembled Sir Tristram.

Fearing the worst, and with Oberon grinning at me, I inspected the White King and Queen. As I suspected, the King had the dragon of Cadwalader emblazoned on his chest, and their faces were perfect replicas of Arthur and Guinevere's.

"You see, Sir Kay, we play for more than just Gawaine," chuckled Oberon, rubbing his hands in glee, "we play for the fate of an entire kingdom. The rules are thus: every time you take one of my pieces, one of my followers dies. If you should take a rook, one of my castles shall fall into ruin. If I should take any of yours — well, I'm sure you can work it out."

So this was the game, and the stakes were higher than I could have imagined. My only hope, England's only hope, was to win the game, but that seemed unlikely. I was a competent chess player from long winter evenings playing against Merlin, but had no doubt that Oberon would be a master.

His grin threatened to split his face in half. "Come, mortal," he said eagerly, "let us play."

I did my best, and in a few minutes had taken one of his pawns. The moment I took the piece off the board I thought I heard a distant scream, far away in the depths of the castle, and Oberon's brow furrowed.

A couple of moves followed, and I had another of his pawns. There was another scream, this time a lot closer, and the sound of a body falling to the ground. Oberon was positively frowning by now.

I noticed that he had only moved his pawns so far. Realising this, he picked up one of his knights, hesitated, and then held the piece up to the light.

"How does this one move?" he asked, looking puzzled, "it does a sort of hop, skip and jump to the right, is that correct?"

For a moment I just gaped at him, and then relief flooded through me. Oberon had barely any clue how to play chess!

Again, I heard Merlin's voice. "Fairies are capricious, lazy creatures. Born with gifts and talents beyond any human, they make little effort to learn anything new, and cannot abide the discipline required for real work and concentration."

Now it was my turn to grin. Within a score of moves I had committed a mass slaughter of his pawns — accompanied by a whole host of screams — and killed a bishop.

"Be still," commanded Oberon as my fingers reached for the knight I intended to slay his rook. They froze in mid-air, and my entire body went as rigid as a statue. I could neither move nor speak.

I thought Oberon meant to kill me, but instead a book appeared on the table next to the board. It was a dusty, leather-bound tome, red plush flaking from its spine, and on the cover it bore the title 'THE ART OF CHESS' in faded gold lettering.

Oberon licked his index finger and began leafing through the yellowed, crackling pages, frowning irritably as he turned the pages faster, too fast for any human eye to absorb the tiny, cramped handwriting and complex diagrams of chess boards and tactics.

"How very tedious," he said at last, snapping his fingers. The book disappeared, and at the same time I regained the use of my body.

"You can make your move now," Oberon smirked, "I have digested the art of this game from the masters, and am now an expert."

Well, he wasn't that, but his game had certainly improved. Within a few minutes three of my pawns had joined the casualty list, though thankfully without any accompanying screams.

"Don't fret," said Oberon as he plucked the third pawn from the board, "no humans will die for rubbish such as this. I'm not interested in the fate of pawns."

He gave me a knowing look, and an icy stab of fear passed under my ribs. "What of my other pieces?" I asked, trying in vain to read any sign of intent or feeling in those green fairy eyes. I may as well have looked for compassion in a cat.

"Play on, Sir Kay," he replied, and so we did.

Half an hour later, and I was still the better player, but had to work for my advantage. All his remaining pieces had been pushed back into a defensive pattern in a corner of the board, and I had my eyes on snatching his Queen. I hunted her across the board, but she kept evading me, until at last I had her trapped. She had taken cover behind a wall of pawns, and to get to her would mean sacrificing a knight.

I hesitated, and Oberon's eyes bored into me. "Your move, Sir Kay," he said, wearing his most insufferably complacent expression, "how close you are to victory, and rescuing your friend. A hundred years in a fairy prison is not a pleasant experience. Take it from one who knows. When I was a mere Duke, some of my enemies locked me away in the Dolorous Tower for three centuries. Three centuries in a nasty, damp little room with no door or windows. It's a wonder I'm sane."

He was testing my will, I knew that, and for the first time I detected a hint of nervousness in my opponent. His Queen on the board could only represent Oberon's wife Titania. If the stories are to be believed, she was a hot-tempered creature, and unlikely to take kindly to her husband bartering with her life in a game of chess.

Victory was within my grasp, for without his Queen all he had left was a rabble of pawns, a single miserly Bishop, and his King. But to sacrifice my knight meant sacrificing the life of a human knight.

"It has to be someone you know," he said, watching me with avid fascination, "you have to choose from the faces in your memory."

The pleasure in his tone disgusted me. "For Christ's sake," I exclaimed, looking away from the board, but Christ could not help me here. We were in a place apart from Heaven and Hell, the Otherworld, a land that abided by its own rules.

However, if I had to go through with this obscene ritual in order to free Gawaine, then so be it. I chewed my lip, trying to think of a suitable sacrifice, a death that would make the world a better place. The face of Arthur's bastard son Sir Mordred flashed before me — Mordred, that twisted, scheming, coddled streak of villainy, forever conspiring to overthrow his father and take the crown for himself. His death would remove a grave threat to the realm, and disperse the dark clouds slowly gathering over Camelot.

His name caught in my throat. I couldn't do it. Vile as Mordred was, he was also Arthur's heir, his only living son, and in his generous folly Arthur thought he loved him. Mordred's death would break his heart, and I would rather have sacrificed myself than cause my foster-brother pain.

Oberon cackled, and tapped his finger-tips together in mockery of applause. "Human mercy!" he jeered, "what an impractical, useless concept! So you would spare Mordred, eh? I am glad of it. That young man is very much like a fairy in character, and I predict great things for him."

I ignored him, rifling through a mental list of the worst, the most expendable men of my acquaintance (I never considered sacrificing a woman: I am a knight, after all). At last, one man's name sprang ahead of the rest.

"Sir Bruce Sans Pité," I said. Oberon looked at me with dismay.

"Are you certain?" he asked, and now there was a definite wheedling, pleading tone to his voice.

"Yes," I replied confidently, "Sir Bruce is one of the worst knights in the realm, and takes delight in murdering innocents. He breeds especially fast horses, so whenever a true knight comes along to avenge his crimes he always escapes. You may kill him, and hear no objection from me."

"Wait, wait!" cried Oberon in panic-stricken tones as my fingers closed around the head of the knight I intended to sacrifice. "Desist, I beg you!"

"Is something the matter, Your Majesty?" I asked blandly, "the game must be played out. Those are the rules, are they not?"

He looked at me with loathing and, I flatter myself, a touch of admiration. "You are a nasty, vicious creature," he said, "and should have been born a fairy. You really must go away now. Begone!"

He suddenly stood, sweeping his hand across the table and sending the pieces tumbling across the floor. His face twisted in wrath and a spectral seven-pointed crown appeared on his brow. This was the true Oberon, King of the Underworld, and for a moment I thought he meant to destroy me.

King, castle, chessboard and all vanished in the blink of an eye, and I found myself standing in the forest glade. The tower was still there, though now it was a darkened, crumbling ruin, its walls covered in moss and creeping ivy.

There was no sign of the corpse of the knight that Gawaine had killed, and the shields hanging from the trees had vanished. Gawaine himself was lying stretched out on the grass, covered from head to foot in decaying autumn leaves and bits of twig.

I pondered on the most effective way of waking him, and settled for a swift boot to the ribs. "Get up," I barked, "I've risked enough for you today, and I'll not risk dying of old age waiting for you to finish your nap."

His eyes fluttered open and fastened on me. "Kay, man," he whispered, coughing through a mouthful of leaves, "what happened? I had this terrible dream."

For a moment I thought about describing recent events, but gave him another kick instead.

"I'll tell you on the way back to Camelot," I growled, turning away, "where I intend to stay until the roof falls in. Sir Kay is done with Questing!"

DAVID PILLING *is an English writer and researcher, addicted to history for as long as he can remember. He spent much of his childhood dragging his long-suffering parents up and down the misted ruins of castles in Wales, and the medieval period has always held a particular fascination for him.*

His first published novel, Folville's Law, *followed the adventures of Sir John Swale during the dying days of Edward II's catastrophic reign. It was followed by twelve mini-sequels.*

His novel, The Half-Hanged Man, *was told from the perspective of three characters and focused on the mercenary Free Companies that plagued Christendom in the latter half of the 14th century.*

The White Hawk *is a series set during The Wars of the Roses, and chronicle the adventures of the Boltons, a family of minor Staffordshire gentry, as they attempt to survive this particularly bloody period of English history.*

Caesar's Sword *tells the story of Coel ap Amhar, King Arthur's bastard grandson, and his adventures in the glittering, lethal environment of Constantinople and the Late Roman Empire. This was followed by a series of indirect prequels titled* Leader of Battles *that chronicled the story of Arthur himself.*

Recently he published a novella, Reiver, *based on the tales of the Border Reivers in the reign of Elizabeth I, and his first non-fiction work, a textbook on the military campaigns of Edward I. He's also written a series of fantasy novels with co-writer, Martin Bolton. His books are available as ebooks and paperbacks.*

A Song For the New King

BY S. BOYD TAYLOR

Archimandrus was fifty when the commission first came. A poem, a psalm
for the new coronation. Oh how glorious! He had waited so long for
this. Years. Decades. Had pushed away wife and child alike. Locked
himself in dark rooms for months at a time. Writing. Mumbling rhymes
under his breath. Until he fevered from the fire of song. Until his
hands bent like meathooks and could not unbend. Until his fingers were
quillstained with the blood of words.

Two weeks he had. Two weeks to compose his magnum opus. He would forge
a crown of words, a masterpiece unrivaled. Words like gems blazing and
vast inside. Phrases of gold bent into perfect shapes.

He began immediately. Scribbling images and themes on a page. Digging
out old scrolls filled with his notes and scribbles. Sifting them.
Panning them. Turning each word one by one, peering deep into its
flaws. Crossing out the ideas too weak to use.

Only two days later, they were all crossed out. Every inspiration and
insight of the last thirty years. Some were good to be sure, but none
good enough for this. The color was muddy, the luster too dim, or the
gleam too pallid. He tore scrolls in half in a fury and raged across
his room uptilting inkpots until not a single thought still gleamed in
his head. In his skull, once a mine filled with gold and gems, only
dark and barren rock remained.

He retired alone to his garden and sat among the bright-maned flowers there and spoke to them and told them that he was a bounder and a cad and his truest artistry was fraud. For three days he miseried there and peered up at the clouds as if in prayer and hoped the sun would shine down through his pupils and into the shadowed caverns of mind and cast light down a new tunnel that he had overlooked. But the sun refused to peek from behind its mantle of mist.

Then he fell ill. Fevers forge hot. Hammers pounding his skull apart. He woke every night screaming the name of his golden-haired wife, whom he left so many years ago. Remembering the faces of his children with jewel-like eyes. Without his servants and the soup they brought him he would have perished there, seared from the face of the earth by his sins.

When he roused himself at last from his illness it was his fifty-first birthday, and only two days remained. Still aching and still shivering and sweating he sat at his table and his fingers shook as they crawled around the quill. The ink on his fingertips, somehow, had faded. Part of him had faded too.

He began to write then, long continuous lines of song. Passion and fever and perhaps even madness spilling through his eyes onto the pages. Within two hours he was done. He had something. Or the beginnings of something, at least. Something wonderful.

The next morning he set to work again. Shaving each syllable and phoneme over with a gem-cutter's precision. Polishing each shining letter. Pinging dented lines back into place. Twining in the sparest hints of filigree. Forging the gold purer and purer still. Shaping the crown of sound for his king.

He worked this way until noon, when only the last two lines remained. A couplet, a bit strained. Then, exhausted, he lay down for a nap.

When the royal couriers knocked on his door that evening, he did not answer. His servants tried the door, but it was barred. Under orders from the courier, they pounded the door down.

There they found Archimandrus dead in his sleep, wrapped up in blankets three layers deep.

S. BOYD TAYLOR *lives in Dallas where he writes, plays Go, and studies random esoteric subjects. You can find out more about him and his fiction at www.sboydtaylor.com*

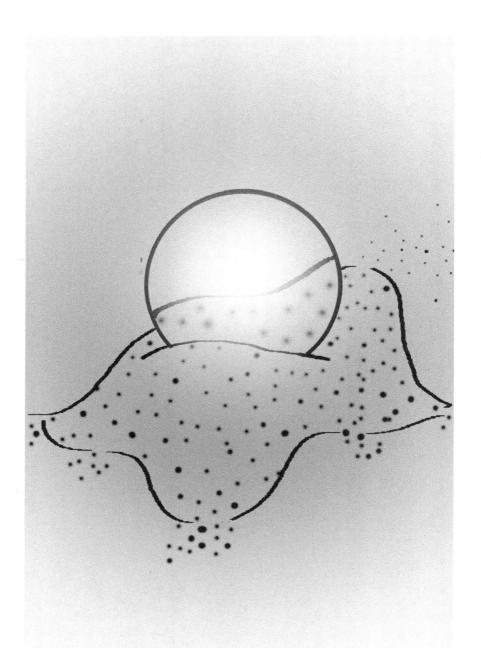

Dusts of War

by Ben Godby

The cart creaked, its wheels full of summer dust, as the peddler pushed it gently up the slope of the road, past the first houses, and onto the main street of the village.

It was late afternoon, nearly dusk, and the sun had a lazy warmth to it. It was the sort of heat that invited the farmers — who left their country plots and visited the village square at the noon hour to trade — to remain longer beneath the shade of the great canopy tree in the very centre of the plaza. They sat on the small lip of stone that surrounded the circle of earth that was home to the tree, sharing bottles of wine. They hardly looked up when the peddler pushed his cart to the tree and thumped the wheels against the ring of stone.

This part of the land was far from the war.

The peddler stopped and pushed back his hood. His head was shaved and his grey eyes were so distant you would think they saw other realms. Those eyes took in the whole village in a great sweep that began at the stables, where the farrier was drinking water in the yard with his wife, to the cool heights of the church steeple where the bells snoozed, to the tavern — in front of which were set tables and chairs that had been deserted in favour of the shade of the great canopy tree. The whole village was taking break, blacksmith chatting with carpenter, mason smoking pipe, women whispering by the gate of the graveyard — which was overgrown.

The peddler slowly bent and opened the cabinets that were set into his cart. It was a little cart, and he removed from these cabinets little treasures: spoons, forks, knives, a teapot, small dishes, and earthenware. All of his wares were old, having the appearance of having drunk the dust of summer many times and never expunged it, but all of them were yet in good repair. Some of the cutlery was silvered. Having taken the things out, he set them on a scrap of green cloth that he laid on the top of the cart, placing the items with the careful, unhurried pace of a child setting table at mealtime.

It was altogether too fine stuff, the peddler thought as he arranged his wares on the cloth. He gazed over the roofs of the village and over the lands that surrounded it, and saw that the only gold here was the wheat, the only rubies the wine, and the only emeralds, beside his cut of cloth, were in the hedgerows. Seeing this, the peddler rubbed gently at some of the spoons, and they tarnished; he prodded the teapot, and a crack grew in its side. He took a jug and shook it, and an odour drifted up from it as though it had not been cleaned in some very long time.

Satisfied, the peddler put his wares back in order. They were far from the war, but some parts of the war came to all parts of the land.

"Pardon me."

The peddler turned away from his cart. A farmer stood behind him, dressed in work-clothes stained roughly brown. There was some white beard on the farmer's chin, and his grey eyes seemed to look right into the other man's soul.

"Some nice things you've got there," said the farmer.

"Thank you," said the peddler. "Would you like to look?"

"Just wondering how long you'll be in town," said the farmer. "If I come back later, will you still be here?"

"Probably only a day or two."

"Glad to hear it," said the farmer. "This town could use you. A merchant, well, can sometimes be a breath of life."

The farmer smiled and took the peddler's hand between both of his. They were surprisingly soft, and he shook the peddler's hand almost womanlike. Then he turned and strode down a back lane and out of the village, up some path that would carry him higher up into the hills — toward the mountains.

The peddler watched him go. Then he slowly unfurled the scrap of paper the farmer had left in his palm and spread it on the emerald covering of his cart.

You will know him, read the note, *when the man in the red cloak speaks with him.*

* * *

The peddler slept beneath the great tree in the square that night, and, on the morrow, decided that he did not need the man in the red cloak to identify his target.

The man the peddler sought came to the square the next morning, at the same time the farmers' daughters came up from the barns with milk, eggs and cheese. Their fathers would be along later, with the meat if there was any to be had — though more likely it would be bread. (The war had not passed through here, but some of the land's better things had passed on toward it.) The peddler watched as a man strode into the square with a beautiful woman on one arm and a young girl hitched up to his shoulder in the other. The wife and child did not fool the peddler, for on this man's hip was a sword. It was not decorated with scrollwork or jewels; its hilt was plain wood and iron, its tabard stiff leather. It was every bit a craftsman's device as the blacksmith's hammer or the farmer's sickle.

But this part of the land had no need for swordcraft. Swords belonged hung on walls, or in the packs of departing first-born sons — or else turned into horseshoes.

The swordsman smiled at the tavernkeep, leaning in his doorway, and spoke to him about wine and fried potatoes. He set his daughter on the ground, and she chased a rooster that strutted around the square. His wife crossed the plaza and spoke to the other women clustered in the shade of the church. The peddler watched and smiled gently as they all glanced in his direction, one by one — not to take in the condition of his wares, he was certain. Then the man with the sword talked to some of the farmers' girls, laughed and flirted, and paid them for eggs and cheese.

His wife re-crossed the square and whispered to him. The man with the sword frowned. The man with the cart carefully polished a spoon.

"Good morning."

He looked up from the spoon. The swordsman was good-looking and rugged, though his clothes were as plain as the villagers'.

"Good morning," said the man with the cart.

"What are you selling?"

"This and that. Would you like to look?"

The man with the sword picked up the teapot and turned it into the light. He set it down and picked up a knife.

"You never know when you will need a good knife," said the peddler.

"But this one is silver," said the man with the sword.

"Only a clever disguise. She is iron at her heart."

The man lifted the knife and let the sun play off it. "How much?"

"I'm sure we can come to an agreement."

A handful of copper coins rolled onto the emerald cloth, a dozen of them, navigating the avenues between trinkets before falling silently.

"What do you say?"

The man with the cart looked at the coins. Simple things. Many common, simple things. No more out of place than the summer dust.

"You are too kind, my lord."

"I am not a lord," the swordsman said, harshly.

"But," said the peddler, his eyes drifting to the weapon at the man's side.

"There is a war."

The man with the cart nodded. He put his hand to his heart and, for a moment, the organ ceased to beat. "I hope it does not come here."

"That is what we all wish," the other replied, drawing himself up and sniffing. His gaze passed across the top of the cart once more, as though to find some artifact he might have missed, and then nodded. "Good day to you. I don't imagine you are staying here long?"

The peddler sighed and looked around the square. "We will see what business I have," he said.

"Little, I expect," said the swordsman. "The people here do not have much."

Sticking the knife in his belt, the man with the sword crossed back to the woman and the child, and, with his cheese and his eggs in brown paper, left the square.

* * *

The morning yawned and afternoon came. The farmers returned as the day proved another warm one. Already they had adjusted to the presence of the man with the cart — if they had ever been disturbed by him at all. The women might talk, and the man with the sword worry, but the farmers and craftsmen knew they had nothing to worry over one man, and so nothing to say about it. Their greatest worry, in fact, which they mulled over as they broke bread over beer, was that no one had brought meat up to the village today, and the tavern's sausages — of which there were few enough left — were not only gamey, but being sold dearly.

The peddler sat in the square and watched every colour. The villagers' clothes were brown, white, black, and green. There was an occasional brilliant flash where precious stones, rinsed clear of rivers or unearthed by the plough, had been turned into jewellery, or where a tattoo had marked a man for some conviction. But there was no red cloak, and so the man with the cart — who had been not just to the lands where the war had not gone, but also to the lands where the war had been bad, and had earned a living with his wares by being careful and patient — waited.

"Are you selling these?"

The man turned to see a young woman had approached his cart. She had picked up a small stack of dishes — little plates, the kind on which a gentlewoman might serve biscuits or sliced fruit — and was sorting through them like cards.

"It is all for sale," said the man with the cart. "That is what I do."

The young woman smiled. She stood out from the farmers' girls and the old women of the churchyard — not because of angelic grace or divine beauty, but for her sense of fashion. Her eyelids were painted green, her lips red, her cheeks powdered silver. A scarf of gentle purple fabric was wrapped around her head.

"What?" the girl said, touching the headscarf self-consciously.

"Nothing," said the peddler, "only I have not seen you here before."

"Well? Aren't you just passing through?"

"I am," said the peddler.

She looked into his gray eyes for a moment. "My name is Keera."

The man with the cart looked back at her, and he knew his momentary silence was heavier than hers. "I am Jarl."

"Pleased to meet you," said Keera. She fiddled with the plates. "So, how much?"

The man that called himself Jarl looked at the plates, then folded his hands. "For you. they are a gift."

Keera shook her head very quickly. "I could not," she said. "They are too beautiful! We don't get things like this, here."

Jarl knew this was not a lie of particulars — the plates were, in fact, unique — but certainly it was untrue that Keera, who was more worldly than the rest of the village combined, could be impressed. She seemed, rather, to be bored. She reached into a purse at her side and placed a large golden coin on the emerald cloth. "How does that suit you?"

Jarl felt his muscles clench — mostly in his shoulders though also his hips and abdomen. He was very careful not to show it: it was good business sense not to reveal too much of one's emotions, even aside from the additional importance it held for his particular profession.

"I did not expect gold coins." He looked up at Keera. "Here."

Keera shrugged. "I am only visiting, also."

"Oh?" said Jarl. "From where?"

"The city is my home," said Keera. "But, my man — he has business here. It suits him for me to rent a lodging here, and he gives me money enough to live by."

"He does not stay here with you, in the village?"

"No. He is a traveller, too. You would have much in common, I think. But he is coming home tonight."

"You must be glad."

"I am."

Jarl picked up the coin and rubbed it between his thumb and forefinger. "And what does he do, your man?"

"A trader." She laughed. "Didn't I say?"

Jarl nodded. The gold was good. It did not belong here, though. It belonged in this sleepy place like a sword plunged to the hilt in a man's guts.

"Your man is lucky to have someone that loves him so," said Jarl.

"No," said Keera, "I am the lucky one."

Jarl smiled. Perhaps, he thought. But gold was not a game of luck. One did not spin gold from summer dust.

"It was a pleasure meeting you, Trader Jarl."

"And you, Wanderer Keera."

She smiled again and curtsied, as out of place as the rest of her. Then she slipped away down the road, the plates clutched between both hands.

The man with the cart, who called himself Jarl, played with the gold coin, wondering, until nightfall.

He would know him when the man in the red cloak spoke to him.

* * *

Night came, but the man in the red cloak did not; and the man with the sword, too, stayed away. The peddler tidied those of his wares that remained, watched the sun bleed away on the horizon, and then climbed the slope of soil to the base of the great canopy tree.

It was a very old tree. Surely it had seen more than any man. But its many knots and tough bark told the same story that did the knots and tough bark of men: the tree had seen enough. It was content to give shade, to confine itself to the rim of stone and the soil below, and to dwell in the village forever.

The man who called himself Jarl sat with his back against the tree and drew his cloak about himself. The cloak was the same gray as his eyes, the same gray as steel, and it wrapped him up with the same vacant distance with which he took in the world. Soon, the peddler was not but a lump against the base of the old tree — another of its knots, another lump of flesh cased with bark.

But still he watched.

Darkness crept across the village slowly, crawling down from the mountains and leaching over the valley, following the sun. Jarl wondered if the dark was ever sad, that it could never catch the light. Then night stole over the village entire, and lanterns, candles, and torches were lit in windows and on street corners. The dark had its consolation, then.

The tavern was filling with mirthful noise. Farmers came — most alone, though some with wives or women on their arms. The men from the village also arrived, their works for the day done and squared away — dough rising with a near-inaudible sigh in the bakeshop, nails rustling with fear in their communal bed. From the foot of the great canopy tree, Jarl watched; and, as he suspected, the man with the sword did not come.

A familiar laugh pulled his attention from the door of the tavern. He looked down a side street and saw Keera. She leaned against and laughed with a man who had a narrow face and shining eyes. He was no taller than she, and wore a leather cuirass, and there was a dagger at his belt — two hands long. They strolled up the lane, careless lovers, kissing now and then, and passed the peddler as though he weren't there. They went into the tavern, letting the noise rush out momentarily into the quiet village before it was muffled again by the door.

The peddler felt an itch in his brains. The man with the sword had not come, but another soldier had appeared — and this one dispensed easily with gold. Perhaps he had misjudged the swordsman; perhaps the swordsman was only a ranger, a sheriff left behind the lines to watch for men like Jarl. A reactionary, in short. But it was another sort of man entirely with whom Jarl usually had his dealings.

Still, Jarl waited. He wondered what happened inside the tavern, but he had made a career of frequenting such places no more than was necessary. After all, he had not made a career of drinking, and he had not made a career of carefreeness. He had not made a career of societies, either. Some cares a man had to abandon in the name of good practice, and, in exchange, there were others he had to hold ever more tightly.

The moon came up over the trees that bristled on the mountainside behind him. An owl hooted, though otherwise no animals came close to the village. There were no crows, no wild dogs, no wolves. In another lifetime, thought Jarl, the village might have been peaceful. But far from the war was never far enough.

The peddler's head came up when the door opened again. Keera came out, her head wrapped in the scarf; and the man with the dagger came after her. He kissed her on the lips, and she pressed her hands to his chest.

"You won't be long?"

"Not long at all," the man said. "I'll just finish up with the boys, and I'll be there."

Keera kept her hands on his chest for a moment longer. "I wish business didn't keep you so — "

"Lora," said the man, stopping her.

Jarl leaned forward to listen. The girl with two names leaned forward to kiss her man. Then she turned and, with quickening steps, went down the lane whence, previously, she had come.

The man with the dagger watched her go, fingering the hilt of his long knife. He looked around the village square, his eyes lingering only a moment on the peddler's cart abandoned by the canopy tree. Then he went back inside.

Jarl counted to two hundred, then stood. As his cloak fell back round his shoulders he became a man again, rather just a curious lump of wood. He went to the tavern and opened the door, letting the sounds of celebration wash over him. He looked back over his shoulder once, but he was not fearful of missing the man in the red cloak: such figures always found him.

Jarl was used to empty taverns, but this one was too full. The tables were crowded and so was the bar, and the serving maids had to shout to be let through the crush and wait their tables. It was only unremarkable in that there was no music. Perhaps the players, too, had moved on.

Jarl went to the bar and slid some of the coppers that the swordsman had paid him onto the sticky, polished surface. "A beer, please," he said, and the barman, recognizing him from the square, nodded, smiled, and passed him a mug.

"Do you need a room for the night?" the barman asked. "I have some, over the stables."

Jarl shook his head. "I am used to sleeping in the rough."

The barman grinned. "Been far then, eh?"

"To hell and back," Jarl said, gripping the mug's handle.

The barman nodded, suddenly very solemn. "Far enough, then?" he said quietly.

Jarl stared into his cup. His watery reflection had no contiguity. "Aye," he said, "far enough."

The barman walked to the other end of his counter, already laughing and joking with other customers. The peddler slowly turned, cup — still full — balanced in his hands. His eyes searched the room for Keera's man, Lora's man, but couldn't find him. Jarl frowned. He turned his ears into the tumult of conversation, hunting for the voice, but it was not there. Then, through the screen of noise, he caught the sound of the door hinges squealing. He turned, and saw the man in boiled leather going again through the front door, out and into the dark.

Jarl put down his mug and slipped between the press of people. In a moment he was in the quiet of the street again.

Quiet but for the quick steps of the man leaving the bar behind.

Jarl moved quickly, but the other man could move faster: he knew the twist of the streets that followed the cliffy contours to which the village clung. Jarl's cloak fluttered behind him, making him a sort of greasy smear against the landscape of shuttered houses and darkened shops. His booted feet made no noise, though sometimes he ran. The torches became fewer as Jarl followed the man with the knife and the gold and they descended toward a disused part of town, buildings where once fish and meat were smoked, pies baked, and leathers worked, but abandoned with the coming of the war and the settling of summer's dust.

Up ahead, the man's footsteps suddenly stopped. Jarl pressed himself against the bricks of a little house instinctually. The ground around it was strewn with broken wheel parts. He slipped to the corner and peered around.

There was an intersection between four of the lost houses. The street had been dug up as though to be cobbled, but then filled back in with loose rock and dirt. There were trees, though none so ancient or shade-giving as the one in the village square; a few young saplings pushed through the shells of bricks and beams. Their leaves made a pitter-patter of the moonlight, dappling the earth and gleaming off the figures in the clearing.

There were three: the man with the sword, the man with the knife, and the man in the red cloak.

Jarl held his breath and watched. The three men exchanged words, but the man in the red cloak had his back to Jarl and whoever spoke did so in tones furtive and hushed — too quietly to be interpreted.

It took only a few seconds: the man in the red cloak shook the others' hands, then turned and began walking away. But as he did so he looked directly at Jarl, and, with only the slightest inclination of his head and a little twinge of the lips that veered toward a knowing smile, told the peddler that he'd been seen.

"Good evening," the man whispered, his voice like a corpse's cry carried on a graveyard wind.

And then the man in the red cloak turned down an alley and was gone.

The other two whispered something to each other, and then they, too, disappeared. The man with the knife was obviously taking a different route home than he had taken down to the meeting place, but the man with the sword came toward Jarl, who shrank into the darkness of the abandoned house and let his cloak fall over himself protectively. The swordsman swept past, up the rutted path to the village.

Jarl stayed frozen in that position a moment longer. To whom had the man in the red cloak spoken? It had seemed, to Jarl, to be both. And both men were, from the start, suspicious. Were they in it together, then? A conspiracy?

But the peddler had been told to expect a single target. You will know *him*, had said the scrap of paper, not *them*.

Jarl stepped out of his hiding spot and took a few steps down the alley the red cloak had taken. If he could just ask him — but the alley ended at a pile of disused bricks, adorned with a discarded winch and a rusted pulley for a well that had never been built. The bricks were piled six feet high and made a solid barrier of the end of the culvert. Jarl clambered to their top as quietly as he could.

Beyond, the fields around the village extended for miles, deserted.

Jarl cursed. The man in the red cloak had disappeared.

* * *

They were still celebrating in the tavern when he returned to the square; but Jarl had no time to return for his beer. He swept past the lit windows of the bar and went to his cart, where he crouched. Beneath the trays and cupboards where the knick-knacks and tomfooleries of his disguise had been placed was another cabinet — this one hidden with locks and covers not visible to the eyes. He pressed with his fingers, the tips sinking into the wood, and a door opened gently, causing a drawer to slide out at the base of the rolling cart.

In the drawer lay a piece of green felt, not unlike the one the peddler rolled out on top of his cart to display his wares. But there was only a single item in the lowest drawer: a many-faceted crystal ball.

The peddler picked up the ball between both hands and stroked it carefully. As he drew his fingers across its surface, the many faces seemed to smooth, and the polygonal ball become a true sphere. It was clear as glass and exuded an inner light, though its interior was deeply obscured by thick roils of smoke.

"How many targets are there?" the peddler hissed at the ball. "What is their number?"

The smoke drifted lazily until slowly it parted. Behind it was a sky filled with stars, white-gold, blinking uncertainly across the midnight blue.

"How many?" the man who called himself Jarl whispered again.

Slowly, the lights in the ball began to wink out. Those that were faintest faded first, leaving only the great bodies of light. The number of stars counted backward, down toward nothingness, until only a single remained.

"Who is it?" the peddler demanded. "Which one? Show me his face!"

The ball did not answer, but filled with smoke again — though it took some time for the single remaining star, burning painfully brightly, to be finally smothered behind the grey screen. The shine of the ball faded also, and soon it was nothing but a many-faceted lump of semi-spherical crystal.

"Damn you," the peddler cursed. He threw the ball into the drawer and shut it roughly, listening only half-consciously for the subtle click of the latch.

Jarl stood. Of the townfolk that were not celebrating, the rest were asleep. But — as though his crystal had set a joke on him — two houses in the village were still lit by lights.

He reached under the folds of his cloak and withdrew a wand from his belt. The shaft was obsidian, but the handle was simple oak — as much a craftsman's tool as the blacksmith's hammer or the farmer's sickle.

He would do it carefully. It was one of two; and those odds, in war, were not so bad. The wand shivered in his grasp. There were rubies not only in wine, but sometimes, too, in blood.

"To work, then," the peddler muttered.

* * *

The home of the man with the sword was made of white stone, and the structure swam in the moonlight. It was more beautiful than any of the other homes in town, and larger, also. There was a small patch of earth, bounded by an iron-wrought fence, in the front — a garden. But it was untended, long overgrown with thorn and weeds. There was a pile in the yard, too, wooden crates and barrels. They were empty.

This might be the one, then, Jarl thought hopefully. He might make do with even better odds than he'd figured. Curse the man in the cloak and curse the crystal ball: tools of mysterious men in places yet further from the war, fickle and unreliable and useless as always. No, Jarl was a craftsman, and, one way or another, he would do this job right — just as ever.

Jarl pushed through the gate and into the yard. The gate was rusted and withered — there were no servants to oil it, evidently — but it moved silently beneath the peddler's command. He gripped the wand tightly, and his grey eyes stared no longer at other realms but surely flicked between the ephemera of the real: the doorway, the windows, the darkened garden path. A crack of light spilled forth between the shutters that looked out across the garden.

He crept to the window, but saw the shutters were latched from inside. He could just catch a glimpse of a table and a stove, a candle burning on a mantle above the hearth. A flicker of motion caught his eye, but then he saw it was a mouse, stealing breadcrumbs — or, perhaps, leftover cheese — from the cabinets.

Jarl reached for his belt. There were many purses and bottles there, though none were for sale and none held the coins a man of his peddling profession might make his primary concern. They were for fluids and powders, tinctures, petals, and roots. Jarl grimaced a little, remarking at the little inventory he had left: the war had been long, and supplies were drawing low. But he had enough that he might succeed in this mission. He drew a phial of juice that shone greenly of its own accord, uncorked it, and let a few drops spill between the shutters to land upon the wooden latch. The wood smoked heavily, then silently fell away.

Jarl peeled the shutters open and slipped across the lintel, as silently or more so as when he chased Keera's man through the alleys. His feet touched the floor and the shutters closed gently behind him, the servants of unseen hands.

Only the slightest wavering of the candle's flame indicated that a new body was within the household. It guttered for a moment, then stood straighter, taller, and reached into the air. A puff of black smoke curled from it toward the ceiling.

Jarl straightened.

The kitchen, like the town, was full of summer's precipitates. The big stone oven was dark but exuded the scent of warmth, as though it had been just working or was ready to do the business of cooking whenever it suited its masters. There was a row of wooden cupboards with stone countertops along one wall, and these were immaculate and spotless. A brace of knives were sheathed in a block at the far end, near a basin.

"Daddy?"

Jarl spun, his wand primed and pointing. In the doorway across the room stood a girl.

She was very small. Working from memory, Jarl would have said that she bore no relation to the man with the sword. She was just enough darker than he was, her hair too coarse. So perhaps she was like the sword and the gold: she did not belong here, though the forces of others — whose real goals lay elsewhere — brought her here with them.

But Jarl had not committed the image of the woman (the mother? the wife? or only the disguise?) with the same alacrity. Did this girl possess her skin, her hair, her eyes, her mouth?

The problem, knew Jarl, was that the best disguises were not fake in the least; and so it didn't matter.

But this land was far from the war. When a child died in the village, it would be from disease, a broken bone that brought infection, a fall, or — if very unlucky — a wild animal attack. They would not be used to the sights of the battle zones, of children blackened and burned, of grinning skulls without faces.

Without saying anything, Jarl reached into a pouch at his belt and took a pinch of powder in his fingers. His hand snapped out and the granules flew across the room, slowly, dancing iridescently in the light of the candle — guttering once more.

He watched the powder fly, and regretted what must be done. He regretted that this place might have been peaceful — a place to live in a lull between histories, distant from the war, surrounded only by summer dusts. But the war spread its ashes far; when war was, it was never so very distant and now, the man who called himself Jarl was here.

The girl started back as the powder struck her. It stuck to her hands and face, to the nightgown that she wore. It stuck to the stuffed doll in her arms, stayed stuck to the doll as it dropped to the ground and bounced noiselessly from the tiled floor.

She reached up and touched her face, her nose, her throat. Her eyes were wide.

It is the most painless way to die, Jarl told the child silently. *And when you awaken, it will be to another life. One without any suffering. Without any pain at all.*

There must be some world, thought Jarl, where such things were true. Or, at least, he had committed these phrases to his mind so frequently that, now, he believed in them.

The girl hit the floor with a thump. Her body was harder, more real than the doll. But, lying beside it silently, her face as still as her toy's, it might be as though that she wasn't.

"Ah!"

Later, Jarl would wonder whether the scream was one of anguish or merely a battle cry. The answer would be imperative to his interpretation of the situation, of the mission; but there was no time to clarify it, no time to think, because the man — the man with the sword — flew through the doorway, over the corpse of the girl, and bowled into him, sending Jarl crashing against the cabinets with the force of his furious charge.

Jarl's head cracked against the wood and the force rang in his ears. He spun his head round and saw the long gleam of candlelight off the edge of the sword, raised high in the air. Jarl rolled to the side and the swordsman grunted as his metal smashed into the floor. The swordsman raised the weapon again and drew it back as Jarl fled to the far side of the room.

"You bastard," the man swore.

Jarl did not hear the curse, nor did he see the man's tear-stricken face. His heart was too heavy with the fact, the undeniable evidence, of the man's incompetence with the blade: how it drooped, how the balance was off, how he stood like no man who'd ever stood in a line of battle, nor like a one who'd fought duels. Jarl's spirit sank with this man's incompetence, and the weight that causes have over their effects.

But Jarl had not made a life as a philosopher. He flicked out his wrist, the wand already hot in his hands. A bolt of fire — red flames nearly liquid — jetted forth and flew across the kitchen. The swordsman ducked and the bolt went overhead, smashing the shutters open and leaving scorch marks across their boards.

The man charged again, screaming.

Jarl knocked the sword aside with a brush of his arm; his cloak was more than strong enough to resist the workmanlike steel. But he could not resist the force of the man's bluster, and he stumbled backward through the doorway, tripped over the corpse of the child, and fell into another room.

The steel flashed again as the soldier stabbed it forward, but Jarl rolled again to avoid it. Another scream filled the house: the woman, this time. She stood at the base of a stairwell, a lamp in her hand casting oily beams across a divan, a bookcase, a short table, and a body.

Jarl pointed his wand and fired before he could think. The bolt struck the woman in the chest and consumed her. Her shriek disappeared in the crackle of flames as her whole body lit like a torch, and she stumbled madly around the room, battering herself against the walls as though that might save her.

The sword came down again and chopped Jarl across the back, but his cloak resisted it once again. The force of the blow drove him forward rudely, but he caught himself, stood and turned. The woman, still flaming terribly, struck a bank of curtains, and they burst into flame, curdling blue and yellow to the ceiling.

"Fucking wizard!" the swordsman screamed.

"Kill me, then," said Jarl, peeling apart his cloak and hurling it the floor.

The man roared again and charged, but Jarl was ready this time. He kicked the low table by his legs and threw it in the pretend-soldier's path. The man grunted and fell, but Jarl caught him as he flew toward the floor. While he was still in the air, he grabbed him by the hand and the shoulder, twisting his hand back so the blade gripped in its fingers tilted back, then cut cleanly through his throat and out the back of his head near the base of the skull. The swordsman fell over on the floor, blood rapidly soaking the rug.

The killing done, Jarl looked around. Already the ceiling beams were aflame: the dust of summer came with dryness. The woman lay, a charred heap at the base of the stairs. The bookcase was smouldering. Jarl looked at the wand in his hand: it, too, showed signs of burning, and soot and blisters had appeared on his hands. The war took life out of everything — even its own weapons, its own agents.

Jarl rushed to the small library and began flinging tomes to the ground, his eyes flicking across titles and tearing open spines — looking for a clue, any clue. But there was nothing but fairy tales and ancient histories, books full of drawings of butterflies and heraldic symbols. He coughed, the smoke fighting to overtake him.

The fire was convenient. But he'd have preferred to choose his own moment to ignite the flames.

He rushed up the stairs. He had to know who the man was — if he was the right man. The bedroom at the top of the stairs was simple and unadorned: no extra weapons, no suspicious notes, not even a writing table on which to produce them. Jarl tore open the drawers, looking for gold — the telltale mark of the mercenary trade. But there were was nought but a few silvers and some more brass and copper change.

The peddler swore. Whoever the man was — for there was no doubt he was someone — he had done his best to cover his tracks. Or had he been a lackey — and Keera's man the real target, the real threat? His presence at the congress with the man in the red cloak just an accident, one of the unexpected circumstances that arises in the business of war?

Or maybe...maybe he was a lackey of the man in the red cloak.

It did not bear thinking about too much. One in two, that was better than you'd get on a battlefield. And there were some cares a man had to abandon in the name of good practice — even if the only exchange was that there were other cares he had to hold on to ever more tightly.

Jarl hurried down the stairs and returned to the man. Carefully, he pulled the sword out of his throat. It would have to look like an accident, even if his head was nearly severed; only so many could die on one night of violence. He leaned it against the wall in the kitchen, grabbed his cloak, and looked once more at the body of the girl.

Then he fled.

* * *

Keera's man had put her in a small house at the periphery of the village, at the end of a track that led up a slope of scree toward a scuff of higher hill. The cabin's windows exuded a soft ruddy light, but Jarl heard them — Keera, Lora, and her man — before he could look in.

He stood under the shadows of an old pine, his cloak making him just a lump of rock or forest-flesh in the night. The shutters of the little cabin were thrown open, and the man and woman inside shone slickly with sweat in the light of the candles burning about the room, sliding up and down one another with the same enthusiasm, the same mindless concentration, of a battle.

The woman with two names moaned.

Jarl threw back his cloak, man again, and kicked the door open with his foot. Splinters of wood flew like missiles across the room. The cabin was but a single chamber, and at the sound of the door exploding the man with the knife jumped off of the bed and turned, still hard and wet with passion. His face and body were suffused with the heat of it, but he was no amateur: naked, he scrambled for his weapon.

Jarl grimaced and aimed his wand.

"Jarl!" Keera said, her voice surprised rather than frightened.

And then the fire jetted.

It swept around Keera's man, wrapping him up like the arms and legs of a woman. He screamed and dropped to the ground, his dagger still sheathed on the bedside table. Keera screamed with him, covering her mouth with her hands as she pulled herself backward on the bed, desperate to get away from the fire; and Jarl, too, screamed as he stalked forward, punishing the man further, watching the flames curdle him black, flake his skin away in ashy chunks, drain his voice to a puddle of sizzling blood. Jarl only stopped when his own pain, the pain in his hand, became too much: the wand shot through the core with arcane energies now spilling its heat back onto its bearer. Jarl stared at his scalded hand, but all he could see was the little girl, dying painlessly in the house of the other man.

When he looked back, Keera's man was nothing but a sticky pool of ruin.

Keera kept screaming until Jarl smashed her face with his free hand. She flew back, dripped down the wall, and blinked spastically.

"What did he do?" the peddler shouted. "What was his business here?"

Keera's face was streaked with tears, her eyes watery, her mouth contorted with horror and with blood.

"A trader! A trader!" she screamed.

Jarl raised his wand. "A trader? Are you telling me the truth? *Lora?*"

The girl raised her hands as if she might ward off his assault, then unleashed an anguished gasp. "I don't know!" she sobbed. "I don't know! He told me not to use my real name!"

Jarl tore open the drawers, rifled through the man's clothes. There was more gold, the knife, but nothing else.

"What did he do?" Jarl said again, turning. "Who did he work for?"

"I don't know," the girl wept. Finally, she raised her eyes. "You're one of *them*, aren't you?"

Jarl ignored her. He reached into his belt and drew a small ring, then walked to where the naked woman flinched and curled, terrified, in the corner.

"Here," he said softly, taking her hand. She howled and thrashed, punching his face with her free elbow, but Jarl gritted his teeth, pushed her middle finger back so it broke with a sickly snap, and slipped the ring on the waggling finger. Her eyes rolled back in her head. Asleep, she slumped in his arms, and Jarl let her down softly.

He sat on the bed. Despite the reek of charred flesh, the air was still full of the smell of fucking, and Jarl felt a repulsive jealousy of the immolated man. He thought he smelled oil, too — the kind a man draws across his blade to keep it quick in the leather. That made him feel slightly better, but not enough. He looked at the puddle of wasted flesh on the ground. The man must've traded weapons, Jarl told himself. Had he sold them to the man with the sword? Or had they worked in concert?

In the town below, screams and shouts were raised up. Flames danced along the lower cliffs of the mountains. The man with the sword, and his entire family — if that is, truly, who they were — would soon resemble the man with the dagger.

Jarl looked back at the girl and drew a phial from his belt: a glowing, green phial. It would make a living being fall apart just as much as a wooden sash.

But he couldn't kill her. He didn't even know if he should've killed her man. One for two was the odds, and it wasn't his place to ask questions: he was not a soldier. He was a peddler. And that meant he had wares to sell — specific wares, at a specific price. One death had been bought, and he'd already crafted four.

Perhaps it was only sentimentality. Perhaps it was only the smell of sex and her nakedness. But he drew another phial, this one lightning blue. He went to the girl with two names and carefully poured a few drops down her throat.

At the cold splash of the fluid, the woman stirred. She had said that she didn't know. When she awoke, it would absolutely be the truth — and the ring on her finger would be a mystery of some mist-shrouded evening never to be remembered.

* * *

The cart creaked and its wheels clattered over the cobbles. Night had already fallen, but the town was lit by thousands of torches and there were men everywhere — men laughing, drinking, fighting and swearing in the red, pulsing light.

They were soldiers, sated on blood and war and yet, it seemed, never sated enough. Carts passed through the streets, carrying provisions, stacks of arrows, spear staves and corpses. Women called from street corners, as did beggars and refugees.

This part of the land was close — far too close — to the war. The man with the cart was not even sure whether he was on their side, or his.

The peddler pulled his cart to a stop and pulled his hood back. His head was stubbly and scarred, and his grey eyes were so distant you would think they saw beyond the tragedy of this great city brought low. But they took it all in with one great sweep, and soon their gaze was absolutely rooted, fixed in the present reality — in all of its blood and viscera.

"There's a man looking for a good time."

The peddler turned. The woman who spoke had her breasts hiked up in his face, her clothes as ragged and threadbare as any casualty's — though with design, it seemed, not necessity. Grinning, her face a mask of powders and paints, she grabbed the peddler's hand and drew it up along her inner thigh.

"There's something," she said, still smiling. "You know where to find me, don't you?"

Then she swept into the night, only the small twist of paper that had been fixed to her garter left behind.

The peddler sighed and pushed his cart into an alley. Slowly, carefully, he unfurled the note upon the top of the cart.

You will know him, read the note, *when the man in the red cloak speaks to him.*

162

"Excuse me."

The peddler turned — and froze. The man in the red cloak stood there, at the mouth of the alley. A troop of soldiers hurried past behind him, guffawing, swigging from full bottles of wine.

"Who are you?" the man who called himself Jarl whispered.

The man in the red cloak frowned. "I believe we have a meeting?"

The peddler stared at the note in his hand, but its text was unchanged.

"No, no. Not me!" Jarl hissed. "You're mistaken. I'm the one who's on your side!"

"Ah," said the man in the cloak, shaking his head. "Say no more. I understand." He smiled gently. "Good evening."

He slipped around the corner.

"Wait!" the peddler cried.

He rushed around the corner, but the man in the red cloak was gone. Soldiers moved up and down the streets, their steel flashing gold in the light of torches. Their steel, their gold, one and the same.

"Move on, old man, eh?" laughed one fighter, shoving the peddler. The man who called himself Jarl fell backward and sprawled painfully on the cobblestones. The soldiers laughed and walked on.

The peddler dragged himself back to his cart. He had placed it among the rubbish heaps of the alley, and the stink made him gag. Carefully, he poked and prodded at the hidden cupboard, and, slowly, the secret drawer emerged. He had to ask the crystal ball. Something was gnawing at the back of his head, some words said both now and long ago: *Good evening.* The man in the red cloak had said the same thing to him, that night in the village far from the war. *Good evening.*

Something moved in the alley behind him. Jarl flinched and spun, drawing his wand. But nothing was there except a lump of garbage, a black mountain of waste that faded into the alley's surroundings of squalor. Jarl's wand wavered, and a pitiful spurt of flame lashed out to lick the garbage. Its oily smoke roiled off the surface of the pile, unfazed.

Had he angered them? Were they coming for him? Or was the man in the red cloak just as fallible as was he?

Slowly, Jarl turned back to his cabinets. He picked up the crystal ball, ran his hands over it. "Who is the target?" he hissed. "Who is it, damn you? Show me his face!"

The smoke gathered and spread, and it seemed that the glass of the ball thinned — became like gossamer, the merest barrier between this world and the next. The fog parted to reveal a sky filled with stars: white-gold, blinking uncertainly across the midnight blue.

"Who?" Jarl sobbed.

The lights in the sky in the ball began going out. Those that were faintest faded first, leaving only the great bodies of light. The number of stars counted backward, down toward nothingness, until only a single remained.

"Who," whispered Jarl.

The smoke in the ball rolled, and the eternal fog covered up what once had been shown. The ball went dark again, and soon it was not but a lump, a worthless polygon of leaded crystal.

Jarl let the ball fall among the others. Other crystal balls, other wands, other phials; the cart was full of them. They were less numerous now than when he'd begun, but he understood them no better; he had only new scars to show what he'd learned from the weapons, and the only catalogue of faces the divining tools had given here were the masks of the dead that haunted his dreams. He looked over his shoulder, watching the shadows of the alley and shivering. Then he looked back at the ball where it lay, dull and silent, in the drawer, but it was still just the same: just a ball, and one that never showed its true face.

BEN GODBY *writes mysterious thrilling pseudo-scientific weird western adventure fantasy tales. He lives in a house in the woods near four very tall pines.*

Everywhere the Serpent Slain

by James Frederick William Rowe

The thunderous passage of heroic feet
Has crushed under heel
The skulls of serpents

The hills were once alive
With their slithering
But no more
For all are dead

Slain in antiquity
That we might live unmolested
Safe and sheltered
Freed of their threat

But the knife unused
Turns dull in time
And never tried
Its virtue is discarded

As fire tempers steel
So does suffering temper man
And we, untempered
Have become brittle

Thus, I foresee a day
Far off from now, yet near in time
Where from the hills again
The serpents shall descend

And there shall be naught in the way of heroes
To stand against them
To strive against them
To succeed against them

We shall become in that day
As they in our own
Our skulls
Pounded to dust

The Monster
Will be an omen
Of the heroless age

JAMES FREDERICK WILLIAM ROWE *is a Rhysling-nominated poet and author out of Brooklyn, New York. His poetry and prose are known to bridge the gap between the philosophical and the fantastical, with work that can be characterized as "literary" and "speculative"—often at the same time. Since first published in 2010, he has seen three short stories and over sixty of his poems in print internationally, with many featuring in the speculative markets* Big Pulp, Tale of the Talisman, Heroic Fantasy Quarterly, *Andromeda Spaceways, and* Bete Noire. *His works have been described as having a "style that is bold, imaginative, crisp, and refreshingly simple, yet profound." He is especially proud to be a Frequent Contributor to* Songs of Eretz Poetry Review, *where his poetry is featured on a monthly basis, and which has done much to foster his growth into a contemporary, literary poet, drawing abundant inspiration from his thoughts and surroundings, while nevertheless retaining roots in the speculative field.*

He is often found writing his poems on the subway commute to his position as an adjunct professor of philosophy at Baruch College. His website can be found at http://jamesfwrowe.wordpress.com.

Kingdom of Graves
by David Charlton

lague had come to the lands west of the river Elakk, and so Rakhar the Half-Orc came, too. He came to their towns with only his spade slung over his shoulder, taller than any man and uglier than most. His brow was heavy and hung low over dark, sunken eyes, and pointed teeth poked up from his protruding jaw. Even stalwart souls did not linger over his brooding and fierce visage.

It was called the Red Death for it came on in a fever, blistered the skin and cooked the brain. No one knew how it spread, but once the boils and rash began, life was measured in hours. Folk cared for their loved ones as best they could at first, but few recovered, and eventually, lest they become sick too, children abandoned their fathers, and mothers left babes to wail and gush out their life. Most died, sweat slicked and gnashing their broken teeth. As the Red Death swept the countryside, whole villages and towns were wiped out, but the graveyards filled up.

That's where Rakhar came in. He was a gravedigger, and he cared not for the plagues of man, for they did not touch him. When he came to town he had plenty of employment, filling the earth with the bodies of strangers, taking their families' coin and spending it on drink while Death made Her fearful rounds. The gravedigger did not look for trouble, but once, a mob of plague-crazed men had accused him of bringing the Red Death to their town. They soon discovered that Rakhar's stout spade could speed a man to his final rest in more ways than one.

It was raining when he trudged up the muddy path into the village. If it had a name, it soon would not matter: there was a telltale stench in the air, and Rakhar knew his coin purse would soon fill up again. Ramshackle huts lined the roadside, and scrawny dogs rooted in the mud for food. In the doorway of a house, a pair of naked children huddled together against the cold and wet, whimpering; above

171

the lintel of the door was a crimson 'x' painted in lamb's blood, the sign of a plague house. The children's faces were splotchy. They would not be orphans for long. The gravedigger walked on.

In the village square, there was a shrine to the Dead God. Scorched bones lay scattered on a stone table, and bits of burnt animal flesh were steaming in the rain. Gathered around the shrine were a few devotees in threadbare robes, kneeling in the churned ground. The downpour kept them from making a proper offering, but they raised their voices in an atonal dirge.

Of what use a dead god could be, Rakhar did not know, nor did he dwell on the question. He looked around for a tavern, and soon spotted a house with a cluster of grapes painted on its windowless door.

"Stranger," a voice rasped, barely heard over the weird singing of the votaries. Close by the shrine was a pillory, and trapped there, his head and hands poking out from between the two hinged wooden slats was a dwarf. To keep from being strangled, he was forced to stand atop a dead tree stump that had been set on the ground there, though he strained on his tip-toes. Rakhar was going to ignore him, but the dwarf called out to him again, "Ha! You're a halfman, too."

That got his attention. Rakhar trudged across the square and planted his spade in the soft, wet earth by the pillory, regarding the dwarf. The head stuck through the stocks was bald and freckled, and the rain washed into a wiry red beard. Despite his predicament, the dwarf's eyes had a mischievous glint to them as he returned the other's stare.

Rakhar leaned one elbow on the crossbar of his spade and said in his rough voice, "You're not in the best position to be shouting insults, dwarf."

"I meant no insult, stranger," the dwarf explained, stretching as best he could in the stocks. "Halfman is what they name my people in these lands, ignorant sots that they are; but I ken that you have some real Mannish blood watering down that good Orcish vintage in your veins." His face brightened a little. "Unless, of course, you are so offended you feel the need to use that bloody great shovel to lop off my head and put me out of my misery," he said and nodded his head toward the caterwauling worshippers at the Dead God's shrine. "In such case, allow me to impugn your mother's chastity, your father's honor and your own no doubt deviant sexual habits. Please, they've been at that for hours."

"It's a spade," Rakhar said.

The dwarf blinked rainwater out of his eyes. "What's the difference?"

Rakhar's shrug was all the response he bothered to muster.

"Well, it's a fine spade." The dwarf eyed the long, iron-banded tool. "Good oak shaft. Solid, scalloped blade. Would take my head clean off, I'd wager."

In spite of the circumstances, Rakhar found himself amused by the dwarf.

"Why did they put you in here?"

"I dallied with a lass in the lord's woods."

"That seems no crime," Rakhar remarked.

"It was the lord's daughter." The dwarf's lips spread in a smile displaying a sizable gap between teeth. "And no more willing and lusty a lass ever there was. But Lord Varvatos wants no halfman grandchildren. I had to do some fast talking to keep him from taking my stones."

Rakhar gave a noncommittal grunt, pulled his spade from the ground, and made as if to walk away.

"Hold a moment, stranger," the dwarf called after him. Rakhar paused, but did not turn back. "As I seemed doomed to suffer the discomfort of the stocks until dawn, and there's no telling how long these shrill fools intend to keep it up," this last the dwarf directed toward the shrine of the Dead God. "And since you seem unwilling to strike me down, how about a swig from that wineskin on your belt? A kindness from one halfman to another."

Rakhar fixed the dwarf with a long, steady look. "What is your name, dwarf?"

"Iolo," said the dwarf, his gap-toothed smile returning. "Called Ironarm, by friends and foes alike."

Pulling the wineskin from his belt, Rakhar told him, "Iolo Ironarm, if you call me 'halfman' one more time, I really will have your head." He held the mostly empty bladder up to the dwarf's bearded mouth and squeezed. Iolo gulped it down, tilting his head as far back as he could to catch it all. Still, some splashed his lips and beard, and when the wineskin was wrung dry, the dwarf licked around his mouth for the last few drops the rain did not wash away.

"Ah! Good gravedigger! May your root never wither and your blade never dull."

Without waiting for further thanks, Rakhar made for the house with the sign of the grapes on the door and ducked inside, out of the rain.

The tavern, as usual in such times, still did good business, and was not empty. Lean men with tired, pale faces cast wary glances toward him. Rakhar ignored them and made for a table by the glowing firepit; two men sat there playing at knucklebones, but as the half-orc approached, they scurried away. Leaning his spade against the smoke-grimed wall, Rakhar sat, his chair creaking against his over-large frame.

"Ale," he grunted toward the barkeep, and scattered his remaining coins on the tabletop before him. The barkeep, a squint-eyed man with long greasy hair, came over, scooped up the chipped and bent coppers and set a clay mug on the table, sloshing some.

Most watched him from the corner of their eyes, though some were bold enough to stare outright: though he was taller, and walked upright, like a Man, there was no mistaking the newcomer had Orc blood. Rakhar ignored them, and downed his drink in two thirsty gulps. He shoved the empty clay mug away, and called out across the room in his rumbling voice, "Another."

The barkeep had not gone too far, but eyed him with apprehension, keeping his distance. "Can you pay? Looks like your purse is empty."

"It will be full soon enough," Rakhar did not look up. "Another, barkeep. The work I do is best done with drink ."

Perhaps taken aback by such reasonable yet ominous words from such a fearsome stranger, the barkeep snatched up the empty mug and trudged away to refill it.

Rakhar drank in silence, keeping to himself. Around him, the muttering started. It wasn't long before one of them found his voice. "You're that gravedigger, ain't you?"

Rakhar looked up to see a scrawny man with red-rimmed eyes and a dirty beard standing on the other side of the firepit. Rakhar nodded.

"I heard about you. My sister's son lived in Mezzek." The man wiped his eyes, but his jaw was set firmly.

Rakhar took a long pull on his cup, and stared back down at a puddle of spill on the table. "No one lives in Mezzek anymore."

"That's right," the man's tone held an accusation. "Because you buried 'em all."

The room got very quiet. It seemed like everyone was holding their breath, the words of the man with the red-rimmed eyes hanging in the air.

"Would you prefer I left them all to rot, stinking, where they fell?" Rakhar still did not look up.

Men stirred, muttered under their breath at the harsh words.

"Jek, let it lie," a man sitting at a table nearby implored the man with the red-rimmed eyes. But Jek ignored his fellow, his shaking hands clenched into fists now.

"Why ain't you stinkin', gravedigger?" asked Jek, his voice shaking with anger. "They say when you come to town, the Red Death follows you."

With a sigh, Rakhar looked back at the man. "You've got it the wrong way 'round, friend. Yes, death has always been a close companion of mine, and it's always red in the end." He fixed the man with eyes so brown they glowed crimson in the light of the firepit, his lips twisted in a slight snarl. "But only a fool seeks Her out."

Jek could not return that fierce stare for very long. After a moment, his shoulders slumped and he staggered out of the tavern, out into the rain and his private grief.

Some of the tension left the room, and conversation resumed. Rakhar returned to his drink, swirling the dregs around in the bottom of the cup. He called for another, and this time the barkeeper did not question him.

It wasn't long before someone approached again, tentative this time. Rakhar was not surprised to find a woman staring at him, her hands clutched tightly in front of her. She couldn't have seen thirty winters, but her face bore testament to hard years. He looked up at her.

"Please, sir," she began in a quiet voice, thick with emotion. "My husband lies dead at our farm; I fear for the little ones. " She sniffed and seemed like she wanted to say more, but only added, after a moment, "I can pay you."

Rakhar nodded and got to his feet, reaching for his spade. "Lead the way, mother."

* * *

Rakhar buried the farmer, and later he buried his widow and all four of their children. It was not long before the Red Death swept its cloak over the village. Bodies were thrown out of doors by weeping, fearful families, and soon flies and dogs competed for the feasts in the stinking town. Two days after his arrival, Rakhar was hired by Lord Varvatos to bury the dead and was paid handsomely for it.

In the morning, the Half-Orc would load a cart he'd taken from the dead widow's farm with the bodies of those who'd perished the night before, and he would pull it himself across the shuttered and woebegone town, out to the graveyard behind the old smithy, just under the eaves of the lord's wood. In the afternoon, he'd dig the holes and lay the bodies down, each to their own grave; Rakhar always gave them this last dignity. In the evening, he would return to the tavern and drink at that table by the firepit, until he passed out and it was morning and time to collect the newly dead.

It was late on the third day when the rain stopped and the clouds parted to reveal the red orb of the sun hanging low in the sky. There was no one still alive who remembered when that sun burned yellow and wholesome, but songs were sung of those brighter days before the Withering, when the Unkindled Flame still burned in the North. Rakhar's mother sang him a few of those songs, before his father had her put to death.

He was stripped to the waist and in broadcloth breeches, chest deep in a new grave, shoveling dirt out of the hole. His skin, like his father's was thick and jaundiced, and slick with sweat and grime. The body that would rest in this grave lay uncovered on the ground, waiting for its final resting place. It was the last grave he would dig today, and he was tired. His limbs were heavy and his muscles ached. A distant clatter caught his attention, so he climbed out of the earth and squinted up the road. From the small castle that sat on the hill overlooking the town emerged a cortege of wagons and riders. Rakhar tracked them down the dirt road and through the now almost-deserted town and away. Lord Varvatos, no doubt, and what was left of his household, fleeing before the inevitable and ugly end. The Red Death had already claimed the lord's daughter, who lay now only feet from Rakhar, as if asleep. The gravedigger looked down on the body. The girl had been young and very pretty, though her delicate features were now twisted in her final agony. He glanced up into the trees and thought how not long ago she had trysted with that dwarf under those very boughs. He wondered if Iolo Ironarm knew or cared his lusty lass was bound for the worms. Perhaps the dwarf himself had already succumbed, but after that first rainy afternoon, Rakhar had not encountered him again. If he had any sense, he had fled the town, just as Lord Varvatos did now.

Satisfied with his work, Rakhar lifted the dead girl off her bed of rotting leaves and placed her in the ground. He began shoveling the mound of dirt back into the hole, covering her up, and it was just as the sun was setting that he became aware of the sound of horse's hooves again. He wiped sweat from his eyes and looked around, expecting to see more riders from the castle, or perhaps some returning. But the sound came not from the road, and he was greeted with a wholly different sight, one that caused the hairs on his chest and arms to rise.

From out of the sunset across empty fields of long grass they came, five riders on bone-white steeds, taller than Men and clad in tattered robes of the blackest sackcloth. They rode toward the graveyard, straight for him. Their faces were hidden by hoods, but there in the failing light of the day, Rakhar thought of the dread *Lornael*, ancient enemy of the Orc race. In his youth, he'd listened to Orc skalds weaving nightmare images of their long-extinct foemen. An Elder Race, they were, Tenders of the Unkindled Flame, born in the dawntime and as beautiful as the Orcs were dreadful. It was said they all died when the Flame in the North went out. For a certainty, all their cities lay abandoned and toppled into ruin. But, sang the skalds, some few of the *Lornael* had slipped Death's grasp, and had returned to ride their ghost-steeds upon the earth, to hunt the Sons of Orguz as they had in life, not resting until Orckind was wiped from the earth.

Surely these were not spectral slayers, sprung from misty legend into the waking world, but as Rakhar watched them closing the distance, a fear grew in him; spectral slayers or not, the riders bore down on him with increasing speed, and showed no sign of slowing. Did they mean to run him down?

He had no time to think about it further. The spade fell from his hands and he sprinted for the cover of the woods. The naked-limbed trees were a barely-glimpsed blur as he ran, the pounding of horses' hooves growing louder and louder. He plunged deep into the woods, only once risking a look behind him, and what he saw made his blood run cold. The horses reared up at the edge of the woods, their forelegs kicking the air; and though it was not yet winter, icy breath came from their flaring nostrils. The hooded figures dismounted and continued their pursuit. So long were their robes they seemed to glide across the forest floor after their chosen prey. And they were faster than Rakhar, gaining on him, spreading out to flank him, cutting off all avenues of retreat.

Rakhar put his head down and ran. He was faster than typical of one of his size, but he was not fast enough. A glance to the side revealed one of his pursuers had drawn almost even to him. The figure turned its head toward Rakhar, and from the depths of the hood, glinted twin pinpricks of blue light, like reflections on ice.

Lornael.

He was not going to be able to escape them; they were gaining on him too quickly. Icy breath tingled against his neck.

"*It is the end, Son of Orguz,*" came a soft exhalation, and something flashed by him, knocking him slightly off his stride. He stumbled and almost lost his footing, and where it had touched him, his shoulder burned like frost bite. He ignored it and the silky, taunting voice, running as hard as he could, trying to stay even a little ahead of them to buy himself some time. If he could not outrun them, he'd have to fight them. If only he had not left his spade behind.

The next instant he burst into a clearing, where the ground sloped up beneath a rocky mound, making it a natural wall; if he put his back to it, they could only come at him from one direction. It wasn't much, but it was all he had. He made his defensive position and turned, hands poised to rend, his lips curling back from his thick, pointed canines.

They emerged from the trees, five hooded figures in tattered robes, all at least as tall as he, drawn up against him. The blue lights of their eyes burned brightly in the gathering gloom of dusk as one figure set itself apart, gliding forward. The hood fell and long silver hair flowed out from a face so sharp and beautiful it hurt to look upon.

"What do you want from me?" Rakhar spat at her, one hand shading his eyes.

The woman wore a thin silver circlet that bound her long, wispy hair. In answer, she turned to one of the others, and spoke a single, musical word: "*Jaranthasalasar.*"

The *Lornael* she invoked raised his arm and in his hand there manifested a javelin of crackling power. Drawing back his arm, he hurled the bolt at Rakhar. It struck the Half-Orc's upraised left hand, pinning it to the wall of rock behind him.

"*Laelandras,*" hissed the lady of the *Lornael.* Another of her band raised her arm and caught a burning spike of blue power in her hand and sent it, unerringly, to pierce Rakhar's right hand, binding that arm, too, to the wall.

Rakhar groaned and heaved against the nails of weird energy trapping him beneath the slope. His hands were afire with pain, and jolts of agony traveled down his arms, and into his chest.

The lady whispered two more names: "*Neochamanderan. Zaballaxiaster,*" and the remaining two *Lornael* sent their luminous spears of power, one into each of Rakhar's legs. Like a bug on an alchemist's table, the gravedigger was splayed, straining but bound tight.

Only the lady had refrained from hurling a bolt. Now she approached, fixing him with her eyes of chipped ice, hair blowing back from gracefully curved and pointed ears, though the wind seemed to swirl only around her.

"What I want from you, spawn of Daemonium," she answered his question at last, "is for you to die, like all of the treacherous and misbegotten Sons of Orguz." She raised her arm, and gathered from the whirling motes of icy air a spike of sizzling blue power. She was poised to deliver the killing stroke, to drive the shard of energy into Rakhar's heart or brain — but something stopped her.

He was laughing.

It was no half-crazed, panic-laced mirth, but a laugh of genuine irony. It stayed the lady's hand. She regarded him with interest. He had, apparently, surprised her.

"Why do you laugh?"

Through pain-filled eyes, Rakhar turned his gaze upon her countenance, looking as long as he could bear upon her heart-breaking loveliness. "Because, lady, I have beaten you to many of your prey. We share the same desire."

Almost before he had gotten all the words out, the blue shard in her hand slashed across his face. It cut a swath from his brow, over his broken nose and across one cheek, slicing and cauterizing the flesh in the same stroke. Rakhar gritted his teeth against the blow, and the chill that suffused his body already made him swoon now.

"What do you know of the desires of the *Lornael*?" Demanded the lady, her words all but freezing the air between them. "What but the basest desires would drive an Orc?"

"My mother was a human woman," gasped Rakhar, shivering in the preternatural cold. "Captured by Orcs. My father killed her, and when I was strong enough, I killed him. Then I slew every Orc I could find. Even now, where I find them, I slay them."

The lady of the *Lornael* regarded him intently. The spike of power in her right hand did not flicker or fade, but with her other hand she made as if to touch his face. It burned where her pale fingertips brushed his scarred cheek, dark blue fingernails leaving scratches even at this lightest of touches. Her sapphire-colored eyes widened almost imperceptibly and she pulled her hand back.

"This Kinslayer speaks the truth," she said softly. The *Lornael* behind her stirred, and it seemed that some sort of conversation passed between them, but it was swift and sibilant, and soon cut short. However, Rakhar caught another name, spoken with respect bordering on reverence: Amandalainion, they called her.

The Lady Amandalainion held up her blue bolt and it flared, casting shadows across the clearing. "Rakhar Kinslayer, we are not monsters," she declared in a loud, strident voice. "You do the work of the *Lornael*, but the Orc stain must not be allowed to spread. This is our Doom. Thus it falls on you, too!"

The blue shard of energy swept down and then drove upward between his legs, burying itself in his loins. Amandalainion held it there long enough to catch his bulging eyes with hers; there was no comfort in that gaze, but the revulsion with which she'd regarded him was replaced with something like pity. He thrashed, impaled on her power as she withdrew the shard. His last sight before he lost consciousness was of her face, beautiful beyond compare, as she drew up her hood and turned away.

* * *

That face was etched in his brain, burning and freezing him at the same time. It haunted his feverous thoughts, watching with impassive elegance as he faced his father again, within a circle of Orc berserkers, all of them banging the hilts of their curved blades against their shields, marking time with the beating of his heart.

Nagarakh Grimjaw was as big as his half-human son, but like every Orc of pureblood, he stood hunched over, his heavy knuckled hands brushing the ground. Torchlight glinted from canines that had ripped out the throat of more than one pretender to his throne of bones.

"Come at me, milkblood," growled the Orcish chieftain. "I'll add your bones to my chair and tonight I'll feast on your guts."

It had been a bloody and fearsome battle. In the end, father and son had grappled close, Nagarakh's mouth slavering for his son's throat, Rakhar's arms binding his father across his chest and back. The loud crack of the chieftain's twisted spine signaled the end of the fight. All that was left was for Rakhar to stamp his hobnail boot upon his father's neck, to the maddened and guttural yelps of the berserkers. The throne of bones was his, but he would not keep it long. His eyes had scanned the ring of Orc warriors, and there she was, inside the circle, the Lady Amandalainion, watching him with eyes that were like a cool wind after a fire.

He fixed the image of her in his mind, and woke up, still pinned to the rock face. It was full dark now, but the bolts of the *Lornael* in his hands and legs cast an eerie flickering glow onto the night. His whole body thrummed with pain, but worst of all was the cold numbness between his legs. She had done something awful to him, he knew. Taken something. The Orc stain must not be allowed to spread— He thrashed savagely against his bonds, gnashing his teeth. Lances of agony ran up his arms and legs, converging in his bowels and chest. He passed out again.

All that he had ever known of beauty and comfort had been his mother, and sometimes he dreamed of her, as she had been, soft and pale, with long brown hair like wheat, and eyes that lit only for him. Her voice was all the balm that had ever been granted to him. Once, after his half-brothers had branded his arms and back with hot irons, she had rubbed soothing ointment over the scorched and sizzling flesh, and sang to him a lullaby of the homeland she knew she would never see again. It came to him now, echoing in his head:

> *Lush the rivers of Galad flow,*
> *Where tall the trees of elder grow,*
> *O, sing to me of sweet surcease,*
> *As down the stream we slowly row.*

> *The rivers of Galad will keep,*
> *In cool blue grottoes still and deep,*
> *All the tears and fears you hide,*
> *So hush now, dear, and go to sleep.*

The ache that dwelt deep in his chest expanded into his throat. He became gradually aware of a burning thirst, and knew if he could not free himself from the rock wall, he would soon perish. The rivers of Galad flowed only in his fevered hallucinations, tormenting him, but the face that hovered before him now was not that of his mother, but of Lady Amandalainion. Had she come back to release him? The steady, sapphire-eyed gaze softened, the sweet pale lips curving into the suggestion of a smile.

Something like a croak bubbled up from him. Cool water splashed against his mouth, and he drank it, letting it slide down his throat and neck, reviving him. Blinking against the light of the setting sun, he opened his eyes, and the beautiful face of the lady of the *Lornael* that swam before him resolved into the bald pate and gap-toothed grin of a freckled and red-bearded dwarf.

"I never thought to see you again, gravedigger," the dwarf grunted and raised the waterskin back to Rakhar's cracked lips. "Seems our fortunes are reversed since last we met."

The clearing was empty but for them, and the sun bathed it in a warming red light. He had stood, crucified on the rock, for a night and a day. Rakhar gulped down the water the dwarf offered.

When he drank his fill, Rakhar found his voice again, though it was thick and rough. "Get me down."

Iolo Ironarm took a step back, capping his now empty waterskin, one eyebrow cocked in grim amusement. "What sort of sorcerer's mischief is this? Did you get surly with the wrong man, gravedigger?"

"No sorcery." Rakhar strained against the sputtering spikes of power pinning him to the wall. The water had revived him a little. "*Lornael.*"

The dwarf let out a low whistle. "The Lost Kindred? You expect me to believe those fey ghosts were here? That they did this to you?"

"I don't care what you believe," Rakhar snarled, "only help me down. You owe me a debt, dwarf."

"Might be I do," the dwarf said, but made no move except to scratch his bushy beard. "But what good does it do to return a kindness and earn the immortal enmity of phantom Orcslayers?"

"They could have killed me," Rakhar rasped. "I was spared."

"Mayhap they expected you to die, thusly?" The dwarf gestured to the crackling blue bolts. "Of hunger or exposure? Or nibbled to death by forest creatures. Pretty perverse of them, granted, but then you are an Orc. Or Half-Orc, anyway. Not that I ever had a quarrel with the Sons of Orguz," Iolo added hastily, casting a glance behind him, into the trees, lowering his voice. "But nor do I want one with *Lornael.*"

"It was mercy," Rakhar muttered, his eyes drooping, remembering that last look from the Lady Amandalainion. "They spared me. She spared me."

Iolo snorted again. "There are many legends of the Lost Kindred, gravedigger; none of them mention mercy. Especially toward your kind. Still, I might be persuaded to risk helping you — for a price." There was a hard glint of cunning in the dwarf's eye now.

"My coin purse is full. Take it all."

"I don't want your money, gravedigger," the dwarf scoffed, all trace of his former bemusement gone now. "I want to hire you."

Another wave of pain rippled through Rakhar's body, causing his chest and arm muscles to spasm. "Yes, yes, whatever you want," he said through gritted teeth. "Free me!"

Iolo approached, rubbing his thick hands together briskly. Planting his boots firmly on the ground, he reached for the bolt in Rakhar's left leg, and before he could think twice about it, grasped it tightly. A cold so intense that it burned raced up Iolo's arms into his chest, but he braced himself and heaved with all his strength. The bolt flared in his hands, sticking stubbornly at first, but then it gave and slid out. The coldfire flickered and was snuffed, the bolt vanishing completely.

The dwarf shook his hands to get his blood flowing again. "They don't call me Ironarm for nothing," he told Rakhar with a confident grin. But Rakhar was too distracted to pay him mind; there was no blood where the bolt had been, no wound at all it seemed. Just the pain of feeling returning to his leg.

After several minutes, the dwarf had the rest of the coldfire bolts out, and Rakhar slumped, weak-limbed to the ground. He was alive. She had spared him. But he was not whole. He clutched at his groin, where her knife had pierced him, and he groaned.

The dwarf squatted by him, giving him an appraising look. Rakhar watched him through heavy eyes, gratitude warring with suspicion for the dwarf.

"What do you want of me, Iolo Ironarm?" he muttered warily.

The dwarf clapped a big hand on Rakhar's shoulder and his lips parted to reveal that space between his front teeth that gave him such a wolfish smile. "What else, gravedigger? I want you to help me bury somebody."

* * *

Lord Varvatos whipped his horse to greater speed, glancing behind him as if he expected to see the Red Death personified nipping at his heels. It had been two days since he had fled his castle, and the sickness that carried away his slut of a daughter and most of his wretched village had caught up to him; last night, as his household train rested by the Elakk River, his wife vomited blood and collapsed. While his sons had rushed to comfort her, he had backed away in horror, holding the edge of his cloak up to his mouth and nose.

He could find another wife. He could make more children.

Not waiting for his horse to be saddled, he had ridden bareback from the camp, past the startled men-at-arms who were already scratching at splotchy rashes on their necks and arms. Nor did he stop when the sun went down, urging his mount faster and further. If he did not rest, he could reach the lightning-struck tower by dawn.

In his prime, Varvatos had been a man other men feared. Broad of shoulder with a mane of wild black hair, he had driven away the brigands and reavers who had ruled the lawless towns west of the river, claiming lordship as his prize. But though his breadth turned to girth and his mane to grey, the fire of his ambition did not die. Richer towns had escaped his grasp, including that jewel of the lands watered by the river, Lakkia, fat with merchants rich off the crossroads trade. The damned merchant-princes hoarded their wealth, spurning Varvatos' offers of protection and guarding well against the day when it might come to a test of arms.

But Varvatos had grown more cunning than the youth who had in years past carved himself a demesne with sword and axe, and what he could not take with steel, he would win with sorcery. Whispers had come to him that weird lights had been seen from the parapet of a ruined tower on a blasted heath, and that gibbering voices could be heard coming from it from miles away. It was said, his poor doomed wife had reminded him, that they who crawled into bed with sorcerers awake twined with serpents. Varvatos rode to the tower anyway, and there he met Xalbulba.

Foam flecked the mouth of his horse and a sheen of blood glistened down its flanks from his spurs. Ridden past endurance, the beast's heart burst and it fell, throwing its rider. Varvatos hit the ground with a jarring jolt, rolling into a tree hard enough to make him cry out. No matter, he thought, I am here.

Rising before him was a dilapidated tower of ancient stone and crumbling mortar. Vines crawled up the length of the structure, which leaned precariously to one side. The top was blackened, as if burned by fire or lightning, and whole sections of wall were gaping open, making it seem a rotting skeleton of a once-hale body. The whole thing was enclosed by a grove of dead trees and brambles, so thick together as to make entrance impossible. This grim, enchanted grove, the necromancer had told him, would admit entrance to no man.

"Necromancer!" Varvatos called up to the top of the ruined tower. "Damn you, Xalbulba, let me in!"

His cry stirred a flock of birds from some nearby treetops, but otherwise it merely echoed off the old stones of the tower. No lights could be seen glowing through the windows and holes; all was still.

Varvatos was drawing breath to yell again when the wall of trees and thorn bushes surrounding the tower rustled. The curling stems of the brambles twisted and moved, the trees themselves shifting in such subtle ways that movement was difficult to detect in the dappled light of the day, but after a moment, a path was cleared and a figure in a scarlet robe could be seen emerging from the tower gate. The sight of the necromancer always disconcerted Varvatos, for Xalbulba had no arms and a weird, loping gait, so that when he moved he swayed from side to side, like the serpent of his wife's warnings.

Varvatos found his hand going to the hilt of the sword buckled to his waist.

The necromancer stopped at the edge of the dead grove, his body arched slightly to one side, his head cocked to the other. Wispy white hair wreathed his head and wrinkles lined a cruel, sybaritic face. His eyes were clouded with rheum, but on his forehead was painted a third eye, and it was that eye that Varvatos felt was watching him now.

"I had not thought to see you again so soon, Varvatos," the necromancer said in a quavering voice through thick lips. A line of drool trailed down his bony chin. "Has our bargain not proved" — his jaw worked, as if searching his mouth for the words — "advantageous?"

"It has not!" said Varvatos, taking a step toward the necromancer. "You told me the Red Death would kill only my rivals in Lakkia, Trant and Mezzek. Instead it has swept from town to town, laying waste to all who live. How can I consolidate my rule when all my warriors bleed out in their beds? Shall I rule over a kingdom of graves?" His voice shook as he spoke, and before he realized it, he had drawn his sword, brandishing it at his wayward ally.

Xalbulba made a low, thoughtful sound, and swayed so that he leaned to the other side; he seemed unconcerned by the naked steel before him, and sneered. "The magicks you called for sometimes have a will of their own, hmmm? Have I not fulfilled my end of the bargain? Are your enemies not dead?"

Varvatos gnashed his teeth. He gripped his sword so tightly it trembled in his grasp. He closed the distance to the necromancer, spitting into his face. "Everyone is dead, damn you! What good is lordship if you have no one to lord over! I only just escaped it, myself!"

"No, you didn't."

Xalbulba exhaled a stream of noxious breath. Startled, Varvatos flinched back, but too late: red-tinged breath continued to stream from the necromancer's open mouth, filling the air between them, getting in Varvatos' mouth and nose. Varvatos stumbled backward, sword falling from suddenly nerveless fingers. He clawed at his throat, pulling his collar down to no avail. His eyes rolled up into his head and he fell to the ground, his heels kicking in the dead leaves. Blood gushed from his mouth and then he was still.

The necromancer loomed over the body, peering curiously down at it. Varvatos had played his part well. He had seen that the brass oil lamp bearing the Red Death spell had been delivered to the guildhall of the merchant-princes in Lakkia. From there, the plague had spread further even than Xalbulba had dared hope. Thousands had died. And now his time had come.

Ravens cawed, took flight, and the necromancer cocked his head, staring into the sky with his Third Eye. He saw leagues distant, into towns silent as death, villages empty of any living soul. He directed his vision to the rotting bodies in the street, to the freshly-dug graves of Varvatos' so-named kingdom. Rats and maggots reigned. The necromancer's Third Eye fixed on one giant rat, gnawing at a loop of guts spilled from a corpse left unburied in a forgotten street in Lakkia. The dead man twitched and snatched up the rat. It squealed as it was squeezed into pulp and chunks in a pitiless grasp. The corpse got to its feet, joining others like him in the streets of the dead city, as they made their slow way, as one, heeding their master's call.

Thousands had died. Thousands would rise. Xalbulba had his army.

* * *

"This is it, then." Iolo Ironarm picked his way through the lifeless camp, stepping over the body of a man-at-arms who simply lay where he had fallen still clutching his spear. "Looks like the plague got them after all."

Rakhar stood by the embers of the smoldering cookfire, taking in a scene he had encountered too often in recent days: unattended horses were tied up nearby, and corpses left to rot out in the open. There were a few tents, the wind having torn up a post or two, leaving the cloth to flutter, adding to the forlorn sense of abandonment. There was a steady buzz of flies in the air.

The dwarf ducked into the largest tent, one bearing the batwing sigil of Lord Varvatos. Rakhar hoped this ended it. For three days they had tracked the runaway lord's procession, the dwarf intent on his revenge.

"I can live with what he did to me, and call accounts settled," Iolo had told him soon after he had taken Rakhar down from the rock. "But he beat poor Varla," he had said, his face growing clouded. "Whipped his own daughter, and turned her out. It's no wonder she got the plague. Ruined the sweetest ass I ever had." He had paused for a wistful sigh, then his expression had darkened again. "A man like that needs killing." And Rakhar could not disagree.

Despite the dwarf's tendency to chatter, or sing bawdy tunes, when Rakhar was especially laconic he had proven a good enough traveling companion, quick to share his meat and drink. The dwarf had even retrieved Rakhar's spade for him while the Half-Orc recuperated from his ordeal. Rakhar would bear scars on his face, hands and legs, but he was otherwise intact, even his manhood, for which he had feared. Yet he felt different. Marked, somehow. And he could not get the image of her face out of his head.

"He's not here." The dwarf emerged from the tent with a puzzled expression on his bluff face. "Some woman who's probably his wife, and two boys, his sons, maybe. But that black-hearted bastard isn't in there. No doubt he abandoned them all at the first sign of the plague."

"There's a horse missing," Rakhar said.

"How do you know that?"

"There's an extra saddle and bridle with the wagons." Rakhar nodded back to where the horses munched on some grass. "He must have left in a hurry."

A slow, satisfied smile appeared on the dwarf's face. "Seems you're still under contract, then, gravedigger. Let's go find the tracks."

Absorbed in his thoughts of vengeance, the dwarf did not notice the figure that shuffled out of the tent behind him. It must have been Lord Varvatos' wife, for it was dressed in fine clothes, but its skin was tinged with a greenish pallor, and worms crawled from its nose and mouth; its eyes were filled with blood, and its hands reached hungrily for the dwarf.

Alerted either by instinct or the stunned expression on his companion's face, Iolo spun around in time to grab the dead woman's hands just before they closed around his neck. It bore down on him with a strange vitality it surely had not possessed in life, its mouth gaping wide to bite or suck at him. Perhaps a hand taller but weighing half as much, it nevertheless drove the dwarf to his knees, its teeth snapping close to his face.

Rakhar swept in with his spade, delivering a ringing blow to its head that all but crushed the skull. It dropped, but two more figures crawled out of the tent, the boys, apparently, and just as dead as their mother had been.

"Beards of the Saltfathers!" Iolo gasped as Rakhar pulled him away. "What the High Hell is going on?"

The two boys crawled over the wreckage of their mother's corpse, arms outstretched for the companions. They weren't moving especially fast, but Rakhar's thrusting spade did not deter them at all.

Iolo swore, some hysteria creeping into his voice. "There's more."

All around the camp, bodies were stirring and picking themselves off the ground or stumbling out of tents; all of them had the same sickly green cast, and all of them — despite their animation — were undeniably still dead. Flies swirled around them, and maggots continued to eat their flesh, but they sniffed the air and turned, unerringly, toward the only two living beings in the camp.

"Undead," Iolo said in a voice he managed to keep steady. He reached behind his back, under his cloak and withdrew the massive double-ended warhammer he kept slung there. "I've come across them before, in the spellsinks of Cthona. Bash their brains in, only way to stop 'em. And don't let 'em bite you!" With a loud cry, the dwarf charged the closest knot of the undead, swinging his hammer and scattering them.

Rakhar spared him only a quick look, then a swipe from one of the boys got his attention. Lord Varvatos' oldest son grasped the shaft of the spade, just above the blade and was trying to pull it out of the gravedigger's hands, an exhalation like a hiss coming from its slack-jawed mouth. Instead of pulling back, Rakhar simply shoved forward with an unexpected jab, stabbing the scalloped blade into the boy's face, cracking the bridge of the nose and turning the eyes to jelly. The revenant slid back, off the shaft, but its brother lunged forward. Rakhar met his attack with a slash that opened its throat and caused the head to wobble, barely clinging to the body by shreds of flesh and tendons. The thing lurched at him again, but Rakhar finished the job with a second swing of his spade, the head bouncing back into the tent.

"This is why they call me Ironarm!" the dwarf yelled over to his companion, laying about with his warhammer in all directions, drawing a crowd of the undead to him. Though he stood a full head or more shorter than his foes, he smashed at them with abandon. He caved in chests, which did not stop a revenant, but it certainly kept it from advancing on him, and on the backstroke swung his hammer into another's head, splattering brain and skull across the ground. Sometimes he had to use the strap, whirling the hammer in a winding-up motion, then striking out at a foe with deadly accuracy when it was close enough. He swept out legs, then two-handedly hacked down to drive the spike-end of his warhammer through a head.

"There's more coming," Rakhar called out to him, pointing into the distance. A large crowd of figures were making their way over a hillside, straight for the camp. Rakhar stepped into a heaving slash, sending another head flying. "We can't fight off all of them. We have to go."

Iolo put his boot on the chest of a fallen revenant and plucked his warhammer from the cavity of a dead spearman's eye socket. The camp was all but cleared of the undead, but the respite would not last long. They made a dash for the horses. Iolo had his sturdy hill pony already saddled, but Rakhar did not have a mount yet. He chose the only one still wearing saddle, bit and bridle, and leaped onto its back. The drab-colored beast was spooked by the Half-Orc, reared and would have thrown Rakhar, had he not seized the reins and steadied himself. Rakhar yanked hard and pulled it about, then kicked at its flanks. The horse shot off after Iolo and his pony.

The dwarf looked over his shoulder at Rakhar, and barked a harsh laugh. "Not much of a rider, are you, gravedigger?"

Rakhar shot him a dark look and reflected that he hated horses probably as much as they hated him.

When they were some distance from the camp, they pulled up and came to a momentary halt. The battle fever waning in him, Iolo was sweating and taking deep breaths, his eyes still a little wild. "The undead make my skin crawl." An involuntary shiver ran through him. He eyed the gore-encrusted spade slung over Rakhar's back and shook his head. "That was a nasty little scuffle back there. Next time, you might want to think about wading into it with something a little more deadly than a shovel."

"It's a spade."

"You made the best of it, I'll grant you that, gravedigger. Still, I'd feel better if you had my back with three feet of steel rather than some pitted iron on the end of a stick." The dwarf reached into his saddle bag for a waterskin, took a gulp and tossed it to Rakhar. The Half-Orc did not comment on the slight tremble in his companion's hand, and drank in silence. Talking seemed to steady the dwarf's nerves. "If there are undead, there's a necromancer involved, somewhere. And I'd bet my beard that weasel Varvatos is wrapped up in this somehow, too."

Rakhar threw the waterskin back to Iolo and said, "Look."

The dwarf followed his pointing finger straight ahead, and squinting, saw a mass of people coming toward them. They were not moving very fast, nor did they seem to be particularly orderly, as soldiers would have been. But there were hundreds of them — maybe more — and they were directly in their path.

Iolo cursed. "More of the moldy buggers. They're coming from all directions, looks like. Except east. A thousand of them, maybe more. Looks like all your hard work was for naught, gravedigger. Not many of them are stayin' in the ground."

"There are more dead than alive in these lands," Rakhar muttered. "Since the Red Death came."

The dwarf glanced sharply at the implication. A rank smell blew through, causing their mounts to whinny and paw the ground nervously. The two shared a look of mutual concern, both knowing Rakhar to be right. If indeed those who fell from the Red Death were rising now, the reanimated would outnumber the living. The lands west of the River Elakk would be a haunted kingdom, a nightmare-place.

"We have to get out of here," the dwarf said, glancing at the approaching horde. "The river is our best chance — the undead won't cross it."

Rakhar shook his head, gesturing vaguely toward the distant ribbon of blue in the east. "Neither can we; the Elakk is too wide and swift here. But the nearest ford is not far away, just a few hours ride. Across the Blasted Heath."

"That place has an evil reputation," Iolo muttered. "But it looks like we'll have to take our chances. Come on, gravedigger. Time to quit this woebegone land. Damn my beard, but it galls that Varvatos goes unrewarded for his villainy."

* * *

They rode hard the rest of that day, not daring to stop for even a moment's rest. Though they had outpaced the revenants from the campsite, they soon spotted more groups of them, and in greater numbers. At one point they were forced to ride through a knot of them. They marched in no order, in clumps or by themselves, but as Rakhar and Iolo galloped through their midst, they seemed to try to close ranks, grasping at them as they tried to navigate the labyrinth of bodies. Before they broke clear, they had ridden down many, and once again bloodied their weapons.

"I don't like this," Iolo yelled to Rakhar over the sound of pounding hooves. "These things are supposed to be more or less mindless, but they all seem to be heading in the same direction."

Yes, Rakhar thought darkly. Ours.

As the sun was bleeding its last light across the horizon, the ground become hard-pack and devoid of almost all vegetation, but for some hardy weeds; the few trees or shrubs there were stood out in stark contrast in the dusty grey waste. Rakhar had never traveled through the Blasted Heath, but he knew its reputation as well as Iolo: local folklore told that long ago, a people had lived here that were so obscene, so vile, that their own gods had struck them down, laying waste to the entire kingdom, so that even centuries later it was still uninhabitable. Rakhar didn't know if those legends were true, but the land was strewn with the remains of rock walls and crumbling stone fortifications of a long-forgotten civilization.

"It's going to be too dark, soon, to risk riding." Iolo reined up his pony, Rakhar rearing to a halt beside him. "We're going to need shelter, someplace defensible if those things find us."

Squinting off into the dwindling light, Rakhar spotted beyond a grove of dead trees, a ruined tower, perhaps a mile away.

The dwarf shrugged and flicked his reins, grumbling, "Looks like more shelter than anything else I've seen in this benighted land. And that grove should slow down the udead. Come on, gravedigger; I'll let you have the first watch."

The closer they got to the lightning-struck tower, the more Rakhar did not like the look of it. There was something wrong about the dead trees that stood sentinel around it; their mounts balked at the edge of the grove, refusing to go further.

"Come on, damn you," Iolo said and kicked his pony, but the animal would not budge, yanking his head away from the sight of the grove.

A sudden fluttering of wings erupted close by. Black feathers swirled around them, and Rakhar was forced to throw up an arm to shield his face. The air around them was filled with ravens, all of them circling and crowding the dwarf and the half-orc.

"Halfmen!" came the intelligible cry of a bird, in a voice pitched like no human's. "Halfmen beat the spell! Xalbulba beware!"

Rakhar and Iolo all but fell from their saddles and rushed into the grove, fleeing the swarm of birds. Almost instantly upon reaching the cover of the trees they left behind the squawking menace. The birds rose into the dusk, cawing out their alarm, even as the horse and pony galloped away in fright.

"What in the High Hell was that?" Iolo demanded, beating dark feathers out of his beard and cloak. Both he and Rakhar were covered in little cuts and scratches from beak and talon. "That bird spoke! He called us Halfmen. Something about a spell?"

The little hairs on the back of Rakhar's neck rose. He hefted his spade, staring through the gloom toward the open portcullis of the tower; something stirred in the darkness there. "Dwarf, that necromancer you mentioned earlier, the one behind the undead? I think we've stumbled onto his holt."

A figure emerged from the tower, approaching them through the trees. He wore good leather boots, and a fine red cloak, bearing a batwing sigil.

Iolo swore almost joyously and brandished his hammer in recognition of the man — it was Lord Varvatos.

But Varvatos was much transformed. His skin was pale, almost translucent, and stretched taut over his bones. His graying dark hair was lanky and framed a face devoid of human expression: the eyes were clouded over and his jaw was slack. In his hand he bore a notched longsword. A stench rose from him that made Iolo gag and take a step back.

"So much for your revenge, dwarf." Rakhar raised his spade and stepped forward. "Someone's already killed him for you. All that's left is to put him in the ground."

Rakhar rushed to engage Lord Varvatos, but the revenant lowered his sword, lips retreating from decaying teeth in a warning hiss. Rakhar held his spade two-handed, eyeing the undead lord closely.

Varvatos stepped aside, and pointed with his sword to the open portcullis. An invitation.

Rakhar and Iolo exchanged glances.

"He has made of me a slave, " said the man who was once Varvatos in a dry exhalation of breath. "A lich-king to lead an army of dead men against Xalbulba's wizardly rivals." The stiff head turned and they followed his gaze through the trees of the grove and across the Heath; hundreds upon hundreds of undead could be seen approaching from every direction, all converging on the tower. "I cannot resist his will much longer; soon, we will all be in his power. Avenge us, halfmen! Quickly!"

Varvatos' body trembled as if he struggled to assert his own will. Rakhar and Iolo needed no further prodding; there was no escape the way they'd come, so they rushed past him, into the tower.

They entered what looked like had once been a guard hall, sparing hardly a glance for anything but the staircase that spiraled up from inside the wall. Rakhar took the steps two at a time, Iolo laboring to keep up with him. Portions of the wall had fallen away, giving them a clear view of the Blasted Heath below as they climbed. By the light of the new-risen moon, they could see the grey wasteland was filled with shambling forms, drawn like moths to the lightning-struck tower.

At last they came to a landing. By the time Iolo climbed the last step, Rakhar had already put shoulder to the iron banded door that barred their way. It rattled but didn't budge.

"Out of the way, gravedigger!" Iolo cried, twisting the haft of his hammer in a two-handed grip. "Let me show you why they call me Ironarm!"

The wood splintered and cracked under his first blow; his second tore the door off its hinges. Rakhar saw the flash of light just in time to tackle the dwarf to the ground. Serpentine trails of lightning crackled out of the opened doorway, scorching the wall behind them, directly in the path where Iolo had been a moment before. The two of them lifted their heads only when the attack had ceased, in time to spy a grotesque figure in red swaying weirdly away. They surged upright and charged through the smashed doorway.

It was an open-aired room at the top of the tower, most of the roof and one large section of wall ripped away in whatever cataclysm that had destroyed the ancient kingdom so long ago. Now it was the necromantic Xalbulba's foul bolt-hole, dead leaves blowing across a floor scrawled with arcane symbols. Torches set in wall sconces lit the night, a rising wind causing the flames to flicker and cast long shadows. The armless necromancer himself stood now in the center of the chamber, hunched over an object on a brass pedestal. It was a smooth-surfaced crystal globe, the size of a man's head, completely opaque, but alive with opalescent colors that throbbed and pulsed from a source deep within. Energies crackled around it, like little worms of light.

Xalbulba lifted his gaze to the intruders, the light of the sphere reflected in his milky eyes; but the painted Third Eye on his forehead exuded malevolence.

"Halfmen," the necromancer chewed the word with profound distaste. "No human man could have penetrated my ensorcelled grove, so they send an orc and a dwarf."

"He's a half-orc," Iolo corrected with what sounded like forced bravado. "But twice the man of any I've ever met. You might try looking in a mirror, sometime, yourself, you red-robed inchworm."

Xalbulba's eyebrows shot up, but it was the Third Eye that tracked Iolo as he moved to the right, then back to Rakhar as he edged to the left.

"Very soon you both will be just two more soldiers in my undead horde," said the necromancer dismissively, looking from one to the other as they tried to flank him, seeming supremely unconcerned by it. "But first, tell me: which of my enemies do you serve? The Coven of the Black Wyrm? Shegaal? The Warlocks of Cthon? Ah." He tilted his brow toward the advancing Rakhar, the better for his Third Eye to regard the half-orc. "Curious! I see the mark of the *Lornael* is upon you. Can you truly be serving the Lady?"

The words had an unexpected effect on Rakhar, bringing him up short, filling him with a heady brew of shock, trepidation, disgust and something like hope. The image of the Lady Amandalainion's face swam before him, chastising him, entreating him, harrowing him.

Taking advantage of Rakhar's momentary lapse, the necromancer attacked. He opened his almost toothless mouth, neck extended, and exhaled a gout of flame. The fireball engulfed Rakhar and the half-orc fell back, screaming. Iolo sprang forward with a battle-cry, but his hammer rebounded off an invisible barrier around the necromancer. However, he managed to get Xalbulba's attention, and the jet of flame arced toward him. The dwarf escaped immolation by ducking and rolling to the side, the fire sweeping over him, the necromancer having miscalculated Iolo's height.

The sound of the necromancer's triumphant cackling filled the ruined room at the top of the lightning-struck tower. Rakhar rolled frantically on the floor to put out the flames, the only thing saving him the thickness of his Orcish hide; a Man would already have succumbed. Iolo pressed the attack on Xalbulba, striking at him in swift, smashing blows that glanced off the necromancer's wards, but nonetheless drove him back from the crystalline sphere on the brass pedestal. No longer laughing, Xalbulba barked a word of power and a whirlwind rose up in the room, so powerful it plucked the dwarf off his feet and hurled him against a wall.

But the whirlwind had an unintended consequence: before it abruptly subsided, it had blown out the flames that clung to Rakhar. Across the room Iolo moaned and struggled to rise. Rakhar pulled himself from the floor, his skin red and raw in places, horribly blackened in others, his face a mask of dreadful rage. The necromancer shrank back from him, muttering quickly to strengthen his wards. Lifting his scorched spade in both hands, Rakhar lurched forward.

Xalbulba's Third Eye flared. But the sorcerer was not the target of Rakhar's fury — not directly. The flat of his spade sent the crystalline sphere sailing off its pedestal, striking sparks where it bounced on the stone floor, rolling to a stop at the unsteady feet of Iolo. The dwarf saw immediately what the Half-orc intended. His eyes wide, Iolo heaved his hammer up, then brought it crashing down on the sphere. The blow shattered the crystal, sending shards and mist in all directions.

The necromancer shrieked, a great portion of his power broken. His Third Eye burst into flame, and he howled, falling to his knees, swaying crazily from side to side. He was probably blind to the Half-orc looming over him, but turned his head toward the sound of the ragged breaths.

"I guess that's why they call him Ironarm," Rakhar said, and with one swing of his blackened spade, swept off the necromancer's head.

Waving one hand to disperse the cloudy trails that had escaped the sphere, Iolo shuffled over to inspect his comrade's handiwork. The two exchanged a look of shared exultation and weary exasperation.

"I was right," Iolo grunted, his hand flopping toward the dripping spade in Rakhar's grip. "That thing could take a head clean off."

A noise from behind alerted them. They spun around to find the lich who in life had been Lord Varvatos, watching them. Behind him, in the ruins of the doorway, they could see a crowd of revenants, slack-jawed and dead-eyed, waiting.

Iolo clutched his hammer, though his stiff and sore muscles could barely bear the weight of it now. Rakhar raised his spade, and a deep, rumbling growl worked itself out from him as he faced this new threat.

But the lich Varvatos made no threatening moves. In fact, as it looked from the crumpled form of the necromancer to his slayers, something like a smile spread across its ghastly face.

"You have freed us," came the shuddering declaration. "The wreaker of the Red Death is slain."

"Necromancy is the father of plagues," spat Iolo, looking from one dead-faced visage to another.

"Aye, and sire of much else that was evil in these lands," said Varvatos in a husky voice. "Xalbulba may be dead, but his malice lives on. Thanks to you, we are not pawns in the feuds of wizards, but neither shall we know rest or comfort, joy or light. My people will know only hunger, and a long rotting walk into oblivion."

"Your people?"

Varvatos' lips drew back, exposing bloody gums receding from yellowing teeth. "I alone of the necromancer's thralls possess a will of my own. I was to lead his horde across the lands, and only my will directs them now. I am all that stands between you and ten thousand reanimated corpses hungry to feast on your guts. What say you, halfmen?"

Before Rakhar could speak, Iolo sputtered, "I say you owe us one, O king of dead men!"

The Lich-King Varvatos regarded them through eyes heavily lidded, pressing cold, blue lips closed again. There was movement among the undead behind him, and a space opened up. For the second time that night, Varvatos stepped aside for them.

"Go, gravedigger and Ironarm, go and let the account between us be settled. Go and tell the world that these lands are mine, and we will brook no trespassers. Leave this sad, haunted demesne to its dread new lord, and pray we do not seek to expand our borders."

So they fled the lightning-struck tower, slipping past the new king and his worm-eaten subjects. Empty, hungry faces regarded them as they walked through the dead grove, but they were not molested. On the Blasted Heath they found their mounts, slaughtered and being eaten; the undead reavers merely smacked their lips and watched as the dwarf and the half-orc looked back once, then ran into the night.

DAVID CHARLTON *is a graduate of the University of South Florida, works in the financial services industry, and lives with his wife and four cats in southwest Florida.*

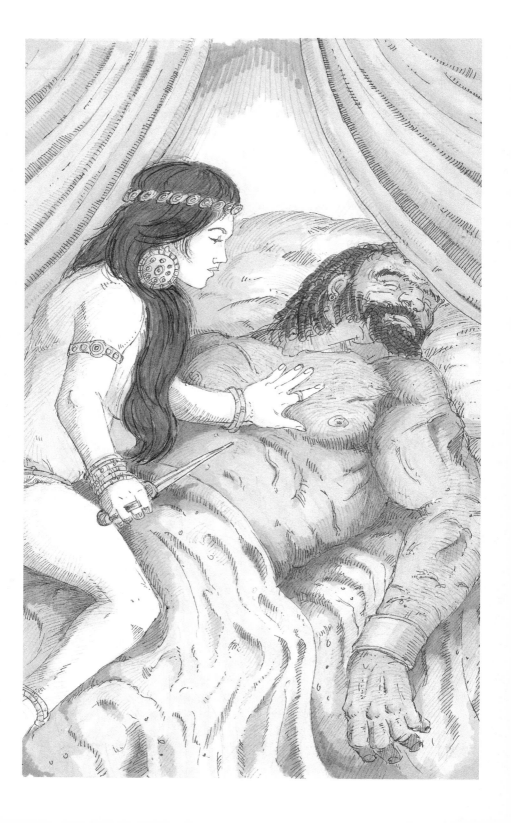

Shadakar

by Barry King

Shadakar! Shadakar! Can you hear me?
Your head, so heavy, so loose upon your neck.
Shadakar! Wake up!

Ah, but the liquor has taken you away, Oh, Shadakar,
Shadakar the mighty, whose weight of gold,
whose thrice-heavy sword, whose swarm of spies,
whose stolen life of luxury warms my bed.

Time it is for quiet words, now. Shadakar, listen.
Listen as you will not, your head upon my breast,
your mind ploughing the fields of your largesse,
lost in the mirror of your greatness.

Listen.

Shadakar, listen. Four and thirty years
you have swelled upon your foe. Liars, thieves,
beggars and worse, you have despoiled, made bare.

But also fine men who met the sword as duty,
poetry upon their lips and grace in their bearing,
heart partners torn in your brief pleasure.
As was I. Forever and anon. Snuffed out.

Hear me, Shadakar. A child I was when you took me,
took me away. A feather-light spoil among your hoard,
a slim-limbed girl among dozens, somehow favoured.
I grasped that favour, in fear, in the knowing of you.
Lost myself in your glory, my mind emptied by your gaze.

And yet, I remember. I have been to that land, now,
that paltry space that birthed you.
No different you were, not noble, not grand.
But now you give yourself airs, as if a lion among beasts.
You exult yourself, and yet it gnaws at you,
how others, older, wiser, see fearful shadows in your face.

You are defeated, Shadakar, by the failing in your heart,
by your father's disapproving brow,
by the scorn of the woman you love.

You care for naught but the treasures of others,
and so...will never exceed them.
How much blood has been spilt
in the name of your mediocre greatness?

So here I have this dirk, sharp as a vengeance-tooth.
Oof. You are heavy. What if I lighten you by a breath?
How if I end this travesty, this fool's quest?
How if I underscore the ebb and flow of your life
with a fine red line of perfect equality?

Equals then. But I will never equal you, Shadakar.
I will not do this thing for your mercy nor mine.

BARRY KING *(Sept. 8, 1969- November 18, 2015) was born in Greece to U.S. diplomats and grew up in Tunisia, Pakistan, Brunei, and the Philippines. He studied Philosophy and Technology in Athens, Georgia, and spent several years working in Washington DC's refugee policy community. After moving to his wife's hometown of Kingston, Ontario, and converting to Canadianism, he worked remotely around the world from his basement in the company of a small blind red dog (who accompanies him still). The rest of his time was spent messing about in the kitchen, puttering in the garden, and indulging his interests in archery, photography, and writing. On November 18, 2015, while recovering from a severe bout of pneumonia, Barry died suddenly and unexpectedly from a pulmonary embolism, aged 46. His fiction and poetry can be found in such diverse venues as* Unlikely Story, Polu Texni, The Future Fire, Heroic Fantasy Quarterly, Imaginarium: The Best Canadian Speculative Writing, Andromeda Spaceways Inflight Magazine, Crossed Genres, Lackington's, Ideomancer, *and* See the Elephant Magazine.

LORD OF THE TATTERED BANNER
BY KRISTOPHER REISZ

By the time they took Orsten Keep, the pretender had already escaped over the mountains with half her army. After the battle, the smell of blood and smoke lingered. It was a strangely fertile smell, like fresh-tilled earth.

Fengr Tall-As-A-Mounted-Man felt his war-rage cool, leaving him with the familiar, limb-trembling exhaustion. He couldn't rest, though. The plunder would be picked clean within an hour. Every soldier who could still walk trudged through the battlefield harvesting jewelry, gold teeth, and bits of nice leatherwork.

Fengr followed the northern wall with Pig-Ugly, ensign of the Brazen Tusks. Frost gave the churned mud the dull sheen of metal. A knight lay in the slurry, his helmet torn off and most of his face gone with it. He wore an amulet bearing the pretender's sign — a pelican in her piety, piercing her own breast and feeding the blood to her chicks. The amulet was silver, the blood drops rubies.

"Ca...Captain?"

The white-tooth orc slumped behind the knight's dead horse. The sword pierced his belly and came out the other side. "I came on him like a summer storm, captain," he chuckled. "Knocked him right off his stupid horse. I earned my brass."

Pig-Ugly glanced at the white-tooth, then at Fengr, silently shaking his head. Fengr turned away. Tugging the amulet loose, he tried to remember the white-tooth's name. "You fought bravely, soldier."

Blood crusted the white-tooth's hands. He motioned to the sword. "I didn't pull it out. You told us...let the surgeons do it."

Walking over, Fengr looked at how the white-tooth's toes pointed toward each other. He kicked the white-tooth's leg, but the paralyzed orc didn't flinch. "The surgeons can't do anything for you. And we can't carry you on the campaign." Kneeling, Fengr pulled a thick-bladed knife from his belt. "You fought bravely. May you meet the strigidæ with equal courage."

"Wait!" The white-tooth grabbed Fengr's wrist. "Captain, please, take me to the surgeons. Maybe they can fix me. If...if not, I'll go back to the mines. Captain, please, please."

Fengr glanced over his shoulder. The surgeon-priests were in the keep. By the time they hauled him up there and came back, the plundering would be done. Fengr shook his head. "Better to die on the battlefield like a true orc than waste away in some mine."

"No! I don't — " The white-tooth struggled, but Pig-Ugly grabbed his wrists. Forcing the white-tooth's chin up, Fengr delivered the *coup de grâce*. As the blood pumped down, the white-tooth wheezed, "You basta — " then grew still.

"These white-teeth from Low Haven aren't worth the meat we're feeding them," Pig-Ugly said. Fengr grunted, cutting the straps off the knight's breastplate. The tabard underneath bore a noble crest: a red and yellow sun. "Still, he bagged us another lord. That's something."

Cutting the tabard off, Fengr tossed it to Pig-Ugly. Pig-Ugly glanced past Fangr. "Lord Cal's coming."

The crown prince's aide-de-camp barreled up on his gray destrier, its fetlocks slathered with mud. Lord Cal's paige and another human rode behind him. "Fengr, his highness has need of you. Come."

Fengr stood. He spoke carefully. "But my lord, the pillaging. The Brazen Tusks have the right of plunder, given to us by the crown prince him — "

Lord Cal lashed out with his rod of office, striking Fengr across the shoulder. "You think you can question a lord because you're the crown prince's favorite pet? I said to come with me."

Dropping his eyes, Fengr grumbled, "I forget my place, lord."

Lord Cal glared at him for a few seconds more, then turned his horse. "Quickly. Come."

Leaving his ensign to the loot, Fengr followed Lord Cal past human companies of footmen and archers. Some men looked up and shied away. They passed a pair of drudge orcs chained to a baggage cart too. The drudges never glanced up, though, thinking only of their next bite of bread or wink of sleep.

The crown prince and his favored commanders stood outside thekeep's chapel. Shimmering with rings and silks, clutching gold cups, they'd been drinking and plundering Duke Orsten's apartments. They had pink-cheeked women with them, the duke's maids or lesser nieces. These were war plunder too.

Despite the cups and gold and women, the commanders wore long faces. As Fengr approached, one of them murmured to another, "...the pretender has stooped to, we must — " He stopped as the shadow of Fengr spread over him.

A woman let out a choking gasp. That made the crown prince laugh. "Hush now, hush. Fengr doesn't eat anybody until I tell him to."

Fengr sank to one knee. His highness boomed, "Fengr Unquenchable, Fengr Tall-As-A-Mounted-Man! Your orcs fought bravely today."

"The Brazen Tusks live to earn you glory and crush the enemies of your illuminated father."

The crown prince nodded. "Rise. Come and tell me what you make of this." He led them into the chapel. The windows were covered with stiffened cloth, and shadows held the reek of old blood. The crown prince yanked one of the cloths back. Hard-angled light fell on scarred stone walls. Mosaics of the God-Who-Sacrificed-Himself-To-Himself had been chiseled away. His face was gone, but Fengr could still see his out-stretched hands. In the god's place, images of strigidæ were scratched into the stone: spear-sharp beaks and round, watching eyes gazing down upon the altar.

Once, both orcs and humans offered sacrifices to the strigidæ, the lords of the hunt and high mountains. Then the God-Who-Sacrificed-Himself-To-Himself came, and men turned away from the strigidæ. Some turned back, though, when their own god didn't give them what they craved.

"These are their names, yes?" The crown prince pointed to the sigils scratched below each face. "Which ones are they?"

Fengr shook his head. "I don't know, your highness. The Brazen Tusks don't follow the strigidæ. We live to earn you glory and crush the enemies of your illuminated — "

"Yes, yes, but when you were young, your mother taught you these things, didn't she?"

"I was brought to the arena when I was young, your highness. From then, I only learned to fight." And what little Fengr did learn before then, he knew it best to keep to himself.

The crown prince flung his goblet. Grabbing Fengr's brass-sheathed tusk, he tilted the orc's eyes down to meet his own. "Duke Orsten was a lack-wit. He didn't come to this by himself; one of the orcs in this castle showed him the rituals, the names of those...things. Find out which one."

"I will, your highness. I swear it."

Because orcs had rejected the God-Who-Sacrificed-Himself-To-Himself, the god gave humans dominion over orcs. Fengr's kind were to be kept as slaves for ten thousand upon ten thousand generations, serving humans just as humans served their self-slaughtering god. Many orcs toiled in Duke Orsten's tin mines, but less than a dozen worked in Orsten Keep itself, most as stable-drudges and strappers. Lord Cal and his men herded the drudges into the chapel where Fengr grilled them. In man's language, he demanded, "Who defiled this holy place? Which one of you repaid your master's kindness with heresy?" In the old tongue the commanders didn't know, Fengr said, "I'm tired. I'm hungry. Maybe I'll just pick one of you at random. You think these humans would care? Tell me who it was before my patience ends."

The drudge orcs stood in a silent group, squeezed between Fengr's shout and the sarcophagi the ancient Dukes Orsten. Except they didn't act like drudges. Standing silent and still while Fengr screamed, they kept exchanging glances, trying to work something out between themselves.

Fengr didn't have the patience for whatever game they were playing. Snatching a son away from his mother, Fengr heaved him off his feet. "Was it this one?" The boy wailed and kicked. His mother's cry bounced offthe chapel stones. The others kept glancing around. "Confess, boy!" Pulling the knife from his belt, Fengr sawed into the boy's ear. The child's scream sharpened to a teakettle whistle. Blood dribbled over Fengr's hand. Suddenly every eye darted toward an ancient dam.

Her skin was knobbed and warted. One tusk had been torn out. She clutched a charm against her chest — a pouch filled with fur and mouse bones. Fengr's mother once had a charm like that, a gift from the strigidæ.

Fengr dropped the boy, his ear dangling by a strip of cartilage, and reached for the withered dam. Just as he touched her, another orc yelled, "It was me! I confess!"

Fengr turned. The other orc had dropped to his knees and crawled toward the crown prince. "I — I taught Duke Orsten the names of the strigidæ. I taught him the ritual sacrif — "

The crown prince kicked him away. "Lord Cal, bind him. Have this defiled place torn down with him in it."

The drudge whimpered in the dust. Fengr glanced at the old dam clutching her charm. When Fengr had been scared at night, his mother let him hold the leather pouch. She told him how she'd met the strigidæ while fetching water for their master.

If the orc who'd confessed wanted to die in the dam's place, what did it cost Fengr? As long as an orc died, the crown prince was happy.

"Fengr, your soldiers fought bravely today, brave as any man." The crown prince shook Fengr's tusk playfully again. "Tomorrow, go to the mines and refill your ranks. We can't stay here long. We must chase the pretender to ground before winter comes."

"Yes, your highness."

"In the meantime, take a cask of Duke Orsten's wine to your soldiers. And this one is for you." Pulling a girl from Lord Elmore's grip, he handed her off to Fengr. The girl was thick hipped and plump breasted. Taking her by the trembling arm, Fengr bowed. "Your generosity is beyond all measure, your highness."

* * *

In their camp, the Brazen Tusks gambled their loot. Fengr staked the knight's amulet against rings and foreign coins, even a false eye carved from lapis lazuli. The dice proved his boon companions, coming up drakes every time he needed them most.

Pig-Ugly knotted the knight's red-and-yellow-sun tabard onto the banner-pole, along with the crests of two other noble houses. The Brazen Tusks, not led by any lord, weren't allowed to fly a true banner. Instead, the orcs marched into battle under the tattered, slashed, and blood-blackened colors of every lord they killed.

They drank Duke Orsten's wine and watched the white-teeth who'd proved themselves in the day's battle get their tusks sheathed in brass. Some howled as Grun hammered the nails in, others roared and laughed. It was a good show either way.

Sometime past midnight, there was a scream of stone. Fengr felt the earth shudder as the chapel was pulled down. Soon after, he tired of dice and carried his double handful of winnings to his tent where the human girl waited.

Her name was Isolde. She trembled when Fengr touched her, but she accepted the cup a wine he gave her and let him slip rings onto her fingers. She said, "The emperor must truly be great that even his slaves drink wine and drip with plunder."

Fengr laughed. "Not all slaves. Only the Brazen Tusks. We eat beef every day like lords. Even the emperor's human soldiers can't claim that."

"He honors orcs above men?"

Fengr nodded as he unhooked Isolde's dress. "Because we break the people's love for the pretender."

The pretender's symbol was a pelican in her piety, stabbing her breast to feed her chicks. And the pretender herself inspired that sort of self-slaughter. She rode into a town, spoke to the humans, touched their hands, and they rose against the emperor. Peasants and noble lords gave their blood for nothing but her words. The emperor's highest priests declared her power came from witchcraft, that strigidæ rode her at night, that her nether parts had teeth. But their pronouncements fell as harmless as dust.

After the loss the Chalk Coast cities, the crown prince raised the Brazen Tusks. He pulled the biggest, worst orcs up from the mines and gladiator arenas. They didn't justkill rebellious soldiers. They filled their towns with fire. They filled their children's sleep with nightmares, their wives' bellies with bastards. Their sworn duty was to slaughter, terrify, and show everyone that the pretender couldn't save them.

The crown prince made sure that stories of the Brazen Tusks swept before the army like a herald. Laying with Isolde in the dark, Fengr asked if stories of him had reached Orsten Keep ahead of the crown prince's host. He took great pleasure in hearing tales about himself. The girl nodded. "Even before the duke cast his lot with Princess — with the pretender. People said the Brazen Tusks were cannibals, that arrows couldn't harm you. It was why the duchess begged Duke Orsten not to join with the rebellion, why the duke locked her in the oubliette."

"Your own people heard these stories as well, Fengr." The withered dam slipped into the tent. "Of the Brazen Tusks marching below their tattered banner. Of the scores of men you have slaughtered in battle."

Three talon-tipped rings flashed in the moonlight — two on her fingers, one on her thumb. The dam also wore a peaked crown of feathers. These emblems meant she spoke for the strigidæ. Fengr snapped at Isolde to find him more wine. Once the girl had hurried from the tent, he told the dam, "If the lords see you dressed like that, they'll cut your throat. I saved you once; I won't save you again."

"You'll save us all, Fengr. Your people, your gods, scream for a champion."

"I live to win glory for the crown prince, nothing more." Fengr wanted her gone; the dam talked too loosely of rebellion. But the magic she might posses made him afraid to send her away.

"The strigidæ have sent me dreams. They say Fengr Tall-As-A-Mounted-Man will become king of all orcs. We will be free once again, and we will flay the meat and smash the bones of those who enslaved us. King Fengr, we of Orsten Keep stand ready to rise with you."

Fengr snorted. "I came to crush the enemies of the emperor. I came because Duke Orsten sided with the pretender, that's all."

She chuckled. "But who convinced Duke Orsten to side with the pretender in the first place, hmm? I had to bring you here somehow, Fengr. We cannot expect the strigidæ to do everything for us."

He stared at her. "You're mad."

The dam said, "I am here to help your rebellion, to do whatever is needed."

"I'm not — there is no rebellion!" Fengr snarled, low and angry. "Leave or I'll slit your throat myself."

Just then, Isolde reappeared with more wine. The dam said, "You will lead us. The strigidæ do not lie," and slipped out into the night.

* * *

The host stayed at Orsten Keep while the priests flogged themselves bloody and searched their dreams for signs of the pretender. They had to chase her down soon, before winter made the mountains impassable.

While they waited for visions from the priests, Fengr refilled his ranks with orcs from Duke Orsten's mines. The Brazen Tusks drilled every day and kept their gear always ready to march. The dam never returned to their camp, and for that, Fengr was glad. He told no one about what she'd told him. Her promises had led Duke Orsten to his doom. Fengr would not follow.

Finally tiring of the priests' too-vague dreams, the crown prince began flogging them himself until their backs were like raw sides of beef — meat and ribs and connective tissue exposed. At last, after days of infection and delirium, one holy brother howled about seven great strigidæ emerging from stone. Locals recognized the place as the Gorge of the Parliament, a narrow defile high in the mountains. There, ancient hands had carved towering statues of the strigidæ into the cliff face. There, they would find the pretender's host.

The priest gifted by the vision died a few hours later. The crown prince declared him a saint and ordered that the new chapel to be built at Orsten Keep bear his name. Commanders consulted their maps and rangers, and the order went out to strike camp. By dawn, the army was on foot and hoof once again. Entering the mountains, winter pulled out her knives. Lords shivered inside furs. Camp followers shivered in wool stuffed with grass. The orcs plodded along, though, skin thick enough to ignore the slashing wind, splayed toes gripping the ice.

On the fourth night, a drudge orc pulling one of the crown prince's supply wagons escaped. Three human soldiers gave chase, but quickly turned back in the face of the cold and dark and steep mountain terrain. Furious, the crown prince had all three of them chained to the supply wagon in the orc's place.

The host crawled up the mountain like an iron-clad millipede. Wagons got stuck, and horses broke their legs. A gang of drudge orcs and human prisoners were put to work laying down planed boards for the horses and baggage train. It was endless, exhausting work, and they could never move fast enough for the lords. Every day, more collapsed into the snow and were left behind.

On the sixth day after leaving Orsten Keep, Fengr marched along — letting his mind go numb, legs moving with no more thought than a waterwheel — when one of the white-teeth from Duke Orsten's mines edged up to him. He touched Fengr's elbow and whispered, "When it is time, what will the signal be?"

Fengr turned. "Huh?"

The white-tooth, Nordy, leaned close. "When the orcs rise? What is your plan? How will we know it's time?"

Fengr snatched him by his throat. "What do you mean 'rise?'"

Nordy sputtered. "Th-the dam. She says the portents have been good since we entered the mountains."

"The dam? She's with us?"

Nordy nodded, his eyes starting to bulge. "In — baggage train. Yesterday, the strigidæ — a charm. The bones inside told her — "

The other Brazen Tusks looked over.

Pig-Ugly trotted over. "Fengr? What's he done?"

Fengr ignored him. "You orcs from the mines, how many believe the dam?"

"All of us — why we — volun — teer."

"Fengr?" Pig-Ugly asked again.

Fengr smashed Nodry's nose, letting the blood pour down. "Tell the others I am not your king. Tell them the next one who speaks of it, I will pull out his tongue. A soldier doesn't need a tongue to fight."

Glancing up, he barked at the Brazen Tusks to keep marching. Nordy fell in with the others, pressing a handful of snow against his broken nose. Fengr walked back along the column toward the baggage train. His thick-bladed knife pressed against his skin with every step. The blade felt terribly cold. But Fengr didn't know if he would use it yet.

He found the dam yoked to one of the priest-surgeons' carts. It was filled with unguents and lancets for bloodletting. Bending to her task, she pulled the cart through thick mud.

"You," Fengr snarled. "What are you doing here?"

The dam had to catch her breath before she could speak. "Your Lord Cal pressed another of ours to this job, a mother of young babes. I took this yoke for her."

"You will die for her."

The woman shrugged. "I will die for the young who need their mother. I will die for the future of our people. What will you die for, Fengr?"

Fengr ignored the question. "Stop telling orcs I'll lead them in rebellion. This talk will earn us both slit throats if it reaches the lords."

"But don't you see? The strigidæ are leading you to the Gorge of the Parliament." Straining against the weight of the cart, she spoke in grunts. "We made sacrifices to the strigidæ there. When we were free. Here, on top of the world."

"When we were free. An age long past."

"An age that will come again, Fengr. You must sacrifice the human army to the strigidæ. Offer them the blood of the crown prince."

"You're mad."

"Madness is bowing and trembling before a pack of squealing pink piglets. Look at how the humans shiver. Watch how they die from the cold. Listen to me, King Fengr, we have allies now. I've sent an orc to seek out Princess Eadwynn."

Fengr tensed and glanced around. Saying the pretender's name out loud, admitting her royal lineage, would get an orc whipped. Only after he saw nobody had overheard did Fengr let himself think about what the dam had just said. "Seek her out? The drudge that escaped, you sent him to find the pretender at the Gorge of the Parliament?"

The dam chuckled merrily. "They know we are coming. They will hide close by and wait. Look down here, King Fengr." Tucked above the cart's axle, the dam had ferreted a tight bundle of oil-soaked rags. "When the moment is right, call out to me and I will light the rags. That will be the signal to the princess and her army to attack. We will be free! Other orcs will hear about you, Fengr Tall-As-A-Mounted-Man, slayer of princes, lord of the tattered banner. They'll rise up to join you. I've seen it in my dreams!"

Fengr grabbed her, shoved his face close to hers. "Your dreams are lies. After Duke Orsten allied himself with the pretender, how many orcs did she free from his mines?"

The dam pursed her lips and didn't answer.

"I have been to the cities she takes over. Humans are free, but orcs remain slaves. The pretender holds to the human's covenant with the God-Who-Sacrificed-Himself-To-Himself to keep orcs as chattel."

"Then you will bargain with her. Agree to fight on her side if she frees orcs as well, gives us the mountains as our ancestral home. Are you mad enough to fight for those who locked your people in chains rather than fight for their freedom?"

Fengr snorted. "Fight for the crown prince, fight for the pretender, fight for you; seems I'll spend my life fighting no matter what. At least the crown prince offers wine and whores for the between-times. What do you offer? Cold and hunger on a miserable mountaintop?"

Hoofbeats made Fengr turn. Lord Cal rode up, coming to see why the baggage train had halted. "Fengr, what's all this?" he demanded.

"Nothing, lord," Fengr said automatically. "This orc slipped in the mud." The dam annoyed him, but Lord Cal made Fengr smolder with hate. He wasn't about to offer Cal the fame of quashing a rebellion against the throne.

Lord Cal grunted. "Get back up with your soldiers. We're nearing the gorge."

Fengr hurried back up the column. Behind him, he heard the thud of Lord Cal's rod striking the dam. "Hold the train up again, and I'll hang you as a warning to the others," the aide-de-camp snarled. "We've left fine warhorses to die out here; you think there'd be any ado about an old drudge?"

Fengr didn't look back. He rejoined the Brazen Tusks at the head of the column. Within an hour, scouts returned from the Gorge of the Parliament. Word quickly spread through the army: the pretender had been there, but her camp had been hastily abandoned. Fengr chuckled to himself. It seemed the mad dam could even get the pretender to dance on her strings. No wonder she seemed so certain Fengr would fight for her.

It took another day for the army to reach the gorge. Ages of snowmelt had created a curved throat of stone. The walls rose up, shielding the gorge from the worst of the wind and cold. A narrow meadow of tough grass and blood-purple flowers grew there. As they marched, soldiers pulled off caps and loosened cloaks.

The shlu-shluff of footsteps and the jangle of tack echoed up the throat. The sound came back down warped and corroded. Then one of the Brazen Tusks gasped, "The Parliament! Look."

Where the gorge widened, the seven strigidæ stood in cliff-face niches. The statues were dizzyingly tall. Wings folded to their bodies, they stared down at the Brazen Tusks passing by their feet. The orcs stared back up, mouths dangling open. A few of the white-teeth stopped dead to stare at their stone gods. Fengr snapped, "Eyes front! Bushwhackers could be anywhere."

Fengr kept his soldiers in formation. He refused to look at the giant statues himself, keeping his eyes peeled for signs of an ambush. The pretender's host had left horses butchered for meat and bodies hastily buried under cairns of creek stones.

"They're starving, eating their horses," Pig-Ugly said, prodding one of the corpses with his axe. "If we catch them soon, it won't even be a fight."

The commanders sent scouts to search every ridge and canyon east of the gorge. Only Fengr and the dam knew the pretender hid somewhere close-by, desperately waiting for a signal that would never come. As night fell, Fengr ordered his men to keep their weapons at hand; they might muster out any minute.

It was a bad night. Soldiers grumbled about cold and dwindling stores. They were anxious for the chase to be done. All through camp, they heard the crown prince screaming and throwing things around the command tent. When Lord Longlane's paige said something foolish, his highness plucked out the boy's eye.

Playing dice below the stone strigidæ, Fengr ran his thumb across the pelican amulet he'd pulled off the dead knight. The knight had been wealthy. He'd likely had land and slaves. Why did he fight and die for the pretender's words? Fengr didn't know, but the dam insisted he would do the same himself: give up meat and mead just to win other orcs a future Fengr would never enjoy himself.

It was madness or maybe witchcraft. Fengr remembered the orc in the chapel, throwing himself at the crown prince's feet. Maybe the dam knew the same magic the pretender knew to sully minds, to make orcs love her even though she offered nothing but death. Fengr resolved to avoid her. He would keep the white-teeth like Nordy away from her too.

But as he gambled and lost, Fengr felt the stone strigidæ watching him in the dark. The echoes through the gorge started to sound like murmurs from above. Maybe the dam's visions were right — Fengr had been destined to be a hero — but something had gone wrong.

When Fengr was four years old, one of his master's foxhounds bit him. Fengr snatched the dog by its ear and kicked it to death. Instead of beating him, his master took Fengr away from his mother and sold him to the local noble to be trained as a gladiator. In the arena, Fengr Tall-As-A-Mounted-Man had fought and slaughtered fellow orcs while humans cheered and threw silver coins.

Maybe if he'd stayed with his mother and learned the secrets of the strigidæ, he would be different. Maybe if he'd ever learned anything besides killing, Fengr would be the hero the dam and the strigidæ thought he was.

The maybes bit at him like lice. But every maybe in the world didn't tip the scales against one sword. For a soldier, a slave — for an orc — it was better to deal with what was, snatch what he could from this life and do what it took to survive. Let the bards worry about what might have been.

Dropping the amulet into the circle, Fengr took the dice. He couldn't keep his thoughts on the game, though. He lost the amulet. Trying to win it back, Fengr put up Isolde but lost her to Nir. After that, Fengr stomped off to his tent where the statues couldn't see him.

He had troubled dreams mazed with steep defiles and the strigidæ crying huhuu at his back. He awoke and reached for the girl, then remembered she wasn't his anymore. Pushing off his furs, Fengr stumbled out into cold, cobalt dawn. Pig-Ugly sat by a low fire, tightening the straps on his armor.

A witch had cursed Pig-Ugly's mother when she was pregnant, causing Pig-Ugly to curdle in her stomach. He'd been a breech birth. His mouth was tilted nearly sideways and bony growths sprouted from his jaw and chest. The night he was born, his father left Pig-Ugly on a mountaintop. "I died for a couple days but got bored. So I walked back home and kicked that piker's ass." Pig-Ugly always laughed loudest when telling that story. Fengr didn't know the truth, just that his ensign only answered to "Pig-Ugly," refusing to let his family name slip between his crooked lips.

"Any word from the scouts?" Fengr asked, sitting down. A pot of beef grease sat by the fire. Fengr smeared some on a hunk of bread.

"No." Pig-Ugly glanced up. "You look worse than a Cilian paige's buggered asshole."

"Grim dreams."

"About the coming battle?"

Fengr shook his head and ate even though he wasn't hungry.

"About leading all orcs to glorious freedom?"

Fengr glared. Pig-Ugly laughed. The way his mouth twisted, his laugh always came as a gurgle.

"Quiet!" Fengr hissed. "If the lords — "

"The lords are drunk and tucked in with their whores."

"Where did you hear?"

"The white-teeth from Orsten all believe it. Some of the others are starting to think it's true too. At least, they wish it was. Last night, you were so insistent they keep their weapons handy, they were convinced it would come any minute. After you went to sleep, a couple of them asked me what I thought."

"And?"

"I told them you were the biggest bastard I'd ever met. Told them you don't have any loftier goals than drinking, whoring, and chopping down any fool standing between you and the first two. I told them you were a pitiless killer and a passable commander, but I'd wager on Lord Cal becoming king of all orcs before you."

Fengr nodded. "My thanks."

As the sun rose, soldiers sharpened weapons and adjusted their armor. Others drank, gambled, or fought. Fengr hoped the battle came soon. Some slaughter and pillaging would keep the orcs from dreaming of rebellion. In the meantime, Fengr patrolled the Brazen Tusks' camp. He snarled and struck out at any knot of soldiers becoming too relaxed. "Keep that gear ready! When the horn sounds, we have two blasts to muster in! If you can't find your axe in that time, your helmet, it's gone." Fengr kicked the white-tooth's helmet across the grounds. "You fight without it."

A clang of metal against stone shivered across the gorge, making Fengr swing around. It wasn't the pretender attacking, though, just a trio of human spearmen clustered at the base of one of the strigidæ statues. They stabbed at it with knives, chipping off souvenirs. Fengr went back to yelling about gear, tossing a white-tooth's shield in the mud.

"Uh, commander?" Pig-Ugly touched Fengr's arm and motioned to where the humans continued hacking at the statue. The white-tooth Nordy strode up behind them.

"Stop!" Nordy snapped. "These statues are sacred."

The humans were drunk, clinging to one another to stay upright. They laughed at Nordy and made ape sounds. One of the three, chubby as a piglet, bellowed, "Piss on you, orc. Piss on your filthy bird-gods." Unlacing his trousers, he pulled out his manhood. Fengr started running, but it happened too quickly. Nordy snatched the spearman up and swung him against the statue. There was a wet crunch. The piglet's head split like rotten wood. Orcs and humans rushed toward the commotion. There was yelling, cursing, then the clamor of horses through the low purple heather. Lord Cal's paige and a knight Fengr didn't know charged up, swords drawn. Some infantrymen had to dive out of the way.

"Kneel, orc! Kneel!"

Nordy dropped the dead soldier. "You think you are mighty? We will grind your bones! We will — !"

They slashed at him with their swords. They kept their horses moving in different directions so Nordy couldn't see both of them at once — like dogs baiting a bear. The paige lost his blade between Nordy's ribs. Nordy took a trembling step, crumpled to his knees, but kept snarling. "You can't keep us in chains. You can't piss on — " he struggled for breath, finding Fengr in the crowd. "We must — Must rise! Our moment is — !"

The knight dealt the final blow, dropping Nordy to the earth beside the fat spearman. Turning, he yelled at the paige to bring Lord Cal.

As the paige galloped off, the knight clutched his sword in one hand and his dagger in the other, ordering the orcs back. His horse whickered and twisted, close to panic.

Fengr slipped away. Instead of returning to the Brazen Tusks' camp, he headed toward the baggage train. Pig-Ugly followed at his heels. "Where are you going, captain?"

"To kill the dam. Offer her head to the crown prince, and show the drudges and white-teeth I'm not their champion."

Pig-Ugly sneered. "About time."

He was right. Fengr should have killed the dam the first time she spoke her mad prophecies. But now Nordy had killed a human, and the crown prince would be hunting for a conspiracy. Fengr was a fool for letting it go on this long.

Entering the curve of carts making up the baggage train, Fengr felt all eyes on him. The thickest knot of orcs was near the surgeon's cart with its sun-faded red canopy. Fengr moved toward it and saw the dam crouched in the cart's shadow. She saw him and bellowed, "Fengr!" Slipping on her bladed talon-rings, she spoke for the strigidæ now. "Fengr Unquenchable has come to free us! The colors of every human nation will fly from the Brazen Tusk's ragged banner!"

The drudges pushed in around Fengr, shouting over one another. "Is this it? Do the Brazen Tusks stand with us? What do we do?"

He shoved them away, trying to reach the dam, but she moved too fast. Running away on bandy legs, she yelled, "King Fengr, Lord of the Tattered Banner, strikes! He will crush all enemies of the orcs! Rise! Rise! Now is the moment we take our freedom!"

Pulling his thick-bladed knife, Fengr tried to catch her, tried to silence her, but the drudges were in bedlam. They grabbed mallets, iron wheel wrenches, heavy cleavers. Panicking humans scrambled out of the clearing, screaming for soldiers. Fengr saw one human snatched by a green hand, his neck snapped back and his cry cut off.

"Rise orcs! Now is your time! Fengr Unquenchable stands with you! The merciless Brazen Tusks stand with you!"

Fengr saw them and halted — Lord Cal led a chevron of soldiers stabbing toward the baggage train. The dam didn't care. She charged the knights before they could figure out exactly what was happening. Shrieking, she slashed at Lord Cal with her talon-rings. She bloodied man-flesh and horse-flesh until Lord Cal's stallion bucked and threw him to the ground. One of the other lords bashed the dam in the head, making her drop like a stone. Still, she looked around for Fengr, screaming, "Mighty King Fengr! Avenge me! Avenge your servant!"

Lord Cal pushed himself off the ground, clutching his bleeding thigh. He saw Fengr standing, knife drawn, and shrieked, "Kill him!"

The knight with the bloody mace spurred his horse forward. Fengr tried to scream, *No! I serve the crown prince! This is a mistake!* But the knight was charging him. He swung his mace, and Fengr barely twisted out of the way, falling to the ground. The knight reared around and lifted his mace for another blow. Fengr did what he had to do to survive the moment. Grabbing the human's leg, he wrenched him off his horse. The man squirmed like a puppy, grasping for the mace that had fallen out of his hand. Fengr plunged his knife into the knight's armpit.

Another knight had pulled Lord Cal onto his saddle as the drudges surged around them. Several more foot soldiers were struck, stabbed, kicked, and punched. Seeing they faced a full-flowered revolt, the lords fell back, racing toward the command tents. Fengr stood. The knight he'd killed lay with his mouth open, showing small, square teeth. Pig-Ugly watched the rebellion spreading around them like a grass fire and said, "This is bad, captain."

Fengr limped over to the dam. She was dying. The mace had crushed her jaw and torn arteries in her neck. Blood spread across her tunic as thick as dye.

"Why did you do that? I am not your hero!"

"Yes, I know." Her breath sounded like somebody squeezing a wet rag. "But now what choice do you have, Fengr?"

Fengr raised his knife, hungry to kill her, but he realized he couldn't. He'd murdered a knight. There was no explaining anymore, there was no going back. He had to escape into the mountains. To escape, he needed the drudges to fight with him. To keep the drudges on his side, he couldn't murder their dam. "This isn't fate," he said stubbornly. "I'm not your hero."

"No." Blood stained her beatific smile pink. "You're just a big bastard that's good at killing. That's what our people need now. But they must also believe you are their chosen champion, Fengr Tall-As-A-Mounted-Man."

He stared at her. "The strigidæ never sent you dreams about me. You made it all up. Me, the drudges, Duke Orsten, you lied to all of us."

Her laugh grated like wet sand. "Lies now, but a legend tomorrow. Tomorrow and for ten thousand generations, our people will sing the song of King Fengr, Lord of the Tattered — "

Fengr walked away, leaving her to die. The subtle witch had pit him against the crown prince. He felt like he was back in the arena, stepping through the gate, ready to kill another orc just because his master ordered him to. At least his master never expected Fengr to be thankful, at least the perfumed goat never tried to gild Fengr's enslavement with promises of becoming a legend after he died.

"Somebody bring me fire! Quickly!" One of the drudges had a fire-horn. Fengr grabbed it and ran toward the surgeons' cart.

Fengr didn't care what orcs said about him after he died. He didn't care about their freedom. He would fight because he didn't have any other choice. And the crown prince would fight back because he didn't have any choice. The pretender, the emperor, Fengr wondered if any of them were truly free. Maybe the whole world was an arena. Maybe the strigidæ and the God-Who-Sacrificed-Himself-To-Himself gathered around, cheering their favorites and tossing silver coins.

But Fengr would let the bards worry about what might be. Reaching the surgeons' cart, He found the bundle of rags hidden below and set them alight. Then, finding a sledgehammer nearby, he heaved it up. "Hear me, orcs! Hear me!"

The drudges, gathered in small groups, armed with axes and chains and ripped-out cart yokes, looked up. Fengr said, "Our time has come. The Brazen Tusks stand with you, the strigidæ stand with you, but we must strike now. The humans are scattered and scared. Grab any food you can, burn the rest of the supplies. Then we must move to join with the Brazen Tusks. Move, move, move!"

A deafening shout rose up around him, "Hail our king! Hail Fengr Unquenchable!" The drudges snatched barrels of food, set carts ablaze, and killed the last humans cowering on the ground. Pig-Ugly grabbed Fengr's shoulder and pointed to the burning surgeons' cart. The oil-soaked rags had some magic in them, and a dense finger of green smoke rose high above the gorge. "A signal?" Pig-Ugly asked.

"The pretender lies nearby. She'll attack the crown prince from the east."

"We're in alliance with the pretender?"

"She thinks so, but this rabble won't last long in an honest battle. The pretender attacks the crown prince from the east. While they're busy slaughtering each other, we retreat west, as high up into the mountains as we can go. We harry whichever side is the victor, keep them trapped up here without supplies. If these drudges can survive a week, all the humans will die." And curse the dam, curse the strigidæ, but it felt delicious to say. Fengr could get drunk on the words alone. "All humans die."

Pig-Ugly gave his gurgling laugh. "Fengr, you're the biggest bastard I've ever met."

Fengr nodded. He was just a big, mean bastard who was good at killing. But as the ragged phalanx of drudges surged forward — many straight into the blades and maces of the on-coming knights — they drove one another on by screaming his name. "Strike! Strike for Fengr Unquenchable! Strike for Fengr your king!"

KRISTOPHER REISZ *is the head of reference at the Athens-Limestone county Public Library and has written three novels for young adults,* Tripping to Somewhere, Unleashed, *and* The Drowned Forest.

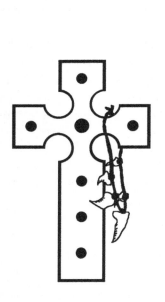

Saint Aedh and the Teeth of Slaibh Scoilt:
An Epic of the Ancient Irish

by Adrian Simmons

How did Aedh Mac Carthin fight and win such glory to stretch from Ireland to Rome? It will be told.

There were sad days at Armagh as Patrick lay dying. And the saint on his deathbed called to his household. Blessings and prayers he said for each, wishes and instructions as well.

Then came Aedh Mac Carthin, the strongest man, Aedh Mac Carthin, a great and prideful prince of Leinster who carried the Saint on shoulder over river and stream. To him Patricus spoke:

'My journey cannot be made
In chariot or on foot
Nor will your arms carry
me to God's house.
A final pilgrimage I make
and after I am under way, you,
Son of Cartin, strong and humble,
will be tasked with
greater weight than mine.
The benighted and ignorant
the druids and their plots.
Rivers you will cross
and the sea as well, bearing
the holy word as you bore me.
The Lord grants me these visions
that I may share them and you may
turn the right side of your face
to honor His will.'

For a month only had Patricus lay in the earth when a chariot drawn by wretched horses and bearing a wretched messenger did come to Armagh. The driver upon hearing the saint had died wept bitterly and cried out:

'Woe to all my people,
murder and pestilence devouring
mother and son to the last.
Brutally are we oppressed
merciless our enemies,
hard their treatment of us.
Our own gods let us suffer
and the god of the saint
takes him from us.
Bitter news must I take back,
lots yet will be drawn,
sacrifice yet will be made.'

'And where is your tribe,' asked Aedh, 'to labor still under the yoke of false idols?'

'Our lands lie beyond the river Bandon, unvisited by saint or priest.'

Aedh Mac Carthin heard this and spoke:

'This river I will cross,
your people I will teach,
God will drive back your enemies.
Make room in your chariot for me,
Make room in your heart for courage.'

A hard journey, flying across plain and over mountain. The horses became so gaunt that a child could lift them with his two hands, and one hand only for the lean driver. The chariot's wheels creaked and shook, its walls offered no shelter. At the Bandon's banks the water rushed and flooded, the charioteer worried and fretted.

'So weak are we,
that men and horses will be carried to sea.'

Aedh Mac Carthin had stayed fit and strong and lifted horses and chariot in one hand, the driver in the other and so carried them across the swift flood.

On the other side they found
the people in sore grief,
the house of the chief in disorder.

Said the charioteer: 'They draw lots to choose who will go to our enemies, as tribute and sacrifice. Fire and sword will they bring if the victims are not gathered and delivered swiftly.'

But Aedh Mac Carthin prayed outside
the hall of the chieftain.
Tasach the king welcomed Aedh
His people took heart and gathered
What numbers they could and went
to meet their foes.

With the Bandon between them, the two armies taunted one another, King Ferchu
and his druid demanded their tribute. This was the force of King Ferchu, eager and
swarming on the far side of the river, that waited for King Tasach and Aedh Mac
Carthin:

Swarming and fierce, haughty with strong arms
Legion overwhelming enraged
Flaming shields, brave spears
Shouting challenges, eyes mad
Charge of a horse
Fury of boars
Taller than oaks
Sprung from giants
A great ivory tooth to
Fill a fist hung about the
White necks of Ferchu and
The thirteen greatest warriors
The very teeth of Sliabh Scoilt
The giant that sired their race.
The Fourteen gathered at the bank
Armies stretched behind them.

The Avenger of Patrick stepped into the ford, answered their demands with a
challenge of his own. The Fourteen laughed at him.

He who stood with no sword,
stood with no shield,
stood with no spear.
Cúlfhaicail they chose, a mighty
wrestler, from their number
to go into the ford and duel.

The water boiled with their struggle. Fish leapt from the depths to escape in such
numbers both armies did not want for food that night.

Aedh Mac Carthin at last gripped Cúlfhaicail
he thrust him into the churning water
and there he drowned.
He took the tooth from Cúlfhaicail's neck
and prayed on the shore for as much
strength in the battles to come.

'Well does this please me,' said King Tasach to Aedh, 'but there is as much work to be done tomorrow.'

Across the Bandon, the Thirteen grew alarmed and chose Meilteoir to fight the next day. So hard was the fighting that no stone was left in the river and both armies built houses from the plentiful rocks.

But Meilteoir met the same fate as Cúlfhaicail
and was drowned in the ford and
Aedh Mac Carthin took the tooth from about his neck.

The Twelve took counsel that night, Ferchu and his eleven warriors. They choose Cnaígh, swift and sure. So hard the struggle that only a hand's-breadth of water was left in the river and both armies crowded atop their stone houses to escape the flood.

Cnaígh was a mighty fighter but
at last Aedh Mac Carthin gripped him and
held him upside down, drowning
him in the hand's-breadth of water.
A third tooth was taken from the
heathens and the Eleven that remained
slept little that night.

'Well have you done, Patrick's arm,' said King Tasach, 'but these are merely the baby's teeth — truer challenges lay ahead.'

In the morning Aedh Mac Carthin donned St. Patrick's breastplate and went to the ford. And while he performed baptisms in the water the remaining Eleven took counsel among themselves.

'Most hard, this,' spoke King Ferchu 'but let us use cunning and deceit:
'The teeth of a man's head work best
When they crush meat between them
And so will it be with us.'

And so while Corrán Séill went forth to fight at the ford with honor, Leiceann, Drandal and Teanga hid in the tall reeds, and there waited with cowardly hearts and cruelly cunning heads.

Hard was the fighting that day so that the river rolled in its bed and flowed uphill in its fear.

Aedh Mac Carthin at last gripped Corrán Séill
and crushed him so that all his bones broke.
Wearily he walked back to shore
were an otter swam to him and

said, 'Beware, man of Patrick.
Onne fang you have pulled but
three more await.'

The otter then brought the
champion the last three
stones in the river.
With three good casts Aedh Mac Carthin
knocked the three warriors
dead in the reeds.
The foolish only, from that
day to this dare to trap an
Otter from the Bandon.

Upon seeing this, Tasach embraced the saint's champion and bade him to baptize
him, which Aedh Mac Carthin gladly did.

Of the remaining seven warriors six fell, one the next day, two the day after, and
three on the third day. Tasach threw down his idols of clay and ordered all his
people to follow him. Across the water Ferchu chief of the heathens grew sore
afraid and went to his druid, chastising him for the loss of the prized warriors of
the tribe.

'Only Géarán remains!' he said.
'Great his skill,
powerful his anger
no fear crosses his brow,
no weakness nests in his arm.
'But still I worry, druid. Use your magic and great cunning to aid this last best
fighter.'

The next day a messenger crossed the Bandon and came to Aedh Mac Carthin,
saying that Géarán feared he would be killed like his brothers and begged to be
baptized before the fight. The holy man could not turn from this request and
waded into the river Badon, crossing to Géarán who waited on the other side.
The druid crept to the bank and slipped into the water. His skin turned to scales
and he changed his form to a great pike and swam beneath the surface where
Géarán stood.

Aedh Mac Carthin crossed the river, fording to his doom. Géarán drew his blade,
the sword seeking the strong-man's head above, the pike biting and pulling at his
feet below.

Aedh Mac Carthin dashed his hands into the water
deep into the current and seized
the druid. No thrashing could free
him from that grip, no cunning could save him
from being lifted, and Géarán's blade

cleft through scale and fin,
meat and bone did not slow it.
Aedh Mac Carthin caught Géarán up in his arms
so fierce did he shake him
that his limbs broke and his ribs
cracked. In the churning waves the strong man
hurled him where he struggled and sank.

The saint then went to the bank, tooth in hand, to rest from the struggles in the ford. Tasach led his people against their enemies and a great slaughter did they make of them.

Aedh Mac Carthin built a church in a fine valley and to teach them the story of their Savior took each tooth and had carved the Stations of the Cross upon it. Tributes to the last day of Christ from the condemnation of the Savior to His burial in the rath, so that the pagans of the land might learn.

Ri Tasach had each of the holy relics mounted in a base of gold, to show his devotion to his new faith, turning pagan idols into holy Christian symbols, as Aedh Mac Carthin had converted his own people.

It is known that Aedh Mac Carthin was brave until the very end of his life. Hear the tale:

Saint Aedh stayed long in the lands of his adopted people before traveling to Clogher to become bishop there. Miracles and wonders he performed so strong was the passion of the Lord upon him. And always with him he bore the fourteen teeth of Sliabh Scoilt with him.

In a vision he saw his fourteen relics strung on a necklace about the bosom of the world, from Armagh to Rome. He determined to take a pilgrimage to the holy city then, leaving his war-prizes to mark the way for those who would follow. The first he left at Patrick's grave, and then turned across the sea, bearing his great load. He had not the luck that his master and teacher Patrick had, and to Rome he never has come. He wanders still, building that pilgrim's road.

Adrian Simmons *is a founder and editor of* Heroic Fantasy Quarterly.

NICOR

BY MATTHEW QUINN

Crows cawed in the distance. The Danes sitting in the longship began muttering ominously. Geiri Jorgenson, a dark-haired beardless boy of thirteen summers, leaned forward to listen.

"Is that the other ship over there?" he asked his friend Halvor Skallagrimson, a big red-bearded man who sat across the aisle.

Halvor nodded. "Aye," the older man said. His ordinarily-jovial face was hard as rock. "Something's wrong." He pointed.

Geiri's gaze followed his gesture to the riverbank where the other longship lay beached. Blood soaked the second ship's sails. A mutilated hand peeked out between two of the shields lining its length. A cloud of crows rose from the beached vessel as the longship drew near.

He swallowed.

Annar Svendson, the towering Danish commander, rose from his oar. "Take us to the side," he ordered, teeth gritted and hand on his sword. The steersman obeyed.

Geiri rose from the rowing-bench as they pulled alongside the other longship. Upon seeing what lay inside, he sank back down, his morning meal fighting its way into his mouth.

Mutilated corpses lay scattered throughout the ship and on the ground nearby. All of them bore long slashing wounds and their empty eye sockets indicated the crows had been at them for some time.

While Geiri struggled with his roiling stomach, scarred and swarthy Ejnar Olafsson vaulted into the second ship. Annar followed. Geiri forced himself to peek over the side and watch the two inspect the dead. Annar tore through the bodies, as if he were looking for someone.

"This is strange," Ejnar said. "Nobody stripped them."

Annar continued rooting through the pile of dead, apparently oblivious to his subordinate. Then, suddenly, he cried out and sank to his knees.

"Sir?" Ejnar asked. "What's wrong?"

Annar turned to Ejnar. Geiri could see his lord's face twisted with pain. When he spoke, his voice sounded empty and flat.

"Do you remember who we were supposed to meet?"

"Fálki Snorrason, sir?"

Geiri's eyes bulged. *Annar's foster brother!*

Annar nodded and pulled something from underneath a corpse. It was a cracked sword with the image of a dragon worked into the blade. A severed hand heavy with rings hung from it.

"Whose do you think this is?" Annar asked gravely.

Geiri's heart leaped into his throat. *Oh gods! That's Fálki's!*

"I'm sorry, sir," Ejnar said quietly. The big man thought for a moment. "He might not be dead."

Annar snorted. "He wouldn't show any man his back." He shook his head. "We can mourn later. Right now we need to figure out what happened." Annar rose to his feet and surveyed the ruined ship. "Do you see any unbroken weapons?"

"No sir. Whoever attacked these men must have taken the best for themselves." Ejnar thought for a moment. "Perhaps they didn't get everything."

He whistled and two more huge warriors jumped into the ravaged longship. Geiri watched the foursome rummage through the heaps of slain, not reacting at all to the stench of excrement from opened bellies and the rotting flesh.

They found only two unbroken weapons, both buried under several dead men. One was an ordinary spear, the other a fine two-handed axe with writhing serpents cut into the blade.

"You were the first one over the side," Annar said to Ejnar. "The axe is yours."

Ejnar grinned and took the weapon from his lord. "Thank you, sir."

Annar picked up the spear and tossed it into the ship.

"Whoever gets it first can have it."

The other men threw themselves after the weapon. The rush for the spear quickly turned into a brawl. Geiri hung back. He didn't need an extra spear *that* badly.

"And when you're done," Annar called out, "Come down here and help gather wood and brush. We'll give these men a good send-off to Odin and then bed down for the night. We can search for whoever did this in the morning."

* * *

"Kill the whoreson!"

The shout tore Geiri out of his dream of gold rings and a naked Anglish woman and cast him into muddy, bloody reality.

He scrambled to his feet, fumbling with his spear. *You're too damn slow. Enemy should be all over you.* Ignoring the pain from his rowing-blistered hands, he got a good grip on his weapon.

Something roared behind him. *Loki's balls! What's that?*

Geiri spun, spear out. The tip of his weapon nearly caught Kerr Throatcutter as he rushed past. The skinny hatchet-faced Dane turned and fixed Geiri with a one-eyed glare.

"Careful, *boy*," he growled.

Geiri began to stutter an apology, but the older man cut him off. "Someone's attacking the camp. Follow me."

The pair approached the edge of the clearing where they camped beneath the half-moon. Ahead of them, through cottony fingers of fog creeping in from the surrounding reeds, Halvor and another man struggled with an attacker Geiri could not quite see.

"You go left," Kerr ordered. "I'll hit him from the right."

Just one attacker? Geiri wondered. *Is it a berserker?* Geiri gripped his spear tightly. Fear-sweat soaked his hair. If the intruder was one of the savage men who wore the bearskin, he might not come out of the battle alive.

Despite his fear, Geiri obeyed, drawing near the pyre where they'd burned Fálki's men. Kerr circled to the right and then charged, sword ready to drink blood.

Geiri hesitated a moment, drew in a breath, and joined the attack.

He managed only three paces when something big slammed into him, sending him tumbling. He crashed into the mud and found himself pinned beneath Halvor.

"Halvor?" Geiri asked, poking at his friend's shoulder. "Halvor, get off me." The fallen Dane did not respond.

Grunting with effort, Geiri pushed himself into a sitting position. Halvor's body slid downward, leaving a trail of something wet and hot on Geiri's leather jerkin.

"Halvor — " Geiri began. Then he saw what the intruder had done.

Dark wounds marred Halvor's face. The moonlight reflected off bone peeking through the gore. The cuts on Halvor's neck looked less severe than those of his face, but the red-bearded man spattered blood when he breathed.

Oh gods. Glistening organs peeked out of a massive gut wound. Geiri scrambled up. He had to get old Sven, or Annar. They'd know what to do.

Halvor's head rolled back. The skin split open around the neck wounds even further. Blood spilled into his furs.

"No," Geiri gasped. He knelt by his dying friend and shook him. His hands came away sticky with slime. Geiri gagged. *What in all the hells is this?* None of the sagas ever mentioned slime on a dead warrior.

Something hissed from the reeds. Geiri looked up and saw a figure silhouetted against the fog. He got the impression of a man, but he had never seen a man hunched over like that. He had also never seen a man with slime dripping from his body.

The figure stepped forward, but shouting erupting behind Geiri stopped it in its tracks. The young Dane glanced behind him. Men were running his way, torches and weapons in their hands.

With a hiss, the intruder vanished back into the fog.

* * *

The following morning, the camp buzzed with activity. Several warriors guarded the edges of the clearing, weapons in hand, while others tramped through the swamps looking for the attacker's trail. Geiri just sat near Halvor's body, stunned.

Weeping is for women, Geiri thought, blinking back tears. *Crying will dishonor him.* He stared out onto the stagnant river.

Annar's shout grabbed his attention. "Hearken to me!"

Once the men quieted, Annar whistled. Sven, a white-bearded warrior older than Annar himself, stepped forward. He looked at Halvor's corpse and the slime spattered on it and spat on the blood-drunk earth.

"A *nicor* attacked last night," the older man declared solemnly. "Probably attacked the other ship too."

A water-monster? Before he left his impoverished village to serve Annar, Geiri remembered his father and the old men talking around the hearth-fire about flesh-hungry creatures from the bogs. But the stories, like the words of men who drank mead to escape the hard farming life for awhile, had an unreal quality to them.

The figure in the fog was very real.

Geiri watched as Annar gathered his oldest, most experienced warriors to his side. One of them was Kerr, whose ugly visage had been further marred by bruises and cuts. They spoke quietly among themselves.

Eventually, the conversation ended and Annar stepped out from among his warriors. "We sleep on the ship tonight," he ordered his men.

The Danes muttered among themselves. Several of the men grumbled about how this was running away. Some spoke of leaving on their own to hunt the mysterious attacker through the swamp.

Annar raised a hand, silencing them all. "We're not running away. I have a plan."

* * *

Whunk, whunk, whunk. Something climbed the side of the longship.

Geiri clutched his spear tightly and feigned sleep. Through squinting eyes he could see a shadowy form clambering over the shields. Moonlight glinted in its great froggy eyes. Panic-stricken thoughts raced through his head. The creature from the fog had come calling.

Thunk. Thunk. One scaled foot ground on the deck, followed by another. The intruder drew near. Fear squeezed Geiri's stomach.

Not me. Not me. Not me.

It stepped over him and approached Egill Fasteson, another youth of thirteen summers. It bent down, a lethal array of claws emerging from its long fingers.

"Kill it!" Annar roared. The supposedly-sleeping Danes surged upward all around the creature. The interloper recoiled. It was then Geiri got a better look at it.

It had the shape of a man, but men didn't have green scales instead of skin and mouths brimming with fangs. It hissed and snapped as they crowded it toward the stern.

Ejnar struck first, slamming his new axe into the monster's cheek. The blow sent it staggering, but when its head snapped back, Geiri's jaw dropped. Ejnar's blow, which would have halved the head of any Dane, had barely scratched the creature.

Murder lit its bulging eyes as it retaliated. The creature's lashing claws did unto the Dane what he would have done unto it. Ejnar's hulking body slammed into the deck, minus most of its head.

The creature wasn't finished. Its eyes locked on Annar. It surged forward, swatting a man over the side.

Kerr stepped between the *nicor* and his lord. The creature tilted its head and hissed. Kerr's grip tightened around his sword. "Remember me, you son of a whore?" Kerr growled, lips drawn back in a nasty snarl. "We finish it tonight."

Yes we will, Geiri agreed as he crept up behind the monster. His spear, a gift from Annar, had never tasted blood before. Perhaps the creature was more vulnerable from behind.

Geiri lunged. Kerr lunged.

The *nicor* was faster. It spun, backhanding Geiri. He crashed into several others, sending them sprawling. With its other hand, it caught Kerr's sword and twisted it away.

Kerr lived just long enough for a look of surprise to cross his face. Then the nicor rammed its lethal claws through his leather and furs, straight into his chest. The creature tore Kerr's ribcage asunder and hurled his mangled corpse into the river.

Geiri saw the moonlight reflected in the creature's eyes. An idea hit him.

"The eyes!" he screamed above the din. "Go for the eyes!"

The Danes surged forward, jabbing at its face. They could not get close enough. Two men who tried went down, rendered headless and gutless by whirling claws.

Then their luck changed. The nicor slashed and missed, burying its claws in the wood behind the row of shields. The creature shrieked and tore at the wood, but could not get loose. Eske Carrson, a stout Dane with a missing nose, seized the opportunity and drove his spear straight into the monster's face.

Though the spearhead caught on the socket, its tip neatly split the creature's right eye in two. Blood and fluid spattered Geiri's face. The *nicor* shrieked.

Its claws took a bloody revenge, ripping five long wounds in Eske's chest. However, a blow meant for Annar missed. Annar took advantage. He rammed his sword straight into the creature's remaining eye. The *nicor* tried to dodge, but the glancing blow it received was enough.

The eye burst. The monster howled and blindly lunged. The warlord ducked under its attack and sent it tumbling.

The men swarmed about the fallen creature, hammering it with spears, axes, and swords. Although they inflicted many small wounds, no one attack did significant damage. Though the nicor tried to rise, the Danes kept knocking it down.

They could not keep up the blizzard of ineffective attacks forever. The monster managed to squirm between two men and scramble to its feet. It lashed out blindly. Its claws caught the ear of short Arnlaug Thorsson, who barely had time to swing at the beast before it stepped away, carrying his ear with it.

Inspiration glittered in Annar's eyes. "Force it over the side!" he roared.

Geiri stood beside two other Danes and rammed his spear into the creature's gut. Though their weapons barely penetrated, the force of their blows lifted it over the shields. The creature toppled howling towards the water and managed to grab hold of a shield.

Eske, still wincing in pain, snatched up the great axe from Ejnar's corpse. He cried out to Odin and brought the weapon down onto the creature's hand. With a scream, the monster tumbled into the river. A scaly severed finger clunked on the deck at Eske's feet.

"It's running away!" Eske shouted. Geiri rushed to the side to see the creature swimming down the river, trailing ribbons of blood.

Annar's eyes narrowed in fury. "After it!" he roared.

The Danes rushed to the oars. Geiri strained alongside the others. The ship ground off the riverbank. Soon the longship bore down on the monster. It cocked its head in the direction of the longship and snarled, then bolted into the bog.

"Beach the ship!" Annar shouted. "We'll take the bastard on foot!"

The men ran the ship aground and spilled over the side, literally baying for blood. Geiri forced himself to be among those first off the boat. *Annar's noticed me*, he told himself. *If I kill that spawn of Jormungand and the village whore, he'll surely reward me*. His heart pounded in his chest, but he forced himself on.

"It went this way!" someone shouted. A trail of slime andfootprints, some filled with blood, lay ahead.

They followed the gruesome trail until they came to a sudden stop. Geiri pushed himself to the front of the group and saw what delayed them.

A rocky promontory lay ahead. In the center of that hill yawned a cave. Blood stained its rocky mouth. Their prey had gone underground.

Annar muscled his way to the front. "What are we waiting for?" he shouted. "Let's go down there and kill it!"

Geiri swallowed a lump in his throat. "Yes sir," he said. He stepped toward the *nicor's* hole, only to be rudely shoved aside.

Arnlaug stepped into the cave. "That scaly son of a bitch took my ear," he growled. "I'm going in there to get it back."

The other men shouted and clapped at his bravery. Geiri scowled, but a small part of him he tried to ignore was actually thankful someone else went in first.

Coward, he reproached himself.

The Danes followed Arnlaug into the cave. Darkness fell around them, broken only by shafts of moonlight entering through holes in the ceiling. They had not gone far when they discovered the passage ahead was flooded.

"It's gone for a swim," Arnlaug growled.

"Should we follow it?" Geiri asked. The creature had come out of the water, after all. Even blind, it could have the advantage.

Arnlaug glared at Geiri. "You don't want to finish what you started?" He snorted. "Fine. I'll go in myself."

Arnlaug climbed down into the pool and vanished below the surface. A long moment passed before he came back up. "The passage opens up at the end. There's air there, and I bet the bastard's there too." He grinned. "Let's kill him."

Arnlaug disappeared back under the water. Several others pushed past Geiri and dove after him. Geiri gripped his spear, remembered Halvor had not yet been avenged, and followed.

The water seeping through the gaps in his leather and furs was not too cold. Geiri's clothing pulled him down as he swam, and he had to kick upwards periodically so his knife did not catch on the cavern floor. Moonlight glimmered on the water ahead as the tunnel rose up. The Danes ahead of him emerged from the water without trouble. If the *nicor* was there, it was not attacking.

Then one of the Danes fell back into the water. Blood poured from his savaged throat, surrounding Geiri with a crimson cloud. The red warmth caressed him through his clothes. He choked back down vomit. Ignoring his nausea, he forced himself forward.

When he emerged from the water, he saw the others had gained the upper hand. They hemmed in the blinded monster and hewed at it with their weapons, sometimes drawing blood and sometimes not. The *nicor* lashed at them with its claws, but the men easily dodged its attacks.

Despite its wounds, the creature was still not without its strengths. Eske was not fast enough and caught a wicked slashing blow on his thigh. He staggered and the nicor leaped, knocking him aside and fleeing into the shadows.

"After it!" Arnlaug shouted.

Geiri followed them into a dark passage, keeping his hands tight on his spear in case of ambush. He felt his heart in his throat but forced himself to keep his breathing steady.

The tunnel opened up into another cavern where moonlight streamed in through cracks in the ceiling.

"Where is the bast—" Arnlaug began before the creature dropped shrieking on them from an overhanging ledge.

Unfortunately for the monster, two of the Danes had their spears up and caught the creature on the spearheads. They tossed it forward, slamming it onto the stone floor of the cavern.

Geiri rushed forward to join in the renewed attack, but then the glint of moonlight on metal caught his eye.

A row of swords lay neatly against the cavern wall near a pile of rotten bog plants. Many bore nicks or notches, just like the weapons the Danes themselves carried.

Oh gods. It takes trophies. Just like we do. He thought back to the captured Anglish weapons hanging above Annar's seat in the timbered hall back home.

"Son of a whore!" Annar shouted.

Geiri turned to see his lord behind him, kneeling next to a mutilated corpse. "Who is—" Geiri began before he got a good look at the face.

Though the dead man's nose was crushed and his jaw hung sideways, enough of the face remained intact for Geiri to recognize him. *Fálki!*

Annar turned away from the corpse, his expression murderous. He strode toward the struggling mass of man and monster.

As his lord approached, Arnlaug got lucky. The *nicor* twisted away from another man's sword-blow, exposing a gap between two thick scales on its belly. Screaming with anger, Arnlaug rammed his spear forward. The long iron spearhead buried itself in the creature's vitals. Arnlaug twisted it, raising the monster's screams to new heights. The maddened Dane leaned on the spear, forcing the creature onto the ground.

Annar approached Sven. "Spear," he demanded. The older warrior handed Annar his weapon, then stepped aside and allowed the warlord to approach the dying monster.

"This is for Fálki, you horse-humping bastard." Annar rammed the spear through the nicor's throat. Geiri winced at the sound of the metal spearhead grinding on the stones beneath the monster's neck. He forced himself to watch as Annar slowly worked the creature's head off with the wide spearhead. The warlord then knelt, slipped his hand into the creature's fang-lined mouth, and took up the fallen foe's head.

He turned to the assembled Danes. "Back to the ship," he ordered.

* * *

"Six men lost," Annar said when the warriors gathered around the voyage's second funeral pyre. "Can we take a rich monastery with only nineteen?"

"Bah!" Arnlaug shouted. He hefted the serpent-carved axe Annar gave him.

"The fat monks of the White Christ will be easy pickings!"

"And let's not forget cattle and women of the villages!" Eske shouted, his wounds weakening his voice. "We've got two ships now! More room!"

Annar nodded. "Perhaps. But what if they raise an alarm? Nineteen warriors might be fine to raid a monastery or village, but what happens if we encounter some real men-at-arms? Might be prudent to stop at the Orkneys first, pick up more men."

The others muttered among themselves. More men would mean a greater chance of survival, but it meant a smaller share of the loot.

Halvor and Geiri had once talked about all the rewards fighting could bring: cattle, golden arm-rings, and women to cook their meals and warm their beds. Geiri tried to summon up all the benefits the coming raids would bring, but the visions of loot faded, soaked with the blood he had seen shed by the monster's claws.

Geiri inhaled, steeling himself. *The Norns had spoken. It was their time to die, and they died well.* The images of the dead men receded, but they did not vanish.

Annar's voice seized his attention. "We'll get more men at the first settlement we find. Then to Angland!"

The Danes roared. Geiri cheered too, trying desperately to think about monastic gold and Anglish wenches, but his cries were half-hearted. The night's battle with the nicor had been his first taste of combat, and it was bitter indeed.

Annar motioned Geiri forward. He had apparently spotted the young man's long face.

As Geiri approached, Annar fished into his furs and withdrew a silver ring. "Arnlaug is not the only man who deserves a reward, my boy. Your idea helped us kill the beast and avenge Fálki." He handed Geiri the ring.

"Th — thank you, sir," Geiri stuttered. He slipped on the ring. The other warriors cheered. Geiri smiled sheepishly, but his heart hung heavily in his chest. I thought the Viking life would be better than scraping a living out of the bogs, he thought. It doesn't seem so grand right now.

Annar raised a hand to silence his men.

"Now get back to the ship!" he roared.

* * *

Six weeks and a detour to Orkneyjar later, the Danes fell upon an Anglish village. They'd looted half the town and a nearby monastery before someone managed to raise an alarm. Then it was time to run, before enemy soldiers got there.

Geiri and the others rushed to the longships, carrying gold, sheep, and the occasional struggling woman.

"Quickly!" Annar shouted.

They vaulted over the side of the beached ships and rushed to the oars, a few remaining on land to help push. Slowly — too slowly — the longships slid into the ocean. Once the oars bit water, those already aboard added their strength to those behind and both vessels slid into the river. The men behind scrambled aboard and joined their compatriots at the oars. By the time the Anglish soldiers arrived, the Danes were well away.

Geiri watched the Anglish brandish their weapons futilely as they rushed toward the shoreline. The Danes had only lost one man during the raid and they'd gained much.

But despite their victory, Geiri wasn't happy. His gaze returned to the column of smoke behind them, his thoughts returning to the screams and blood.

"All right, my boy?" Annar asked.

Geiri nodded. "Yes sir."

Annar slapped him on the back. "First time you've fought against men, eh?" The Danish warlord smiled. "This'll lift your spirits."

He turned and reached into a sea-chest. He pulled out a silver arm-ring, carved to look like a coiling serpent.

"You deserve another," he said. He gestured expansively to the loot behind them, gold in many cases still slick with the blood of the men they'd killed to take it. "None of this would be possible without you helping kill that monster, and you performed just as well against the Anglish too."

Geiri remembered the screams of surprised Anglish as the Danes spitted them on their spears, but his lord was watching. Hesitantly, Geiri slipped the ring on. Back home, he'd seen men at the village wandering around with the arm-rings. How proud they were to have gone a-viking, how the pretty girls marveled at them. It would be nice to have a wife — preferably two, or even three — and raiding the Anglish would go a long way toward getting one.

The first thing coming to his mind, however, was not glory or the possibility of wooing, but the coldness of the metal arm ring. It was cold like the flesh of the men who died fighting the nicor. Cold like the bodies they'd heaped on the pyre.

He forced the thoughts away. It was dishonorable to be ungrateful to one's lord. "Thank you, sir."

Annar laughed. "You earned it, my boy."

A squabble broke out on the other end of the ship. Geiri craned his neck to look over Annar's shoulder. Two of the older men fought over a girl roughly Geiri's age. She was comely and would be even more so once her bruises faded.

But she whimpered. Her sounds of pain reminded him of Eske, whose wounds had festered. He'd slowly died in the days after the battle with the *nicor*, before they got to Orkneyjar.

Annar walked away to restore order, leaving Geiri alone. He looked once more back over the water, toward the smoke rising from the ravaged Anglish village.

We are *nicors*.

MATTHEW W. QUINN'S *imagination has taken him on many different paths. "Nicor," which premiered in* Heroic Fantasy Quarterly *in 2013, was his first foray into heroic fantasy, followed afterward by "Lord of the Dolorous Tower" and "Lord Giovanni's Daughter," both published by* Digital Fantasy Fiction. *But Matthew has published in other genres as well, including his horror novel* The Thing in the Woods, *available from* Digital Horror Fiction, *his short independent horror stories "I am the Wendigo" and "Melon Heads," and the Lovecraftian "The Beast of the Bosporus," also available through* Digital Fantasy Fiction.

Outside the fictional realm, Matthew holds a masters' degree in world history and works as a high school social studies teacher. Before that, he was a freelance publicist and marketer, a newspaper editor, and a small-town journalist.

The Lion and the Thorn Tree

by J.S. Bangs

My husband's voice came through the door of our house in the night. It was a ghost voice, muddled with the baying of wild dogs, and so I knew he was dead. I was four months pregnant.

I followed the echo of his voice for half the night until I reached the thorn tree. When I found him he had been beaten by Wuluju's warriors and impaled on the thorns, his wrists and legs bound by leather thongs to the spiny branches. Vultures huddled in the tree's crown. In haste I cut the knots and let his body fall. He was too heavy for me to carry, but I could not leave him. That thorn tree was an evil place, unhallowed by the sorcerer Wuluju's magics and murders, and the ghost lion that he summoned to hunt there. So I stayed, swatting away the vultures that approached, until the sun broached the eastern horizon and burned away the night. I prayed for the aid of my mothers and grandmothers, but I did not think they heard me.

Just before dawn I heard the ghost lion roar for the first time. I wished then I could summon the lioness, as our mothers and grandmothers had done in the old days. But our ancestors had forgotten us, and the old magics had died. So I fled.

The sun was high when I finally returned to our village. Wuluju's men had passed through earlier that morning boasting of my husband's murder. I knew this, because the women of the village wouldn't speak to me, honoring my rank as a widow. For a while I sat in the shade and listened to the krik-krik of locusts. You may think it strange that I didn't cry. At a funeral a widow is expected to beat her breast and tear her clothes and crawl after the bier of her husband casting dirt onto her head. If there had been any funeral, I suppose I would have done all of that. But there had been no proper funerals for some months. Wuluju was afraid of the Nande lineage even in death, and he forbade them to be buried or mourned. Perhaps he thought they would return from the dead. But my husband was the last man of that name.

Yet not the last. I put my hand on my belly.

My nearest relatives were my half-brother and his wife in Kunante, eight days to the south. Wuluju's empire was long settled in that region, but for that very reason his warriors there might be less vigilant. The thought of walking alone smothered me with dread, but I drove the feeling away.

I whispered to the old men of the village to find my husband's body and bury it if they could, and set off that afternoon.

The roads were full of warriors and thieves, cut loose by the long war, so I followed the flood pan of the river to the south. I slept with my knife in my hand, the knife which had been a wedding present from my Nande sisters. Our troubles had already started when I wed, and they had taken to giving brides a knife of Madekkan steel in place of a hundred yards of red-dyed wool. I used to joke with my husband that he had married a scorpion rather than a woman, as I had no wool to weave, but I carried a sharp sting. He would smile and say, "All the Nande women have become scorpions these days."

At the time I could not weep, so I weep now at the memory of my loneliness.

The lion roared at dusk during the ghost hour, when the moon and the sun mingled their light in the sky. This proved to me that it was no fleshly lion, and that it hunted me. A real lion will not follow the same prey for three days. A ghost will, though it must wait to attack until the ghost time when the moon is full. I had most of the month left to reach safety.

* * *

When I reached Kunante I found my half-brother's home. The whitewash on the exterior had cracked and crumbled, a tattered curtain hung over the door, and the spirit niches were clogged with mud. I called out the names of my half-brother and his wife: "Dede! Kawaku!" No one responded. Then a shadow moved in the door, and the ratty curtain parted.

"Dede!" I ran and kissed my half-brother's cheek. His skin was rough as a dried leaf, and he did not return my kiss. I saw no one in the house beside him. "Where is Kawaku?" I asked.

"Kawaku is dead." He peered at me the way a man looks at an adder in the grass, then grunted. "Come in."

The home's interior had not fared better than the outside. There was a single bed laid on the ground and a few dusty gourds filled with salt and starch. Before the troubles, my brother had a rifle and an iron spearhead and a stack of hides ready for tanning, and the house was rich with food and Kawaku's laughter. "What happened here?"

He told me: Wuluju demanded tribute of food and valuables even after the village was reduced to poverty, and his warriors had seized my brother's rifle. Now the houses were all desolate, except for those where Wuluju's lieutenants lived. The young women all gave themselves to Wuluju's men, because who wanted to marry a poor man and starve with him? In the last dry season the food in Dede and Kawaku's house had run out, and Kawaku fell sick with fever and died.

He said all of this in a flat, toneless voice like a dead man.

The news of Kawaku's death wounded me like a thorn in the palm, yet I had my own wound to share. I told him that my husband was dead.

He shrugged as if he had expected the news, but his shoulders slumped a little. "Our hope is finally gone."

"There is one thing," I said. "I am carrying a child. I'm sure that it's a boy." I had been sure even before my husband had died, which is why I knew I was not merely wishing.

"We should go to the fortune teller," my brother said. "To know for sure."

"Is there one in this village?" Wuluju drove out most fortune tellers, for he was jealous of their power, and afraid. When he had first become a sorcerer and began to oppress the upriver country, a simple bone-caster had prophesied that a son of Nande would kill him. He had hunted and killed every Nande man after that, down to infants suckling at the breast.

"One. Her name is Gwana. We'll have to go to her in the night."

* * *

The nights in Kunante were quiet in a dead, uncanny way. I should have heard the chattering of birds and young men boasting around fires, but the villagers hid in their homes, and the birds had fled. Dede and I moved through the shadows like thieves. Dede whispered Gwana's name at her window, and a husky voice bade us enter.

There was a low, red fire burning in hearth, making the hut very warm. It smelled of old smoke and burnt animal hair. Gwana crouched near the coals playing her fingers across her fetishes, a sour-faced woman with gray hair and flat breasts. "You have a child," she said as soon as the curtain fell over the door.

"You have a good gift, Grandmother," I said.

"Huh! You don't need a gift to spot a girl flush with her first baby. How long?"

"Four months."

Dede broke in. "Grandmother, she and her husband were of Nande's lineage. Wuluju killed him. He was the last one." It is important that I was also of Nande's line, for when a name becomes weighty with power it can no longer be given by the father alone, but must come through the mother's line as well. This is also why my half-brother was not Nande, though we shared a mother.

The red light made Gwana's face look ghastly and severe. "So you hope for a good fortune? Foolish girl. There is no good fortune left for a woman like me to give. Our mothers and grandmothers have forgotten us."

"Please, Grandmother. I want to know if I have a son, and if he will — "

She hushed me. "You are a fool. Come here."

I knelt next to her. She held an oracle stone carved like a fat pregnant woman, which she passed over my breasts and belly muttering prayers. After she had done this several times she drew out the pouch of bones, shook it three times, and threw them across the hearth. Her breath hissed through her teeth as she looked over the heap. Twice more she cast. Then she spoke in a low, creaking voice. "Oh, oh, oh."

"What is it?" I asked.

"What did I tell you about good news? Listen: your child will not be natural born, but cut living from his mother's womb."

Dede drew in his breath. I said nothing. If that was my fate, I would not fare worse than many women.

Gwana continued. "If the child lives, Wuluju must not see him nor hear his name until he is circumcised, or else Nande's blessing will leave him." She paused and scratched the dirt. "But if this condition is met, he will destroy Wuluju and deliver our people."

"That is not much hope," Dede said.

I said, "But it is a little."

Dede paid her with a pigeon, and we crept through the shadows back to Dede's home. As soon as we reached it I told him, "I'll go to Madekka."

Madekka was a city far to the south, whose name reached us mostly as rumor. Their sages had become wise, and they made guns and books and medicines, and had doctors who might save a child unnaturally born.

Dede's face was dark. He kicked at the empty gourds against the wall. "We have no food for the journey. But if we put down the yams first, we might."

Listen: I was a fool. Though I knew I had to leave, I was disposed to listen to my half-brother and linger in the land of my mothers and grandmothers. I had spent many nights in that house, grinding flour and laughing with Kawaku while the men threw dice, back when we thought our troubles might pass quickly. Plus, young yams take only a few weeks to harvest. It would be good to have food for the journey.

So I stayed. At the next full moon, I heard a lion roar. Wuluju's men fired their rifles at it and swore. The second night there was no sound, and the moon wasted away without the ghost roaring again. I grew comfortable and stopped fearing the lion, and kept putting off my trip to Madekka.

Another month passed, and there came a night when the moon lit the village in bone-colored light. The lion roared as I squatted over the dinner pot. I was not afraid. Then a second roar, closer.

Dede looked up at me. "Don't go outside," he said. He took a spear and left.

I pulled the doorway curtain aside and spied the village men gathered around the well, shouting and gesturing and pounding their spears on the ground. Beyond them, from the north end of the village, approached Wuluju's garrison, rifles in hand. They too seemed afraid. I felt a chill of doom seeing them. You cannot kill a ghost lion with a rifle.

I took my knife and banked the fire. I put on sandals and an extra dress that I could use for a blanket, and I packed the food we had saved. This was all we had, but if I had to run it would have to be enough. I heard a rifle fire.

The men at the well had disappeared along with Wuluju's soldiers. Another gunshot sounded, then the thunder of many guns at once. The sounds of screaming reached me. Men came running into the village, howling of a ghost lion. More men bearing spears came from their houses. Then a second group of runners arrived, and behind them roared a white, evil shape.

I didn't stay to look. I had a chance — a ghost lion is still a lion, and in pursuit of one prey it will ignore another. I bolted. Behind me mingled the screams of men and the crackle of rifles and the yowl of the hunter. I couldn't tell whether the lion's roar grew closer or further away, but I didn't dare look back. A quarter-mile from the river I heard a voice call to me, "Sinka!"

It was Dede's voice. I stumbled and nearly fell. Dede leapt from the bush and caught my shoulders.

"I have to go," I gasped. "It's following — "

"Take this." He pressed an oiled, heavy object it into my hands.

"What is this?"

"I took it from the soldier's store when the lion attacked. You'll need it."

I stammered for a moment, feeling the heft of the rifle. Dede pushed me to the south. "I will stay and fight the lion. Find someplace safe." He picked up his spear and headed back to the village.

I ran until dawn with one hand on my stomach, lest I provoke the child to miscarry. My stride was clipped by the weight of my womb, making my gait crooked and ungainly. My feet were swollen and chapped. Sweat greased my grip on the gun. When at least the yellow dawn brightened the east, I collapsed in the brush, covered myself with the blanket, and slept.

* * *

This was the beginning of my great journey. I knew no kinsmen to the south that might take me in. So I traveled alone, staying close to the river and foraging for food. Once I killed a coucal with a lucky stone's throw, and I roasted and devoured every scrap of it but the bones. I passed by many villages, and when my hunger grew too great I crept into a garden at night and stole yams. If anyone saw me, they saw a wild woman, hair uncut, face blackened by travel, ponderous with a child and milk-heavy breasts, digging in the dirt with a knife. They left me alone.

I never fired the rifle. My brother had given it to me with one bullet in the chamber.

The full moon came again, and I stayed awake all night with my finger on the trigger. I heard no lion's roar. When the dawn broke, I turned my face to the south with more confidence than I had known for weeks. With a little luck, I would reach Madekka and bear my child before the moon grew full again.

I did not have luck.

Between Madekka and the upriver country there is a girdle of wilderness in which no village stands. Four days after I passed into that wild place I stepped into a snake's hole and fell. I caught myself before I landed on my belly, feeling a moment of relief that gave way to a scream of pain from my twisted foot. My ankle was purpled and swollen when I pulled it out of the whole. I staggered upright and tested it on the ground, but the pain came fierce and hot. At the same time, a tremor tightened my belly. It was not the beginning of labor, but one of those harbingers that trouble a woman as she nears her time, a reminder of my peril. I had no time to wait or to heal.

I planted the butt of the rifle in the ground, leaned forward on it as on a crutch, and hobbled onward.

I will not dwell on those black days. My foot healed slowly. Every scrap that I ate nourished the child, leaving me thin and sickly, and prolonging my lameness. Every night I slept hungry. My breasts withered while the child stirred and kicked. I fell mute with horror and despair that even if I had the strength to birth the child, I had no milk to nurse him.

And then the moon grew full again. I watched it creep above a thorn tree to the east, a disk of bone in the bruise-colored sky, and I heard a long ways off the roar of a lion. I despaired. I had not reached Madekka. I could not run. Tonight the lion would overtake me. I lay on the ground and waited for death.

But my groin quickened, and a cascade of water washed my thighs. A groan of anger and surprise bubbled up from my gut. The child was coming.

I would not die. The rifle struck the ground again, and I pulled myself up.

In only an hour, I came in sight of an outpost of the guard of Madekka. Two men with rifles and dark green cloaks slouched in the door of a hut. They raised their guns, shouting warnings at my approach, though neither of them fired, too surprised at the sight of a starving pregnant woman hobbling along on a rifle. I came right to the post-house and collapsed across its threshold.

"Who are you?" one of the men demanded. "What are you doing here?"

"My name is Sinka. I am having a baby. You must take me to the *hospital.*" I repeated the word I had heard travelers use.

"What?" At that moment the lion roared again, this time very near.

The men exchanged a glance and began to argue in their local dialect. Finally one of them said to me, "Get into the hut. We'll send for someone to escort you to the hospital."

I shook my head. "The lion's coming for me. I must — " At that moment a pang tore through me, and speech fled. I seized the doorpost and screamed. They started away, more frightened of me than the lion. More words passed between them in dialect, then the elder spoke.

"We can't leave the post. In an hour our commander will visit us, and he may send for a midwife, or give you an escort to the hospital. Can you wait until then?"

I shook my head. The child could wait — even in the wake of my pain, I knew that the boy wouldn't come in the next hour. But that was not the danger. "The lion. We must leave now."

The men exchanged a gesture that meant that I was crazy. The pain had ebbed, and I hobbled to my feet. "How far to the city?"

"You can't possibly go out by yourself."

"Tell me how far!"

"Thirty minutes on foot to the outskirts. But you — "

The lion's roar swallowed his last words. We all fell silent. Night air confuses distances, but there was no doubting that the monster was near. The younger soldier lifted his rifle.

"A lion does not roar while it hunts," the elder said.

"This is a ghost lion," I said. "Your rifles will not harm it."

"A ghost lion," the younger said. His tone affirmed that I was crazy. But they held their rifles at the ready and watched the approach. When their eyes left me I slipped out the back door.

A few shouts chased me when they realized that I was going, but true to their word neither of them left their post. The moon lit a well-trod path through the grass. I hobbled a hundred yards before another labor pang toppled me. The grass alongside the path muffled my groans. When it passed I struggled again to my feet. Thirty minutes to the city. Perhaps an hour in my current state. The lion would find me in less than an hour, but it didn't matter. I walked and kept walking even when the next spasm flogged my weakened legs.

I heard the crack of rifles far behind me, then the screams of the soldiers. The lion roared, not in terror but with the snarl of slaughter. A bolt of agony struck me again. I fell to one knee. Behind me the screams turned to a gurgle, then, terribly, the rifles quieted. The pain did not leave me. My fingers tore tufts of grass from the ground. I ground my teeth.

Even if I could stand, I couldn't outrun the lion. But was I not also a daughter of Nande? The edge of the pain wore away, and I rose to my knees. A growl rattled through the dark. I cleaned the dirt from the muzzle of the rifle and raised it to my shoulder, futile though it might be. I lay my knife on my thigh. Though these might not kill the lion, at least he would not take me unarmed.

"My mothers and grandmothers, remember me," I whispered.

A white shape moved through the grass. I could not see it clearly, but I felt the tremor of its approach. It roared. The ground quaked. I pointed the rifle at the source of the sound and fired.

A shudder of pain lashed my womb in that moment, and I closed my eyes and moaned. The beast roared, and in a moment I was thrown to my back and felt its teeth in my flesh like a kiss in the violence of labor. Then the first roar was met by another. The pain was such that I did not know whether I was consumed within or without, and only when the pain ebbed did I realize that the ghost lion did not devour me.

I opened my eyes and saw the lioness.

Her hide was as white as silver in the moonlight, her muzzle wet with blood, and she fought with the lion. They traded roars in the grass, shredding each other with their claws.

"You have not forgotten us!" I cried. Courage filled me. I seized the knife from my thigh and leapt forward. The bade tore though the lion's hide as surely as if it were flesh. He twisted toward me in rage, and I fell. His claws raked my thigh. But that moment of distraction was enough.

The lioness leapt atop his back and crushed his head in her jaws. His final roar died in his throat.

I could not stand. My ankle was bruised, and my leg bled. The lioness came forward and licked my face, then took my shoulder gently in her jaws. She dragged me down the path toward Madekka. At my gasp she dropped me and licked the marks her teeth had made.

She roared. Her roar stirred new strength within me. I rose to my feet. She nipped my ankle, and I began to lurch toward Madekka.

The lioness brought me the rest of the way to the city. When I fell, she kissed my face and dragged me onward. When I flagged, she spurred me on with her roars. I crawled the last mile to Madekka with the lioness always beside me. When at last the lanterns of the city blessed me with their light, I fell and screamed for help, and the people of the city heard me and brought me to this place. I do not remember after that.

I woke up here in the *hospital*, in a bed with white sheets. A basket lies next to me with a baby boy, tiny but alive. I bear the scar across my belly where they cut the child from me — and the medicine here is so great that I still live! A nurse-maid suckles my son while I heal from these harrowing weeks. It will be long before I leave the hospital. Longer still before I repay the kindness that Madekka has shown me.

I told my story to the commander of the army, and I hear that they are sending soldiers north, thinking that men with guns will intimidate Wuluju. They will probably die. It doesn't matter. My son is a child of Nande. I will give him a gun and teach him to summon a lion, and when he is a man we both will go north to free our people.

THE LION AND THE THORN TREE

J.S. BANGS *lives in the American Midwest with his family of four. When not writing, he works as a computer programmer, and he can occasionally be found gardening, biking, or playing Magic: The Gathering.*

His short fiction has appeared in Daily Science Fiction, Beneath Ceaseless Skies, Orson Scott Card's Intergalactic Medicine Show, Heroic Fantasy Quarterly, *and other venues.*

About the Artists

SIMON WALPOLE is a freelance illustrator whose works primarily in pencil, pen and watercolours and whose work can be seen here:
http://swalpole6.wix.com/handdrawnheroes

MIGUEL SANTOS has years of experience illustrating for RPG's, magazines, books and comics. Major themes are Sci Fi, Fantasy and Horror, he has done multiple illustrations for *Heroic Fantasy Quarterly*.

KATARINA DEGGANS, 16, balances high school, art, and a science-fantasy webcomic, "The Phoenix" (https://www.tumblr.com/blog/crescentstarpath). She currently works on the iPad, and uses digital for most of the things she posts. She aspires to be a full time artist, whether it be for book covers or comics, and hopes experience will make every picture better than the last.

RAPHAEL ORDOÑEZ is a mildly autistic writer and circuit-riding college professor residing in the southwest Texas hinterlands. His short stories have appeared in several magazines, and his paleozoic adventure fantasy novels, *Dragonfly* and *The King of Nightspore's Crown*, the first two in a planned tetralogy, are available from Hythloday House. He blogs about fantasy, writing, art, and logic at http://raphordo.blogspot.com/

ROBERT ZOLTAN is a first generation American born to Hungarian immigrant parents. His artistic aspirations began at the age of four when, left unattended for a short time by the locked basement door, he proceeded to cover it with crayon from the bottom of the door to as high as he could reach.

During his career, he has done work for a wide variety of clients, including Simon and Schuster, and Disney. He creates in various media, both traditional and digital, and specializes in illustrations of fantasy, adventure, and science fiction. He is also an award-winning music composer, fiction writer, graphic designer, owner of Dream Tower Media, and host of *Literary Wonder & Adventure Show*.

He holds a Bachelor of Fine Arts Degree in Illustration from Washington University in St. Louis, and currently lives in the Silver Lake neighborhood of Los Angeles.

View Zoltan's work at http://zoltanillustration.com/.

About the Founding Editors

ADRIAN SIMMONS is a Norman, Oklahoma, based reader and writer. His essays, reviews, and interviews have appeared in *Internet Review of Science Fiction*, *Black Gate*, and *Strange Horizons*. His short fiction has popped up in *Allegory Ezine*, *Strange Constellations*, *James Gunn's Ad Astra Magazine*, *Heroic Fantasy Quarterly* (after a fashionable wait of four years), and the *Apotheosis Anthology*. An avid backpacker, he has hiked over 800 miles.

DAVID FARNEY studied architecture and science in college before earning a journalism degree. He works in medical sales, and enjoys writing epic and historical fantasy, as well as speculative poetry. He lives in Oklahoma City but dreams of living farther north — which might explain his fascination with Norse and Viking lore.

About the Designer

KEANAN BRAND has been a proofreader for a small science fiction press, a member of the editorial teams on a handful of ezines, including *Ray Gun Revival*, and later an associate editor for an independent press. He is the author of the first half of an epic fantasy duology — *Dragon's Rook* — and is at work on its companion, *Dragon's Bane*.

KICKSTARTER CONTRIBUTORS

SUPPORTERS

Adrian Coombs-Hoar
Bradley Halweg
Brian Rock Hubbard
Christopher Dunnbier
Daran Grissom
Dawid Wojcieszynski
Dietmar Schmidt
Edward Potter
Eric Priehs
Guest 2115119531
James Schmidt
Jamie Manley
Jeffrey Shanks
Jordan Berghauer
Josh Olive
Keith West
Marc Rasp
Mark James Featherston
Mark Robinson
Matt John
Michael De Plater
Mick Gall
Newt
Nolabert
Patrick Bboyle
Paul McNamee
Rhel
Ricciardi Luc
Scott Edward Nash
Sean Reisz
Shawn Scarber
Spencer E Hart
Thalji
Troy Chrisman
TS

Benefactors

Made in the USA
Las Vegas, NV
24 June 2024